Sharecropping
The
Apocalypse

RON FOSTER

Alabama, USA

ISBN-13: 978-1501081255
ISBN-10: 150108125X

Printed in the United States of America.

Preface

About the cover of book 1 "The Preppers Lament".

In the fall of 1845, the potato blight in Ireland began. By 1847, there was massive death and famine. The Irish were only permitted potatoes by the English authorities, and when the potatoes perished, so did they. As many as a quarter of the Irish population either starved or immigrated under the worst of circumstances. Many of those who left Ireland never arrived at their destination. Ships were known as "coffin ships."

British colonial policies before and during the crisis exacerbated the effects of the potato blight, leading to mass death by starvation and disease. For example, in March of 1847,

Preface

at the time of the Choctaw donation, 734,000 starving Irish
people were forced to labor in public works projects in order
to receive food. Little wonder that survivors referred to the year
as "Black '47." What potatoes were harvested was shipped, by
the English, outside of Ireland. There is certainly some question
about whether these acts were intentionally genocidal, the same
questions that apply to the US policy driving the Removal Act
which led to the Trail of Tears.

Famine' (1997) was commissioned by Norma Smurfit
and presented to the City of Dublin in 1997. The sculpture is a
commemorative work dedicated to those Irish people forced to
emigrate during the 19th century Irish Famine. The bronze
sculptures were designed and crafted by Dublin sculptor Rowan
Gillespie and are located on Custom House Quay in Dublin's
Docklands.

The photo depicts the Famine Memorial in Dublin today
near the docks. These pathetically thin people are portrayed
walking towards the ships on the quay, their desperate escape to
anyplace. The story of the man on the right, carrying the child,
is that by the time he arrived where there was soup, he
discovered that he was carrying a dead child.

I'm always amazed at the degree of cruelty humans can
carry out upon other humans.

As an academically influenced prepper fiction author, I
have studied in depth the sociological and psychological impacts
of how disasters influence the populace. Many of the post
apocalyptic books I write include a specific story line that the
books' title refers or alludes to. I have decided to call this
particular book "The Preppers Lament". This reflects our
community. A strong central underlying theme of the books'
purpose and lessons to learn is to construct or deconstruct just
what that titles' implication or meaning applies to the reader's
own perspectives about surviving a disaster, as well as life in
general...

Preface

Just what is a lament one might ask? Well, according to Webster's, we find the word to be defined as:

la·ment

Verb

1. to express sorrow, regret, or unhappiness about something

2. To express sorrow, mourning, or regret for, often demonstratively

Now being a country boy that sometimes forgets some of his education on exactly what a word means decided that if something is done "demonstratively", it must therefore be important that it be well   defined and so I looked this word up also.

. de·mon·stra·tive

adj.

1. Serving to manifest or prove.

Author Note." We preppers hope we will not have to prove our skills or depend on our preps if a disaster should manifest itself but serve ourselves and others by preparing for a perceived likelihood of inevitability".

2. Involving or characterized by demonstration.

Author Note." Preppers are all about involving themselves with the community and learning from and demonstrating preparedness and survival skills.

3. Given to or marked by the open expression of emotion: an affectionate and demonstrative family.

Author Note "The Prepper community as a whole characteristically tends to be open about their enjoying the sharing of knowledge and camaraderie that defines the movement.

4. *Grammar* Specifying or singling out the person or thing referred to: the demonstrative pronouns these and that.

"By definition we are singled out by the media and referred to as these Preppers or that Prepper and of course even those Doomsday Preppers but it doesn't matter, we define ourselves by our actions and our deeds.

So having defined that Preppers express sorrow and regret strongly what exactly would entail qualifying some thought process specifically as a Preppers Lament?

America has become increasingly angry, confused, depressed, sick, deranged, conflicted, addicted, suicidal, faithless and hopeless. The aftermath of 9/11 highlighted how unpredictable disasters can be and how unprepared we are as individuals as well as a nation to cope should we lose any of our precious infrastructure. This is something for everyone to lament about.

The prepper movement seeks to obtain an individual or personal level of well-being by having people take control over their own destinies and try to mitigate the numerous threats we ourselves and others perceive as risks or hazards to us and our families. By preparing for ourselves to be more self- reliant, we assuage our psyche and calm our nerves.

A lot of us utilize the prepper community as a hobby and a social platform to share similar views and beliefs under the banner of preparedness. The uncertainty of what lies ahead - and our inkling to know what lies ahead - is the perfect platform for the grassroots community to take on not only personal preparedness but also influence state and federal emergency management agencies. The Prepper community is vociferous in its dire warnings that put the challenges ahead in the spotlight and in so doing, we hope in some small way that it prepares the authorities to plan to ensure that them gloom and doomer Preppers are wrong.

The orgy of ominous predictions that greets us on the internet and news drives prepper newbie's to the internet forums and other social media daily as our community of awareness increases. Is to lament about risks, disasters, unpreparedness etc. what makes us a prepper? Surely not, most people lament about such woes and worries so it's not exclusive to preppers.

Preppers do and will lament about those who do not prep because of many reasons. People who concern us are those that refuse to be informed about the need to prepare for disasters, people who are too lazy to prep, maybe they are just self absorbed with daily living, or maybe they are just plain naïve and out of touch, also lets don't forget about those who for no fault of their own are economically challenged and can't afford supplies. Does speculating about whether these people are a threat to us and our preps or that we will mourn for them after a disaster makes this a "Preppers Lament"? To mourn death is to lament, remember?

But the battle to define a "Preppers Lament" is simultaneously being waged on another plane: Lament can mean to want. Every time the government creates another "crisis," it promotes and enlarges the societal stress, the emotional instability, the cultural anxiety, the brooding anger, uncertainty, dread and growing national self-doubt and gives us yet another reason to prep. The news about natural disasters and terrorist threats fuels our prepper psyches while it drains our bank accounts for latest got to have items. Prep to live folks, don't live to prep, please, or you will find you created your own economic collapse and living a preppers lament. For some folks, there needs to be a Preppers Anonymous like they have for shopoholics or gamblers. Remember that your mind is your biggest asset to invest in and it needs words of wisdom not dollars to enrich your survival. Your mind is better than any survival gadget you can buy.

What is your "Preppers Lament"? How about wishing you had purchased long-term storage food instead of all that out of date canned food you are holding on to? How about the number of times your water storage has sprung a leak because of shoddy made containers? How do you prepare for life's laments versus prepper laments? The one thing though that I bet none of us ever laments about is becoming a prepper

Imagine That A Coordinated Cyber Attack Has Taken Down The Majority Of The Electrical Grid In America.

Imagine That This Disaster Happened Two Weeks Ago and Your Home's Water Quit Flowing a Week Ago.

Imagine That You Started This Catastrophe with Only a Month's Worth of Food and Water Stored.

Imagine That Your Neighbors Only Had About Three Days Worth Of Food On Hand Two Weeks Ago And Now They Beg You To Share What They Think You Have Put away But you Do Not Have..

Imagine That You No Longer Wish To "Share" And That Today Is The Day Of Reckoning To Tell Your Friends And Neighbors "No More" And Draw A Line In The Sand.

Preface

Imagine For Instance That You Had Somehow Already Imagined This Event Or Disaster Day and Prepared For It Because You Were A Prepper.

Would Your Disaster Survival Plan Work?

What Happens If It Does Not?

What Happens To Those People Without Anything Put Away For These Hard Times?

"Who Dies, Who Lives, And For How Long?"

Acknowledgements

SilverFire Rocket Stoves

Sun Oven

Henrey Repeating Arms

1

NOW IMAGINE IT!

David the old prepper/farmsteader considered that his community was only just now starting to experience the kind of chaos, mass confusion and social difficulties he expected from a power failure of only a few weeks duration in his part of the southern United States. Several of the large northern states industrial cities had already been off grid much longer than his state and those over populated cities had already begun to succumb to mayhem, smoke and death as society began to panic after the great cyber attack took the electrical grid down.

"Just imagine what will happen when the power stays off for many MONTHS! Common folks normally take electricity so much for granted that they fail to fully realize

for themselves that without it, we are literally soon to be thrown back a century in time. I am positively sure myself, that by now a lot of people sitting are home in the dark have had time for a few minutes careful personal reflection on that particular reasonable assumption and are scurrying their asses off now to get the hell out of the cities and get themselves and their family to whatever safer place they could imagine. Didn't much matter to some where that was, just get out of the big city and go anywhere that seemed like a more likely place to have a chance to survive. No gas (pumps) or heating oil, no more transportation of food, water shortages, failure of computers, medical equipment, banks and the monetary system, no ATMs, no TV, limited radio and other communications -- in short absolute and total chaos and panic is setting in for good and the fuse is lit. Society was going to implode." David thought to himself a bit alarmed and wondered exactly just what indeed was the state of mind of his neighbors were in at this moment. Thinking about going, thinking about staying, thinking about robbing, thinking about looting, hunting, prepping, going crazy hell there was no telling.

"Were they still thinking more Sane than insane? "David wondered to himself.

"Were the neighbors on this dead end road remaining relatively rational or perhaps they were becoming foaming at the mouth dangerous folks to be around as starvation began to affect their minds? For that matter what was his state of mind? How was his thought processes holding up compared to those other folks whose normal realities were being shattered? He knew one thing though for himself, he was sure he could switch or adapt faster than most people to this crappy existence. He had already developed his own personal kind of "situational acceptance" of the disaster and went into his survivalist mindset and by doing so, he let his ideas of normal life and expectations of soft living go, thus greatly increasing his own chances for survival. Choosing to be a survivor is an action step that creates a mental change in the way we think and the way perceive or act towards a situation. When one chooses to be a survivor they have made the decision to distance themselves or step out of a" victims role" and are using positive energy to actively pursuing alternate means to live through the problem." David reflected, confident his knowledge and preps would allow him to hang on as long as it was humanely possible while waiting for the electricity to come back on some year...

He squinted and adjusted his old brown eyes to the suns glare and then somewhat causally looked out the window across the old drink glass stained oak dining room table for the umpteenth time today. He looked out about 50 yards towards his driveways entrances in quasi alertness and was feeling a bit forlorn and apprehensive about his sorry state of affairs. His mind churned and it wandered constantly back to the subjects as to what he could be doing, or what he should be doing to prepare his home further for long term survival.

He dreaded the routine of keeping up this boring, as well as nerve racking, peek and watch, paranoid or not so paranoid vigilance today. He was trying to stay focused and keep an eye on the main points of access to his property. He continually grumbled all the while about the need for him to be watching out for strangers or friends to approach his prepper shack.

"Damn your soul David! You just had to go and tell a bunch of folks around here that you were some kind of a prepper didn't you? Oh yea, you made a buck or two doing it as a marketing technique. You also enjoyed informing other folks to prepare for calamities like this and you knew the risks before hand of advising them that you practiced what you preached in regard to preparedness. Now, all of his dispersing that advice for whatever reason other than also

trying to make a buck off selling prepper supplies to build up
his own preps didn't sound so smart for him to have done at
this moment. No, he should have been more careful. The less
interaction he had with people outside of his prepper shack,
the better off he would have been now." David muttered,
while admonishing himself gloomily. He then adjusted the
balance of a green camo 12 gauge pump shotgun he had
leaning against the table next to him and looked back towards
kitchen window in case anyone might just come in from the
woods.

There are many ways to "spread the preparedness word" or get the message about prepping out without unnecessarily endangering your family by being less public. He could have been a bit less lazy and more resourceful in lowering his profile. But he had always figured that it's kind of hard to do anything secretive at all if you want to advertise products or sell articles about survival and preparedness to the prepper community. You got to get known as an expert for it and you got to live it as a lifestyle. Also for kind hearted survivalist fools like David, it is just a simple fact that it is hard for some people to just shut up and prep and try to keep a low profile. A bunch of drinks with the boys or girls and parties on regarding survival tricks or what it takes to get an article published. For some folks like David it's counterproductive to their incomes or their psyches to just hush.

Some people make survival so much a part of who they are, that they want to share every little experience with others, just like campers or hunters often do. For many people who enjoy talking publicly about prepping and sharing survival knowledge, it is something they do to help spread preparedness warnings or mitigate a perceived risk, for others it's just a teaching or sharing moment. In David's case it was all the above and more as he considered it partly pure interesting entertainment to participate with the community.

Many times some people see or hear something about preppers in media, then give that thing a name such as when we break the supposed prepper taboo of operational security (OPSEC) and that's it. The speaker is belittled and is chased away by internet trolls or sternly warned by other preppers of their impending doom by neighbors coveting the speaker's goods in a disaster. Loose lips bring the zombie hoards or whatever. The worst thing about prepping for disaster is the stigma it gives if you let labels affect you.

Oftentimes there is much more sense behind the way that you yourself have chosen to spread the word of preparedness and prepare for yourself, than observing some top secret doomer rational. CERT training, Red Cross, Prepper Conventions,

Forums etc. are all good places to learn and interact in, just use some common sense.

David's in your face, I am a prepper rationale was based on his belief that if you are thinking about gathering preppers in your community for when SHTF happens, then start doing it today. You do that task by talking to people and talking about how to prepare for disasters. He figured it was better to end up being with (close like family) people when SHTF or failing that, at least be known by other likeminded people that prepped and might cross his path someday, then for him to be left all alone and a stranger to others. At least they knew him as someone who cares to prepare.

David had no way for himself of knowing, or for that matter even finding out the actual magnitude of the cyber attack that had taken out most of the U.S. electrical grid. He didn't have anywhere near enough information for him to even try to hazard a guess about the effects of the media reported scalar or cyber terrorist attack on the electrical grid. He himself wondered like many other preppers if this could end up being the real deal true cataclysmic event that ultimately caused the actual destruction of all the power grid hubs in the US. But with out any hard facts, his speculation was about as good as anyone else.

If it was the feared big grid down, double" damn damn" apocalypse occurring in the country and all of the power plants were fried beyond 6 month repair.. Then he knew things would spin out of control quickly and with a swift and definite finality. The outcome of what once was a technological and civilized world would soon be a smoking ruin in no time and of that he was sure.

However, the event he himself personally was experiencing of a darkened world without power could easily be nothing more than a localized disaster or a geographical grid down thing. You know one that could be recovered from in a few months if a concerted organized effort amongst the utility companies could get the grid back online even a few blocks at a time. The type of event that some radio announcers might say after a major disastrous event, don't worry, the power will only be out for X many months in certain areas of the country until the problems were isolated or fixed.

Some more skeptical or informed scientists and engineering experts were saying perhaps the power would be out at most a year until efforts to restore it were successful on an attack of this magnitude. Of course one significant tangible thing to consider strongly and also, it is one strategy or theory that for some reason strangely no one in authority was talking about publicly, was that as the electrical power distribution stations are repaired, or as they were being repaired, these were the same facilities that can also be hit and attacked, time and time again with either cyber-attack or physical destruction. The choice of keeping the grid down just depended on, but was not limited to, how the original power disruptive attack was done the first go round by whoever had the ax to grind and said lights out America.

"I can't believe this government was actually being foolish enough to think that the impacted and darkened cities could try to survive an entire year without power. Really? No freaking way anyone is that stupid. There have been plenty of their own studies performed and by all kinds of Federal agencies as to expected causalities and costs occurring after an EMP attack takes out the grid for example. That type of a dark world scenario is basically the end of our modern civilization as we know it and according to most scientific predictions and assumptions a staggeringly enormous number of the population will have died in the first six months from starvation, dehydration and violence. As well as one must stop and strongly consider the devastation and aftermath from the unstoppable fires generated from societal unrest and ignorance. These types of things will force a bug out on you. Look at how much of LA burned from the riots and that was when electricity, water,

communications, National Guard, Police and Firemen were on duty to handle one segment of one big city acting the fool.

I think the estimate in the government sponsored studies for the United States casualties was something like 300 million dead or 90% of the population dead within a year if a EMP strike took out the power grid.. Put a fork in it folks, we are done and our butts are baked!" David though morosely. He knew that the turmoil and chaos of a long term grid down situation could not be contained and would be spilling over this country like a plague of flaming locusts."

A 119-square-kilometer (46-square-mile) swath of Los Angeles was transformed into a combat zone for 6 days in one riot called the Watts riot in 1965. Times have changed and so has weaponry and attitudes. The government is going to have to be everywhere showing they are doing something about the cause of this disaster and will pick out a focus to scapegoat on at first before the food riots start. People are angry, they want revenge, better to direct this energy towards some other enemy than the racial, rich or anti government grievieances that will get expressed with fire and destruction. A distraction or a real need response will be used by the President to try to call the nation unsuccessfully together to fight a common cause. Problem is everyone's common cause is to live for themselves another day.

"I wonder just what in the hell the government has in its devious little mind as to what it is going to do for, or to the general populace? Well they are going to first fill up the detention camps and prisons most assuredly and I bet they start with the various foreign terrorist cell member watch lists DHS has somewhere. Those are long subjective lists filled with religious radicals, terrorist wanna be`s, subversives etc. Probably that list will include a whole lot of south of the border illegal immigrant folks who will be trying to come in to this country now in droves because that now, even our lax but somewhat effective hi-tech security is down. No grid power to run surveillance cameras and sensors on the border, greatly reduced border guards, fuel shortages, armed drug cartels, oh yea we will have all kinds of unwanted visitors aplenty. Hurray, now it's easier than ever to get into the U.S.A, gringos are such dumb asses.

Mixed in with all the would be poor but descent hard working immigrants taking advantage of the situation will be disaster refugees seeking to leave their countries who are also without power etc. and the terrorist like or state sponsored foreign military special forces who somehow manage to get through the borders everyday anyway and they are not coming as tourists anymore. There will be a whole fresh new shit load of assorted terrorist cells moving up their troops from their bases in South America to create more mischief and a actual militaristic invasion of the U.S. of sorts which is not out of the question A few hundred dedicated soldiers or terrorists could easily keep us tied in knots as they blew power stations, upset shipping etc.

Damn right those savage people need rounding up first and detained somewhere in a concentration camp like sized affairs. As far as David was concerned, hell they need to just be shot while crossing the border and he wasn't adverse to summarily declared executions if found to be foreign agents in a round up. This was a touchy subject with him, As far as he was concerned as a former soldier, a soldier was a soldier and deserved the rights and privileges of the Geneva Convention. But he had no problem throwing out the rule book when dealing with the festering politically and religiously radically influenced insurgents that might come to our shores.

David thought that regular Mr. or Mrs. John Q citizen shouldn't worry too much about some of the more oddball internet conspiracy theories on FEMA camp reserving a place for them should the whack jobs in Washington somehow feel threatened about preppers or patriots right now. The government was going to be entirely too busy and have their *hands full dealing with real active threats and challenges to care if they been complaining on face book too much or about which citizens was ever on the DHS list for expressing patriotic sentiments that somehow the justice department found to be subversive .Hell us good old boys and Constitution wavers are now the first line of defense and they can worry about us taking our country back later.*

David thought disgustedly that the terms the media bandied about causally labeling folks like him or those following a lifestyle of self reliance as being some kind of a nut job right or left wing prepper, homesteader or survivalist, you name it was treasonous to our history as a nation. Did they think our fore fathers never prepped or what? The label or name they wanted to put on you these days usually depended on what kind of firepower, guns and such you might have personally on hand and what they thought this subjective term might imply to their political aspirations or sensationalism.

Well no one would probably label him or call him an excessive armament stocking doomsday prepper or some kind of bunker conspiracy fearing commando survivalist. He believed in the common core Minute Man theory our leaders should have learned in elementary school regarding his guns but he just had what he considered basics.

However, you could also easily say about him that he had more than a sufficient range of firearms and ammo to deter most folks from trying to take his stuff and encourage their thinking that he was far from an easy target or mark to be strong-armed or robbed should someone get such an ill advised strangely misbegotten notion... Couple shotguns, some pistols, a few rifles, more than some folks, less than others, nothing special.

Whatever the label someone used to describe those survival oriented folks like him who were trying to become more self-reliant while becoming less reliant on big government was redundant. The common thread about it all concerning the survival movement and self reliance community was that things are going to hell, we see it for ourselves everyday in the news and feel that you should and can take measures and steps to defend and provide for yourself and your family.

It didn't matter what you wanted to call David, to him it was enough to know he just tried to live a lifestyle that mattered. He was a survivor, someone who believed in the Boy Scout motto of "Be Prepared." and he dang sure planned on keeping it that way. He knew deep in his soul that the societal glue that held everything together was dissolving faster than he might be realizing and if he was taking unnecessary precautions to deter someone at this stage of the game, well then you could bet your sweet bippie he didn't give a damn. It was open carry season in his neck of the woods now.

Practicing his battle drills in anticipation for what threats or risks he knew would come later in his direction as this apocalypse progressed didn't seem to him to far fetched either..

Tactics or drills he envisioned and had rehearsed from his old Army days might just become necessary soon enough as cities burned and people migrated. There were oh so many half remembered or tried to be forgotten memories of mayhem and battles that needed to be practiced and planned for by him, He had an edge and some practical experience if such extraordinary measures were required to hang on to his homestead should it be challenged and he didn't plan on making any forgetful or newbie mistakes.

A loaded semi auto black AR 15 rifle with an adjustable stock and his old green canvas H pattern harness military web gear sat next to his boogy bag in back of a black futon not far from him. The field gear was positioned somewhat out of sight should the need for him to decide to go full military battle rattle. He looked over at its familiar comfortable presence of the web gear to once again reassure himself that it was handy and that the straps and rigging remained untangled for quick donning should the need to put on his rig in a hurry occur.

"That is if, the big if", David considered. This wildly obscure depending on his luck big "If", was something that might be his opportunity to flee should he somehow be lucky enough to be forewarned, or "if" he possibly saw a large group of folks approaching his place, then he hoped he might, just might mind you, have enough time to get the hell out the backdoor of the house unnoticed and deal with the threat from his now hopeful unscathed and miraculous escape to the wood line.

David could decide if he made it to a safe position with a survival pack and his battle rifle if it made more sense to take flight or fight from there. Running away from indefensible odds or escaping to fight another day was not cowardice but hard earned wisdom and survival. He could always bring the fight back under his own guerilla warfare rules another day if it made sense. Live to fight another day, haul ass, avoid confrontations when you can and let folks know the devil might follow them back home if they knocked at his door with hate or theft in their hearts.

"After all, the ants should be ready when the starving grasshoppers start running around in the woods or vice`versa." David mused grimly with a wicked smile. He knew you had to prepare for the fact that true aggressors are not going to use the normal way to your house, knock on your door or unlatch your gate hollering to come in etc. If they were intent on robbing you, you were going to get robbed, but folks just looking for a soft or unguarded target of opportunity were a different matter. So were folks with murder already in their hearts who were most likely on the prowl taking by force already. That's why countries have different uniforms, so enemies recognize each other and shoot on sight remains an option. Thing is, whose uniform you going to shoot at and why now?

David wasn't ignorant of the messy facts facing him or even considering deluding himself in anyway that he or his girlfriend could do anything much more than maybe performing a heroic vain attempt at temporarily holding off a determined enemy. If people wanted something from you, eventually they can get that from you, your food, house, wife, it does not matter what. You are not omnipotent or ever awake and ready; it's as simple as that.

Only chance for him and Julie in the unlikely, but still very possible event of being directly targeted was that the imagined adversaries did not notice his escape. He also considered Psychological warfare. If there was an opportunity that he could convince others that they might think he had enough men or firepower to protect his goods from loss they might decide whatever it is they wanted from the house was going to cost too dearly and avoid him and his house.

"Now then, back to this stupid stagnant reality I am trying to sort out. At this very moment I am looking good." David said to himself while admiring his gaunt but wicked looking form in the mirror.
"Yea, handsome indeed." David kidded with himself comically posing with a shotgun and six shooter like some Wild West photo shoot.

"If I spied someone coming in the gate and it was just a neighbor that was looking for another hand out coming to see me, this .357 mag hogleg style pistol on my belt and this 12 gauge pump shotgun I would be holding should more than

suffice to get my point across that this" mothers *"cupboard was bare and guarded by some redneck cowboy shooter in a unfriendly mood about the notion of giving up any of his vittles."* David mused admiring himself in the mirror once more while making mock threating faces.

"Hopefully who ever it might come visiting unannounced desperations would not out shine their realization that it might be very unhealthy to hang around and not take his firm no way José for an answer." David thought while considering where he was going to conceal his extra 9mm backup pistol on his body.

"Hey, extra knife too, he surmised checking that he could easily get to some kind of a weapon with his left or right hand in an instant.

"Humm, how about that brace of OSS Phillips head looking knives he had pit back from his crazier times thinking about this day? No that was frivolous and unnecessary. He had what he needed weapon wise and if it wasn't sufficient he would be dead anyway." David thought why was it that no one was considering that just plain dying of old age was no longer an option and that helping each other in mutual kindness to hopefully not meet too much of a untimely or very painful death was much more important than

27

dreaming up things to die over? Of course if a lot of people just remembered the fact that survival skills are not just for war, they're needed in our daily lives as well, then we might all get through this.

.

That it was a well known fact by some that David had military grade weapons around and readily available to him was a pretty much known or a guessed fact by most folks in his small rural community.

The residents of this backwater were also precariously somewhat aware or had been forewarned about his alleged prowess and marksmanship in using said firearms tactically and effectively. For him to have pondered on his small arsenal of guns and having chosen as his daily carry for today an old western style six shooter and a 12 gauge pump shotgun also spoke volumes about his shoot them if I need to mindset.

Nothing like having a shotgun in close quarters battle. David also stood a pretty good chance at shooting a deer at 50 yards or so with the flat trajectory of his potent .357 magnum pistol. He could at one time back in the day, he thought whimsically also place an accurate lightening quick follow-up shot with the single action pistol if needed. He wasn't really to sure how much of his previous prowess and accuracy he retained with it though, because he hadn't fired that particular weapon in years. However he was comfortable with it and hoped his muscle memory and brain sighting of it remained.

David loved the old simple six shooter pistol and had learned and practiced several western trick marksman shots with it over time, but that had been with a younger mans eyes and a much longer time ago than he cared to think about. A lot of water had passed under his bridge and time and age had sneakily caught up with him as the years faded and he mellowed.

David had been prickly as hell though lately, hinting about or directly telling the few folks he had seen around that his "well was running dry" regarding any food supplies and that his "well bucket" had had itself a big hole in it for weeks in regards to leaking out any more morsels of food to the needy non preppers looking to him for a hand out.

Oh, give him a little credit now. He had given away some basic foodstuffs away like a few pounds of rice and beans to assuage his conscience and other folks hunger and he use some goods to try to gain some time and allegiance with one set of not so savory neighbors, but he had judged this little bit of foodstuff loss as a necessary evil and not a total loss entirely.

The old late seventies in age couple across from his property had taken in the grandkid and his girlfriend a year ago and the boy had walked over about a week and half ago to ask David would he mind helping dig a grave for his grandmother that had just passed. She had been on a cord plug in oxygen generator and had bless her old heart, expired within a day of switching to bottled emergency oxygen. This tragic event had happened not to long after the grid was shut down and was a surprise to David just because he had not considered her fate or plight until then. Too many things affecting his own life and others made him remiss in his considerations of some neighbors he rarely saw.

David didn't really have to ask the surviving relatives exactly why they wanted to bury her on their homestead, but like an old goombah he was he asked them anyway. Sometimes you just don't think things out. The boy said him and his grandpa had decided it was neither fitting nor proper to bury the old woman in the city mass graves that were filling up if they had their own land to pick a peaceful plot on. Said the old women would be happier that way in only the way the living can relate to last wishes.

The radio had advised in no uncertain terms awhile back that the closest town's community mortuaries were full up and that the morgues were way over capacity in the hospitals and with no fuel to run emergency generators for refrigeration that mass graves were a necessary sanitization issue and services were being held to bring out your dead for civil affairs disposal. The National Guard was setting up numerous grave registration rosters to try to keep up with the deceased so a record could be kept of those who had expired and gone to the great beyond, but the boy and his grandpa like many others of like minds or hearts chose not to waste the gas or energy notifying anyone of the women's passing. They were just going to handle the laying of the woman to rest matter quietly themselves in a more meaningful manner.

.

David thought of the boy begrudgingly as an arrogant nare do well occasional hardcore druggie that under normal conditions he needed to avoid and not associate with. However, under these conditions he would not refuse anyone in there time of need and one thing lead to another and soon they were both digging the hole with a self serving passion while sweating profusely preparing to give the old woman's bones back to the earth in a solitary respectable grave in a backyard clearing.

David had allowed himself to cough up and donate to the surviving relatives a bit of food. He made the gesture stating it was to help stabilize the boy's sick grandfather who was grieving for his wife. David by this act of generosity actually quietly hoped it would buy him some small space of time before he had to do the same kind of funerary duties again for the old gentleman. Old couples have been known to die a week or so from each other.

The boy and his girlfriend acted grateful and friendly enough for David's kind acts but he had rebuffed any of their efforts to befriend him any further or answer many questions about how he was getting by. He knew all too well that now was not the time for him to be evaluating or accumulating new friends and took on a persona of aloofness and icy suspicion in their regard.

The boy's (should say mans) name was Will for Willard and the girls or woman's name was Sally and both had the tattoo freak thing going on that David despised somewhat. His generation considered tattoos as something for the lower class criminals to advertise prison sentences or for the more hardcore type fringe folks to evidence their toughness or something.

David had ever so slowly become much more accepting to the inking your skin fad overtime but generally speaking his first instincts had been proven to right all too often regarding folks he knew wearing piercing and ink to be pretty much disreputable types. Particularly if they were into extremes of this funky trend which in his opinion was nothing more than a distasteful fetish. David particularly didn't like to see them on women at all. This was because he considered the female form to be the most beautiful creation on earth and it was almost sacrileges to him to watch pretty young women deface themselves and their loveliness in what they considered his uncool geriatric old mans view on how their tattoos looked

His personal opinions aside of the couples constitutional rights to do freely with their own personal appearance as they wished notwithstanding, he could not overlook the feeling all those dreadful tattoos and piercing they sported gave him of the couples chances of being industrious and employable in this world or any other.

That wasn't the worst feeling he ever had about them though. The feelings he got about them when just barely a week had gone by after they buried grandma and they had stopped for a visit were far worse. The couple had come over to ask of him once more to dig deep and provide for them some rations in a way that felt like, well to him anyway, that they thought they were somehow entitled to it offering nothing in return.

At the funeral he had given to them in his opinion, graciously and without reservations 5lbs each dry weight of parboiled rice and beans, a few cans of corn and 2 cans of spam. That was before they had come to his front door knocking loudly and announcing themselves the following Monday morning wondering if he had anything different to donate to them. Apparently a diet of beans and rice sucked and was not good on their or the old man's digestive systems and they were wondering if he couldn't diversify the contents of his next donation to them.

David had not even tried to explain the benefits of Parboiled rice to them. How it actually was better on the old mans stomach etc. Parboiled rice might sound like it's precooked, but it's not. Instead, it's processed quite differently from other types of rice. The resulting grain is cooked and served just as you would white or brown rice. However, because of the special processing, parboiled rice is a better source of fiber, calcium, potassium and vitamin B-6 than regular white rice.

Parboiled rice is especially rich in niacin, providing 4 milligrams, or 23 percent of the recommended daily intake in 1 cup of cooked rice. You'll also get 19 percent of the daily intake of vitamin B-6. These values are about double the amount you would get from non-enriched white rice. Your body needs B vitamins to metabolize food into energy, but they also fill other roles, such as helping make hormones and neurotransmitters.

Vitamin B-6 removes the amino acid homocysteine from your bloodstream by turning it into other substances. This might help keep your heart healthy; high levels of homocysteine are associated with an increased risk of cardiovascular disease.

These reasons alone were all well and good with David but his thought on the matter were parboiled rice stores on the shelf longer and is more nutritious. That's a no brainier for a prepper like him. Hell you can even get it in white and brown.

"White rice has a shelf life of up to 30 years if it is stored in a cool dry place sealed in a container with oxygen absorbers.

If stored at higher temperatures it will still last for about ten years. Any added nutrients and flavors will be retained.

Brown rice from the store typically only lasts about 6-8 months due to the oil content in it. If you choose to include this in your food storage make sure you rotate it very aggressively. Commercial packaged instant brown rice designed for longer term storage can have a longer shelf life. Thrive Life has Instant Brown Rice with a 7 year shelf life. That is the longest we've ever seen for brown rice according to Food Storage made easy by Jodi and Julie at http://foodstoragemadeeasy.net".

"My *NEXT* donation?" David drawled out and asked while raising one eyebrow askance at the pair but otherwise looking quite deadpan.

"Well yea, I mean, well uh... David don't get me wrong now. We are really grateful man for the rice and beans you gave us and appreciate the kindness. But you know how it is; we were just hoping that you might maybe throw a few cans of something different in this time to break the monotony" Will sort of whined as he looked like a weasel to David.

Sally backed him up in his efforts to get on their seemingly well prepared neighbors good side and added

"David it was so nice of you to help bury Me-Mah and Papa said to give you his heartfelt thanks again and tell you that you would be in his prayers, but we are almost out of food once again and he would be terribly grateful if we could maybe have some more canned spam or something today." Sally said hopefully.

David regarded the pair of them evenly for the moment while displaying very little of the uncomfortable emotions he was feeling inside before he spoke.

"I think we need to discuss why it is you think that I offered to donate to you somehow on a regular basis. I admit I gave your family a gift and offered some small help in the future if I could possibly, but I didn't say it would be a regularly occurring thing." David replied looking aghast at the presumptions they seemed to be still holding. Bits of humor from the gallows of humanity were David's mainstay, but this conversation was going in entirely the wrong direction and his brow began to furrow...

"I thought that you were one of them survivalists. What they do they call them? You know, a Doomsday Prepper like on NatGeo. Don't you have yourself a ton of stuff all stored up like those people on the show do somewhere for a disaster like this?" Willard said in a "what-cha talking about Willis" like voice. Just as if to be refused by David had never even been considered by him.

"No hell I don't! I never have said that I did either! Get this straight. I don't know what Hollywood fantasy notion you are thinking I got put away but I am telling you here and now that just giving you that little bit of shit I gave you the first go round took food out of my belly as well as Julie's! You two go sit yourselves down over at the picnic table a minute while I think about this and go see what my lady has to say about giving you another care package. Listen, hear me out. I am telling you that I hardly got enough food for myself let alone any extra to spare for anyone! That includes some neighbors that I hardly even know if you get my drift. Now then, I will still try to do something for you if you would please just go sit yourselves over there for a bit while I break this news to the missus and see what we can do about finding you something to eat? But remember, I never took you to raise son, you neither missy." David advised glaring at Will in an angry exasperated fashion and giving a side-glance at Sally that could have charmed a rattlesnake not to even think about biting or shaking its tail.

Will flinched, dug the toe of his boot in the dirt and directed his somewhat now cowed girlfriend towards the wooden picnic table David had sitting off to the right of his front door. David ignored their mutterings as he closed his front door with a flourish and a with a loud click of the lock went to talk to Julie who was standing guard in a back bedroom with the pistol-handled alley sweeper of a Mossberg cruiser shotgun she had loaded and at the ready if David had needed any help.

David thought to himself "Damned if that couple had any kind of "walk in the front door privileges" now, that is if he ever was even fool enough to invite them into his home under even normal social conditions. Right this minute, they are here by permanently shit out of luck to enter his abode."

The word *prepper* was unheard of just a few years ago. Average people don't relate the word normally to identify the self reliance or prepper community as people who use the word on thousands of prepper-specific blogs, websites, and YouTube videos. No they prefer or expect the NatGeo show version of a rich odd person they were exposed to in a reality show. NatGeo chose some whack jobs for a show about how some people prepare for a disaster and now folks want to add that "doomsday prepper' label on to him and everyone else in the preparedness community. A lot of those people on the show were some kind of rich eccentric survivalist that had all kinds of preps coming out their ears' David mused thinking about the fact that he was far from rich, but his kitchens counters at the moment had evidence of much more food preps than he was admitting to the couple or to anyone else for that matter. He had spent the morning dragging them out of everywhere and the cans and boxes were out on display awaiting him and his sweetie's inventory to do some prepper planning on how they should regulate their accumulated foodstuffs over the days and months ahead. Not a good thing for those two outside to catch even a glimpse of his small hoard.

"David I only caught a small piece of that conversation. Do they really expect to come down here whenever they have a need and you to supply them with food?" Julie said looking angry and then peeking around the corner of the blinds at the couple with the pistol grip 12 gauge shotgun in her white knuckled small hands.

"I guess the fools think so, but I will soon rectify that dumb notion quick enough. It isn't time yet baby to start a war with them or any other neighbors just yet if a bit of threatening or hollering can keep them away." David said ominously in a hushed tone that she evidently picked up on and followed up with an abrupt no nonsense reply of poking a threatening gun barrel forward gesture in their unseen general direction with the scattergun.

"Geezus! " David thought, knowing that the first round out of that thing could sink a boat with its 3 inch shell loaded with 42 pellets of No. 4 Buckshot. Follow up that shot with 5 rounds in succession of 2 3/4 (12) pellet nickel plated double ought buck and he doubted he would not even have a picnic table left if she made good on the threat with any kind discharge towards them ." A very wicked weapon indeed David had decided.

"I chose the right gun didn't I David?" Julie said looking back into the bedroom and seeking his approval as she questioned herself about having not chosen her .22 rifle instead for this possible encounter.

"Yea baby your doing fine. They are ok, nothing much to worry about from them today and if not that shotgun persuader you are toting could of put them in every shot glass in Chicago. Don't sweat yourself about them bothering us at all for now darling, you and I already guessed correctly they were coming back over wanting a hand out. Now they are here and they are and what they are. Thing is now what are we going to do about it?" David said peeking out the window at the couple. They saw him and didn't look away any too quick, sort of like they were still waiting on him to give them an expected invite to come in.

David eyed the pair and thought to himself "Well the nerve of those two!" As far as he was concerned, they were pretty much just strangers when you got down to it. For them to come knocking on his door looking for him to "redistribute" his canned goods in their direction like it was expected of him was ludicrous. Friggin people were just plain crazy".

"David? Did you tell him and tell him in no certain terms that from now on he had to hunt for his own food or that maybe they just needed to move themselves on somewhere away from here more apt to have food for them like a relocation camp?" Julie said uncomfortably while watching the front door like it was going to be kicked in possibly by the unsavory hungry pair.

"No I haven't, not yet. I am still strongly thinking about how best to say that and calm everyone down some. You know when desperation reaches its peak people don't get scared as easy or show any fear to a threat real or not. You can be sure though Julie that he already is trying to hunt some on his own and since we haven't heard a gunshot from their direction he hasn't seen shit to shoot at or he would have been popping caps with whatever firearms he has over there.

That's a weird thing by the way that we haven't heard any shots coming from over to their place. That grandpa of his bragged to me once that he normally has several deer on the property at 5am and more crossing at sundown everyday, but as you know the deer have changed their normal trails and directions it seems." David said pondering the possible causation of the lack of gunshots heard from a house where it was normal to occasionally hear something going off occasionally, even if it was nothing else but celebratory gunfire of a few rounds on a holiday.

"You have been saying David that the deer are acting weird anyway, maybe then going to the camps is for them. By the way, I am not going to let you forget that you wouldn't even allow me to take a shot at that buck standing next to your garden last week.' Julie said grousing about David's adamancy not to interfere in any way with the deer on his property normal migration and feeding patterns for awhile because he felt they needed to be undisturbed and not hunted close in until they really needed them.

"I have explained my reasoning on that to you Julie a hundred times over. I cannot monitor the deer's trails or figure out their numbers if we mess with what they are currently thinking are some safe clear paths this close to the house. What I think has happened to make them so skittish and confused is that these damn hunters around here have pulled out all the stops and are dumping whatever kind of bait or scent they got in their hunting areas to increase the chances of a kill and confusing them with odd smells and signals. The wind and the woods for miles around here are being convoluted with man scent and deer attractant. The problem with that is if you make an artificial salt lick or a rut you scent away the deer herds from a normally traveled trail. Then it is up to the bucks or odd does that decide most everything's not right and they make new trails to seek food or avoid danger just like during regular hunting season. The age old traditional forest trails are all convoluted now except the ones running across my property exiting that low lying boggy area in the back of my property down by the creek. We need to keep them trails as is and put nothing like a snare set up to molest them or even so much as put out a bait to guide them elsewhere for now. We have got ourselves plenty of stored food for a good period of time and like I told you, in deer terms we are thought of as an island of safety or recuperation in these stressful hunting times. Not hunting them now will payoff for us in spades later." David said remembering Julie's excitement to protect the garden as well as put some fresh meat on the table and prove to her and her man that she was

fully capable of ranger living and bagging a deer all by
herself.

She had begrudgingly lowered her gun on what would
have been her first deer and in her opinion could have
performed a major supportive accomplishment to "prepper
shack" by adding some game meat to their diets when David
had unexpectedly put a hand on her weapon and spoiled her
exuberance with a hushed admonishment to "let it pass.' The
deer had noticed them watching her, but the buck had
retreated unhurriedly away from their presence.

Julie more than understood that animals were going to
be soon hunted to darn near extinction like David had pointed
out history had proven in prior disastrous hard times during
the depression. However, she still longed for the missed
opportunity to make the kill and fumed over the loss of food
she would have been able to provide for them.

David had assured her many times over that by her
being patient and not taking that "proving or being helpful
shot" was a very wise and good thing she had done. Not
insisting on taking that shot was paramount to their survival
and that Julie had more than fulfilled her duty to "Prepper
Shack" by using good judgment. She still retained some

regrets and animosity towards David for not taking her prize, but she understood and was soon over it he thought.

"Hell! I bet David is now going to go give a bit of expert advice to the guy across the street on how to take a deer for the pot and he would probably shoot the one David had told her to let pass. Dang David! No matter how much she understood his reasoning for not shooting that deer she had in her sights it still irked her no end. That big buck had been right there in front of her and it would have been so easy! Humpf! Now after all that David was now asking her advice about giving away some more of their storage food to this couple who would be most likely shooting her deer tomorrow!" Julie fumed trying to evaluate it all.

That for some reason David had some kind of hunters natural innate or odd understanding with the deer was a given. He might not have hunted deer nor had the desire to in years, but he kept good track of the herds around his area. When they first met David had taken great joy in explaining to her how to read the faint tracks on the trails the deer used as they traveled criss-crossing trails on his property. David could tell you by the clock what time you could observe a deer slinking through the forest and pretty much exactly where it would appear on his little spread. He also messed with the deer by occasionally chunking a pine cone at them or something else suitable like a rotten stick if they got too brave or familiar when he was present and they didn't politely retreat back to the woods after checking him out. He wanted the deer to not get to familiar with humans for their own safety.

It was that testosterone induced "No Worries" attitude of his that caused Julie so much frustration as well as intrigue with him.

A large graceful brown doe that David had shown her a time or two before had been known to be seen standing just outside his garden in midwinter at four in the afternoon as the sun started to go down before he corrected the animal's s too close for comfort behavior. David had told her on the phone of this magical sighting occurrence more than once. But her not being a country girl and because of David's penchant for playing jokes, she had never taken his clockwork sightings seriously. That is, until over a couple days he had proved it up to her twice for her own eyes joy and amazement to see this forest creature going about its natural state of affairs like it had its own way of telling time.

David had gestured slowly towards her as he put his finger to his lips to indicate for her to be silent and then showed her out the front door of his house and pointed carefully towards one corner of the fenced enclosure of his little raised bed garden. There it was! Julie thought as she beheld the wild deer's magnificent beauty and her and David shared a wonderful Mother Nature moment.

"Calm! Be very calm Julie; don't even think how exciting or lovely the deer is. Watch; just observe this forest being casually. Don't talk to the deer except with your mind. We see each other and it's Ok. No harm no ill will by our meeting, but wish with your mind that she leaves us for now. Watch her, your mind moved her and now she is nervous and scared and wants to take the first way out. David had whispered softly.

See the fence? See how it's bent down in some areas? That's where a panic exit by another deer had hit it a week earlier. Look now; look at her feeling our intents. A graceful leap and a clearing of the wire and a non destructive understanding of deer nervousness and humans had occurred.

"Hey Lady, by the way I ain't the only one around here that can piss around fence posts to "Claim" space in the natural world by the way. You got your own plumbing to help out with the task of keeping critters away; yours just don't aim as well as mine." David said chuckling and reminding her that pissing around the backyard was not only a convenience but a duty at prepper shack and that lady like ways could be forgotten now as it was important to deter animals from the garden...

"I have been telling you all along Julie why I don't need 10 ft fences to keep them deer or other critters out. I only need to be actively patrolling around the place more and mark my territory the same as the other animals, or it helps to be around and watching to war on the ones that don't take the nature's way of subtle or unsubtle suggestions to avoid an area." David advised thinking about remedying any animal that tried to snub his claims on who was allowed around his gardens.

"You remember Julie; I showed you that deer scrape the other day in the middle of my orchard where I tried that experiment of raising vegetables out of a hay bale? That bale stayed intact and unmolested all summer and was producing yellow squash well before the drought hit. Then midwinter arrived and that big buck and his harem of does pawed it down ate most all of it in what looked like a feeding frenzy and then he left a big scrape to challenge any other male in the area. I pissed on his scrape and dug in the dirt a bit myself and left the message for him to indicate I claimed it as 'MINE! No deer allowed this was my scary male human path they were messing with and so they diverted 30 ft away following on new trail but were still regularly using my road crossing. A week later they were back to where I wasn't following up with "claiming" game and munched my lime tree because the game had now changed in their eyes and noses and I had not been around to mark or tromp up the trails." David said flustered his analogy didn't seem to be going anywhere.

"Well if I had of shot that deer those neighbors wouldn't be on our door step so soon wanting food and you wouldn't be asking me what to do with that couple outside" Julie jabbed back at him but then gave him a big hug and wistful eyes to acknowledge his plans might need support and considerations that she had yet to realize and waited on his kind reactions.

"Honey, I can't say your right or that I am wrong at the moment darling, but it might help us to look a bit crazy when we go out to talk to them." David declared while fidgeting with the pistol he insisted on strapping on two weeks ago to alleviate his sense of vulnerability or for increased security he didn't know which.

"I believe you got that line of thinking covered already. You already got that crazy look about you David; lighten up a bit and relax some if you can. I can see your cautions but let's try not to be looking so fierce today. I will back you up and tell Sally in no uncertain terms they got to talk to you about working some fields and doing some hunting if they expect morsel one from us from now on." Julie said patting David assuredly who just said "Damn' and tried not to fidget further with his holster.

"Come on girl we might as well wing this thing and get it over with." David said after his exclamation and made a point to have his own shotgun in hand for looks sake.

Once outside, David looked over at the couple looking at them google eyed like aggressive lost sheep sitting at his picnic table waiting for the outcome of the mysterious discussion that had went on inside his home. Sally noted the casual way Julie was toting a wicked pistol handled shotgun they had not seen before but things seemed ok as she beamed her normal infectious smile.

"Greetings!! You all doing well?" Julie said giving them brief each one handed hugs while still holding the shotgun as David regarded them with a more reserved standoffish sort of alert scrutiny.

"Hey man David, why all the hardware? Are you that worried about us? I didn't mean anything by calling you a Doomsday Prepper" Will said eying all the guns and he hoped Julies friendly greeting might have some influence on David's suspicious and aggressive nature.

"No I am not particularly worried about you, we started carrying guns a week ago just as a precaution and you never know when you might see some game. Anyway, I told you Julie and I had to get in agreement on our food stores and this time you're in luck Willie." David said as happy as a clam that his one handed grip on his own shotgun made everyone a bit nervous as he looked at their eyes when its barrel accidentally pointed in their direction. He mumbled an apology and adjusted it to point up and down range.

Nobody felt right about this meeting and you could cut the tension in the air with a knife as David and Julie settled down at the table and propped their long guns against it just out of reach of the self-assuming neighbor's, but still handy enough for themselves to get to.

Both Julie and David wore pistols on their belts that they could also access easily. They seemed very at ease with their surroundings and armaments while David's "Devil may care" attitude and too familiar handling of his shotgun sort of unnerved the neighboring couple.

"Willard and Sally there is something you need to realize before I give you any more food. We are giving you something to eat don't worry. This world we find ourselves living in has gotten really mean and really crazy. I mean absolutely topsy turvy evil and maniacal crazy and regardless of what you believe are the causes of this blackout and who were the participants, we live in a world where anything can and will happen. You best be deciding where your best chances of long term survival lay and be working on heading in that direction if you don't already have the supplies to hang on here and I will tell you why if you will give me a few minutes." David advised and then looked to the couple for permission to speak further.

"Well we hadn't considered going anywhere David but I am all ears if you have heard any news or can offer any advice. After all you're the prepper author! I said that right didn't I" Will said catching himself after using a term David seemed to scowl about previously.

"Yea I am a prepper author I suppose Will. All the term prepper means is someone who prepares, hell everyone prepares for something, but back to what I wanted to tell you. You remember I said that anything could happen now? Well back in my college days I used to study Emergency Management and terrorism and we looked at all kinds of potential risks or threats. Have either one of you given any thought to the nuclear power plant up the road and what might be going on up there at the moment?" David advised them and answered Julies unsaid question with a dismissive look to tell her not to worry about what he was going to say next.

Sally and Will looked at each other momentarily and then warily asked David if he had heard any news or knew anything about the safety of such Atomic power plants when they were shutdown.

"I haven't heard anything about that particular plant Will. I can only assume and hope the utility company has shut it down safely and are running emergency generators for core cooling or something. I sure hope they have enough fuel for them damn things to stay running until they get re-supplied." David advised but didn't bother to mention the possibility of some of the 440 nuclear power reactors in this country running short of backup generator fuel before the reactors had time to completely and safely undergo an emergency SCRAM shutdown and subsequent cooling. Surely most will successfully shut down – but all of them, too many screwups and operator errors for that. And to maintain cooling? *David reminded himself to put batteries in the old Geiger counter he had.*

"I know from the radio news that they are having some issues and problems of shutting down a similarly designed plant up in the Midwest, but they say they will have it under control soon. Now let's think outside the box for a minute everyone." David said getting ready to lay more doom and gloom on his listeners.

"I told you that right now you need to be thinking that anything could happen and just might happen from now on to make the situation infinitely worse. What if for example, What if those terrorists stepped up there attacks on us and launched a coordinated virus attack on our nuclear power plants. They could you know, they have the capabilities and no qualms about using what's considered weapons of mass destruction or biological warfare if it increases their own political agenda. It wouldn't take much toxin to infect a few workers here and there and instead of just causing a power outage we could face multiple nuclear meltdowns... I mean it's easy to bump into folks at bar or at the beach all the time that say they work for one of the plants. The workers at those plants are freely accessible by anyone once they leave work. Or maybe we should think about the cyber attack we have already experienced, were the Nuclear plants themselves directly or indirectly hacked also? Those plants could now be leaking radiation because of mechanical or technical difficulties that we are unaware of and rather than them being restarted to try to turn the lights back on, we could be dependant on workers scurrying to prevent a major meltdown somewhere. Damn utilities and the government will hush that up long as they can I bet once one starts leaking." David said watching his audience intently for their reactions.

"Hell David, are you saying that the terrorists are going to be releasing some kind of viruses?" Sally said looking around like she might see a poisonous pink fog shaped like a skull or something drifting their way.

"That's not what he meant at all Sally. Let me explain it differently. He was saying that the nuclear plant up the road might be having technical problems now that we don't know yet about it or for that matter, whether or not any plant in the country might be experiencing major difficulties. Nuclear plants are not made to be shutdown and moth balled without a lot of ongoing work and preparation before you hit the switch. What he was saying about the viruses was that whoever attacked us is capable of doing anything and it's not like waiting for the utility truck after a hurricane to get your lights back on. I think the gist what David was talking about is to expect more attacks and expect more technological failures to make life a whole lot harder on us all. Am I right David?" Julie asked looking in his direction for affirmation.

"Yea something like that Julie, but the point I am trying to get across is we got to hope for the best, but expect the worst to happen and plan accordingly. You know Sally; you might want to think about this for a moment. Let me ask you a question. What do most people do when they are at home and the power goes out?... They wait. They wait for the government or state to send help and they wait for the power to come back on. Just sit and wait" " David said letting the notion sink in that a lot folks were still waiting for the Cavalry to arrive and would keep on waiting around for the government to come rescue them.

"What I am saying to you and Mr. Will here is that the two of you, or should I say the 3 of you counting your Grandpa need to start making your plans and prepare for yourselves before the rest of the folks stop waiting on the lights to come back on and eventually start thinking for themselves to go after the same resources you need now for your own survival. Get a jump or head start on the competition if you know what I mean. Anyway, back to the actual situation we have at hand. Those cities which are still operating with electricity out in the Midwest might just be living on borrowed time. I mean there is no guarantee they will remain unscathed and unmolested by who ever attacked us. The power could go out for them also after a progression of cascading electrical events just like it has every other time we have had a major blackout in the U.S. or Canada. The grid system is an antiquated, bulky and weak linked thing. Dosent takes much to throw things out of sync. Think about also when this food shortage we are in worsens because farmers can't get fuel for their tractors or they don't have electricity to power their water pumps for irrigation in order to grow crops? If you can't get the crops out of the fields or ship what ever excess there is that might somehow be grown depending on the rain this summer to a distribution point we got more problems. Lots of things will cause no aid to be coming. No aid to be coming ever for that matter. From fuel shortages, crop failure, disease etc. we must consider that we might also no longer have anyone who can work at the power plants, drive the trucks etc. for the same reasons. I could go on and on but I am not here to try and scare or worry you more than I already have. What I am saying to you is that you best be thinking quickly and hard about how and where you're going to be trying to live out your days, because chances are that whether power stays out for 6 months, a year or 2 years you need to deal with your food requirements for the foreseeable future now.. I don't have any more groceries to give to anyone and this will pretty much be our last food donation we can give you. I mean that now, this is all there is unless I happen to shoot a deer or something if there is any left around here after everyone and their relatives try to do the same thing." David told them resolutely and watched the warring emotions of astonishment, anger and confusion takeover the couple's faces as shock and angst set in that David was basically telling them to starve to death or leave the area. But go where?

Will and Sally looked crest fallen for the moment before their southern pride took over and they slowly regained their composure.

"David I am really sorry I even had to ask you for food and I can say for myself and the family that we are very grateful to you even if we haven't showed it much. Knowing what I know now about our situation and everyone else's around sort of makes me ashamed that I even had to come over here asking the second time. But that's the way it is, we really truly need those supplies. We wont bother you no more after this lot, don't worry about that. You are still going to help us out one more time aren't you David? I mean think of it as giving us a little food to get by on just for now until we can make us a plan to survive for ourselves I mean. I reckon me and grandpa will be talking pretty deep about moving on somewhere, I don't know just what he might suggest, I just hope he has got more ideas than me at the moment." Will said hopeful whatever David was going to give him would last more than a few days while gently reminding David of his feelings about his friendly but aloof relationship with his grandfather.

"Sure I will, Julie grab that box of goods we got together for them please." David asked and wondered if he should go talk to the old man himself.

"You need some help?' Sally asked Julie who was starting to get up.

"No I got it." Julie replied hurrying away from the table as Sally sat herself back down.

"They ain't getting even a nat's ass glimpse of what's behind that door!' Julie thought resolutely as she made her way back to the house. "It is bad enough that they will probably be trying to figure out what we got food wise put up based upon what we are giving away to them" she fumed. They might start thinking something foolish as soon as they got their box of goods like "oh since they gave us two cans of beanie weenies then that must mean they got at least 8 more cans they kept for themselves.

Or maybe they would imagine that this must be the least favorite kind of food we had to give up and what kind of other delicacies were we holding back from them? They damn sure didn't need to see all the gear inside neither. What passed for a living room in the small house had prepper gear like bug out bags scattered about that needed to be secured better.

Julie came back shortly to the picnic table with the box and left the shotgun inside figuring it was no longer being used as necessary deterrent, however she did retain the comfort of her pistol.

"That will get you by for more than a week if you're careful." Julie advised.

"Yea get innovative in the kitchen, chili con carne over spaghetti isn't bad and you will fall in love with cream of chicken soup and rice." David said making some recipe suggestions.

"Humm chili con carne, Chili without beans huh? Never seen it before, sounds like a meat sauce." Sally said examining a can.

"Yea it is, think of a chili hotdog. This is what David used to make them with. Its Hormel brand so the can stores longer than most other brands." Julie told them becoming much more relaxed while talking about hard timing or comfort food. David and she had a ton of made up recipes and ad hoc ways to fix things in the pantry that they ate if they didn't want to go to the store or couldn't afford too already.

"Well we really appreciate it. Thank you!" Sally beamed and gave Julie a hug.

David deftly avoided getting hugged himself and changed the subject.

"Hey Will, do you know anything about trapping or snaring?" David inquired.

"No, unless a box and a piece of string counts." Will said smiling.

Out of his own personal meanness, frugalness or just his own thoughts on his chances of personal survivability he wasn't going to give up even one modern animal cable snare. David had decided to give the neighbors on this case to just supply the bare minimum of knowledge about snaring with homemade snares and said nothing of his stash of commercially made ones. Commercial snares made from aircraft cable could make all the difference in the world in greatly enhancing his own personal chances for success.

He had decided in regards to whoever else came to him or his door in need of or begging for food that he would claim to be only getting food for himself by foraging, hunting and a bit of trapping using what ever bits of wire or strong cordage he had around the place to catch the occasional small animal for the pot with a snare.

His soon to be newly initiated greenhorn neighbor amateur trappers stood much less chance of success with their own clumsy and most likely flimsy attempts to ensnare some sustenance. Thus they were much less competition to his own trap lines success rate in providing game for his table.

Hells bells, he muttered to himself. He already knew they would be most likely thinking about asking him for some spare bits of wire or string to construct a snare once he mentioned the concept and explained the basics. He would tell them he had none to spare of course and also tell them he was sorry for that fact, but he would tell them how to scavenge some usable material that their non prepper minds would have taken awhile to come up with on their own.

The solution to not lending snare wire was very easy and obvious; every household has a bunch of electrical cords. Strip the plastic off and harvest the copper wire and twist or untwist it into the appropriate size wire for whatever critter it is your going after. Pull the wire off of pictures etc. Unwind an electric motor, get your Xmas decorations out just search around where ever your imagination takes you and locate the means to survive for yourself.

David decided he would give the neighbors the old U.S. Army Survival manual he had gathering dust on the bookshelf for whatever good it might do them. Without a seasoned instructor around to explain some of the principles to them of hazy illustrations he doubted they would get much out of it but it would damn sure keep them busy and maybe give them some hope or success while keeping them out of his hair.

Knowing that he was most likely only prolonging the inevitable by these actions and putting the curse of prolonged starvation on these folks weighed heavy on his mind, but he saw no other recourse. He had a very limited supply of commercially made modern snares and had already mentally committed to share some of this finite precious commodity with a different neighbor he had chosen as a hunting buddy.

His neighbor Mike had two young kids and a wife to tend to, as well as an elderly mother to care for at the end of the road. Mike had recently medically retired from the Army as a maintenance Sergeant and had come home to his country boy roots. Despite an occasional bad back ailing the man, his assistance would factor in heavily in David's long term survival plan and keeping that family ahead on the survival game was on his pepper's agenda.

David rarely saw or associated with these neighbors much except to wave to them as they drove up and down the mutually shared dead end road. David had spent some time talking to Mike and his wife about prepping and mutually helping each other out after a hurricane when the couple had first moved in, but nothing really more after that. Now it was time to renew the friendships and mutual assistance pacts before Mike ventured down to David's on his own to ask him if he could most likely help him with some dire food shortage needs.

One thing that worried and concerned David quite a bit in these trying times was the levels of desperation people were reaching. Particularly of concern to him were the family men, the head of households who were hunters that lived in the cities and had families to feed. They must have been already rounding up their hunting buddies and holding meetings if they were able to meet up weeks ago. Some groups of hunters are just occasional friends from work that gather a few times a season, some have always lived in a neighborhood and grew up hunting with their country cousins. Hundreds of different backgrounds and ranges of experiences were represented, but starving groups of men were coming to the woods or were already in the woods silently praying for a shot at some game or trying to dream up some way to feed their brood.

Talking about moving out of the house to the country was being debated in earnest amongst the hunting club squires of the city who had country club like hunting retreats to consider going to as the city began to slowly tear itself apart.

The large and small elite private hunting clubs, big game guides, birddog handlers, professional anglers etc. all had them some personal and professional plans on occupying certain large tracks of prime hunting land.

"The unrealistic among these affluent hunter survivors was that they thought the land could provide for them and their family's needs until the power came back on. Well to be honest, no one really knew or could say when the power would come back on." David mused while thinking possibly that these people were just more optimistic than him about the chances of turning the nation's great cities power back on again. There were lots of smaller cities in states to the west that had anything from regular to sporadic power still on and maybe they could throw some help this way.

Those cities with remaining operable utilities must be filled to beyond capacity as the destitute swarming masses of humanity from the east and west coast tried to converge on them in hopes of warm shelter and some food.

David knew better than try bugging out to get to a working city. There was nothing there for him, no future or self-reliant freedoms to retain. His only hope of surviving was to remain on his land and depend on his preps and luck to hold out where he was at.

He was sure that there were people right now who were making uninformed or mostly bad decisions right and left while making heroic efforts to get to these so called sanctuaries of modern living, but he was not having anything to do with it. Beyond the fact that a cyber-attack had wiped out infrastructure for the majority of the United States, as soon as that swarm of unprepared people hit a city and began to use up its scarce resources the first responders would be overwhelmed in short order and then what? Hell keeping that many first responders helping refugees and away from the rest of the nation and in the rear with the gear as it were, took all the manpower and resources this country had and then some.

You probably couldn't even buy gas and oil within 500 miles of those places now anyway, even if you had the hard currency to travel cross country it was a suckers bet because there was no guarantee you would find any gas to buy. There were already government imposed travel restrictions and from what little bit of chatter David could pick up on the shortwave channels of his AM/FM radio, gas stations as well as all refineries ,stocks and reserves of gasoline and oil were under federal government control. There was no gas around David's small town except what folks had stored in a shed for the lawnmower or had dwindling rapidly in their vehicles gas tanks. Gas rationing for his particular county was thought to begin a month from now if they could get some trucks through and those rations were on a priority for fire and medical .There existed the unknown probability for civilians how much gas might be possibly allocated to them if any.

It was evident to David that strife and brutal lawlessness would soon get the upper hand in the general population and whichever terrorist or state sponsored agency that had hacked our computers was sure to exploit things as best they could by making things much worse.

The world hadn't ended yet for the rest of the nation, but as far as David was concerned, the shit had already hit the fan on his end of the road and was here to stay. When hard winter hits a several months from now, it was a given that untold millions would soon be dead, much sooner for those in snow prone states. He didn't have any second guesses about his status or geographical location, winter kills north or south. I guess the lists of the dead will be getting longer now as each hour passes.

David had anticipated deaths shadow coming for a visit weeks ago, now was the time for him to start barring his door to it. The first door being locked of course was to the neighbors. They would just have to make do until he figured something else out or hopefully they would leave for greener pastures on their own. Putting the fear of God in them about that nuclear plant up the road was hopefully just a mean trick and not a portent of his own need to flee the area.

David and Julie said farewell to Will and Sally and returned to the house and the chores of reorganizing it.

2

Chapter 2

Death Rides A Cold Horse

Whoever had unleashed that cyber-attack or whatever it was that hit America including the possible use of scalar electromagnetic pulse weapons on the US infrastructure, hadn't as of yet, well that was as far as public knew anyway, taken any credit for doing it at this time or given a reason. A Cyber-attack is not the very clear and definable smoke plume coming out of a missile on somebody's foreign shore. ... Also one must consider it's not just the idea of the detection part of it; it's also how you choose to respond, or maybe rather when you respond. ... You may want to watch an attack play out inside your system so you understand more about it, or you might be seeing if it left any backdoors or Trojan viruses on your computer server if you are going to setoff a major counterattack. ... You may not always want to let the other side to you know "know that you know" that they are the ones attacking you and you caught them at it.

Your response may be that you want to hit them back immediately, or maybe you want to let it settle a while and design something particularly devilish or a cyber and electronic attack of your own as a response that totally overwhelms any counterattack...

Whatever was going on in the darkening big world, David knew to wait on several other shoes that were going to drop as battle plans now were most likely being scaled up to what is called increased asymmetric warfare. Something is coming, and the executive branch of our government has been planning for it for a long time. Whether this attack is from without or from within, the chance of a violent end to our way of life is scary real.

Asymmetric warfare deals with vulnerabilities, leverages, and our centralized power grid was America's greatest vulnerability. The enemy, whoever they were, had just played

Death Rides A Cold Horse

their first card in this little game of snuffing the candle out on civilization and David's military background understood asymmetric warfare as the following steps.

(1) A long **insertion phase** in peacetime, when the WMD/weapons-of-mass-destruction and teams are inserted, and then

(2) An **operations phase**, when the inserted teams start unleashing the weapons of mass destruction (anthrax, smallpox, nuclear explosions, whatever).

"The operations phase is now upon us, and the next month or so to use a Chinese phrase – will be "interesting times". *Well we know we had state sponsored terrorists and spies running around in the US of every ilk for some time, just what kind of crap they were going to release now and how we were going to respond militarily was anybody's guess. It is almost certain that some of these portable weapons have also been inserted into the U.S". David mused shuddering and went back to his tasks at hand after one final thought.*

"So this next year or so if he and Julie could somehow survive all its hardships would be almost biblical in scope and its scale of misery and death. These coming bad times will certainly be falling into the realm of what the Chinese so laconically refer to as "*interesting times*".

He and the Prepper community for years had been warning others that there are plenty of ingenious evil minds out there that are at work daily finding nefarious ways in which they can wreak terror and havoc upon other nations…It's a real threat, very tangible and that's the reason why we have to intensify our efforts to prepare, and that's why it is so important to be vigilant and advocate for more safeguards to our power grid system.

David sat up in his deer stand quietly but still impatiently awaiting an animal to come by. He normally didn't hunt so close to the house, instead preferring for deer to think the paths that crisscrossed his backyard and orchard as a free zone to be safely traveled so that he could observe their wanderings and migratory movements. Today though he needed to bag one and he knew their traditional approaches to his property well. He had observed the deer utilizing various trails so many times that if he put his mind to it you could almost set a clock on his predictions of when and where they would be seen.

The squirrels suddenly stopped thumping in the litter. The blue jays quit their shrill piping. And there he was. A beautiful six point buck. The deer didn't weave through the saplings or step into the clearing as he was normally was apt to do. He was just suddenly there on the edge of the woods tentatively looking around and listening. Fifty yards ahead, a bit farther than David liked with a shotgun but fine all the same. David didn't want a chance for the deer to get spooked and return to the scrub so he took the shot. BANG! And it was over and David climbed down from his tree stand after waiting a bit to be sure the animal died and didn't run off wounded before he went to check out his prize.

David positioned the deer's head laying downhill so that when he cut its throat the carcass would bleed out more quickly and thoroughly. While performing the task he grumbled to himself about how hard this pioneering living was if you were trying to stay clean and preserve water. He wiped his knifes blade clean with some fallen leaves and headed back towards the house to inform Julie of his successful hunt.

He followed the winding wooded trail back to the house and hollered" Hey Julie' cautiously before starting to unlock the door.

"I am in the kitchen" she called back nonplussed before coming to meet him half way into the house.

"I saw your happy self coming down the trail through the window as I was finishing up the dishes. I take it you had some good luck?" Julie said having heard the shot and noting David's lopsided grin.

"Yea no problem, that fat deer was just where I said he would be. Hey you still got any water in the sink?" David inquired. One of the things that changed a lot when the shit hit the fan is the fact that everything became really dirty, really fast and cleaning anything up was now a calculated chore in efforts and scrimping on the materials used.

Death Rides A Cold Horse

Preparation of food was all about "how to make it with less firewood" and trying to use less water. Rocket stoves worked for the first part, but clean up and preparation was a never ending task of hauling and purifying water.

Because David had himself a pretty good store of freeze dried and dehydrated food, most of the preparation was simple and took about as long it took to fix boiling water.

"Yes sinks still full of water, but it's kind of dirty and greasy from washing all the pots and pans, the rinse water is alright though. What do you need water for darling? I can heat up some more water for you if you need me too." Julie said bustling back towards the kitchen and pausing before starting to ladle up some water with a saucepan out of a 2 1/2 gallon bucket that was sitting on the floor.

Julie had already been through the slow process of adjusting to the water shortage and the accumulating trash. At first people tried to keep themselves and the yard as clean they could, but without all the normal services, like garbage trucks, running water and all other community services that make normal living simple, soon it became impossible to not value even dirty water and as far as the trash went it either got piled up on a curb or got burned.

"Maybe later I will have you heat some more up but not right now. Just leave what you got water wise in the sinks for moment and maybe I can use it. Mike and I have a deer to clean and it will get kind of nasty and dirty around here for a bit. Come to think of it, let me go talk to Mike first and then we may just decide to put that carcass on my Deer cart and drag it on over to his place. That rationale of doing it off property sort of makes sense to me for a number of reasons at the moment. I won't go into the wisdoms of it all, but I want to get his input on doing it. Julie, I want you to please stay here and hold the fort down for a bit sweetie and I will go walk on over there and roust that rascal Mike for some help butchering that deer." David said glancing at the dirty grey dishwater in the kitchen for a moment and then grabbing a Clorox wipe instead to remove the last traces of grime and blood on his hands. At least getting rid of guts and garbage in the country wasn't that big of an ordeal. David could just imagine the garbage in the cities as it began piling up everywhere, when you add to that broken down or out of gas vehicles on the street, human waste and dead bodies it was a very ugly picture that he was glad he and his nose had some distance from.

"You know those neighbors across the street are going to see you if you start dragging that deer down the road on a cart." Julie stated raising one questioning eyebrow.

"I am trying to decide what to do about that particular bump in the road now. I hate having to deal with them and be all friendly just after trying to put the fear of god in them about keeping their distance from us. Well we will figure it out and if you would please, why don't you spy on their house a bit with the binoculars as I walk past it and see how much attention they give me while I am passing by. They shouldn't even notice me and be out somewhere engaged in their own woods building snares or something but you never can tell." David said opening the front door and glancing off in the distance at what bits he could see of their houses front porch.

"I really think that they took your message to heart David and they will be minding their P`s and Qs trying to fend for themselves or getting ready to bug out. I bet you that they are probably out in the sticks right this moment trying their hand at trapping, but then again they might be curious about that shot you fired and be watching over here out of general or hungry curiosity." Julie said peering over David's shoulder and looking in the same direction for any signs of movement.

"I will probably end up giving them a little roast or something anyway from the deer. But for now they are on their own and best mind their own business until I can talk to Mike." David began saying before catching a glimpse of a figure approaching on the far side of his circular driveway.

"Well damn Julie! Speak of the Devil and guess who comes walking up to my door! "David said before stepping out on his door stoop and waving at Mike who was beginning to walk down the somewhat steep dirt and rock graveled driveway.

Mike was carrying what David knew to be a nice 4x powered scoped bolt action wood stocked .270 rifle slung across one shoulder and he had on a colorful mismatched assortment of multi-layered clothes in order to be bundled up for the chill of late March. As far as David knew that hunting

Death Rides A Cold Horse

rifle was his sole possession of the firearms hunting or defensive nature unless he or his wife over the years had acquired a pistol that he knew that she and her husband had on their wish lists.

Times were tough and military disability pay and odd jobs didn't go far. David knew the couple had hopes of doing some prepping and he had given them a SilverFire Rocket stove and a nice Smith and Wesson Knife from his extra preps that he had accumulated as an occasional survival gear reviewer and evaluator when they first moved in as his housewarming present to them and prepper buddy introduction years ago, but he hadn't kept up with their efforts to acquire goods or more survival tools for themselves over the years. He guessed now was the time they had decided to see if he was serious about his intentions of providing each other mutual aid if the poo did hit the fan as they had previously agreed upon. Mike had probably heard David's gun shot and was coming over to check out what it was he had been shooting at.

Death Rides A Cold Horse

"Hello there Mike my friend! Long time no see, you old soldier." David said walking out a short distance to the driveway and enthusiastically shaking the man's hand.

"Hi there David, nice to see ya buddy. I heard the shot and thought I would come check on you and see what you were firing at." Mike said before Julie gave her friendly greetings and customary hug for all well-wishers or friends of David's. .

"No worries buddy, matter of fact I was just about to walk up to your place and come get you. I shot myself a nice deer and I figured that you might possibly be in the mood to help field dress him in trade for half the meat, but we need to talk more about how we are going to divvy it up before we start fleshing it out." David said stopping a moment before telling him any further details in order to ask him if he wanted some hot coffee on this cold blustery day.

" Coffee would be great, that is if you already got some made" Mike said before being quickly assured by Julie that it would only take her a minute to make a fresh pot and

Death Rides A Cold Horse

then asking the boys if they were coming inside for a visit or staying out in the cold to deal with the deer.

"We are going to go pick up that deer in the woods first Julie and move him closer to the house. He surely should be bled out by now and it won't take us but a minute to fetch him home. We will come in the house for coffee with you and warm up when we get back before getting started field dressing on him. Come on Mike! Let's quit fooling around and go get that part of the task out of the way. I need to go over here and get my deer cart out of the shed first though. That tasty deer is laying only about 75 yards away from here close to the stand. Won't take us more than 10 minutes to go grab it and haul it back." David said fetching his shotgun and leading Mike to the backyard to unlock and open a 20x14 metal storage shed. Mike slung his rifle over his shoulder and followed along scanning the wood line.

"To be honest with you David, I am very glad you got lucky and got yourself a deer today. I was hoping you were not just out squirrel hunting and maybe had a bit of something from your hunting efforts I could talk you into to sharing with us. Food is getting mighty tight over at my place and the deer around my place are so skittish and high strung with all the hunters in the woods that I haven't even seen a clear shot or for that matter a deer in days. My cold bones have been sitting out on my stand every morning and dusk watching and waiting for nothing." Mike said forlornly.

"Well then it's your lucky day my backwoods buddy, that's a fine of a 6 pointer deer that you will ever see that I managed to shoot this morning. There he is lying over there by the gully. See him?" David said jubilantly as he now let Mike take a turn and pull the two wheeled cart down the forest trail instead of him. David was always good at instigating or conniving to get younger folk to use their youthful muscles and enthusiasm to perform a task regardless whether or not he could easily do it for himself.

It was to him, a sort of southern respect your elders' thing that he sort of did to have some mischievous fun while playfully cajoling or tricking someone into sharing the harder part of a task that David needed to work on and that he just as soon get out of.

Death Rides A Cold Horse

"I take it that Mike you didn't get much of a chance to prep for hard times as bad as these ones we are going through now" David said cautiously wondering if Mike had prepared for himself and his family much at all.

"Well David you know how it is; new shoes and clothes for kids, low pay etc. Just seems like every time I was planning on making some prepper purchase something would come along and take away all the extra money. Seems pretty much every time I turned around, just simple everyday living or unexpected bills and expenses would pop up and short sheet my bank account." Mike said wistfully.

"I got some stuff put back for this apocalypse that I might be able to let you borrow, but nobody, I am telling you now, nobody unless they were Rockefeller could afford to prep for something of this magnitude. You wouldn't believe how much it would cost to even try to and like you say a dollar doesn't go very far anymore. The only reason I have the amount I have is that I started prepping several years earlier. You will however be happy to know though that I planned on my stored food running out and prepped extra food procurement items like traps and snares enough for the both of us to use if you're up for it. My motto has sort of been "have it on hand when you do not need it, but get it when you can find it and afford it so that you will have it around before you actually need it. I need you Mike, one man is not going to be able to provide food and security around here by his lonesome. We got to team up together and practice some community survival as I told you a long time ago" David said warily watching Mike's reaction.

Authors note: One of the most basic rules in preparing and acquiring things for SHTF is that you need to have it before you need it. You may think „oh, but that is so obvious"yes and no. Sometimes it is not. When the poo hits the fan you may find out that it is very important to have any number of things you can no longer buy. You need to think and explore more about what weaknesses you have in your own preps and how to fix them before SHTF. Also do not think only about „ what things do I need"? You should feel free to think about what things are other people maybe going to need? "Because you are going to trade in these kinds of items with others if you can.

If you look around at society in general and keep in mind when SHTF actually does occur the term "useful things" takes on a whole new light and meaning. Now we are not talking about the fact that for some people it is priority to loot the mall and steal useless TV sets, stereos or something similar first chance they get. Hopefully during this period of craziness a lot of ammo gets wasted on them idiots from law-abiding folks and by the hoodlums themselves in internal squabbles with their own evil elements. Candles, batteries, lighters, canned food, spices, small tools, pocket knives etc. you know small concealable things are what is valuable and good for barter. Acquire things that are easy to carry and easier to sell later now when their priced cheap. I would say even get visionary about it if you got the bucks or barter. I bet condoms will still sell. Also think of things that you think will gain value over the time, possibly even multiple times over in value. Stuff like seeds, plants and knowledge about medicinal plants and herbal teas for healing etc. When a few months pass and people finally realize that the lights are going to stay out for a longer period than they can imagine and no doctors, no hospitals etc occurs, then diseases will also start spreading of course and you will see that homemade remedies suddenly become very popular and at the same time much more expensive to procure. That is if you can find any or anyone selling such.

"I told you David I would be here for a disaster and now here I am on your doorstep ready willing and able." Mike said with a smile while helping David hoist the deer on the cart and balance the load.

"I know you are buddy and I thank you, but there are a few things we need to discuss further such as just how screwed we are at this very moment and how hard it will get for us to even get out of bed in the morning and try to hunt later .Or for that matter for us to even attempt to make a crop in that big field you have. I know that sort of work don't sound like so much now, but we will soon be expending more calories trying to get food and stay warm than we will be getting from our efforts. We need to watch that. It don't take very long to over exert yourself or become malnourished just trying to survive. We also need to consider how desperate everyone has become around us now or is going to be getting all too soon and try to make ourselves a plan. You know that right now, this minute, some single mom somewhere is probably sitting down with the last can of peas in the house and divvying it up between her three small starving children… Some father or grandfather is pissed about that and out hunting to feed his family and he knows coming back empty handed is not an option….The crack heads and looters are starting to do day time break-ins to businesses and those thieves already rule the night so you got to worry about the home front as well when you are out in the woods. I am telling you the pins already been pulled out of the hand grenade and its smoking!" David said resolutely and pulled the cart along with Mike's help back to his house.

"David at least we can take satisfaction in the notion that we got ourselves deer and other critters to eat in the woods for now and count our blessings. I imagine we should be alright for some time to come as long as the other hunters don't wipe out or scare off all the game in the area". Mike said confident that he thought that between the two of them that they could procure enough food to feed themselves and their families.

"There is something to be said about that bit of good fortune for now Mike. However, I don't think you have really considered just how much game that is going to take us hunting and trapping to just keep ourselves above the starvation level. I got an article I want you to look at and study by Russ Gilmore called Living Off The Land: Delusions and Misconceptions About Hunting and Gathering. (Full article is at end of this book) Anyway if we look for example at what this deer means to us food wise we get an estimate. "Deer: a mature buck typically yields about 70 pounds of meat (1,120 ounces) (University of Wisconsin study 2006). Venison is a lean meat, with about 53 calories per ounce (USDA SR-21). The meat of a mature buck will therefore give you 59,360 calories, which will be sufficient for 18 days of food at the 3,300 calories per day requirement. If you are eating the internal organs as well, that will probably get *pushed to about 20-21 days of food. (Gilmore 2014)"*

"Now think about it Mike, take 18 days of food for one person then divided by your family (two adults 3 children) add Me and Julie, you get 18 divided by 5 leaving us with about 4 days worth of food if we were eating like lumberjacks to keep up with all of the wood cutting, water hauling, trapping, hunting, gardening etc." David concluded

"I never threw that calorie count calculation into the mix before and that don't even take into account if we can keep the meat preserved, share any of it with neighbors, waste or feed the dogs some etc." Mike said rubbing about a week and half's

Death Rides A Cold Horse

worth of beard stubble worriedly.

"They got some emergency food relief coming into the cities Mike, but I am telling you right now that will be depleted in probably a week or so and then its spin in the wind time for everyone. Hell man ,you know yourself it's already far too dangerous to even get around those food drops with your family these days with all the desperate folks both old and young pushing and shoving to get something, hell anything for that matter they can yell about, scuffle over or grab to eat or drink. The surrounding area sidewalks and roads coming to and going away from aid and disbursement stations has opportunistic punks with a mind for criminal stealing, mugging folks or worse gathering and lurking about. Sorry bastards will lay in wait for folks like highway men I am telling you Mike with fist, gun or knife to take what they can. No compassion for or value of human life at all, those people are just hell bent to rob and take. Keep in mind a favorite of those damn thugs is that they will try and rob you in your own driveway like you're some little old lady who just got back from the grocery store. This has happened in the city several times before around here when times were not this tough and cops and helping neighbors were something for a thief to fear. There isn't any gas to be had for any price once whatever you got in your cars tank is run out. The

Death Rides A Cold Horse

National Guard is barely moving their trucks around themselves except maybe to guard distribution points when a relief truck comes in. One of the main plans of that cyber-attack we got hit with was to bleed the U.S. and hemorrhage it economically, causing a catastrophic and utter economic collapse. You can rest assured that other countries are probably not studying our letters of credit to buy imports or finance exports at the moment and that list of goods will include the electric parts and food *everybody needs.* A year from now, most likely the countries entire electrical power grid system will be history, and destroyed, never to work again. No parts, no gas and crews, no food for workers and families, no recovery" David said fatalistically.

"I sort of agree with what you are saying David, but for the sake of my wife and kids let's please just pretend like this is just a long-term inconvenience and not the actual end of the world as you seem to be talking about a lot. Cripes boy! I got my old momma to think about also and she needs all the hope she can get and hold onto about now. She is worried to death that her meds are running out soon and that we don't have anyway for her to get anymore when they are gone. It's got her thinking and talking about dying and she is worrying all of us around the house no end" Mike said advising David to try and candy coat his words about doom and gloom if the subject of government emergency response or assistance came up.

"Sure, Mike I will watch it, just chattering at you." David assured him.

"Hey, David, did you hear on the radio about China invading and taking the island of Taiwan and the Chinese's also shutting down the Panama Canal in South America? What's that all about anyway?" Mike said as they parked the deer trailer and went in the house for coffee.

"Wouldn't surprise me in the least. Hell the Chinese already controls the canal. They have inserted more than 200,000 Chinese into Panama over the years. Lots of folks are going to take advantage of this situation like I said. Supposedly China declared that they traced their own terrorist cyber-attack on their grid system back to Taiwan but that could be anything from truth to propaganda. China has been spoiling for a reason, pretty much any reason to do just what they are doing now and invading that country for a long time. Don't worry; this global war has just begun! I doubt anyone will start slinging nukes or are contemplating having themselves much of a traditional Land, Air and Sea war or anything to dramatic, nope asymmetric strategic warfare will rule the day and you don't know where it's coming from and it's damn hard to identify by whom. *The insertion phase has been successfully completed* for the long asymmetric strategic warfare plan and we have now moved into that final year *operations phase*. It's kind of like the horseman of the apocalypse got together for a game of chaotic chess." David said letting his statements sink in and thanking Julie for the steaming mug of black coffee she handed him.

"So in your opinion what's next in this 'war of the worlds' scenario buddy? I mean you mentioned that we already had plenty of insurgents, terrorists, mole spies, radical religious groups and every other kind of nut case running around here in this country with the lord knows what kind of weapons of mass destruction. You think some kind of WMD is next?" Mike asked very carefully trying to not appear as rattled as he actually was about that insidious notion.

"I have been thinking on that thorny subject quite a bit lately and have concluded that basically it just depends on who whacked us and why. Somebody is pissed off at us that is for sure, just depends now on who and what for. That there will be more attacks and that will create more anarchy is an assured outcome, yes most definitely assured I am sorry to say. However, I sure hope and pray the shit doesn't start falling like dominos around the world with every evil soul taking up arms to take advantage of a situation and drag the world down into a deeper burning hell with them. Think about it this way, in Los Angeles you got to contend with on any given normal day the armed gangs who roam the streets and terrorize the neighborhood. Every few inter city blocks are controlled by one of more than 30 armed different factions doing some kind of warring drug lord thing while murdering and robbing folks.

The gangs have been able to survive and shoot at each other every single day for decades and that's mainly because they were being only somewhat marginally contained by the cops and the modern legal system. Now it's a no holds barred world for them without law and order and it takes just one firebomb (which you know somebody will think to use) to set the whole city on fire because the fire department can't respond etc. So the survivors of this damn cyber-attack in LA are toast now because somebody else's political agenda or culture tried to take advantage of the situation for a little revenge or to influence a little druggie control over another warring faction. What freaks me out is that Smallpox is already in the hands of the worlds terrorists, and it is the nasty Soviet-modified kind that is resistant

Death Rides A Cold Horse

to most countermeasures. I can tell you from my emergency management studies that whenever smallpox is unleashed in a single large city anywhere on this planet, it will eventually kill one-third of the human population. Things are going to get real freaking strange around here no matter what happens and we may as well plan to be pretty much on our own for the rest of our lives in my opinion. But then again I must say it's a wait and see affair whether or not it ever escalates into WMDs, all I can say now is pray it don't." David said ominously to his evidently shocked and afraid listeners.

"That bad? Really, David? You really really don't know the chances of someone taking advantage of this situation like North Korea or Iran attacking us with biological agents either directly or through one of their proxies? Those fanatics are not sane on a good day I remember you saying. " Julie asked somewhat confused that he hadn't given a comparative statistic or risk assessment on the probability of the situation.

"Too many if's, ands or but's in the works to give you any kind of decent percentage guess of that possibility Julie. I am sure both countries are making noise and saber rattling right now to do something just like that, but they do that kind

96

of threatening all the time anyway and then we threaten them back with massive retaliation, but we just do it not as publicly or as aggressively." David said dismissively before resuming his banter.

"Propaganda takes on many different forms and I am guessing about right now that we will be hearing lots of it on the radio soon from everyone with any kind or type of agenda to serve. I believe all of them lousy bastards, the government, the terrorists and the huge utility corporations as well as the sorry ass media will just talk about turning off and on the lights slowly before the whole works goes poof! The government and FEMA will hand out little pocket lights of hope so that people can peek at a small area around them, but they will never give the people enough light to see the big picture of a permanent blackout occurring and lasting for years. We will all have to try to endure varying degrees of the slippery slimy slow descent of this societal collapse until we get to the point of complete anarchy worldwide. The Dark Ages will look like a romp in the park by comparison to the crap we got coming. Does anyone really wonder why it is increasingly only the ignorant and oblivious that still trusts the government anymore?" David said going into the kitchen

Death Rides A Cold Horse

to retrieve a dark curve bladed Old Hickory brand skinning knife from his kitchen drawer that he had honed to a razors edge.

"Mike checks this out. If I am not out in the field or woods using my sheath knife, then this is my blade of choice for the tasks at hand of skinning that buck neatly." David said changing the subject and showing Mike the knife.

"Dang that thing looks older than my Grand Pa, how long you had that weird looking knife David?' Mike said seeing that the dark blade had been significantly thinned over time from constant sharpening, but the edge looked true and it looked like it could split frog hairs if David had a mind to.

"I don't know, I have had it 20, 25 years maybe? They still make these knives you know and their reasonably priced special carbon steel blades that gets dark with age and that aspect of them reduces rust. "David said taking the knife back.

"The sharper your knife, the easier your life." Mike quoted peering at the assortment of blades David had in a kitchen drawer.

"Hadn't heard that one before Mike. That saying makes a lot of sense though." David replied pondering upon its country wisdom meaning.

"Did you ever end up deciding whether or not you're going to clean that deer here on the property David? I thought you said you were going to take it down to Mike's place to do it?" Julie asked while trying to speculate on what it David was had in mind to do with the deer at the moment and why.

"I haven't really had a chance to talk about that subject yet; we sort of got sidetracked dragging the deer back here. Mike I got lots of swamp deer that use my place as a trail crossing point from the woods to the paved road and up until now my land hasn't been hunted in 10 years. What I propose to you is that you clean the deer up at your place and dispose of the offal and other nasty stuff on your property. If you want to use the scraps for snare bait we can do that also but you best keep track of whose dogs are out and about running loose." David said not really wanting to have to deal with processing possums or getting involved with a lost neighborhood dog dispute just yet.

"I wish we had us some wild hogs close by. I could use them deer guts and such to attract them into shooting range with. I guess I will talk to my wife and see what pot she is willing to give up out of her kitchen and cook up something for the dog. I don't want him eating raw meat and taking a chance on worms. Maybe if that husky gets a taste for venison he will become a good deer dog! Ha!" Mike said thinking that dang dog of his was fast enough already to catch one if he had a mind too.

"Hey, now that reminds me! Charlie up the road might know if there are some wild hogs in the area Mike. Me and him have got us a sort of prepper pact going on between us also. Me and him have drank ourselves many a beer and played with various prepper toys over the years while discussing how we might be able to help each other out in a situation like this. I thought that I would have seen him come around here to my place by now and come to think of it I am starting to wonder if he is even at home at the moment. He has been among the missing anyway. You want to take a walk up there with me before you head back or do you want to go ahead and get started on cleaning that deer? Hey. Charlie's got himself a big barrel smoker by the way that we could use. That smoker would be handier than what I had in mind for preserving some of the venison." David declared.

"Sure David, I will walk up there with you. I take it that since you are giving me half of that deer in barter that I am on my own to transport and butcher it?" Mike said not caring one way or the other if David wanted it that way, just as long as he ended up with some much needed food for him and his family.

"I can help you drag it up to your house. Besides I wanted to come down and say hi to your family anyway. I would even venture to say butcher it up at Charlie's and we all have a big cook out, but I am not comfortable leaving my house unattended at the moment. I got some neighbor trust issues going on I need to remedy or at least get myself comfortable about. By the way I have already talked to them questionable neighbors across the street from me, but I know little or nothing about them or the ones living on the other side of me. Charles knows the neighbors on my left personally and does not have much regard for them. He told me awhile back to steer clear of the "prison family" when I first moved down this way, but he never said much more to me about them. Wish I had of asked him for some more detailed information on them people now. That other couple who lives up from them on our road before you get to Charles place I don't know very much about them either. I met the live in girlfriend from that trailer parked up there in the pines one time and she seemed a kind of shady character but she was nice enough. Talked a lot of alcohol induced trash about whom she knew was a prostitute or dope fiend up in the city that hung out around the day labor places if I remember that day correctly. I never have seen hide nor hair of her boyfriend though. He supposedly raised some bulldogs up there on that ridge but I haven't heard much barking to support that theory and only saw the one dog next to their trailer when Charles ex-girlfriend had me give them a ride to take her home onetime. You can't even see their place from the road at all." David said envisioning the uphill walk to his friend's house.

Death Rides A Cold Horse

"I don't know much about them folks next door to you either. The moms sickly and she has been to prison for something or the other and I heard they got one mentally challenged kid as well living there as well as the two brothers that have done some penitentiary time for drugs or burglary. You never see them folks outside their house, kind of reclusive types. You have any problems with them people you let me know." Mike said staring off at the couple acres of woods separating the neighboring house. You couldn't see the neighbor's house from David's but it was easy enough to hear its occupants if their dogs barked or if music was played loud.

"Yea Mike we got to figure out for ourselves some kind of communication signals or something between us. Establish us some better communication between us someway. I got one set of Midland handheld radios that I figured we could share with Clancy at the entrance to the road but I haven't thought that exchange all the way through as of yet. "That way if either one of us gets wind of suspicious activity we can warn each other. It's beneficial to have an extra set of eyes and ears even if they don't live right next door.

I got to also get myself up to see the "Mole Boys" eventually. I don't know how they are making out these days or even which one of them boys are around. They will get the notion to all walk or drive down here soon enough though I bet, but those danged dogs of Clancy's will mess with you if they walk past his house on the way to mine. Those ill-mannered hounds of Clancy's have always been free ranging country dogs, but me and Clancy disagree on how much manners those dogs actually have. If you are used to dogs you can sort of control their aggressive behavior by hollering at them, but they are still squirrelly enough that even though I have met them hounds before and have been formally introduced I don't like getting out of my truck unless Clancy's around when I go to visit him. That SOB Clancy likes it that way and thinks that it's in some way amusing that if the dogs don't know you well, they tell you whose property they think it is by quite loudly barking and challenging you". David said reminiscing on the meet the dog's routine at Clancy's which you were never quite sure how it would turn out.

Death Rides A Cold Horse

"To be honest, I hope it stays that way." David said picking up his pace to pass by the house quicker and hopefully not be observed by the occupants.

"You know Mike, in a normal grid down situation, like one caused by a hurricane or something, I would have been the first one to finally walk over to that house and see that they were doing all right after a bit of reflection on their welfare. Now a days it feels weird to hope I never have to see them or visit that house EVER." David said unsure of the wave of feelings and emotions coming over him suddenly that apparently caused him to have such low opinions of folks he had never met.

"I can understand your wanting to do something helpful or be sociable to people David, but don't you be letting folks take kindness for weakness. Like you said," its dance with the devil time and the ox is in the ditch". You can't just go help out whoever you want these days without some kind of unexpected or unwanted repercussions possibly coming from it. Besides, you got nothing much food wise put away for yourself and for that matter, I will remind you that

you are now sharing game as hunting partners with me!"
Mike said giving David twinges of guilt on how much food
he had hidden away from his quasi, well up until now
anyway, friend.

"We're living in a time of constantly evolving
instability David." Mike said, adjusting the hunting knife
sheath on his belt. "It doesn't take long for people to turn into
animals. I seen it in Iraq" he concluded.

"Look when we get back to the house Mike, Julie and
me set you out a care package of sorts. Nothing much mind
you, just a bit of food to tide you over until we get the
hunting and trapping routine down and hopefully start
producing some regular meat from our trap lines. Before we
go any further with this conversation, I can tell you here and
now buddy that you're likely going to want to turn your nose
up at most of what it is that I have reserved for you." David
said before gently hushing the rising protests from his friend
and fellow soldier that Mike was never going to turn his nose
up at anything David ever offered or happened to discard as
surplus food stores or garden produce in his direction.

Death Rides A Cold Horse

Mike paused to reflect.

"Hell on earth, I would bet that some people were probably already wishing they hadn't fed rover that last can of dog food and had instead saved it for themselves and their own bellies by now . Or for that matter if they didn't have a pet themselves to care for themselves then they might most likely be eying their neighbors pets by now as possible a la carte menu entries. It is a dog eat dog world now. I can not even imagine what folks will be doing or thinking in the big cities when there are no dogs, rats or cats left to eat." Mike thought with a shudder before quickly clearing those bad thoughts out of his mind. However, Mike still worriedly kept thinking about of his own dog's safety in these trying times. Once it is matter of your life or that of a dog, opinion can change as to property rights or to someone's normal loving nature and view of them.

"Look Mike, you're a meat eater and a have a hardcore male appetite the same as me that does not under any stretch of the imagination think we even ate a meal if we are forced to partake of a vegetarian diet. No meat on my plate and eggs don't count, I didn't eat a meal is the way I feel about it. Which, old buddy, you and I might be stuck eating grazing food like a cow for more days than I care to think about later on in this disaster. I really don't know how in the hell women do the salad thing entrée for dinner or lunch and claim they get their tummies so full, because as far as I am concerned that only works if you are a rabbit. I have got a variety of canned and bucketed crap stored for long-term last ditch emergency rations like 5 gallon buckets of different types of wheat. You know the kinds of wheat I mean like soft white summer and hard red winter wheat that the emergency food stores sell you in order for them to puff up the numbers of the daily adult required calorie counts on those high priced year supply packages of dehydrated or freeze dried long-term storage foods? Yes wheat is tried and true real nutrition and yes you can live off it long-term, but we aren't going to be none too happy with it or without it I am afraid. The bible says supposedly "wheat is the staff of life" or so I have heard. I had my wheat stored for when things were brought to a level where we eat just to survive. You know, sort of as iron rations to keep me from seeing my ribs too soon should the game disappear for a season. I have this belief in regard to preps, "if it's all you can afford, then buy wheat and have SOMETHING!" The day will come or might come along when you say to yourself I really want to eat SOMETHING, but it is not too important WHAT

Death Rides A Cold Horse

that SOMETHING is and if that's all there is to eat anyway, it won't matter." David said, regarding Mike before carrying on.

"However buddy, we can be somewhat hopeful about the menu we are going to likely get stuck with someday. I have some recipes for wheat that knowledgeable folks swear makes it sort of taste like meat, but I have never tried any of them dishes myself personally. I do know however, that I can pour hot water over wheat and wait a few minutes and end up with something like cereal if need be, but that ain`t even close to oatmeal from what I gather. As far as I know the stuff might taste like grass, but I will eat it and be thankful for it when we get to that level." David explained, regretting that he couldn't do more than share some of his precious iron rations with his survival neighbor.

"Iron rations were my last line of defense preps and could be considered a make or break starvation solution while Julie and I were trying to make it through a tough winter." David said while hoping somewhere in the back of his mind that he could make up for the loss of some bucketed and canned grain now by producing and growing his own replenishment come summer .

Death Rides A Cold Horse

"I remember you telling me about us needing to plant a bit of that wheat and oats rather than eating it up awhile back David. When do you plant and when do you harvest that wheat grass stuff anyway? I never known anyone to grow it down south and closest thing I might know would be Rye that is raised around here." Mike asked trying to grasp the amount of seed and labor it would take to even raise an acre of the commodity.

"We have ourselves a wheat cook book and a farmer's almanac for reference is about all I can say on that subject. I have about three hundred pounds of the stuff stored around here to experiment on or get creative and process further. Come spring we will give planting some kind of wheat a shot. What we got to have us Mike is some kind of grain crop as a staple to preserve and put away for hard times as well as supplement our daily diets with. The land around here is not good at all for growing vegetable crops and we don't have much fertilizer to help it along. I have tried to raise corn before here and other places and if you don't have a ton of fertilizer for this poor soil and plenty of rain, you are just wasting your time and energy. At least wheat is lot like growing grass and we can do that I hope. I have some canning jars stocked up, but I don't have very many to spare. We are going to have to try and dehydrate or sun dry what we can with the fruits from the vegetable gardens. I have never tried sun drying myself before, but I have some muslin and mosquito netting to try out in order to keep the bugs off of the veggies while they are baking and drying under old Sol. I also got some of those dollar store plastic picnic, white netting looking food table tent things to try. Hopefully I won't need to try my hand and patience at that lost art of air and sun drying. I have a truly modern approach to solve my preservation and drying needs though utilizing two small electric food dehydrators that I can run off my marine batteries and solar panels. I also have a Sun Oven that has dehydration capabilities which I haven't tried out yet for that purpose, but I have the directions and recipes that came with the oven and I have watched a lot of YouTube videos on the subject. I want us to try our hands at making some jerky in the Sun Oven using some of the deer meat this go round. We shouldn't have any problem doing it I don't expect, that is if we get it sliced nice and thin along the grain". David explained trying to envision the ramifications of trying to plant a crop in spring and hopefully being able to store something for next winter from the gardens as well as put up any kind of meat some way or the other. If he and Mike couldn't through their toil and labor produce and preserve some kind of surplus from the gardens this summer, then they were going to have nutrition problems aplenty no matter what kind of meat they could secure from hunting or trapping efforts.

"Damn, first thing I want to trade for if I can find them is a few live chickens" David mused, mad at himself for not preparing properly to raise a flock someday. Other than previously buying 25 foot of chicken wire on a very limited budget, his plans for having the material like wood and nails on hand, or having the completed project done by this time evaporated into one more of those would da, could da, should da, sentiments he seemed to lament a lot about lately. He didn't give such wishful things much further thought though. He had done his best to balance his prepping and his regular life as well as he could. What he now had on hand in the way of preps was as adequate or not as it will ever be and no sense fretting about anything missing or depleted. No one could possibly afford to buy the supplies that might be needed for this level of disaster. What you had to invest in was knowledge and practicality to even have a general idea of

Death Rides A Cold Horse

*how to "ad lib in the danger zone" as David referred to some
of his MacGyver like tendencies of his using a common
household item to overcome the lack of a tool or
technological solution to get the basics of life like food, fuel,
shelter, clean water etc.*

"What's a "Sun Oven'? Is that something you can run off your solar panels and batteries also? "Mike inquired trying to envision some kind of low wattage appliance like device.

"Oh no, a Sun Oven is not electric at all, my friend. Regular appliances require way too much wattage to even consider. Think of a sun oven as basically black steel or iron pot nestled in an insulated box with glass over it that uses the suns energy to cook with. Mine is far from being that simple though. I have what I am standing here proud to say, the Cadillac of all solar cookers with the trade marked name "Sun Oven". How spectacular is that? That fine technologically advanced cooking and baking solution is an alternative energy marvel with many hidden as well as evident craftsman oriented attributes. I will show you my sun cooker later and maybe we can talk about building you something to cook in but it will be much less efficient and elaborate as my commercially made one." David responded thanking his lucky stars and doing a mental happy dance he had such a resource on hand for his post-apocalyptic and intriguing off grid kitchen setup.

"Apocalyptic nothing" David mused with a grin. He used that trademarked Sun Oven year round. Not only did it keep his kitchen from heating up in the summer, but reducing his electricity bill was also a key factor anytime. It was so efficient that he had no problem in his southern winters producing some of the most flavorful and juicy food you ever had. Sun-baked foods stay moister and have less shrinkage than conventional oven-cooked foods.

Death Rides A Cold Horse

https://www.sunoven.com/foster-coupon

"Oh I know what you're talking about David! Seems that I remember something about the theory of them kind of solar cookers from a science class I once had. I have never seen a commercially made one however, what's it made out of? Hey, It looks like Charlie is either out and about somewhere, or he might of moved in with that girlfriend of his around Dothan. Looks like no one is to home." Mike said noticing no vehicles in the driveway in front of the trailer on the hill.

Death Rides A Cold Horse

"I haven't seen him around for a few weeks now come to think of it. He *was* here when the power first went out, we chatted for a second in passing. Back then I wasn't sure how long this blackout was going to go on and just stopped by for a few minutes to check on him. He hadn't made up his mind then if he was going to the girlfriends or having her come down here. I would have thought if he was taking off long-term he would have come down and told me something, but there is no telling with Charlie. He has his own ways and might have just left without a word and will pop back up whenever." David said and after a quick look around the property he and Mike headed back to start processing the Deer.

3

Gardens, Bug Bites And Water

Julie had been listening to the news on the radio while David was gone with Mike and besides the bad news about uncontrolled fires in several major cities along with the litany of boil water warnings and various announcements that the government wanted you to know they were doing everything they could to restore power there were some new things to add to the list. Flu pandemics, Cholera, Famine, late season Ice storms.

"Damn depressing to listen to the station, but it was indeed some news, life still went on and they were not alone." Julie mused. Life was going on elsewhere and folks talked about it over the airwaves and gossip fences. How long it could remain so as a norm seemed to be becoming more questionable by the day. For

119

Gardens, Bug Bites And Water

now, she and David had food and they were not physically sick so they regarded it as being blessed with a future. The hope of spring planting seemed a far away and distant thought but they had faith in their self-reliance and hopefully all their stored preparations would win out the day. Not many complaints or laments to despair regarding these rehearsed plans to grow a victory garden of sorts in the face of adversity.

The thought of growing a big garden was treasured and this hope shone like a beacon to them as the hopes of an early spring approached. They held solid hope in their knowledge of raising a crop this spring and their stock of precious vegetable seeds appeared to be adequate to achieve their goals.

David and Julie spent odd evening hours occasionally pouring over his library of gardening books looking for new tips or tricks to help them insure a good crop by gleaning some wisdom from some tidbit of knowledge forgotten or yet undiscovered. Long gone for the pair were the days of jumping in the truck and running to the seed and feed store for plants or insecticide. Whatever things they had on hand now garden wise on this particular day, was all they could

Gardens, Bug Bites And Water

expect to have for the foreseeable future and beyond. Anyone who has ever gardened before can tell you that there were a million and one things that could go inexplicably wrong come planting and growing season. That weather was often fickle and contrary was a known fact to think about and prepare for.

David's big three worries for the garden were drought, insects and disease. Drought was the easiest to handle because there was a certain amount of preparation you could do for it like strategically placing rain barrels at the perimeter for the hand watering that would soon be necessary.

Insects and disease were another matter. He had lost the seasonal war with insects like squash borers more than once and had lost plenty of tomatoes and squash to fungus like diseases over past growing years. Often times he blamed the wilt on possibly already infected plants he got from the nursery; other growers' problems in his area supported this theory. Julie and David hoped that since they were raising this year's garden straight from seeds that the risk or threat of disease or infestation was nonexistent. However, the gut wrenching thought that his raised bed gardens had once held disease and bugs before and might yet remain to infect the new plants nagged at them. David was practicing crop rotation and he and Julie had spent the previous day trying out and implementing an idea Julie had found in one of his books.

The concept for cleaning up the old beds was called soil sterilization. They had spread clear plastic sheeting over his dozen or more garden boxes in hopes that the sun's ultra violet light would get the ground hot or UV saturated enough by spring planting to kill any lurking viruses or insect eggs. David should have done it more towards the end of summer to maximize the positive effects the book said would be heightened but that was hindsight now.

He had done his customary burn off of most of the raised garden beds when the vegetation had died down during late fall and it was dry enough now to catch fire again after having accumulated enough fallen leaves and pine needles to get a small blaze going. He burned the surface of each bed to its 2 by 6 wooden soil line one at a time because a grass fire if it got out of control could also catch the leaf litter of the nearby forest on fire and wildfire was the last thing anyone needed..

All those raised growing beds had previously produced plenty of veggies for David and his household's consumption and he proudly declared it also grew a decent amount to spare that he could give away to friends. However, the area he had planted did not produce that much extra, NOT near enough surpluses to think about canning or drying to try to fill a pantry for winter.

About the only thing David could think to do about this shortfall of produce was to till up the ground outside the edges of his garden fence and hope something would grow in the farmed out Alabama red clay soil with no fertilizer or soil amendments added by him to improve it. One thing David did have plenty of was leaves and pine straw in his woods and he and Julie had decided to start trying to build up a layer of debris around the gardens fence in hopes it would compost down some and even if it didn't they would till it into the soil come spring. David said pretty much anything they did would be an improvement and said use the area as a dumping ground for anything organic within reason from now on.

The outside of the garden facing the back of his house consisted of a slight downhill slope and David had a trick he wanted to try out called "Swales" to increase production along its length. A swale is basically a series of little C shaped "dams" that catch and hold water in small depressions in front of them.

He had considered doing this landscaping project for some time in order to up his chances of self-reliance in food production as well as he found it aesthetically pleasing to landscape the area in this intelligent way. David had accumulated a small stack of bricks leftover at a jobsite to build himself a more permanent lower maintenance landscaping project to take advantage of this particularly advantageous growing system by terracing up the slope properly.

The small inclined slope, which was about a 100x 20 or so feet in length, lent itself to a unique swale arrangement. He could make a series of swales traditionally going downhill but he could also tweak on the principle and do some terracing as well as in order to create some catchments sideways to feed water into his main growing area.

He had a shit load of what he considered dubious germinating seeds left over from years gone by and other growing seasons that he planned on just willy nilly planting around the garden in hopes of creating a food forest of sorts should even 10% of them produce a sprout he could coax out of the ground he would have something amazing if it worked..

He had purchased a couple boxes of seed mixture recently from the dollar store of French double mixed color marigolds and he had high hopes and plans of interspersing them all around his garden to deter insect pests. Dwarf Marigolds are pretty much as good as regular ones to help keep them damn squash bugs and other crop destroying insects away. You need to companion plant marigolds, but you need to grow the French ones, they have the most scent those nasty bugs hate.

Planting all those marigolds was damn sure going to screw up any OPSEC ideas he had of doing any gorilla gardening as far as concealing the glimpse of the 35 or 40 foot of his garden you could see from the road and he pondered on that.

A bunch of bright pretty flowers in a landscaped setting would draw someone's eye dead toward what he wanted to remain more obscure he had realized. After giving it some practical thought, he had decided for himself that the

Gardens, Bug Bites And Water

solution would be to plant the area in mostly Seminole squash that you could see from the road about 75 yards away.

To the uninitiated eye, at least for part of the growing season, it would look damn near like a patch of the noxious weed Kudzu to the country boys around here. That acreage eating nasty weed scourge of the south was something to be avoided and despised by most folks with any walking around sense.

Having Kudzu on your property dropped your land value to nil because it was so damn hard to get rid of, that is unless you managed to find the main root in a field full of it and dose it with used motor oil or some other toxic substance equivalent to Chernobyl. That stuff was so voracious in its growing patterns it covered up and ate telephone poles, cabins, farm equipment, barns; you name it in a period of less than a few years unless you fought it with determination and hateful diligence.

It was also snaky looking as hell and no sane country boy dove off in a patch of it without a pair of armored snake boots and stick to whomp four legged and slithering creatures as well with. What was worse than ducking and dodging the

Gardens, Bug Bites And Water

possible venomous and otherwise snakes was the most assured fact that at certain times of the year the risk and threat of getting a master case of the "Red Bugs" was alarmingly high. Once you got that you knew you were in for a case of the worst itching and needing to scratch you were ever going to get.

Now for those folks that are not experienced with southern climes might not know what a red bug is. It is an anthropoid, what northern folks call a chigger and they are a force to be reckoned with and to be avoided at all costs if you can. This biting blood sucking microscopic insect actually digs into your skin and lives there until it dies or you get rid of it. The resulting round the clock itch of them son of a bitches will drive you bug eyed crazy even if it was just a couple of them little tiny red spiders that jumped on you. The bite wound starts out as a small red dot and soon develops into an angry looking small pimple affair that just gets redder and itchier as time goes by. You can't stand not to scratch it but you know if you do it will make it worse.

Those that are familiar with this parasitic nemesis perform Herculean efforts for days trying not to scratch these bites for fear of infection or stirring the critters up to dig

Gardens, Bug Bites And Water

deeper and cause even worse itching, but scratch eventually we all do whether consciously when we are awake or subconsciously when we are sleeping. Damn it, it made David itch and burn just to consider them pests. Many memories of the number of times he had got them and had been trying to focus his mind on not to scratch regardless of how good it would feel just for a moment stayed with him. The cure to immediate itch t is to smack it, yea smack the skin like you would a wrist playing schoolboy games to raise a whelp or draw the blood to the surface. That little trick lasts a while and seems to help relieve the need to scratch or rub the itch so incessantly.

David had done some research on the internet about how to get rid of the 2nd worse scourge of the southern pine woods and fields (the first is imported fire ants) and came up empty except for an untried patented medical solution to get rid of the frisky persistent itchy bastards.

What amazed David the most in his research was the number of so called experts or doctors who poo pooed the notion of the number one cure for the bedeviling beasties was somehow ineffective. The general idea of how to get rid of them amongst generations of southerners was you had to smother the nasty's before they ate you alive or reproduced. The experts said for many reasons we were full of it and our concept of the insect and its feeding habits on humans and other animals was inherently flawed because their research said the wretches died after they burrowed in and didn't feed or reproduce the way our country lore suggested.

"Well, bull shit!" David had exclaimed in his own mind or to anyone that would listen after reading such expert bull hockey that was in his opinion bad advice given without tried solutions.

"Why he had been he himself had been dealing with them pesky insect critters for more years than he could count. The number one universally accepted tried and true remedy of the southlands was to put clear nail polish on them, lacking that valuable commodity he had tried using everything from rubbing alcohol, hot as you can stand it showers, baby oil, Zinc oxide cream (if that's all you had, good for poison ivy and oak)Red Devil lye soap, Witch Hazel, mercurochrome, gun oil, turpentine, kerosene, paint thinner, soap (Irish Spring, Life Buoy etc.(strong scented soap to leave on awhile and itch before scalding one's self in hot water.) etc. had all been tried at one time or another in his experiences or overheard by him listening to others at

Gardens, Bug Bites And Water

National Guard drills trying to get rid of the incessant deep abiding itch a bite site would give you with varying results.

If you were a very lucky human you would only have one or two bites where those little buggers would feast wherever your blood was closest to your skin like where your socks or underwear connected to your body. That's the places where they would start to first get you as they traveled up a pant leg after attacking and milling around the tops of your well tied or bloused boots. *It was wherever your clothing got closest to your skin they would attack. The closer the blood is to the surface the more apt something is to get bit. Your waist where your belt, your underwear or your pants contacted waist skin was a favorite for them biological hazardous little bastards.*

There was more than one deep wood hunter around here that swore that wearing women's panty hose kept the red bugs and ticks off of you, but David had not got around to trying that particular fashion. Spraying insecticide on those thin military nylon or canvas belts he wore when he had his army uniform on and spraying the area where he bloused his boots seemed to offer a degree of protection, he had even tried blousing his boots with dog flea collars with marginal effect.

Gardens, Bug Bites And Water

Anyway, basically any area that looked like it contained kudzu was to be avoided and property that looked like it had some on it, usually meant its owner had abandoned it or was just pretty lazy and a poor land steward. The Seminole squash he had in mind was perfect to imitate Kudzu in the early growing season. That stuff quite often put out 50 ft or better vines and he would just let it go wild and maybe even train some of it to swallow part of his garden fence. Now later on when it set small pumpkin looking squash it wouldn't fool anybody, but it was very useful camouflage for a time. Seminole squash is an ideal prepper storage food because if its stem is not damaged that stuff lasts longer untreated than anything else David knew of. He once kept a squash on his kitchen counter for a year and a half and it was still good until its stem got knocked off and then it soon began to rot. David planned on planting this ancient heirloom squash pretty much everywhere around his property and just letting it run wild. He would need to look out for snakes but this particular squash was pretty much impervious to insects and disease and it didn't seem to attract those dang red bugs. Red bugs could be anywhere or everywhere, it was just that for some reason certain areas were more buggy than others.

Gardens, Bug Bites And Water

Getting the garden all tilled up and his various landscape projects completed were constantly on his mind. He hoped his food forest project would take and become almost permaculture, but he had his doubts on nature's cooperation in that regard.

What little bit of precious gas he had available was going to be the big thing to conserve for these tasks. David had about 10 gallons of gas stored in his shed at the moment with the right kind of ethanol reducing Stabil for small engines already mixed into it. The gas guzzling problem he also had though regarding his immediate needs of home heating was that he had only about a half cord of wood stacked and maybe 50lbs pounds of LP gas to see him through the tail end of winter and heat the house. Both his and his girlfriend Julies cars had some gas in them but they had determined that the half tank of fuel in hers needed to stay unmolested in case of emergency's like a bug out, so that left them about a quarter of a tank or maybe 5 gallons of gas in David's vehicle.

David had declared his car and the gas in it their emergency generator because he could hook an inverter to his vehicles battery and run a few useful items like a battery charger to top off his big Sunrnr solar generator if the sun hadn't shined for a while, or some project like running a dehydrator had drained it too much. He also had a few 12v marine batteries as part of his off grid system but they were getting a bit old and didn't hold a charge as well as they used to. Normal electric chain saws draw too many amps to try and run off solar but he had a cordless 18v 6 inch chainsaw he found indispensable to stack his woodpile with thumb size sticks for his rocket stoves.

David always had back up to his backups and was proud to say one of the ones he had chosen was a SilverFire Hunter model rocket stove. This was the only patented rocket stove on the market that had a chimney to vent the little bit of smoke it produced up out through a window or wherever. David had it sitting under a table in the laundry room of his home ready to be vented out a window should the need arise.

David called his little added on backroom to the house his "Prepper Pod" because if needed, he could retreat to it in the dead of winter or the heat of summer and have himself a microcosm of modern comfort with minimal effort on his part.

Gardens, Bug Bites And Water

Why, one could stay in that one little room and except for having to use a bucket or go to the outhouse, have everything you needed at arm's length somewhere in the room, positioned and ready to hand. Actually, you didn't even need to leave the house if you had enough water to flush the toilets because he had an operational septic tank.

On David's to do list was hooking up a 12v D.C. pump to a rain barrel in order to have running water for indoor plumbing, that is if he could keep the barrel filled. He had slowly accumulated all the parts over time for the project and had them around just for this particular day and purpose. David's thought about how he had justified their expense and purpose when he told Julie he was light on cash from buying parts and couldn't afford to buy something else.

"With what is going on in our nation right now, if you're not prepping, you're not thinking, and right now I am thinking it sure would be nice to have ourselves a cheap indoor plumbing backup." David had told her and Julie, being the intrigued prepper that she was, wanted to go play and get the project started as soon as possible. Well, David had not got around to rigging that setup or a couple other things that he had dreamed up and got materials for that he had stored in his shed for just this sort of occasion. He didn't lament much for never having made a dry run at installation, he just hoped he didn't get in the middle of it and find out he needed some cheap insignificant part that he no longer had ready access to at a hardware store. Hell, he had crap stored that he couldn't even find at the moment and wondered where he had misplaced certain items or key parts.

Organization was not his long suit but pack ratting all kinds of stuff to someday make his prepper shack operate totally off grid was his hobby. The acquisition and research was the chase. Now he had plenty of time to play with his accumulated toys and prepper woman Julie would be in hog heaven helping him to do them expeditiously and neatly. The tasks of making the prepper shack as self-reliant as possible had been discussed into the wee hours of the morning many times by the two of them and the plans had been verbally rehearsed, refined and revaluated many times over.

One thing David pondered about and regretted was that he lacked any kind of manual for how to construct a water lifting device out of PVC. He had researched the subject of other means though.

Gardens, Bug Bites And Water

Rowers Pump

David if nothing else was an interesting and inquisitive old soul Irrigation Reference Manual (Peace Corps, 1994

Chapter 3.5 Pumps and water lifting devices

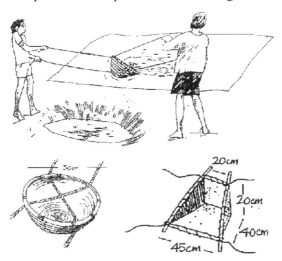

Figure 3.15 Swing Baskets (Ref. 28)

Wicker swing basket of average capacity 8 liters.
Swing basket made from metal sheets

Gardens, Bug Bites And Water

Figure 3.16 eater Scoop (Ref. 28)

David described how in the past in some countries, water was moved from pool to pool or to irrigation ditches using an affair called an eater scoop. Basically, it was a scoop you could make out of wood or an old can attached to a stick to be able to shovel the most amount of water from one place to another. Now by knowing and thinking about this arcane technology as a prepper, he tried to envision various modern uses for it. One thing he had come up with was applying the principal to modern day street gutters. Water runs down the gutter on both sides of a common neighborhood road to the street drains at alarming rate during a storm. The flow of the water is so fast and shallow often times that it makes it very difficult to collect before it's lost to the sewers. No everybody

Gardens, Bug Bites And Water

knows upstream from you god knows what might be flowing in that water and even more so now that you have everybody's stacked up stinking refuse on the curb awaiting a garbage truck that will probably never come again but this trick is useful. Hell dirt roads, suburbs etc. you might not even worry much about really bad contamination coming down the pike. Even in the cities if it's a strong rain the gutters will be washed out some before you try it anyway. What if you just needed water to water your crops or flush your toilet? Just get your poncho or rain suit on and commence to letting the scoop fill up automatically and dumping it in a 5 gallon bucket. You are already probably going to have every pot and pan you have out anyway trying to collect some water and hopefully your prepared for this type of thing and not out trying to catch your death of cold doing it because you lack protective clothing or commonsense. Those pans or buckets you have set out are not going to collect much unless you already made you some kind of rain collection system to increase surface area and flow with a piece of plastic or old poncho.

David and Julie had joked as well as discussed in earnest a purchase Julie had made a while back of ten new Czech military surplus ponchos for seventeen bucks and some change. David had shown Julie the internet ad for them as a great bargain but he was watching his pennies and waiting on a gift card to stack coupons with for what he felt like was a more practical purpose or use of funds.

Julie had made this purchase with much aforethought as only a wonderful prepper girl and intuitive motherly and imaginative woman could do. She had viewed this particular deal as an especially whimsical and practical acquisition to spread a little love and preparedness. LowBuck Prepper`s Prepperstock meet and greet was a few short months away and as she was lovingly wont to do was looking for inexpensive highly thoughtful things to bestow upon new and old friends.

Gardens, Bug Bites And Water

If you have two ponchos, you can construct a brush raft or an Australian poncho raft. With either of these rafts, you can safely float your equipment across a slow-moving stream or river.

Brush Raft

The brush raft, if properly constructed, will support about 115 kilograms. To construct it, use ponchos, fresh green brush, two small saplings, and rope or vine as follows (Figure 17-4):

•   Push the hood of each poncho to the inner side and tightly tie off the necks using the drawstrings.

•   Attach the ropes or vines at the corner and side grommets of each poncho. Make sure they are long enough to cross to and tie with the others attached at the opposite corner or side.

• Spread one poncho on the ground with the inner side up. Pile fresh, green brush (no thick branches) on the poncho until the brush stack is about 45 centimeters high. Pull the drawstring up through the center of the brush stack.

• Make an X-frame from two small saplings and place it on top of the brush stack. Tie the X-frame securely in place with the poncho drawstring.

• Pile another 45 centimeters of brush on top of the X-frame, and then compress the brush slightly.

• Pull the poncho sides up around the brush and, using the ropes or vines attached to the comer or side grommets, tie them diagonally from comer to corner and from side to side.

• Spread the second poncho, inner side up, next to the brush bundle.

• Roll the brush bundle onto the second poncho so that the tied side is down. Tie the second poncho around the brush bundle in the same manner as you tied the first poncho around the brush.

• Place it in the water with the tied side of the second poncho facing up.

Gardens, Bug Bites And Water

Australian Poncho Raft

If you do not have time to gather brush for a brush raft, you can make an Australian poncho raft. This raft, although more waterproof than the poncho brush raft, will only float about 35 kilograms of equipment. To construct this raft, use two ponchos, two rucksacks, two 1.2-meter poles or branches, and ropes, vines, bootlaces, or comparable material as follows (Figure 17-5):

• Push the hood of each poncho to the inner side and tightly tie off the necks using the drawstrings.

• Spread one poncho on the ground with the inner side up. Place and center the two 1.2-meter poles on the poncho about 45 centimeters apart.

• Place your rucksacks or packs or other equipment between the poles. Also place other items that you want to keep dry between the poles. Snap the poncho sides together.

• Use your buddy's help to complete the raft. Hold the snapped portion of the poncho in the air and roll it tightly down to the equipment. Make sure you roll the full width of the poncho.

• Twist the ends of the roll to form pigtails in opposite directions. Fold the pigtails over the bundle and tie them securely in place using ropes, bootlaces, or vines.

Gardens, Bug Bites And Water

•   Spread the second poncho on the ground, inner side up. If you need more buoyancy, place some fresh green brush on this poncho.

•   Place the equipment bundle, tied side down, on the center of the second poncho. Wrap the second poncho around the equipment bundle following the same procedure you used for wrapping the equipment in the first poncho.

•   Tie ropes, bootlaces, vines, or other binding material around the raft about 30 centimeters from the end of each pigtail. Place and secure weapons on top of the raft.

•   Tie one end of a rope to an empty canteen and the other end to the raft. This will help you to tow the raft.

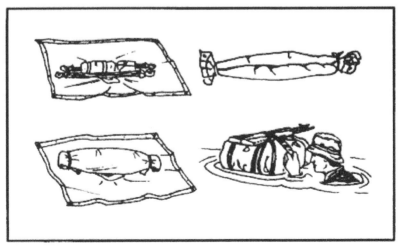

Figure 17-5. Australian poncho raft.

Gardens, Bug Bites And Water

Poncho Donut Raft

Another type of raft is the poncho donut raft. It takes more time to construct than the brush raft or Australian poncho raft, but it is effective. To construct it, use one poncho, small saplings, willow or vines, and rope, bootlaces, or other binding material (Figure 17-6) as follows:

• Make a framework circle by placing several stakes in the ground that roughly outline an inner and outer circle.

• Using young saplings, willow, or vines, construct a donut ring within the circles of stakes.

• Wrap several pieces of cordage around the donut ring about 30 to 60 centimeters apart and tie them securely.

• Push the poncho's hood to the inner side and tightly tie off the neck using the drawstring.

• Place the poncho on the ground, inner side up. Place the donut ring on the center of the poncho. Wrap the poncho up and over the donut ring and tie off each grommet on the poncho to the ring.

• Tie one end of a rope to an empty canteen and the other end to the raft. This rope will help you to tow the raft.

Gardens, Bug Bites And Water

When launching any of the above rafts, take care not to puncture or tear it by dragging it on the ground. Before you start to cross the river or stream, let the raft lay on the water a few minutes to ensure that it floats.

If the river is too deep to ford, push the raft in front of you while you are swimming. The design of the above rafts does not allow them to carry a person's full body weight. Use them as a float to get you and your equipment safely across the river or stream.

Regrets

David and Julie lay in the bed exhausted before attempting a fitful sleep for the night, listening to the dark outside the curtain shrouded window and talking softly to each other as they wound the day down... David had his normal fire duty of tending the woodstove and would have to wake up every three or four hours to go and tend it. David stayed watchful and alert for any would be visitors during the day light and dusk hours but night time was pretty normal and security lax other than observing light discipline.

No lights leaked out his blanket or otherwise shrouded windows to draw attention to prepper shack. He didn't even want to contemplate what he was going to be doing about light discipline come the heat of an Alabama hot summer when windows needed to be open to catch a breeze.

The radio said it was chaos in some areas, mayhem in others and lots of unchecked raging fires in the bigger cities, but it did not relate or generally describe the criminal mayhem one would expect under such conditions. States and cities had declared their own states of emergency and curfews long before that crazy president started wielding his emergency powers to try and control just about everything.

The Board of State Governors had lost their direct controls of their state National Guard units in times of emergency such as this by an executive order long ago. It used to be a Governor could lend troops to a neighboring state or to the Federal Government at his or her discretion. The government usurped these states powers and had federalized the National Guard under the direct command of the President the same as the rest of the military as Commander and Chief long ago.

Oh everybody bitched about it in academia and all 50 states governors voted against it but with the so called war on terror going on it was a moot point. The law was passed and that was that, without even any media fanfare to announce the loss of rights.

Some states wrote into law their own interpretation of emergency powers to block the government from interfering in state affairs and these state laws were being tested now with varying results from the more patriotic or belligerent governors.

The Fed kind of had the upper hand and advantage in breaking down the sovereignty or resolve of the states by threatening to withhold emergency aid and FEMA supplies if their directives were not complied with in full.

All oil refineries had been federalized within days of the cyber-attack that knocked America to its knees in an effort to restart the grid and keep fuel flowing by tapping the national reserves. This process had its own hiccups and delays as bureaucratic red tape met delayed hacker installed malicious software and codes in the pump and power stations operating systems.

That a lot of Midwest cities still had power and were reasonably functioning was known but that couldn't last forever David figured. The cities were being besieged with large numbers of refugees they could not possibly absorb.

There were FEMA manned "Evacuation Centers" that people were directed to for aid and assistance and the government seemed to be trying to move the population towards more centralized and manageable locations, but there were just too many people desperately in need of help. Conflicting travel restrictions and limited gas rationing did little to slow their swelling to over capacity but a little. This policy also left pockets of travelers stranded without gas and living out of their cars awaiting emergency gas trucks that were likely not coming again that way.

Long lines of people can be seen slowly walking or pushing shopping carts towards the cities and transient camps. The skyline has a haze of smoke everywhere and the sides of the road are a dump with bodies and trash fouling the air. Squabbles and fights along the road for food, water. Women, money or countless other reasons occur and usually are concluded violently. The hollow eyed looks of weariness and despair from those you see sitting on the side of the road you know come from those people who have given up on life and can walk no further. This sadness will haunt you, you will lament for them and yourself. You know this, but you can do nothing more for anyone and so you keep pushing yourself towards your destination thinking mostly about putting one foot in front of the other ,and one more foot in front of the other. As your shoulders ache and burn your pack back straps cutting in and your body begins to dehydrate you start looking for a place for yourself to take a rest. This walk will be nothing more than government directed death march for many or just a march to their death, for some.

The economy for all practical purposes had tanked and a dollar didn't really have an attachable or attainable value at the moment. Trading in securities had stopped and unless you were in a 'powered zone" you couldn't get any money out of the banks. About 80% of the population in the US was now unemployed and had no prospects about their future.

Food riots and social unrest were endemic as the seams of civilized society burst and overflowed with desperation and want. People are afraid of each other.

Dealing with everyday problems since the SHTF means that you now have to face a whole new set of uncomfortable situations, from how to take a shower "with a few gallons of water" to thinking about how to use pure violence in response to a threat or theft when violence was not part of your life before.

At the beginning of the disaster people tried to stay together, I mean in the terms of communities or neighbors pulling together and trying to help each other. Folks said people used to have a "normal" way of communication and pretty much normal thought processes when the cyber attack first occurred.

But as weeks went by and cupboards went bare with no end in sight people started to snap. The media broadcasted fake messages of hope of restarting the grid right alongside horrible details of murder, rape and other crime becoming more common, the Peoples trust in government faded quickly and was replaced by fear of the known and unknown risks they faced.

Ever so slowly people had started to move away from each other and there was left a "just us or them" mentality taking over.

Groups were not open anymore. No more welcoming strangers or considering altruistic acts. Folks didn't have anything for themselves and even less for others.

David had prepared for something disastrous to happen for some time. He didn't know what exactly he was preparing for but he had followed his instincts like the universal conscious raising of the prepper community felt that something "bad" was going to happen.

Researchers say that an interest in survivalism can often be used as a barometer of social anxiety; and in many cases, says sociologist Richard Mitchell, it can also be a response to modern stress.

There are many stressors that can bring out the survival instinct in someone. People might be influenced by past experiences surviving or preparing for a hurricane, losing their jobs, fears developed from reading the terrible headlines or absorbing the latest internet theories and conspiracies.

In the end, what it all boils down to for everyone, well at least for the preppers, is self-reliance—this is a concept that is as old as the human race itself? Some entitlement oriented, ignorantly unprepared people think a disaster can't happen to them etc. people, or sheeple as preppers are sometimes wont to refer to them, refused to heed any preparedness messages or warnings. These types of people will suffer the most in a disaster and will also cause undue suffering of others through their inactions and lack of preparations.

David particularly lamented this fact because he had a friend that he thought was a sheeple extraordinaire. She had not always been like this, but somewhere over the years she had developed a panic attack syndrome that caused her to become reclusive and fear even going to the grocery store.

David had tried his best to get her to prep even just a little several times but to no avail. She said in her condition she didn't want to think about bad things and rebuffed any further attempts by him to talk about it. He did get her slightly prepared however because she often asked a favor of him to go to the grocery store for her. Often meant like once a week sometimes. He sort of slowly got the notion over to her to let him add some canned products to her order for when he or somebody else couldn't go to the grocery store for her.

Phones still worked intermittently if you had the old style phone and David was in horror of what that meant now. Beth trusted the media hype that in a few months many cities might get power back on and that she had her animals to think about so she and they were just going to stay in town and pray.

Starvation is a nasty way to go and David shuddered to think of the conversations that he might have to have with someone in that wretched state. Yesterday's conversation with Beth was how to possibly get her some extra heat, he didn't have a clue what she could be eating at the moment and he didn't even consider asking her for obvious reasons. He already told her he had no intentions of coming back into the city and that he was sorry he could give her no help and she was on her own now. It was quite a tearful event on both their sides. He had halfheartedly mentioned the possibility of her coming out to the country should a disaster happen but she wouldn't hear of it and would stay in her home no matter what happened.

Julie and he knew she was going to die there at her home and it was just a question of when and this fact disturbed them very much and often. However, there is nothing they could do other than offer lip service to her plight and suggest what few improvised preparedness tips they could give her to aid in her comfort. Kind of weird being on call and scratching your head to come up with a miracle. One day that phone will quit ringing… too much to think about.

5

Solar Solitude

Now I have heard some folks around here bragging for quite sometime that if we had a sizable disaster (natural or otherwise) that halted the worldwide production and distribution of food that us country people could survive because we have land and could grow our own gardens. But, in reality, now that the tractor trailers of Wal-Mart have stopped running altogether around here it will be getting even more real "interesting" you might say.

It wasn't long ago when I was living here during the week long aftermath of a hurricane that many folks around here would've likely starved to death or killed one another off over the last carton of milk or loaf of bread ... they would have been feuding with each other in the trailer parks like the

Solar Solitude

Hatfield's and McCoy's long before anyone that actually farms around here could have raised a herd of dairy cows or planted a field of wheat to provide our own milk and bread, not to mention other necessary sustenance. Even those of us who already garden would be hard-pressed to grow much more produce than for our own use let alone several more families and with the droughts or torrential rains going on there is no way.

Yes we can. But not without learning a few skills and employing a little well-thought-out preparation. Country folk are more likely to "figger' out" a problem and create a makeshift solution given time, as opposed to their urban neighbors; however we're still prone to being temporarily without resources.

When you wake up one morning in a world where everything that you took for granted suddenly ceased to exist or no longer worked at all, just realizing that one simple little fact could blow your mind and set it to reeling and worrying. People would be reacting to these morning thoughts in different and often times strange and bizarre ways as to how they were handling the losses they were experiencing.

David had not quite figured out what sort of reality he was experiencing and found himself in these days and that fact messed with his coping strategies somewhat. On the one hand he was in the enviable position of living on a few acres outside a small college town and had more than sufficient preps to carry him and Julie for 6 months or so in food and comfort. On the other hand it seemed impossible to gauge what, if any, relief and reconstruction efforts the government was going to be doing or might have any hopes of ever reaching him personally.

Theoretically speaking, the cities and states in the west that still had working power could send aid to stricken areas and the country could start rebuilding one day. To accomplish this, large numbers of people needed to be evacuated just like we do for hurricanes to neighboring states. The cities and towns that have infrastructure absorb as many evacuees as they can and disburse as many refugees as they can geographically to lessen the impact on resources. The storm passes, or in this case as soon as the homes the

Solar Solitude

evacuees left get water and later lights and life resumes again in a disaster reconstruction phase.

There have been huge migrations from the hurricane prone gulf coast states over the years and FEMA and the State Emergency Management folk down south have many models to go by in order to try and make an exodus as smooth as possible.

As far as David knew, pretty much everything on the eastern seaboard as far west as Texas was dark and off the grid for one reason or another. Some of the Midwest and Northeast power was still connected to the grid and offered bastions of hope for America to regain her former glory. The big flaw in that hope was people, there were just too many people from the mega cities like New York etc. that clogged and snarled the highways heading to towns and cities that could just not absorb nor feed these millions of lost souls.

A swarm of locusts coming from every direction can be managed somewhat if Emergency Management has anticipated and begun some formal disaster plans to deal with these herds of humanity but that is an iffy proposition. Everyone knows, or thinks they know, that there is no formal plan for an EMP like event but that is not totally true.

Solar Solitude

There are rehearsed plans such as the "Great Shake Out Exercise" this was the plan for receiving huge numbers of evacuees when the New Madrid fault decides it's time for the inevitable mega earthquake to occur and displace millions of people. The Center for Disease Control works on various policies to quarantine and control whole cities etc. so it's not out of the realm of possibility to just stitch various agencies and policies together and use them for any large grid down situations.

The Army is the expert of operating in a grid down situation and has a long and glorious history of operating in and restoring war torn countries. Just look what we did in Iraq for example? You are naïve if you think the U.S. didn't use some conventional EMP bombs over there, anyway, we came in and restored the infrastructure for the country while trying to keep peace so why not here?

This is where the lines get blurry, they most assuredly will use the Army post conflict reconstruction manual to guide America through this disaster, but that will be an evolving thing brought about most likely by the just plain

Solar Solitude

ignorant, rude and criminally inclined fools in the poor inner cities at first.

Look at the LA riots and just imagine it's been a month since the cyber-attack and the welfare checks and food stamps ain`t coming no more and that would be even if you could find a place to spend them at. Hell during the LA Riots people burned what few grocery stores dared open up in their neighborhoods then. Nowadays I bet you that the residents of those "Hoods or Ghettos" have set the whole damn place on fire again and are fleeing in front of the flames like animals from a forest fire heading where? The National Guard may as well be the Army anyway these days and there is not enough manpower stateside without the military getting involved to even consider trying to quell all the civil unrest and lawlessness that should be starting to be going on full tilt by now.

The bigger cities that have all those unemployed refugees in them will most likely try and resort to civilian labor gangs similar to ones we had as Conservation Corps under the "New Deal Policy" during the depression. Hopefully that will further geographically dissipate people and spread economic stability further.

Solar Solitude

Many FEMA trailer parks would get set up and Federal relocation camps would begin popping up in likely and unlikely places as a means to draw the evacuees closer to the city's infrastructure and political and legal controls. When they evacuated New Orleans after hurricane Katrina folks were bused, flown, trained etc. all over the country and they got lodging, credit cards and cash to survive on for some time. The government most likely now after this latest disaster would begin issuing some kind of military script for goods and services as they reset the dollar and the rest of the world currencies followed suit.

"Money! Now that's a screwed up situation David groused to himself.

David got paid from working off the internet. He had no internet to do his business on at the moment. He didn't know why he didn't have an internet signal even though he could power his computer with his SUNRNR Generator. His signal came from a satellite and had nothing to do with the grid as far as he was concerned. Not knowing the technology of it all made him wonder if somebody might of hacked communication or military satellites as a reason for his internet signals absence.

As far as having a job went David figured that was the end of his and wondered if he even had any funds left from his last paycheck which should have been deposited in his bank account. Not that it mattered at the moment; there wasn't anything much for him to buy and that was even if he could access a working bank to get cash. No for him and Julie and for some time to come they would be operating and trying to live without any funds as their long term reality.

"This is going to suck!" David muttered, and Julie agreed.

Oh David figured he could maybe find some kind of work in the city if reconstruction really did arrive someday in the distant bleak future. He had some marketable skills and academic degrees to compete with for employment, but mostly he figured it was a matter of outlasting and out surviving any of the other would be survivor applicants because at this time things were about to get pretty hairy around here.

Solar Solitude

The town had agriculture around it and a few factories that actually produced something so chances were good that it would rate highly in a reconstruction plan. David looked at his mental map of the United States as hot zones (those places that had power) and dead zones (those places without) and tried to imagine what areas the government might like to first jump start. Louisiana refineries most assuredly, perhaps insure traffic on the waterways like the great Mississippi River, do something with our outdated rail system and start reconnecting the dots to move goods and services cross country. An enormous undertaking to imagine, let alone one to accomplish hastily and that idea was unfortunately going to creak along slowly with bureaucracy and incompetence leading the way. Plenty of labor around let's see how they use it.

"I might, just might see a light go on from the power company in about 6 months if I am damn lucky." David optimistically estimated. But that was if they could get those pump stations for the water back on in the next few weeks. Folks are probably already dying from lack of clean water." He mused.

Solar Solitude

" I can't even imagine how it is in California right at the moment. They were undergoing the biggest drought they had had in a 100 years before the poo hit the fan and the farmers that produced half of the vegetable's for the U.S. were struggling hard and causing the agriculture department concerns recently. David quickly reminded himself to keep one faucet turned on a little so he would know if or when they ever got the water turned back on.

David was watching how they country was slowly dying along with the normal behavior of people. The thoughts of the populace already held numerous opinions, and also numerous ideas about how it was going to look if some crap like what had happened impacted America. They also held opinions on when societal collapse was going to start getting totally out of hand and in what stages it would occur.

The big truth is that the sheeple or those masses of people who are non preppers, you know the non survivalist type folks prepping even a little bit. These people now had no other choices, no food and no means of getting any sustenance or fuel for their cars meant "get on the bus Gus" meant go to the FEMA camps.   Non Preppers or non alarmists were not apt to see this type of event coming so I guess you might have to say these days that it is understandable that they saw their only hope as trying to get to an evacuation center at this point.

The problem also being is that many real or practicing and storing stuff preppers are that they are blind to their actual long-term as well as situational short term needs. They also must get to the camps if they can, but they at least have some awareness and plans for this event. They have themselves personally thought about various expectations or warnings to heed or look out for and are thinking outside the box.

Many preppers become too deeply involved," too fixated" horse blindered or buried in discussions about Bug Out Bags (BOB), Bug Out Locations (BOL) or when the mutant ninja bikers are going to come for their stash post shit hit the fan (SHTF). The countless hours spent in these prepper communities also gets sidetracked on any number of finer points once the basics of 72 hour preparedness are covered.

Certain preppers spend all their time in these forums and other discussions arguing about, what knife, what pack,

Solar Solitude

9mm versus 45 calibers etc. to have when SHTF comes around and gamut of other stuff. They spend their energy oftentimes talking about God knows what else other than concentrating on bugging in or becoming more self reliant. The subjects all have their finer points in addressing prepper related information, I am just saying it is too distracting to go down the wrong rabbit hole chasing obscure information you don't need right now unless you have done a serious risk and preparedness survey of your "bug in" situation. A lot of survivalist types are planning for what they think one day will happen when the lights go out and they find themselves surrounded by darkness all around while waiting on all hell to break loose in the dawn. Doesn't usually happen like this, a disaster unravels and gets compounded at different rates. Many disasters are precluded by a warning; you prepare for the disasters without warnings the same way. Many people haven't thought about an on off switch situation.

They haven't even considered or thought about this type of lights out scenario affecting them. This a rare occurrence, but one that has precedence and it only happens when governments make huge mistakes or nature finally gets back at us and shows her deadly fury and devastation. It can also happen as a political act of repression or warning. Think about Russia threatening to turn off gas and lines in the dead of winter to influence the politics in one of the spin off states obstructing its wishes. Russia also intentionally starved millions in the Ukraine and other areas to fulfill one of its pogroms.

I believe preppers should be thinking about the government and corporations just turning on and off the lights slowly and purposefully and you should feel that most of the time you can pretty much see it coming.

Nowadays, just like it was before the cyber-attack, you see that people are slowly accepting the various miseries of their daily lives and they are thinking that it is normal for them to do without some things and that they have to improvise or are forced to work harder for what they used to have with less effort.

The human psyche can get used to a lot of depravation around them if they have enough time to make the adjustment. But remember this and remember it well, "When people lose everything, they lose it" so consider that a immediate loss can send many into deep depression, fear, anger, jealousy and a host of other emotions.

Solar Solitude

The government and corporations seem to like to use this take away this and take away that until you feel like sometimes they are just leaving you enough air to breathe in order to keep you alive and paying taxes. Smaller packaging, smaller servings, more fine print, lower quality, increasing taxes, higher cost of living etc. Stores won't be offering you green stamps any time soon to get your business and kitchen towels are not attached to sacks of flour anymore. Dish night at the old local movie theater or a free glass in your laundry detergent is an ancient hard to grasp notion in marketing that most have never heard of from bygone times. The days of getting a bit more for a dollar have been replaced with a continuous assault of a bit less, every year a little less.

What I am getting at here my fellow preppers is that for many of us economic challenges makes it feel like the poo was already hitting the fan long before this cyber attack was unleashed. Far too many of us were dealing with our own personal, financial.employment you name it problems that are now even more greatly magnified by this event.

The disaster of not being able to pay for their daily food has already previously hit quietly to your friends and neighbors with job losses and bankruptcies. A national disaster has already insidiously hit the Constitution which impacted all of us with losses of rights and freedoms under the so called Patriot Act along with destructive presidential emergency powers and executive orders that were passed.

All these restrictions, all these economic woes, all the manufacturing shipped overseas, the militarization of our police etc. are only going to get worse and those calamities are slowly gaining in momentum. Most people are not going to realize any of this until martial law, societal break down and fascism blows up in their face. Many of us prep now for such events, most don't. Prepping for a job loss doesn't usually include buying high priced battle rifle scopes and such.

Consider what is the state of your own local infrastructure? How about your individual feeling of safety with increasing criminal activity and elements in your area? Are you finding it hard to cope with Gas prices, food and utility prices? How many folks still have decent jobs and if not what are their chances of getting one?

Solar Solitude

How does this current slow collapse look to you? It is happening you know. Are you going to grab your bug out bag and head for the hills? No of course not, so why fixate on that aspect of survival now? What preppers are most likely lamenting about at this very moment is not having a piece of dirt and some shelter to call their own with some off grid sturdy cooking and heating resources they can rely on.

David's solution was

SilverFire Hunter Natural Draft Chimney Gasifier Stove

The Silver Fire Hunter maybe the most *important emergency or disaster stove* to own, use coupon code Prepper1

Solar Solitude

Preppers are infatuated with the exciting aspect of bugging out. Face it, it just sounds exciting and romantic. If you want to lose that notion quickly, just try it for a few days. The idea of grabbing a pack and heading to the woods sounds adventurous and somehow glamorous to the unaware or beguiled. Be able to do it, but prepare for everything you can in order not to have to. After that, lighten the load in your rucksack and just start with a soldiers basic, poncho, sleeping bag, shelter, mess kit, canteen and socks. Get the silver impregnated socks that are part wool for summer and winter. They also do underwear this way but at the moment it's hard to find silver impregnated cotton drawers from the military.

EXIT STAGE RIGHT

"What type of advice do you think you can offer me regarding those FEMA relocation camps, David? I remember that you said you had worked around some and studied a couple of those trailer parks that were put up by the government after Katrina and other Hurricanes displaced people. I really hate to bother you today but my Grandpa said for me to come ask you about them and he also said if it wasn't too much of an imposition, that he wanted you to come over to the house and talk to him. His breathing is bad as you know and he doesn't want to risk the exertion of walking over here and having to walk back up that hill." Will said as cordially as he could.

"I will be happy to come over and talk to him Will in an about an hour or so if that's alright. I have a couple of chores I am involved in I need to finish first if that would be alright. Will, Are you planning on trying to get to one of them places maybe? Have you thought it through?" David replied scrutinizing the young man.

"Well David, me and the family got together and talked it over some and we come to a conclusion. We concluded that we need to consider for ourselves a backup destination to go to if where we are planning on going doesn't work out as expected. We could encounter a glitch or two, it just depends. You see David we have got us some kin folk that live about a hundred miles from here as the crow flies and they raise maybe 15 head of cattle a year, sometimes a few goats or a hog or two occasionally. They actually live the farm life and have been doing it for generations so it sounds like our best bet to try and see if they will take on as boarders. We haven't been real close at all to them for a long time, but they are kinfolk and Grandpa thinks that they will take us all in if we just show up on their doorstep with our hats in our hands and a growling belly. Grandpa grew up around there and his stepbrother Mani and he used to be kind of close. When I was real young I can remember my Uncle Mani taking me and his boy fishing on the properties pond, but I haven't probably talked to the boy twice since then and pretty much only to answer the phone to Mani. Thing is David, Mani`s daughter got cancer years ago and they had themselves some serious financial hard times to cope with. All the kinfolks and family helped Mani out to some extent on those outrageous medical bills, but because he and Grandpa were a bit tighter back then my Uncle seemed to depend upon Grandpa financially a lot more than the others.

Mani hadn't found that St. Jude's Children's Research Hospital the girl finally ended up at that time; you know the one that never charges parents a penny? None of us knew of that option then and the other bills caused family rifts. Grandpa didn't have much money and him and Mani sort of got into it over Grandpa saying it looked like the child was going to die soon no matter what they did and he needed to keep his cash money for his own family. They didn't talk for a week or so after that and depending on who is telling you the story, Grandpa signed away his interest in the family farm because Great Grandma said everyone should sell off a little acreage from what Great Grandpa had allotted in his will to try and get Mani out of debt. They made Mani executor to take over the real-estate sale and everyone gave him power of attorney and that's where things seemed to go sideways and different versions of the story change...

Great Grandma Elberta died within about three months of that document and since Mani had everybody's power of attorney he sort of did what he wanted to regarding the estate. Needless to say he and Grandpa didn't agree about his actions and to make a long story short they only speak on holidays and once in a great while to yell at each other about money." Will said evidently feeling the cold air while he was standing with his ungloved hands shoved in the pockets of a thin light weight dark blue, almost black mechanics jacket.

"That's a hell of a story, my condolences to you. Money can come between the best of brothers they say. You're sort of between a rock and a hard place I guess Will. I can see why you all have some reservations about going to a camp or to your Uncles. I would suggest to you strongly though that if you can any way work it out with your Uncle, I would suggest that. Work on strategies for staying with your Uncle and try avoiding the relocation assembly areas if possible. As for the camps, well I don't know what conditions are like now. I can tell you about the type of parks evacuee centers and conditions of the ones I am familiar with. Some of them still exist in one form or another or have been repurposed. They are not that bad but you should avoid them if you can. No telling who you going to be living next door to and where the camp will be located often times. You are always subject to transfer, relocation or further processing. One big thing to know about them places is that from county to county and from state to state you can't compare them to each other. It's a too many chiefs and too many tribes of Indians to deal with thing. Think of it as, who is in charge of whom and which tribe has the majority influence under whose authority. Each official or administrator running those places has various levels of experience and various mandates to follow or superiors to answer to and they create different camp rules or types of accommodations for the so called guests or refugees to bed down at.

I am going to give you a paper I wrote in college for Sociology, the Theory of mass Disasters later on if you want, its about 20 pages of how I suggested to fix what was wrong with a particular model of a type of camp that a lot of people don't realize was both an experiment as well as a policy makers influence on the future of disaster reconstruction efforts. This camp I am referencing was in Florida and it was particularly chosen as a field of academic as well as federal agency targeted studies for many reasons. My reasoning for examining it in great depth was mostly based upon my need of graduate credits. It was also part of my Masters Displaced Persons certificate so that I could get the level of degree I needed to advocate for more holistic methods versus the prevailing judicial way of addressing the needs of displaced people.

In the United States or for that matter the World, field experience, opinions and wisdom does not seem to matter in policy reform unless you can evidence a higher degree of learning to be allowed a voice in their august decision and lawmaking forums. You have to evidence your expertise by citing other peers that are already recognized as having some expertise whether or not you agree with them.

In other words if you don't have the accredited sheep skin seal emblazoned diplomas in your resume as a common man or as a speaker then you don't get a voice or consideration as an individual that is worthy of being considered by political appointees for setting policy. Simple as that, uneducated officials, tenured professors, all fulfilling all the qualifications to the letter listed on the job application, or appointment. How the way the public will politically fund or support an independent advocates efforts etc. all depends on a worthless piece of paper that only means you can talk in the stiff regulated voice that has enough literary rules in it to rewrite the King James Bible in order for them to even consider for themselves to deign reading your stuff before dismissal to a dusty file cabinet.

I wanted to change those emergency assembly areas and trailer parks really bad and thought that by me gaining degrees and submitting my scholarly papers it could make some kind of a difference and save some people some unnecessary grief. I have older and wiser eyes and ears now and can pretty much tell you that nothings changed. Good camp commanders use common sense and bad ones try to look good by enforcing bad regulations. Apple and stick routine, stick and apple.

"By the way which of the compass directions are you planning on going in, Will? "David said, while sort of pointing his finger up in the air and wiggling it towards several cardinal points inquisitively, looking like the Wizard

EXIT STAGE RIGHT

of Oz scarecrow.

"I don't know, we are going back roads and heading sort of south west, I guess. Is there a camp that's better or worse down that way that you maybe can suggest?" Will said, confused all the while trying to take in the fact that a one size fits all aspect had nothing to do with an emergency Relocation Camp.

"Well, if you are going south west then it appears to me that are you leaning more towards the panhandle of Florida around Panama city or did you mean more central southwest like towards Mobile, Alabama and Pensacola, Florida? I would advise staying away from Pensacola" David admonished, studying him.

"More towards Opp and Andalusia, hey that's a question for ya, you old veteran prepper!" Will said joking at what he thought he could get by with regarding David's discomfort with the word.

"David you were a soldier, what do you think is going to happen with those damned chemical weapon destruction sites down by Andalusia the Army runs? I know they been incinerating old munitions stores like mustard and nerve gas artillery shells for years down there for various disarmament agreements, but do they perform that with electrical power or natural gas?" Will said enjoying that look David was wearing that he evidently hadn't thought about that particular risk and it vexed him.

"SHEEEEEET! You got me brother! Give me a second here to wrap my head around that particular threat for a minute. Holy smokes boy you just pissed in my pudding, let me think about what might go along with them things being shut down that might pose us some kind of a risk. Ok I can see myself in one mentally as a laborer or operator, working, working and zap the power goes out. What now? Never having worked in one of those facilities before I got to just guesstimate what happens now. There is an official prescribed shutdown procedure and it is rehearsed better than most business continuity plans rest assured. No lights, no problem the emergency lights will automatically come on with backups. I can not see what I am doing as a worker in the dark to perform my regular duties, but I have access to battery operated exit lights and I have mission critical lights illuminating key areas that run on batteries, generators or both, response crews, security, civilian responders ok I am copasetic. No problem, probably the plant workers have practiced the emergency shutdown or clear the area drill a hundred times, its military operated right? I say nothing happens untoward, no gas leaks, no problems the engineers already covered all known toxic safety issues. The plant is shutdown and secured safely and we are now in emergency response mode awaiting further orders." David concluded.

"That assessment sure does make me feel a whole lot better, David. It is bad enough we that might be trying to avoid fallout from nuclear plants, but we also got chemical factories and military bases to think about to I reckon. What exactly is that school paper you were saying that you wrote about FEMA Camps? Were the conditions really bad or something?" Will asked looking very interested at what David had written as the outcome of his studies and research.

"I didn't write much on the actual living conditions like the livability of the trailers or the palatability of the food, I concentrated more on the mandated strict seclusionary polices that were being enforced by private contracted security elements. You see FEMA wouldn't let the media or even any charitable organizations representatives into the gated enclaves to interview the residents for benefits or to inspect and report on living conditions. The people in the camp had to follow very strict rules regarding any type of interactions with anyone out side of the camps fenced perimeter and it caused a lot of problems both for the guests and the non profits trying to help the residents. I will tell you about some of the ridiculous rules that can get you in trouble when I come over to see your grandpa in a bit.

Rambling and Reminiscing

"Julie,
I am ready for a stiff drink, how about you? You ready for one yet?" David said heading for the kitchen.

"Sounds wonderful to me, it has been a long day hasn't it?" "Julie said following him to the kitchen.

"Yea it sure has been a long one Julie, I am starting to get back into shape little by little but I still have to take a lot more rest breaks than I used to when working that garden. I felt like I was going to fallout from unused to exertion several times today while swinging that mattock to cut tree roots and break up the soil. Tomorrow I have decided that I am going to go ahead and use up whatever gas is still left in the tiller and loosen up that dirt so it's much easier to work with. I might even waste a gallon of gas and get the garden as close to spring ready as I can while I have the food to supply my body energy to throw at the task. Let's see, we got about 2 months until spring planting and I am guessing that should be enough time to get the fugelfort garden built and start the soil and wood composting. I have got an idea about trying to plant that little clearing in the woods that you can see from the garden. "David said after handing her his version of a moonshine and lemonade cocktail. That's about the entire adult beverage they had left alcohol wise. David and her had drank up the whiskey and coke about the first week of grid down and had hunkered inside the house to discuss future plans like it was a hurricane party. It hade taken David about another three weeks after that binge to ferment some mash and distill up some home brew fiery elixir. Two big jars of country time lemonade from his preps were reserved for mixer for this fire water because the long-term storage drink mixes were too precious to use because of their calorie count additions to their diets. David had about three cases of orange and apple number 10 sized cans of the long term storage drink mix to augment the meager calories in the premade freeze dried meals he had stored. The extra vitamins and minerals contained in the drink mixes were very important to their welfare. Besides when it came to David's sometimes over indulgent drinking habits, one drink equaled many more in the same sitting and as he put it he was not going to "Piss away dinner and breakfast while catching a buzz foolishly playing with his homemade hooch." The drink mixes were to be rationed for meals and nothing else.

"I know that particular spot in the woods where you are talking about David. You are talking about over by that big sawn up fallen tree right?" Julie said taking a sip from her drink and making a "this tastes wonderful" happy face as she was finally getting able to settle in for the day with a relaxed easy smile.

The area David had referred to was nothing more than a leaf covered small oval woodland clearing about 25x 30ft that had a bark shorn 20 inch circumference fallen tree laid across the edge that had been sawn to lengths but had left laying in the dirt and rotting. The tree looked like it was rotting years ago when David bought his place and he had just left it as it was and let the forest reclaim it however it wanted too.

"I am going to till up the center of that clearing and throw some of the dirt over that tees trunk. We can add more brush and limbs around the perimeter and slowly cover it and those logs with dirt as we go. I haven't made my mind up on that yet. I think we have enough logwood already cut for winter, but I still want to be able to just wander in the woods close by the house and be able to pick up enough fallen limbs and sticks to feed that SilverFire Hunter if we have too. I might just try to compost those logs from the trunk and depend on row cropping for the rest of the clearing to augment the garden." David said settling down on the couch close to Julie and taking a long satisfying sip of his drink after describing part of his plan.

"I can see why you want to use the tiller. That area is probably full of tree roots and you will be swinging that mattock and axe enough just to make paths for the tiller to get through. How about if I gather up tree limbs and such while you work on that project? I could pile the wood up closer to the house around that area and later on you can decide if you want to use them for a garden or we need to save them for cook fires or heating?." Julie said patting his leg and unwinding after the days chores.

They were both pretty tired and dirty from their day's exertions and didn't want to move around much just yet. The sterling powered eco fan atop the wood stove was spinning wildly as the stoked up woodstove radiated its blazing heat in the small place. This tended to create sauna like conditions until a bed of coals was created that would allow David to feed the fire one log at a time from now until it was loading it up to max for bed time.

The excessive heat in the house made David half way consider stripping down with Julie and partaking of a "cat bath" from the water they had heating in a big iron kettle setting on the woodstove. He decided for now he was just too comfortable and enjoying his drink and talking to Julie to bring that subject up and just settled.

186

"David, please point that fan towards the back of the house or take it off the stove if you would." Julie said pulling off her boots and socks and beginning to fan her over heating self momentarily with her hand.

"Sorry baby, you know how it is with that thing. I got the damper closed on her and the air intake shut down but it's not much use. I can't do anything about the excessive heat until it burns down some." David said as he was closest to it to do something about the small fan circulating heat directly in there direction on the couch.

"Julie I got rather an odd idea about that clearing I also wanted to kick with you. If we fooglefort the perimeter of that clearing we will basically end up with a sort of defensive earthworks like they used in the revolutionary war. If I leave some of the tree branches sticking out towards a line of possible attack it would be pretty effective." David shared and to Julie he evidently was already starting to catch a buzz and reverting to his sometimes addled military mind regarding obscure bits of info.

"So you were thinking about building you a fort David? What are you going to call it?" Julie said going along with the strange notion and humoring David.

"Lord knows he had already transformed and tried to fortify the house to a certain extent. *That didn't even include how David's eccentric but good taste in decorating what he referred to as his "Prepper Shack had already occurred before the grid went down." Julie thought beginning to grin.*

David had created an atmosphere in the about 8ft x 25 ft common room area at the front of his house that could be described as Gilligan's Island borrows props from the Korean

War comedy show M.A.S.H. When David first moved to where he was creating his little "Bug-In" retirement home he was sorely regretting that he couldn't afford to move to his love of the beach in northwest Florida so he compromised. This particular property was as far south as he could afford to get to in the direction of Florida and as far as he was concerned he was going to decorate it like Florida to remind himself he was only a couple hours away from the hurricanes and high prices.

The common room took on a nautical theme like a bachelor sea captains inland retirement cottage. A pair of large copper antique ship lanterns graced the top of a beloved and moved too many times old worn mahogany dresser. A large hand painted oil picture of a great four mast sailing ship hung over the couch and above that a hand carved wooden mermaid from Bali graced the wall with her bare bosom
.

A Russian Mosin Nagant rifle with bayonet affixed hung over one window suspended from a gun rack made of welded horseshoes. . Framing it were two solar LED lights with the wires running down to a blue metal battery box. He had some Vietnam era military issue. Flak jackets for chair back covers over two of the four dining room chairs that braced his work and socializing table.

Tent Toters

"David are you about ready to start helping me water proof those tents?" Julie asked.

"In a second darlin, I thought I had me another tube of seam sealer around here somewhere. One tube is enough but I would like to put my hands on my other one first if I can find it" David said rummaging about some shelves.

"So explain to me why you want to set those tents up so they can be seen from the road. Also what is it that inspired this project when you got so many other things to be doing?" Julie said as she started going through a box David handed her to search for the missing tube of sealant.

"Well I grew up during the days when nobody expected floors in tents. When I was in the Boy scouts we had for our use those big yellow canvas baker tents and I camped in many a drip fest and stayed nice and dry. Rarely did we ever need to trench around the tents, to do so usually means you're going to accumulate a whole lot more water from the effort than leaving it alone or better yet sometimes just strategically piling a bit of

189

dirt at a low place. I remember that the tents dirt or pasture grass floor and my poncho stayed dry 98% of the time. I am telling you someone ought to have started a website called all-tents-suck.org because the manufacturers of today now have got the purchasers to do their job for them waterproofing the useless things they sell and they continue to get away with it.

How many preppers or campers got the unique opportunity to depend on a brand new or slightly used tent only to find that in a bit of rain it leaked miserably and usually in the middle of the night? The instructions to the tent supplied by the manufacturer when you buy it says to use seam sealer before actual camping use but this warning also should say spray some other kind of waterproofer all over the damn thing too for good measure. There has been many a camping trip I have been on where I saw people pitching tarps over their tents and putting another tarp under it in order to try to stay dry. Kind of gives you a whole another mindset about people's chances of surviving in a "Homeless Tent City" or being foolish or solely misguided enough to depend on this type of shelter in a bug out.

"I got me a brand new old style two shelter half canvas Army pup tent that me and you are going to depend on sweetie if we decide to go somewhere. If you don't touch the damn roof on the inside they never failed me in all the years I spent under one when I was in the Army. That style of tent was in service about a hundred years and used many wars and for what it is, it just plain works as shelter. I wish I had bought me a few more tents when they were cheap when the army switched over to a different model." David said reminiscing and then brightening noticeably as Julie found the missing sealant and they headed outside to setup the two nylon tents they had as a project for today.

"I already understood the need for us to waterproof the things; I was more wondering why is it that you're trying to make it look like we got extra company coming or have maybe already arrived here." Julie said pondering what scheme David might be up to.

"Oh that, well a bit of curiosity if anyone notices is a good thing I am guessing. Besides, I am only going to leave them up overnight and let that sealant dry well. I want to have our tents ready and in the best working order I can in case we have to bug ourselves out of here for some reason. I doubt we are going anywhere any time soon but you can never tell and I might not be lucky enough to have a vehicle to climb into one rainy night if we get ourselves caught sleeping out in one of these fair weather tents. I am real curious however just how much these tents might get noticed and talked about by the neighbors. Ha! Sounds like fun. Mind games and curiosity, Mind games and curiosity will keep the gossip going around here a bit longer. Well maybe someone will come visit to ask about them or maybe not. Either way, we will get the task done and pack one tent in the van and put one in the prep shed." David said as they began assembling the tents at the end of his driveway in an arrangement like someone was setting up camp there.

"Playing with these tents sure brings back great memories David of when we all camped out at Prepper Stock 2014 doesn't it?" Julie said smiling at the pleasant recollection.

"Makes you wonder how all those fine folks are making out about right now don't it." David said smiling back as he began securing the last tent pole.

"It sure does, I bet all of them preppers are bugged in by now and doing just fine for themselves, well better tan most anyways. Wish we could have gone to the regional event this year but we tried. Makes me sad we had one more chance to see all of them again and missed it." Julie stated sighing in fond memory of all those prepper faces gathered around a campfire or two.

"Me too, I sure wish we could have made it but we just couldn't swing it. We did make a camping trip or two this year though. How much lead time did do you imagine that them cross country preppers, the ones that traveled in by airplane or drove it have to get home before this shit hit? I am having problems with associating this shit to dates and times. They changed the dang date of that thing so many times I am confused. Hell I don't know even what today is, do you?" David said straightening up after securing a tent peg.

"March 22nd I think. I guess folks attending Prepper Stock had maybe a week or so to get home?" Julie said looking in David's direction with her brow furrowed in mental calculation.

"Sounds about right. I wonder if they are ever going to get some kind of phone service working regular, well just fixing the landlines anyway. From now on you and I need to try the phone every once in awhile for service and call Crick Miller (as in "down by the crick (creek.)" any chance that we may get. I want to find out what shape his area is in and how him and his buddy Morgan is making out. Julie, if for some reason we have got to bug out north then we will be heading somewhere in his general direction I am guessing." David said starting to reveal some plans he was considering for their safety and security.

"Ok, if your not around when I get through I will tell him that, but why all this talk of bugging out David? That is not like you at all. I thought we were remaining here from now on. The whole count your blessings, stay with all your stuff and bug in thing. What is it that's seems to be worrying you David? You know that I want to know and I bet you know I want to know now." Julie said looking very anxious and concerned about what ever might be bothering David.

"Nothing special, well maybe just a small concern or two has me puzzled for the moment. Do you know what kind of business was operating about 8 or10 miles up the road?" David asked more subdued than he meant to be.

"Some kind of aerospace thing wasn't it? Are you thinking that it might be a target of some kind?' Julie said trying to understand what it was about the place that David had some kind of apprehensions about.

"Well they build missiles, actual missiles or assemble missile parts for the military I don't know but I am going to ask Mike first chance I get about that. If there is something down there that can explode and make a bigger boom than I can imagine well then I want to know something more about it. Another thing is that if its primary function is manufacturing for the department of defense then maybe our area will get relief attention quicker than somewhere else. I also want to watch that place like a canary in a coal mine for a bit, might find out something interesting." David concluded looking at the little campsite being setup and ready to waterproof.

"Like? What kind of information do you think you might learn from seeing if that place opens its doors or not?" Julie asked thinking about what the possibilities might mean.

"Like whether or not the workers go home after a shift. Probably not, there is not much gas and there is precedence for workers staying at factors in emergencies or during times of disaster. I am wondering if they will work folks maybe two weeks on then a week off or something; remember there are a lot of families attached to those workers. Feeding the plant workers cafeteria style is one thing, but what about the families staying back alone? Folks wont stay on a job very long if they are worried about the families at home. How that situation is handled will be the biggest indicator I can think of as to what our chances are and where the regular unaffiliated folks like us stand in the pecking order of things." David explained.

"Ok I think I understand you David. You want to see like if they bus the workers families in to feed them at the plant or will be holding there own worker family food drops and the rest of us ain't supposed to notice. Yea sounds like a good place to get news about and watch if we can. Are there any other places we need to be being paying special attention to?" Julie asked while spreading some clear gummy seam sealer on the first tent.

"I don't know right off hand; I am still trying to think of some more places that might bear us watching. We probably won't be able to watch nothing much though anyway, why waste the gas if there is nothing to see or gain? I am going to undertake to drive down and ask that farmer with the geese what he sees traffic wise on the interstate once in awhile though. Outside of the radio news we are pretty much cut off. Come to think of it, I might have my apprehensions about driving up to that farmer's house in the state of affairs we are in. I am sure half this road remembers his chickens and geese for sale signs and has already gone over to talk to him one way or another. I wish I had gone over there to begin with instead of putting it off so long and forgetting about it. I think I will just stay where I am at and keep a low profile for now. I have too many unknowns going on outside this property to be venturing out just for news and I doubt he has increased his flock to a surplus yet that maybe I could trade him something for." David said spraying the rain fly with water sealant.

"We need to pack us a box or two and discuss what type of stuff you need to move to a FEMA camp if the occasion ever arose also besides just getting our camping gear together today. You won't see me near one of those camps if I can in anyway help it, but you never know about relocations. It isn't possible to move all our preps with us and we really have no idea how long they will last us until we can somehow replace foodstuffs. I don't want you to have any illusions of never having to go to one at all, that would be foolish. A tornado could come through here and we could lose everything for example. Instead of thinking about not going, think about how you would survive in a camp and build onto your strategies and resources to maximize your comfort. I will give you some examples of bugging to a shelter versus bugging out to the woods. One thing is clothes; take everything you can winter and summer in your car and dress grey man in the trailer park with your older clothes. Think of it as starting out in a new life with just your cars contents and be ready for a ton of rules applying to anything questionable as contraband or not allowed on premises. Some things or rules might seem odd at first, like no outside decorations for your house, any media interviews or social worker questionnaires except government recognized ones on camp premises etc. Living in a FEMA trailer park is easy enough to get the hang of if you don't make a spectacle of yourself complaining or expecting better than you got. Be careful how quick you make friends with those you don't know and try to gravitate in line with like minded folks for lot assignment. One of those big electric frying pans is a good thing to have when traveling because if you get stuck in a hotel, first you have a means to cook and second technically it's not a hot plate so not specifically banned. That reminds me, that induction cook plate is an ideal prep also. It's a low wattage kitchen aide, pretty safe and efficient as well as versatile because you're not restricted in pot sizes; only restriction is the pan you use to cook with metal composition. It mattered using the cook top if your pots and pans were thermo conducting or non conducting metals.

.

9

A S.O.S is Received

"Hey David come here quick, I finally got Crick on the phone!" Julie called out the door to David who was working on the garden fence.

"Hell yea!" David yelled back and dropped his fencing pliers and ran back towards the house.

"Hey Crick buddy! How are you? "David said quickly into the staticy crackling phone after Julie handed him the receiver

"I can barely hear you David. I am fine. Are you coming?" Crick said quickly back.

"Well only if I have to, I really was… Hello? Hello?" Damn phone went dead." David said and put the phones handset back in the cradle momentarily before picking it backup to check the line again.

"Ah Hell! What did he say Julie? "David said looking crestfallen and anxious that he didn't have a chance to talk to his friend.

"Oh David you are not going to believe this! We only talked a little and I missed parts of what he was saying from the static on the line but he wants you to come up there. He said the dams had been blown by the terrorists and that the folks attending this years Prepper Stock had been cut off from the roads leading out of the park and for most practical purposes they were all living on an island!. "Julie said all in a rush.

"They are got themselves stuck on an island? As in surrounded all around by water or is it they just can't use the bridges or dam roads?" David queried.

"Uh, well he didn't really say why they were an island. Only thing he said was that they were pretty much stuck on an island for all practical purposes. . Maybe that means they can walk over a bridge but not drive? But he did say that he had just got home after rafting across the river to that big houses boat dock that you can see from the park. He said he rode a bicycle a few miles to his house after that and hadn't been in long. I don't know, I guess maybe they are surrounded by water or going the way he went was shorter somehow. He didn't elaborate, he only said for you to meet him at his house at 397 Stone Crick roads, I mean creek road. Damn that Crick Miller sometimes his southern accent is worse than yours." Julie said kidding David while checking the scrap of paper that she had scribbled down the address on in order to confirm that she had written the message down correctly.

"He said to be sure and tell you that he would leave you a note and a key where you could find it if he wasn't there to greet you when you arrived. That's about when I hollered for you to come inside the house to get on the phone. I had just finished telling him that you and I had been trying to get through to him for days to ask some questions about bugging out to that area when I passed him and the phone over to you. I didn't get a chance to tell him anymore about why we wanted to know so I bet he thinks we got problems here also…." Julie said looking at David with a raised eyebrow and a tight lip.

"Hell I bet he does. Darn phone." David said as he once again picked up his receiver to check for a dial tone.

"Nothing, nada! Not a damn thing. No signal at all. The phone was just plain dead like he hadn't paid his phone bill. Speaking of which had he paid it? Oh come on now David get serious, did he really think that the phone company had time at the moment to shut him off for being late?" David thought with a slight ironic smile.

David related to Julie what it was that had caused his smile to appear while putting down the phone and after a brief chuckle with her about it, he had a bad premonition come over him.

"You know Julie if someone can hack our electrical grid and shut it down, wouldn't it have made sense for them to also attack the phone system? Nothing much, just some hacker somewhere tell a computer somewhere else that every bodies phone bill this month was in default and to shut down the service on xyz day. That's an easy way to cause some serious stress and worry on the populace as well as insure that it is pretty much impossible to call up people to report for work as well as greatly slow down communications amongst first responders." David said now eying his phone and wondering if his own phone line might be down for good this time.

"Oh David, that means we might not be able to get back on the phone again with Crick! What are we going to do? You think the phone id down for good?" Julie said as the realization that the phone service might be being attacked or hacked at this very moment came to her.

"Well let's hope the phone is just temporarily out of service Julie. You know that the phone service has been very spotty to non existent last couple weeks to say the least, but it sounds like we got a hell of a mess to deal with either way. I wonder what in the hell it is that Crick expects me to do to help if I come way up there. I can't imagine a single thing he could want out of me other than for me to bring a few items of comfort to those stranded preppers and help him out in someway to do the same. Must be something else he wanted from us but for the life of me I don't know what it is at the moment. He knows that 2 ½ hour trip to the Park is far too long and dangerous for me to consider unless I thought I would actually make some kind of significant contribution or difference to those stranded." David said trying his best to get into Crick's mind and critical assessment of the situation so that he could possibly guess what it was that might be expected out of him.

"Maybe he thought you might have on hand more food than you actually do? It could be David that he expects you to share some of yours with the stranded prepper community as you and he try to rescue them off that island" Julie speculated offhandedly while thinking about what might have been behind her and David's friend Crick's reasoning.

"Rescue them folks how and take them now basically homeless refugees to where? I mean if Crick got off of that island somehow and he himself home ok then he is in a far better position to help them than I will ever be. He is from that area and knows the ins and outs of it as well has lots of friends to call upon maybe., most likely he will be rounding up some kind of a boat or boats to either bring supplies back to the castaways or use a boat to evacuate folks from the island. That's kind of like out of the frying pan and into the fire if you ask me. Hell there has to be at least forty of fifty preppers there, maybe more. This years turn out was supposed to bigger than last years. Then you have got to take into account all the other campers that may be visiting the park getting stuck on the same campground along with them that does not include any park personnel that might be present. Watermelon road has small non producing farms and a golf course community development along it but depending on where on that road the park got itself severed from the mainland makes a big difference in resources and people milling around. I bet that the Preppers campground itself got cut off and blocked somewhere around the middle of the reservations access road between that Dam and its locks a mile or two from that spillway and pump station just up the road from the generation plant. There is another Dam around that area I know of that might have also impacted them. I don't know much about that Dam; I just heard Crick mention a time or two that it was also an access artery into the road system surviving another park. That bit of road and campground they might be stuck on doesn't leave them with very much of an operating area and its landscape is mostly pretty hilly scruffy pine woodland until you get to the park from either road." David said trying to mentally picture how exactly big this so called island might be where his friends and fellow preppers were stranded.

"That area of the road sounds about right David. We drove over that shallow but impassable spillway last time and if any part of that road you are talking about got messed up some kind of way I wouldn't know how to get back in or out there from the side they are from town. Maybe I better get us a map out of my car and see exactly what's on the backside of that place instead of the front way we are used to coming in." Julie said rising to go get it.

"I think it's all National Forest or sort of swampy river bottom land with creeks leading to the reservoir. Deer Park sits on a bluff and on the map it looked like it just sort of jutted out by itself between two rives and the dams which made up what was called a lake." David said following her outside to try to figure out more

David remembered the panoramic camps lake view but actually the lot Julie and he had camped on last Prepper Stock looked more like the campgrounds were composed of a series of steep hills above a river."

.

"Yea, you can see that there is no other way into Deer Park except these two roads coming in David and that point right there is that other Dam you were talking about earlier." Julie said pointing down at the map and tracing a road that ran directly over a dam.

"Thanks for thinking about this map Julie. It helps me to clear a few things up in my mind. I wonder if they got water damage or flooding up in that area as well as road damage. It's pretty hard to blow any kind of giant gaping hole in an actual modern dam but somebody with the where with all could have done plenty of superficial damage or caused the dam to open its spillway gates for some major localized flooding. Without talking to Crick who knows what conditions are in? As far as we know, expect flooding and them poor folks are stuck on their own brand new manmade island." David replied

"Not really what you might want want to own in the terms of waterfront real estate right now." Julie said dryly.

"You got that right, hell Prepper Stock was only supposed to last for three days so if you just packed for it and brought your 72 hour kit you would only have food for about 6 or 7 days. When did Crick say that the Dam or whatever else got blown up Julie? I don't remember hearing anything at all about it in the news do you?" David asked pondering just how dire circumstances were for the cutoff and for all practical purposes it appeared, pretty much abandoned preppers and campers.

"I didn't hear anything about Deer Park or anything about the Dam either. Something could have happened to them before or after we heard about the major cyber attack. We were pretty much off grid and out of communication with the outside for a day or two until we decided to eventually cut the radio on when the power first went out. We thought that the power not working was because a thunderstorm had taken down a transformer feeding the house or something and were just sitting around partying or arranging preps waiting for things to dry out and the power to come back on remember David. How dismissive and naïve of us to just not care that the power went out for awhile and just figured it was a normal occurrence after a thunderstorm. Worlds going to hell and it took us days to figure out we were part of it." Julie said as David sheepishly acknowledged the fact.

"Ignorance is bliss?" David offered remembering he had just played music CDs once in awhile on his laptop and chattered about all sorts of things with Julie as they spent the first few powerless days.

"Not in this case. Ignorance is awful! Why is it that that you think Crick wants you to go to his house David? Better yet, have you got any notion of actually going there?" Julie demanded stressing on too many things at once.

"That is what we are figuring out Darling. I think I might have an inkling of the answer. You know last Prepper Stock I had a conversation with a lot of people around there about what resources I thought it might take to feed that many people for a short period and what everyone might need in the way of resources if a community actually could survive there. I bet Crick wants my fish nets and a Trotline or two. Not the easiest items to find in a disaster if you wanted some. Without a net of some kind those survivors' chances get greatly reduced. Probably a few more things he might want me to bring I haven't thought about yet would be good. Damn it I wish the phones would start working." David said and checked the phone for the umpteenth time to no avail.

"That sounds logical. I wonder if they plan on living on that island short or long term. There were lots of folks from Alabama represented there at last Prepper Stock that might be able to bug home if they got off the island, do you think he wanted you to play shuttle service for some of them?" Julie asked examining the problem further.

"Time will tell darling, Time will tell. Let's go get a drink and hash out the pros and cons of leaving here on a few days trip." David said thinking he liked a chaser with his bad news.

"Sounds like a fine idea to me, I think I can use more than one also about now. David we had better be listening closely to the radio and finding out how the travel restrictions are going to affect us should you start thinking about going anywhere." Julie reminded him while getting real apprehensive about the fact that David had not brought up anything yet about the possibility of them not going on a mission to Crick's place. What about all their stuff? What about the gas it was going to take? These questions and a million others flooded her mind.

"I agree, I already got an idea that might work for us to get around that travel restriction thing. I am going to see if Clancy will lend me that old tractor of his with my Van for collateral to take up there and back. I admit a van with barely any fuel in it isn't much collateral but I will sweeten the deal someway. You see if I am driving a tractor pulling a trailer say with a tarped down hay bail or two on it, well then if any official inquires I can always say I was just going down the road to some farm somewhere and not look like I was fleeing a disaster." David said looking very smug.

The End

Book one of a prepper is cast adrift.

A S.O.S. IS RECIEVED

INDEX

I Living Off The Land: Delusions and Misconceptions About
Hunting and Gathering

Ah, living off the land. Thriving in the wilderness with the use
of your skills. It is the ultimate goal of many bushcrafters and
survivalists. Numerous posts have been written on forums about
this subject, and as soon as one ends, another is started. Of
course, actual evidence is rarely presented. We often fall back on
positions such as "our ancestors did it, so clearly I can do it", or
"I was out last week and saw a bunch of cattails and barriers, so
my food sources are secure".

The problem is not made any better by so called experts in the
field, who fuel the myth that they are feeding themselves in the
wilderness. I vividly remember watching Andrew Price, host of
A-Z of Bushcraft in one of the episodes, waking up in the
morning, walking a few feet next to camp, gathering a few
berries, and then turning the camera and saying "breakfast is
served". Ray Mears, aside from his excellent series, Wild Foods,
has numerous instances where he gathers meager resources and
then implies that his food requirements have been met. Of
course, none of them ever bother to calculate or present actual
caloric values, or discuss the long terms consequences.
Similarly, people like Dave Canterbury, who discusses at length

hunting in wilderness living conditions, never actually do the math of how much game has to be killed to justify the weight of that shotgun being carried, or whether the numbers would work out at all.

For the past year I have been attempting to gather some actual numbers on the subject, so we can have a more meaningful conversation about what it would take to sustainably feed a person in the wilderness, and consequently, what tools may be suited for the task. I must admit, I have been slacking with the project because of its tedious nature. Last week however, a reader referred me to a source related to the Chris McCandless post, which provided me with some of the information I was searching.

Samuel Thayer, author of the books Forager's Harvest and Nature's Garden, wrote an essay related to the starvation of Chris McCandles titles Into the Wild and other Poisonous Plant Fables. While much of the essay focuses on disproving theories of poisonous plants, the last section discusses actual caloric requirements for a person living in the wilderness, and what resources that would require.

So, let's assume a scenario where a person will be going into the wilderness with the intention of living off the land. He will practice wilderness self reliance, he will thrive in nature, and whatever other cliché you want to insert here. Let's also assume for the moment that there are no hunting or fishing regulations that we have to comply with, and let's assume that the person has all necessary equipment, including hunting and fishing tools. What would the person need to procure each day in order to live in a sustainable manner for a prolonged period of time?

Well, the first piece of the puzzle is the required calories. Citing *Michele Grodner's Foundations and Clinical Applications of Nutrition*, Thayer calculates that a male who is physically active under wilderness living conditions would need approximately

3,300 calories per day. This number seems consistent with calculations done by long distance backpackers, who usually aim for a bit over 3,000 calories per day. So, to maintain one's physical condition, and prevent weight loss, the person in question must consume about 3,300 calories each day. Of course, there are other nutritional requirements, but at a very basic level, to prevent death from starvation in the long run, this caloric minimum must be met.

The above caloric requirement for wilderness living should not be confused with accounts of short term survival, where a person stays in the wilderness, slowly losing body weight, until they are rescued. We have plenty examples like this from series like Survivorman, Naked and Afraid, etc. Those are not examples of sustainable hunting and gathering situations, and we should not have any delusions about the long term applications of such a starvation diet.

So, sticking with the 3,300 caloric requirement per day, what would it take to meet these caloric needs?

Sources of Calories

Meat

First let's look at animal products, something to which I will jointly refer to in this post as "meat", but should be understood to include both protein and fats. Meat can vary in caloric content anywhere from 40 calories per ounce for lean meat like squirrel and rabbit, all the way to 60 calories per ounce for very fatty meat like salmon. Using these numbers, we can roughly calculate the caloric value of each animal, and how much of it we would need to meet our daily caloric requirements.

Red Squirrel: as Thayer calculates, at an average of 2.8 ounces of meat per squirrel (*Michele Grodner's Foundations and Clinical Applications of Nutrition*), it would take 25 squirrels per day to meet the caloric requirements, or if also eating the internal organs and brain, about 16 squirrels per day.

Rabbit: at about 16 ounces of meat per rabbit (*Michele Grodner's Foundations and Clinical Applications of Nutrition*), you would need about 4 of them per day, or 3 if eating all of the organs and brain.

Salmon: assuming you are catching Sockeye salmon, they average 6 pounds (96 ounces) (*Kenai Peninsula Borough Commercial Fishing Industry State Records, 2012*). Since salmon meat is rich in fat, we can assume 60 calories per ounce (*USDA SR-21*), which would mean one salmon would give you 5,760 calories, or a little under two days of food.

Clams: clam meat varies in caloric density from about 33 calories per ounce to about 42 calories per ounce. (*Interstate Shellfish Sanitation Conference, 2013*). To satisfy the required 3,300 calories per day intake, you would need about 5 pounds of clam meat per day (using 40 calories per ounce for the calculation). In order to get 5 pounds of clam meat, you would need about 320 medium size clams. For each ounce of meat, you need about 4 medium size clams. (*Interstate Shellfish Sanitation Conference, 2013*)

Raccoon: while many people would not eat raccoon meat due to its high content of parasites, it is technically edible. The meat is fatty, averaging about 72 calories per ounce. (*USDA SR-21*) The weight of raccoons varies widely from 10 to 25 pounds for adults. The average listed size is about 25 pounds for an adult. That should provide approximately 10 pounds of meat once it is gutted, skinned and deboned. At 72 calories per ounce, such a raccoon will provide about 11,520 calories. However, keep in mind that these numbers reflect the calories if the animal is cooked to preserve all of its nutrients. In order to make it more palatable, people usually cook raccoon meat to remove most of the fat. If you do that, the caloric content will drop significantly. Assuming you save all of the fat however, a 25 pound raccoon should provide sufficient calories for 3.5 days.

Turkey: a good size turkey will yield about 10 pounds of meat (160 ounces) when processed. The caloric value of processed turkey meat is about 45 calories per ounce (*USDA SR-21*). Therefore, a turkey will produce 7,200 calories in total, or a bit more than 2 days worth of caloric requirements.

Deer: a mature buck typically yields about 70 pounds of meat (1,120 ounces) (*University of Wisconsin study 2006*). Venison is a lean meat, with about 53 calories per ounce (*USDA SR-21*). The meat of a mature buck will therefore give you 59,360 calories, which will be sufficient for 18 days of food at the 3,300 calories per day requirement. If you are eating the internal organs as well, that will probably get pushed to about 20-21 days of food.

Black Bear: a large black bear will produce about 100 pounds of meat (1,600 ounces) once processed. Bear meat has about 43 calories per ounce. (*USDA SR-21*) So, a large black bear will give about 68,800 calories total. That would be sufficient calories to satisfy the caloric intake for 21 days.

| Type of Animal | oz of Meat/Animal | Meat | | Animals/Day |
		cal/oz of Meat	Total cal/Animal	
Squirrel	2.8	47	132	25 (16)
Rabbit	16.8	47	790	4 (3)
Salmon	96	60	5,760	0.57
Clams	0.25	40	10	320
Raccoon	160	72	11,520	0.29
Turkey	160	45	7,200	0.46
Deer	1,120	53	59,360	0.056 (0.05)
Black Bear	1,600	43	68,800	0.047

The table below gives a general summary of the results. The numbers you see in the last column for animals needed each day to meet the caloric requirement, the number in parenthesis represents what is needed if internal organs are preserved and eaten as well as the meat.

Plants

Now, let's move to plant sources.

Cattail Roots: cattail roots, will yield about 8 calories per ounce (USDA SR-21; *Revedin, A., et al. Thirty thousand-Year-Old Evidence of Plant Food Processing, 2010*). This means that about 413 ounces or 26.5 pounds of cattail flour would be needed to meet that daily caloric requirements.

It should be noted (as pointed out by a reader in one of the comments) that Table 2 of the above study, *Thirty thousand-Year-Old Evidence of Plant Food Processing, 2010* provides that cattail (Typha) rhyzome flour contains 266 kcal/100g, or 75 calories per ounce. That is much higher than the 8 cal/oz provided by the USDA and other sources. It appears the difference occurs because that table speaks of the caloric value of already processed and cooked flour. The article specifies that *"The flour would have undergone a multistep processing involving root peeling, drying, and finally grinding using specific tools. After this, the flour needed to be cooked to obtain a suitable and digestible food."* Cattail rhyzome contains large portions that are inedible, such as the spongy layer covering the rhyzome as well as the fibers from which you have to remove the starch. As such, the numbers don't appear to be contradictory. You may very well have a caloric value of 25 kcal/100g (8 cal/oz) for cattail root and 266 kcal/100g (75 cal/oz) for processed cattail root flour where the outer casing has been peeled, the fibers have been removed, and the resulting starch cooked. In the table here I have used the number for unprocessed cattail root, and the quantity you would need to get the necessary calories.

Parsnips and Similar Wild Roots: according to Thayer, at approximately 23 calories per ounce (*Michele Grodner's Foundations and Clinical Applications of Nutrition*), about 9 pounds would be needed per day to meet the daily caloric requirement of 3,300 calories.

Blueberries: again, according to Thayer, at about 16 calories per ounce (*Michele Grodner's Foundations and Clinical*

Applications of Nutrition), you would need 13 pounds of blueberries per day to meet your caloric requirements.

Lingonberries: at about 5 calories per ounce (*USDA SR-21*), you would need about 41 pounds of lingonberries to meet your daily caloric requirement.

Acorns: once processed into a flour, after leaching out the tannic acid acorns will provide about 110 calories per ounce (*USDA SR-21*). That would mean that 30 ounces, or a little under 2 pounds of acorn flour would be needed per day to satisfy the caloric requirements.

Burdock Root: at about 20 calories per ounce (*USDA SR-21*), you would need about 165 ounces, or 10 pounds of unprocessed burdock root to meet your daily caloric requirements. If cooked, a large amount of the water removed, the pounds one needs to consume may be significantly reduced, but would still constitute more than what a person can eat in a day.

	Plants	
Type of Plant	cal/oz of Plant Material	Pounds Per Day Needed
Cattail Root (Unprocessed)	8	26.5
Parsnips	23	9
Blueberries	16	13
Lingonberries	5	41
Acorns (processed)	110	2
Burdock Root	20	10*

The above represent average numbers, both for the calories required per day, and the amount of food which must be consumed to provide those calories. Variations should be expected. Even so, it is evident that a person attempting to live alone off the land in the wilderness has a serious challenge on his hands. The amount of food required seems absurd, but as Thayer explains: *"If this seems like a high volume of food, that's because it is. We have sought, developed, cultivated, and become accustomed to calorie-dense foods for so long that most of us have never been without them. We've never had to eat food in volumes like this. When you realize that a stick of butter has as many calories as two and a half quarts of blueberries or seven pounds of broccoli, you can see why the innate human desire for calorie-rich, low-fiber food developed."*

Gathering

The gathering of food has become a great area of teaching for survival and bushcraft instructors. Unfortunately, much of the teachings create a false impression of what it actually takes to feed oneself through gathering of food in the wilderness. As Thayer also noted, many such instructors teach, or imply through their representations that a very small amount of food is needed for a person to sustainably live in the wilderness. Whether the misrepresentations are intentional, or due to lack of knowledge is hard to say, but the results are the same-people fail to realize how much food must be gathered to sustain a person long term.

We have to make a clear distinction between "edible" plants and "food". Just because something can be eaten, does not mean that it contributes to your caloric requirements in any meaningful way. Many staples of bushcraft teachings, such as dandelions provide virtually no caloric value. You can easily starve to death with a stomach full of such plants. In fact, it is not unlikely that a person may spend more energy gathering edible plants, than the calories he will get from consuming them. To effectively gather food in the wilderness, one has to know not only what is edible, but also what provides meaningful calories.

From the plants available and listed in the above chart, not surprisingly acorns provide the highest nutrition. I imagine it will be similar for other nuts because of the high oil content. If processed correctly, a person can certainly provide enough food for himself using acorn flour. The other plants that are readily available, including the all too popular cattail and burdock roots, are far less than ideal when it comes to providing sufficient calories for a person attempting long term living. Not only would it be difficult to supply yourself with enough of the plant, but consuming such large quantities would be impossible. We should also keep in mind that the plants I have listed here are the ones with relatively high caloric value.

On that subject, Thayer writes with respect to Chris McCandless, *"If he didn't get any meat, couldn't he just eat more lingonberries and get all his calories that way? Absolutely not. He would have needed to eat almost three gallons of lingonberries per day. He'd probably be vomiting before finishing the second quart. No matter how many lingonberries were available to him, his body would have only accepted them for a small portion of his caloric requirement. This doesn't make lingonberries "poisonous"; the same is true of virtually every food, although the appropriate proportions vary... The concept that foods can be eaten only in appropriate quantities is taken so much for granted that, to my knowledge, it has never been given a name in the medical literature. I call it themaximum caloric proportion (MCP). Some foods have a very high MCP, such as milk, meat, and potatoes. They are easily digested and contain few antinutrients or toxins, thus they are suitable as dietary staples. Others, such as cabbage, rhubarb, and raspberries, cannot serve as staple foods and are only suitable to supply small portions of the diet. As one travels north, there tends to be fewer plants with a high MCP; this is why hunter-gatherers from northern latitudes ate meat for the great majority of their calories.*"

As a result, if you can not find the right plants and gather it on a large enough scale, or have simply missed the gathering season, one typically has to resort to meat for the majority of the required calories. So, let's look at some of what is required in terms of providing sufficient calories through hunting and fishing.

Opportunity Cost of Hunting and Fishing

Before we look at specific examples, it is important to note that when we speak of hunting and fishing, activities which require that you bring specific equipment into the woods, we have to look not only at what you can successfully hunt, but also at the opportunity cost of that equipment. What I mean by that is that for each pound of equipment which you bring with you, you have to forego a pound of some other resource which you could have brought with you instead. Since we are assuming a person who is otherwise prepared for the wilderness, the most immediate opportunity cost is food. For each pound of gear that you bring, you have to leave behind a pound of food. So, when you bring a 7 pound rifle with you, you could have instead left it behind and brought 7 pounds of food. So, when we look at the equipment one may bring for such hunting, we have to see not only if it can get us any food, but also whether the food we can procure with it is more than the food that we could have brought with us had we not brought the equipment.

To complicate things further, we have to look not only at the weight of the food, but more importantly at the caloric content of that food. So, a pound of squirrel meat will give us 752 calories. On the other hand a pound of instant mashed potatoes will give us 1,664 calories. For this post, I will use mashed potatoes as a base line for calorie dense food that could have been brought into the woods.

Fishing

First, let's look at fishing. Fishing is a good way to procure calories because the equipment required is not heavy, and is relatively reusable. A large net, fishing rod, reel, lures, and a sizable spool of line will only add up to a few pounds. You guys have seen my lightweight fishing kit, which came in under one pound. A more robust and complete kit can be estimated to around 3 pounds. 3 pounds of gear has the opportunity cost (using the above base line numbers) of 4,983 calories, or about day and a half of food at the required 3,300 calories per day. From a simple numbers standpoint, this means that the first day and a half worth of food that you catch will go to offset the weight of the gear (which you brought rather than bringing food). Everything you catch after that is surplus.

The downside of fishing of course is the limited availability of resource reach areas. For example if you are lucky, and are in an area and the right time for a salmon run, as we saw from the above numbers, a single sockeye salmon will give you about two days worth of food. That means that the first salmon would offset the opportunity cost of the fishing gear, and every subsequent one will be pure food value. If you can catch one every two days, you will be able to meet your caloric requirements. The problem of course is that you may be a week late, and not find a single salmon because the run has ended; or, you may be in an area where no such fish is available; or you may be in an area where there is no body of water which carries any sizable fish at all.

Remember, it takes about 3.5 pounds of salmon per day to meet a person's caloric requirements. If instead of a 7 pounds salmon, you were pulling out 3 ounce sunfish out of the water, the calculations would be very different. At approximately 50 calories per ounce of fish meat, you can do your own math to see how much fish you would need. I remember an episode of Ray Mears Extreme Survival where he caught a small fish while he was in the Rockies, and prepared it with some plants. It may seem like he has prepared a good dinner, but the reality is that the meal probably contains less that 300 calories, about a tenth of what is needed for the day if we are facing a long terms sustainability situation.

Even with all those considerations however, if you have selected an area close to a sizable body of water for your long term wilderness living situation, fishing is a good way to procure food because of the low weight and reusable nature of the gear, as well as the low amount of energy expenditure required.

Hunting

Now, let's look at hunting as means of procuring food. Obviously, a hunter needs his tools. There are a lot of misconception from people who do not hunt that you can use primitive weapons, constructed in the woods, to effectively hunt. The difficulty of such a task is nearly always underestimated. Thinking that a person can construct a stick bow, or carve a longbow in the woods from an unseasoned piece of wood, and then go hunting with it in an effective manner is wishful thinking. Keep in mind that a hunter with a modern state of the art bow, with modern optics and range finder, will rarely take a shot at over 50 yards. If you are hunting with an improvised bow, lower that range to about 25 yards. Now, go measure out 25 yards and try to think of what it would actually take for you to get to within 25 yards of a deer. Then, think of what accuracy would be needed to hit a squirrel at 10 yards with that same bow.

You will quickly gain a healthy appreciation for modern weapons.

Most people who are contemplating long term wilderness living will use some type of firearm, much like Chris McCandless did during his attempt. In recent years, Dave Canterbury, former co-host of Dual Survival, has popularized the single show 12 gauge shotgun as a weapon for long term wilderness living. In this post I will not address any issues regarding whether I believe that to be the best choice, but I will simply use it as a base line for purposes of discussion. A single shot 12 gauge shotgun weighs approximately 6 pounds (*H&R Topper Deluxe with synthetic stock*). Using the number we previously calculated for calories per pound of food which we could have brought into the woods (1,664 cal/lb), we can calculate that a 6 pound shotgun has the opportunity cost in terms of food of 9,984 calories, or about 3 days worth of caloric intake. That would mean that the first three days worth of food which you kill will go to offset the weight of the gun (keeping ammunition weight aside for now). So, if your trip is less that three days, even best case scenario (you being able to successfully kill enough game each day to meet the 3,300 calories per day requirement), you would be better off simply bringing your food with you. That way the availability of food is guaranteed.

For trips longer than three days, the gun would theoretically be the better bet, assuming you can secure enough food with it. So, let's look at what that would entail. Let's assume that you are now hunting small game with lightweight shotgun shells (2 3/4 shells with 1 oz load). Each such shell weighs 1.4 oz. So, for each shell fired, we have to add that weight to the opportunity cost, meaning, for each box of shells, we could have simply brought food with us. We than have to see if the numbers work out.

As I was saying, let's assume you are hunting small game. As we established earlier, it would take 25 squirrels to provide enough meat for a day's worth of calories (3,300 cal). Killing 25 squirrels with the above ammunition would require 35 ounces of shotgun shells. Using our caloric value for instant mashed potatoes from above at 104 calories per ounce, the same 35 ounces if brought in the form of mashed potatoes instead of shotgun shells would give us 3,640 calories, more than what you would get from the squirrel meat. That means that if you are hunting squirrel with shotgun shells, you will never procure enough meat to offset the weight of the gear that you have to bring. You will be better off bringing food with you rather than the equivalent weight of ammunition. That is not to mention the weight of the shotgun itself, for which you could have brought an additional 3 days worth of food.

The numbers of course look much better when we consider larger game. If we are hunting rabbit, 4 of them would give us the caloric requirement for a day. That would mean we would have the expand 4 shotgun shells, at a total weight of 5.6 ounces. The equivalent weight of mashed potatoes will only give us 582 calories. In that instance, again, assuming perfect accuracy and availability of sufficient targets, the shotgun will be the better bet. The numbers of course look even better when hunting large game like deer.

A possible way to address the problem with small game hunting is to use different ammunition. While a shotgun shell weighs 1.4 oz, a .22LR cartridge weighs 0.1 oz. 25 squirrels will require only 2.5 ounces worth of .22LR cartridges, making it a viable option. The solution proposed by Dave Canterbury is to carry an adaptor, which inserts in the shotgun, allowing you to fire .22LR bullets. While the approach is viable in theory, if that is the route you chose to take, keep in mind that this is quite possible the least accurate way to fire a .22LR bullet. A non properly bedded, 10 inch rifled insert will give only marginal accuracy, made even more difficult by aiming only with the aid of a bead sight. You should adjust your ammunition count accordingly. After all, the goal here is to kill game, not to just fire ammunition.

219

Lastly, all of the numbers provided in this post assume 100% accuracy and unlimited availability of any particular resource. Obviously that is not the result in reality, but here I am assuming best case scenario. Success rates for hunting, or hunting strategies are beyond the scope of this post. The only thing I will say on the subject is to be careful when extrapolating success rates for a wilderness living situation based on anyone's success rate when hunting closer to home. A lot of hunting these days is done on people's personal property and close to civilization. That has a huge impact on game centralization. Food plots, open terrain of farms, fields, and roads are a great attractant to animals, which in turn become familiarized with people. Hunting in such an area is very different from going deep into the woods and attempting the same thing. One way is not necessarily better than the other, but there is a danger in trying to extrapolate your possible success rate when hunting in a wilderness living situation based on success rates in the woods behind the house.

Trapping

I have added a trapping section to the post since I first published due to several comments requesting information on the subject. The reason why I didn't originally include a section on trapping is that an animal caught through trapping has the exact same caloric value as an animal caught through hunting. The ease of hunting, trapping, or gathering is beyond the scope of this post. For all of the numbers I have presented here, I have assumed 100% success rate and infinite availability of the particular resource.

I will discuss a few of the legal issue involved with trapping, but I will mention a few things here.

First, it is very hard to get data on trapping in the wilderness. The reason is that most trap lines are run close to home for reasons I will explain in the section on legal considerations. As a result, it is hard to find data from an actual wilderness trap line, so some of the aspects of trapping during long term wilderness living are hard to address.

Also, just like with hunting, be careful when extrapolating success rates for wilderness trapping conditions based on trap lines run close to home. Around where I live, there are large numbers of raccoons. I saw five of them walking through the parking lot two weeks ago. It is a different story when you are actually in the forests.

As I will explain below, trapping, just like hunting, requires gear. You will have to bring your traps with you. What traps you use and their size will vary greatly depending on what animal you are trapping and where you are doing it. Factor that weight into your calculations and determine the opportunity cost to see if the numbers work out under the specific conditions.

Legal Considerations

Lastly, we have to get back to that issue which we put to the side earlier, the law. Assuming we do not wish to be poachers, and are actually contemplating living in the wilderness within the real world rather than some imaginary scenario, we have to comply with regulations. Hunting seasons will vary trough different areas, but for most species, especially large species, it will be quite limited. For example, in the State of New York (southern region), deer and bear seasons are from Nov 16 – Dec 8; turkey season is from Oct 1 – Nov 15 in the fall and May 1 – May 31 in the spring; cottontail rabbit is from Oct 1 – Feb 28; gray and fox squirrel is from Sept 1 – Feb 28; grouse is from Oct 1 – Feb 28, etc. There are a few species that can be hunted year round, such as red squirrel, porcupine, rock pigeon, and woodchuck. As you can see however, the limitations are severe.

Above we calculated that a mature white tail buck will give us about 21 days worth of calories if properly processed and preserved. Let's assume that you can supplement it with other sources of food, and extend that time to a month. If you are hunting deer lawfully, that would mean that to provide sufficient calories for the full year, between the dates of Nov 16 – Dec 8, you will have to kill 12 mature deer in that 3 week period. You have to average 4 deer per week. The practical difficulty with such a task is not the only problem. Most states have restrictions on the number of deer that can be harvested. In NY it is usually 1 or 2 per year.

Now, using New York State as an example, let's see if the necessary calories for a person for a period of one year can be legally acquired through hunting. The generally available large game would be deer, bear, and turkey. In certain areas, the hunting of other large game like elk, moose, duck and geese may be legal and available. In NY we have good access to duck and goose hunting, but no elk or moose hunting. So, let's look at the generally available game. Let's assume that you have two buck tags, one bear tag and four turkey tags (two spring and two fall).

One black bear gives us 68,800 calories. Two bucks, at 59,360 each will give us 118,720 calories. Four turkeys at 7,200 calories each gives us 28,800 calories total. Combined, the bear, deer, and turkey give us **216,320** calories for the annual hunting season.

The caloric requirements for one person for one year based on the 3,300 daily requirement we used above, would give us 365 days times 3,300 calories per day, for a total of **1,204,500** required calories per year.

So, assuming you are a skillful hunter, and luck was on your side, and you managed to fill all of your tags (one black bear, two deer, and four turkey), that will still leave you at a caloric deficiency for the year of **988,180** calories. In other words, you will have no food for 299 days out of the year. If available in your area, you may be able to decrease the deficit by hunting other large game if available, like elk, moose, and duck, although, it appears that a large deficit will remain.

Just to give some perspective, assuming that a duck or goose provides the same amount of calories as a turkey, it would require 137 ducks or geese to satisfy the above caloric deficit (assuming no legal limit on the number you can harvest). Assuming you are hunting those ducks with a 3 inch shotgun shell with a 1 3/4 load, which weigh 2.2 oz each, and assuming perfect accuracy, that would require about 19 pounds of ammunition.

On the other hand, you will have to kill or trap a whole lot of squirrels to make up for the deficiency, approximately 7,486 squirrels, which if hunted with .22LR ammunition, and assuming perfect accuracy, would require about 47 pounds of ammunition.

Trapping is also an option, but you have to keep a few things in mind. First, trapping, just like hunting is regulated and only allowed during certain seasons. Second, the way you can trap is heavily regulated. Deadfalls, snares, hooks on trees, and virtually all DIY traps are not allowed. The regulations are very specific as to exactly what trap you must use for each animal. Third, trapping is generally only allowed for furbearers. In most areas you are not allowed to trap game animals. Some furbearers like beaver are edible, others not so much. Last but not least, regulations typically require that you check all of your traps every 24 or 48 hours. For most people that places serous restrictions on where traps can be placed and limits the size of the trap line. The result is that most trap lines are run close to home with the few exceptions for people who travel deep into the woods and then live there for the trapping season.

The alternative is that you need to systematically exploit another abundant resource such as large scale gathering and processing of acorns when in season, or moving to take advantage of large scale fish migrations and then catching them with nets, fishing wheels, etc. where the law allows.

Do the numbers work out? You do the math. I think we get a better appreciation for why high calories foods such as pemmican and corn meal were so highly valued and commonly carried by woodsmen in the past.

I don't write this to discourage anyone from attempting the challenge, nor do I believe it to be impossible. In this post I am simply attempting to provide some more solid data that can be used to make a realistic evaluation of exactly what it would take to thrive alone in the wilderness. As Thayer writes: *"In a long-term subsistence situation, food is the priority. In former times, the native people of the Far North planned each move according to food availability… In a short-term survival situation, food is of minor importance. However, in long-term survival or "living off the land," it is of paramount importance."*

There was a time when men who ventured into the wilderness knew what resources were required, and how much of them had to be brought along. Their accounts often refer to base camps, cabins, and food stocks being carried on horse back, mule train, or by dog sled teams. Somewhere along the way we seem to have lost the realistic grasp on those requirements, and were left with nothing more than romantic musings and conjecture.

The end book one.

A CYBER-ATTACK HAS DE-
STROYED 80% OF AMERICA'S
ELECTRICAL GRID LEAVING HUN-
DREDS OF MILLIONS OF PEOPLE
IN THE DARK WITH NO INFRA-
STRUCTURE AND NO RUNNING
WATER. MARTIAL LAW HAS BEEN
DECLARED AND IT HAS BEEN RU-
MORED THAT RUSSIAN TROOPS
ARE ASSISTING WITH SECURITY AND CONTINUITY
OF GOVERNMENT OPERATIONS. TERRORISTS HAVE
BLOWN THE HYDROELECTRIC DAMS SURROUND-
ING A PREPPER FESTIVAL STRANDING THE CAMP-
ERS ON AN ISLAND WITH NO CHANCE OF ESCAPE
OTHER THAN USING THEIR OWN WITS AND IN-
GENUITY. FOOD IS ALMOST NONE EXISTENT FOR
THESE CAST AWAY SURVIVORS IN BOOK TWO OF
THE 'A PREPPER IS CAST ADRIFT' SERIES AND DES-
PERATE TIMES CALL FOR DESPERATE MEASURES.

ENJOY A PREPPER FICTION POST APOCALYP-
TIC TALE OF INTRIGUE AND SUSPENSE SPRINKLED
WITH SOUTHERN COUNTRY HUMOR AND ZANY
CHARACTERS SURVIVING A MEGA DISASTER.

Barcode Area

We will add the barcode for you.

Made with Cover Creator

"CRICK"

A PREPPER IS CAST
ADRIFT SERIES

RON FOSTER

Acknowledgements

Eric Smith
Cory and Wendy Evans
LowBuck Prepper

ALL THE FOLKS WHO ATTENDED PREPPER STOCK 2014
1

THE RUSSIANS ARE COMING! THE RUSSIANS ARE COMING!

David and Julie sat their tired, sweaty and somewhat more than a little bit grimy bodies down upon the old wooden picnic table's top and swung their dirt dusted boots over to rest solidly on the worn cracked boards that formed the seats of the table. The couple was knocking off work for the day. They had finished finally putting up all the gardening tools they had used in their labors and they were looking forward to enjoying the taste of an evening cocktail together and just sitting and chatting in the shade.

They sat comfortably and casually on top of the table in front of "Prepper Shack" as David called his home and discussed the day's problems and accomplishments just like they had done hundreds of times before. To most casual onlookers the only difference in the couples appearance and demeanors today, versus that of any other day, was that they both now carried a loaded shotgun and each sported a holstered pistol on their hips. As they talked, the pair looked around the woods casually surveying and checking the property over for movement or signs more than they tended to look at each other, but they didn't seem to be alarmed or edgy about anything in the least.

You could say that they might be talking bit lower in tone to each other than normal and you might also say that they appeared to listen to the woods a bit more closely than they were apt to before the power went down from a cyber-attack weeks ago, but other than that, they were unchanged by the disaster, remaining calm and joking with each other as was their normal familiar nature. The pair just sat there partaking of a well-earned adult beverage as they enjoyed their casual existences daily ritual of listening to the birds and Cicadas sing while waiting for the fireflies to put on a light show in the woods for them in a few hours when the sun went down.

A newer white pickup truck had been observed and watched closely by the couple previously traveling pretty fast down the dead end road they resided upon heading in Michael's house direction. This evenings table top conversation centered on as to whom it might be and not if they were any threat to them or not.

David had speculated that he thought it might have been Michael's cousin who had purchased the small acreage across from him as his retirement property for when he got out of the Army, but he and the cousin had never met, although a white truck coming and going from that direction had been noted by David. His hunch about who it might be soon proved to be correct because in about 25 minutes or so the white truck nosily returned and Michael and his cousin drove up his driveway and got out and approached where David and Julie were sitting.

"David, this here is my Cousin Ray. He bought the land next to you and directly across from me if you remember." Michael said as David and Julie walked halfway down the driveway in back of their parked vehicles to the pickup truck to greet the two men. They all exchanged pleasantries until Michael said let's get down to business and explained the reason for their abrupt visit.

"David you told me awhile back that if I heard anything about that missile plant's comings and goings to give you all a heads up. Well I am telling you now that you ain't ever going to believe this, well I take that back, maybe you would, you always have been kind of up on unbelievable conspiracy type things, but my cousin Ray here says that there are, now get this and listen close now, actually genuine Russian troops running security over there at that missile plant. " Michael said opening his eyes real wide to accentuate the scariness of what he just had said and let the shock value of his statement sink in.

David looked incredulous at everyone for a moment and then he cocked his head towards Ray in order to listen intently to him getting ready to tell the story about what he had somehow managed to observe or had noticed about the plant.

"I know this sounds pretty crazy, David, but please just remember and give me the benefit of the doubt of, that I have spent 23 years in the Army and I can recognize a Soviet "Ivan" when I see one. As a matter of fact the S.O.B. that stopped me at the gate was even named Ivan!" Ray said excitedly and then went on to explain that he had stopped by the plant on his way home from his last duty station in order to see if his friend who was Lab supervisor over there was on duty so he could tell him he was back in town and they could visit for a bit. Ray was supposed to be starting work at the missile plant in a month and he had been on his way bugging home from Fort Sill when the poo hit the fan causing the electricity to go out and all the gas pumps from here to hell and back to give up the ghost. He said that he had hoped that since the Gemini missile plant was probably considered by the Fed as a mission and defense critical facility that he might have lucked out somehow and still had himself a job to depend on while the rest of the world these days most likely tried to find themselves the means and fuel to get to a bread line.

Ray then commenced to tell a very anxious and exasperated story that was filled with his versions of fake Russian accents with added American curse words about how he had stopped at the factories entrance gate to gain access to the plant, just like he had done several other times before and was shocked to see that rather than the normal singular security guard standing duty, he had been approached by four soldiers dressed in foreign camouflage uniforms without insignia all babbling in broken English and asking him for his identification and the nature of his business at the plant at gun point..

"That's when one of the helmeted guards called for Ivan to come give him permission to enter!" Michael interjected with a quick apology to Ray for interrupting the story.

David gave a startled quick "Whoa" look of surprise towards Ray and Michael's direction while straightening his back and then giving Julie a knowing "oh hell we in for it now look!" side glance with a nod to Ray to continue the story and that he himself agreed that they were indeed foreign troops he had met manning that security gate.

"So this big shaved headed Russian came over and asked me to get out of the truck and accompany him back to the guard shack while the guy that had called him over was busy gibbering something that sounded like Russian I guess it was, into his hand held radio. I tell you, that commie reminded me of that big Russian giant that fought Rocky in a boxing movie once. He wasn't as big as that sucker was, but he had the same demeanor and was a pretty stout and tough looking sucker. Once we got back to the guard shack the Stalinist son of a bitch sits down and left me standing there in front of his desk like I was a prisoner being interviewed by the warden at the state pen. He says wait for a moment then he picked up one of them old land line field phones like we had in the service and cranked it to ring another line somewhere. Then it got a little spooky, friggin Ivan Ivanovich or whatever his last name was just says "Mr. Poole please wait a few moments more while Lieutenant Rawlins comes to assist you. Evidently whoever answered the phone asked for some kind of confirmation and Captain Ivan or whatever rank he was read my full name off my driver's license and who I was coming to visit as well as a curt couple word response of "possible worker" before hanging up the handset and staring at me like I was a bug on the rug until the Lt arrived with his aide. Finally a pair of U.S. uniformed and insigniaed soldiers come in and take charge of me and that damn Spetsnaz just waves us out like we were in a base commander's office." Michael said before David interjected.

"Spetsnaz? Real Spetsnaz or are you just labeling the oversized fella?' David asked quizzically raising one eyebrow wondering if indeed the guy was Russian Special Forces.

"Like I said they were not wearing any type of indications of rank or origin but that Ivan character carried himself like a Special Forces soldier that meant business, if you know what I mean. The guards were fearful enough of him, but I don't know if it was his rank or demeanor they respected or feared more. David, you are prior service and from what Michael told me of your own service you know that we military folks can recognize elite forces soldiers by the way they carry themselves in public. Anyway, this American newly minted butter bar of a Lieutenant takes me outside and apologizes to me for having undergone so much trouble while trying to enter the facility and explains that his aide will now take me to go see my friend Paul.

The aide said "We are going to ride over to his office on this little golf cart thing because for updated security reasons your vehicle must remain behind the barrier. You know how it is." the aide tells me "what with the terrorist attempts to bring down the infrastructure and all, its policy now that all critical facilities were now on enforced lockdown." This bone head then explained to me he himself can't even go off premises without a pass." Ray said pausing to spit some chewing tobacco a distance away from the picnic table they were all now residing at.

"Shit, I am dying to hear the rest of this story Ray. But I feel like what you're going to tell me next requires me to freshen up my drink. This is the kind of news that alcohol seems to make it easier to swallow. You all have one with me?" David said rising from the table and turning up his last sip.

"Damn straight!" Michael said and then Ray quickly agreed he could use one too and be much obliged if it was a strong one..

"I will go fix them for you David!" Julie said reaching for David's glass as he seemingly hesitated to leave this little confab that he was having and dreaded having to go into the house and fix them himself.

"Thanks Sweetie, I will bring you up to speed when you get back. What kind of shoulder patch did this butt faced lieutenant you described have on? Did you notice, Ray?" David said relinquishing his plastic cup and sitting himself back down.

"Yea I did, it was a shield with crossed pistols and an X centered on it. Thought maybe that unit patch was Alabama

Army National guard military police but he told me, right branch of service, however that he was from the Mississippi division of the brigade. Seems the majority of our guard troops are now stationed out of state at Camp Shelby Mississippi and for some reason the Mississippi Guard and the Georgia National Guard are all migrating over towards Florida on active duty. All state governors activated their National Guard units for this emergency within hours of being informed the U.S. was under attack but it's the Pentagon and Presidential executive orders under the auspices of FEMA and Homeland Security that are directing troop deployments these days instead of the governors. Michael told me that you have a background in Emergency Management as well as some Special Forces experience that might help you to explain these odd goings on and maybe enlighten us a bit, David." Ray said looking at him speculatively.

David made a long sigh and got a far off stare before answering and then carefully crafted his words to respond.

"It is a case of knowing a shit load about a lot of things that it might possibly indicate but not knowing really anything about what these folks are actually up too. I ain`t trying to be a smartass but I would hate to even take a guess as to what is going on outside of what I consider obvious the obvious occurring. No chance that those were a contingent of UN troops on a relief mission maybe Ray?" David questioned hopefully.

"Well, I didn't see anybody wearing any funky blue helmets or berets and there were no white armored vehicles evident." Ray said rubbing a 5 o'clock shadow of a beard which was darkening with sweat on his face.

Evidently he must have somehow found the means and a place to spruce up for a job enquiry before he got off the road,

David guessed. Most folks basically gave up on any thoughts at all of shaving regular or for that matter at all or ever again when the water got shut off a few weeks ago. David wished he had a whole lot more info to base his guesstimates of the status and risks of the current situation on, but he had already learned enough from Ray to make some pretty good educated assumptions and was torn between stating them and further inquiry.

"I am thinking that most likely the U.S. Government must be utilizing foreign troops to supplement some kind of emergency disaster continuity of government operations exercise." Ray said, looking quizzically to David for affirmation or comment before carrying on. David agreed with him and wondered exactly which continuity of government plan they were using to have them foreign soldiers arrive so quickly.

"Perhaps the social unrest and breakdown of society that was expected in the cities after such a calamity as they were experiencing was much worse than the main stream media or government run news was letting on." David suggested.

"Anyway, the LT cuts our conversation short and tells me to mount up with his PFC aide and driver and off we go to see my buddy, Paul. Well from the front gate to the plant is about a quarter of a mile distance and as I was getting into that golf cart I hear the LT and Ivan arguing and turn around to look and then see them blue green clad Russkie A-holes of a security guard force trying to get the tarp off the back of my truck. I hollered at the driver for him to stop so I could go raise some of my own hell about them performing an unauthorized search on my truck when that asshole of a driver just sped up and grabbed my leg and said I should let it go and that the LT would handle it. That didn't set well with me because I had more time in the chow hall than him and his buddy had in the Army and was trying to insist that he should pull over or I was going to be putting some knots on his noggin when I saw Ivan pointing his finger in the LT`s face back at the gate when all of the sudden the driver swerved the golf cart off the road into a designated picnic area access path. That boy told me in no uncertain terms that he had nothing but my best intentions in mind and that if I wasn't transporting a bomb to blow up the plant in that truck to shut up and listen to him for a bit. After I got my dander down and I told him to carry on and to drive to Paul's office and that we would leave up it to the lieutenant to deal with comrade Ivan. Then this fella explained to me that the rules as I knew them had all changed and that he barely knew what it was all about or meant himself. Thing is he told me, we now had ourselves a very obscure chain of command to operate under that was contrary to anything we would ever expect to occur and the best way to deal with it was playing follow the leader with whatever situation you were told you were in and whoever they said follow. We didn't have time to talk long between ourselves as he then pulled out of the company rest area pretty quick with an odd look over his shoulder to see if anyone had noticed our momentary detour and in a bit I finally got escorted into Paul's office. I am telling you here and right now that you could of cut the tension out of the air with a dull butter knife as we walked into that building. They had door guards posted like you have in Army basic or A.I.T. (Advanced Individual Training) that let us in the doors and log booked our names and time of entry and when we got in Paul's office, my buddy put his finger to his lips and indicated the walls had ears and that we were being listened to. Ray said at this time he felt like he was in the twilight zone and just went with the flow.

"Ray, nice to see you, sorry it's not under better circumstances we are meeting. I am afraid I must inform you now that the position that was offered to you is on hold temporarily as we try to surmount the difficulty's we are having after the attack on the counties infrastructure." Paul said, shuffling papers aimlessly and then looking out the window in dismay or with some kind of weird anticipation a watcher was around observing them.

"No problem, I just wanted to stop by and see if I was gainfully employed not. You sent me an employment contract which we both signed about a month ago, if you remember." Ray said hopefully but very distant in his anticipations of working here any time soon.

"I know! Let me assure you that US missiles will honor that contract to the letter as far as I know but the current situation may cause some delays on your start date." Paul said, pointing a finger at the door like Ray should consider leaving post haste and coming back another day.

"I am not understanding what you are saying at all Paul, my papers say my job starts on April 1, now I know stuff happens and that the situation we find ourselves in indicates that delays are to be expected from both sides of the agreement, however I need this work and you need to speak plainly." Ray said gruffly already tired of this dilly dallying BS that threatened him and his family's existence.

He had spent enough time in the military and worn enough pairs of boots on the ground in foreign countries to smell a political rat a mile away but with this crap going on in his own backwoods of Alabama after doing so much time in service and retiring honorably was way too much to bear. Whenever someone said to him „do not worry, we have got ourselves a system here, just wait patiently we are going to take care of everything reminded him of the VA hospital fiasco and made him want to throw up.

"Thing is Ray, I got to answer in my position to a lot of folks and to be honest I didn't even think you would be here blessing my doorstep today or even coming around this place for a bit, we do have a shortage of workers because of the enhanced pre-employment background investigations by homeland security but your position that was contracted for falls in to a constricted and restricted market." Paul said rather hesitantly as he was unnerved about what to do or say next.

"I am just not following you man, what's up with the weird guards and this screw you attitude they got?" Ray said angrily.

"Calm down my friend. We have known each other for a long time; I will find something for you. Don't forget I helped you get this job, only thing that has changed between us is that we are now no longer a cost conscience capitalist business making missile components but instead now are something of a hybrid enterprise which I will call an evolving part of a bureaucracy that is being created by federal and state war power acts that confuses the hell out of everyone." Paul said trying to control the rising anger that was evident in his lifelong friend.

"Screw that! Do I have a job or not, Paul?" An evidently frustrated and put out Ray responded.

"In a just a singular word or answer I will tell you No, not at this time. Hear me out now before you start you're bitching and getting all huffy and leaving before I can explain.

This nonunion shop was up for a labor union at one time and the workers voted it out, now none of that matters anymore because we find ourselves stuck in the here and now. This facility is under the direct command of, for lack of a better word, Presidential decree as afforded by the Executive Emergency Powers acts that you don't need to be reminded of. No one really knows who is in charge of what, or for that matter anything else these days because the so called interim established State and Federal governments have already pretty much figured out how to be contrary to or good at confounding or countermanding any order given by corporate or State government to run their own business. It is a pissing contest as to who is control of what and who follows and who leads who down this garden path of destruction, let us just say that when foreign troops suddenly appeared to "assist us" the cat was let out of the bag and I find myself in a "do or die situation" that I am feeling my way through as a continuity of government response situation which we are going to get stuck living with and under for longer than I care to think about. All of the sudden I have blank orders to surrender my command or my control over things and a whole bunch of party line reinforcement type meetings I need to attend where some big wig calls the hour and the day and I am told to follow this or that's agencies program or be replaced." Paul said looking miffed but still scared of those in authority and trying to play the game like the good little follower he always was.

"So maybe the new world order doesn't like us old soldiers anymore you are trying to say? They just soon not have us around making any waves and are abolishing the hire the Vet first employment rules." Ray said, considering his dangers as well as chances of being gainfully employed.

"Well I am not saying that at all. "Paul said hurrying to check the window again like someone now must surely have had their ear to it and was eavesdropping.

"It only means Ray that the rules are, shall we say, right now a bit more plastic or liquid and flexible regarding key contractor businesses." Paul said unconsciously wringing his hands at the notion.

"Ok then, Paul, I am reporting for work at your invite and your civilian company's contract, you say there is no work because of the calamity and for me to wait for further approval by some state or federal board. Is that right, buddy?" Ray said flipping a bird at the aide who seemed to be forever trying to remind him with hand gestures that they were being recorded.

"Christ on a crutch, if there was some kind of a listening device in here then most likely it was a sure thing that in these days and times of modern technology that there was also video camera to go with it in here somewhere they had not considered and this hand sign hush farce they were doing was total crap." Ray considered.

"You know we been buddies a long time, your place is here if I can get you approved for a workers pass. "Paul began before a loud snort of derision came from Ray.

"Evidently they seem to have got you by the balls boy, tell me straight now, do I have the job I contracted for or not? It is as simple as that, just say yes or no." Ray responded looking adamant about what kind of answer that he expected.

A very uncomfortable Paul minded as well as minced his words carefully and squeaked out that Ray must first sign on to the "Affiliated Workers" union roster under the emergency

238

powers act in order to be considered for a position at the plant now.

"What in the F~ing hell is an affiliated workers union? Some kind of federalized workers union, some kind of weird crap they dreamed up when they were dinking around with General Motors or putting the boots to the scope dopes in the flight towers?" Ray said watching his dreams of retirement and a better life disappear.

"It's a swearing in thing, just like you did with your oath when you joined the military." The aide said before an "I will kill you look" furrowed the brow of Paul for him to speak no further of oaths or promises.

"It means Ray in a nut shell that officially the Federal government has now set wages, worker benefits etc. and if you're ok with that you must evidence it by adopting the new Constitution and taking a pledge to abide by all executive orders during this emergency if you want to remain under consideration for the job." Paul concluded.

Paul then quickly advised Ray not to make any kind of a decision in haste and stressed that he should go home and take for himself a few days to think it over before giving any kind of response either negative or positive. Paul then nervously but visibly looked around the room to remind him that they were being monitored and to heed his advice. Paul soon after that appeared like a balloon someone had let the air out of and seemed to be relieved now much to his evident chagrin and discomfort that he finally had gotten everything out in the open and that this meeting would soon be over for better or worse. He didn't care, get Ray out of his office and resume his safe existence like a fish in a bowl doing nothing and saying nothing to upset his meal ticket.

Ray paused and put both thumbs in a rubbing motion to his eyes and advised he would indeed have to think things over before making any decisions as momentous as this and thanked them both for their time and consideration. I will come by your house in a couple days Paul and we can share a cup of coffee and share some news. This place just doesn't appear to be as comfortable as it used to be." Ray advised pointedly.

"Oh I can understand you not wanting to come visit me here Ray but I am afraid I don't get home much these days. I need be around here to help with administrative duties as well as my lab." Paul said putting on a brave front for his pal.

"You want me to check on your wife Martha?" Ray offered thinking perhaps he could maybe learn the real story about what was going on from her and away from these prying eyes and listening ears.

"Oh I am sorry, Ray, I forgot to tell you that we temporarily have moved closer to this facility. All the workers here for that matter have. You know it's a matter of requisitioning gas and food these days and you can't have critical people and workers spread out all over the county. You know the old budget mobile home sales lot right before you get to the University? FEMA took that over and is housing whatever transportation workers they need and their families over there. Me and Martha are staying on the university campus with assorted executives from other businesses as well as providing a safe place for various first responders and their families. It's like a big village actually but you need a pass to travel by or go in there. I will get my secretary to get you one while you think over whether or not you want to join the new Gemini family. Oh by the way, I forgot to tell you that even if you live closer than the university to this place, you will most likely be asked to move off your property and join us in a for lack of a better word "gated community". Paul said, letting the implications of such a move sink in that he doubted his old war buddy could stand to abide by.

"Shit must be hitting the fan pretty bad out there? Anything I need to know Paul? It wasn't too bad getting through Montgomery but I was wearing my uniform and just sort of got waved through any check points. What does the real city of Troy look like brother? I ain`t had a chance to make it that far you know." Ray said solemnly.

"It is not a place you want to get off the main drag at, let's put it that way. The main drag of this college town is pretty short as you know but it is also a main artery of the hurricane evacuation routes coming out of Florida. Normal evacuations our small police force used to be able to take in stride and get the state troopers and sheriffs and such to help out with. Right now the road from the Holiday Inn at the interstate, the entrance to alternate 185 to Florida and 231 to Dothan looks like the crossing of the old war era of East and West Germany or the DMZ in Korea. Stay away from there and be sure you got some kind of something evidencing you are a local resident." Paul advised with a raised eyebrow and called a suspicious sudden halt to any further conversation because he was very busy today and that he looked forward to talking to Ray at a later date this week.

"This can't be happening!" Reds in control of security at factories in the US? Old soldier's Kowtowing and accepting a new Constitution without fight or complaint? This shit was

241

unreal!" Ray thought as he was summarily escorted back to the golf cart and off the property.

"He has a lot on his mind Ray." The aide offered as an excuse to Ray as he got into his vehicle scowling and fired it up but not before a momentary look back at a tarp that he now knew to have been removed and placed back on haphazardly caused him more grief and anger as to what had just occurred.

"So do I, Private." Ray quipped and made haste to get the hell out of there and home as fast as he could.

2

SPIDERS AND LIARS

"So are you considering going back to the plant or might you be not even considering going back there at all, Ray?" David asked studying the old war vet who he had not had dealings with before.

"I am trying to decide, danged cousin of mine whisked me over here before I even had time to digest what has happened already. He said you might have some insights into what's going on we needed to talk about." Ray said putting the weight of the world on David's shoulders to answer.

"Ah hell, Man, you are putting me on the spot. That is one hairy ass and scary situation that I never really ever thought could happen while my blood was still flowing. There have been many rumors of Russian troops being deployed over here on U.S. military bases for years but I always thought that they were just training with FEMA for mutual aid and emergency assistance for dealing with a world threatening or impacting catastrophic disaster. I never really gave it much serious thought that they would be actually used for or trained on our soil for security or law enforcement to suppress dissention or opposition of a ruling faction. I am sure it has some mad man's philosophical or could be religious notion of what to do with continuity of government plans so they can try to quell social unrest, but using foreign troops? That is a fools bet at best. To even house and feed UN troops on US soil is treasonous to me. Take the frigging job if you are not taking a side between light and dark at the moment. New Constitution my ass and add I said in a pigs eye! Who is crazier at the moment, me and those who quote that there is no question of justification because in our hearts and minds that an immortal declaration was once made that; "We hold these truths to be *self-evident*" is more worthy of defending today than ever? The militias will be going crazy and rightly so at the moment fighting for a cause without real leadership and wasting their lives. I know it sounds cool to get yourself a job Ray in this hellish situation we find ourselves in, but please try to weigh other options if you can. I can understand maybe thinking that taking an all or none attitude ain't the right thing to do at the moment if it means starving, but let's talk this out. On the one hand you say government has grabbed control of everything they can think of from fisheries and farms to national defense and gasohol, on the other hand folks like me and you believe it's a constitutional matter and will support so called subversive ideas of taking our government back." David said still shocked at the news and trying to figure out just what all the implications of having foreign troops just up the road in his close proximity might mean.

After a second or two of pondering further, David broached the subject about road conditions under the mandated marshal law. Hell he figured he had to leave for a bit anyway he just might make it permanent if the Gestapo had just moved up the road.

"Dusk to dawn curfew is the order of the day unless you have a pass with all the right stamps and seals to go to a relocation camp and be taken in. No gas allowances or subsistence allocations unless you are on and headed down a mandated evacuation route and can find a relief truck with anything left to fill you up. A lot of relocation or evacuation busses and some military convoy traffic get what they need first. I didn't see hardly a car out on the road from here all the way to Montgomery today traveling down. I saw only a cop car or two in the city proper heading this way and they were mostly parked waiting on a call from the dispatcher I guess. Military bases are officially closed for entry or exit to anyone but active duty personnel. I tried myself every gate to get on Maxwell Air Force base or Gunter to see if the commissary was still operating but they turned me around at the gate and refused me flat out." Ray groused about the ordeal of trying to seek military assistance in his time of need.

"I told my cousin about our mutual hunting and trapping deal. David. Ray is a pretty good hunter when it comes to deer and I told him we all needed to team up to try and get through this by sharing our luck and skills." Michael advised trying to gain David's acceptance to what to him was currently a stranger in their fold..

"I need to talk to you about that further, Michael. Lots of surprises are happening today I haven't had a chance to inform you about yet. I had a phone call from a friend the other day and it seems I need to go on a mission and help some folks out of a bad situation if I can manage it." David said watching the confusion and mixed emotions from Ray and Michael from his last statement.

"How long are you going to be gone? I mean hell man; this is awful sudden isn't it? Where do you have to go to, not far

I hope? Montgomery?" Michael asked while trying to guess what David was up to and wondering if the introduction of his cousin had anything to do with this sudden revelation.

"Well no Michael, I can't say I am going directly to or through Montgomery, I got to go about 120 miles to cover going towards Tuscaloosa. I managed to receive, when the phones were working, a rather odd call from a friend of mine the other day asking me to come up there and help out with some kind of emergency he was involved in and asked for my assistance with. Give me a few minutes guys and I will bring you up to speed as to what is also rocking and rolling my little world besides what you just advised me of." David said sipping his drink and trying to decide for himself just how to approach describing the touchy situation he had recently found himself in.

"Now David if it can wait until later today or tomorrow, me and Ray really need to get back to my house and help my wife with a few things needing some help and our attention. We can come back in a couple hours if that suits you and discuss plans then or sleep on it and pursue it tomorrow." Michael said uncomfortably.

Ray had studiously rerouted his trip home to pass any and every military base he could after he heard of the news of the cyber and terrorist attacks that had devastated the country's electrical grid and infrastructure and had come up with a brilliant solution to help him and his cousin out with the current circumstances. Ray had by wit or guile managed to take full and possibly devious advantage of the initial confusion and chaos the disaster had caused to get what cash he could and buy as much can goods and food as he was allowed from the various commissaries on the bases he visited on the road home.

The military was uniquely capable and set up to handle the nationwide bank cash shortages for goods or services if anyone was accepting such for goods or services and set up their own paymasters to issue an emergency draw of green cash against a personal check of $250 for its service members to ameliorate the crisis. Every training or front line base anywhere had a system at one time to avoid mass people of going to a commercial facility to receive their pay from a government check. It had taken him 99 forever's to stand around in several well-ordered pay lines to receive his cash against a check and then go shopping for whatever picked over can goods and sacks of flour that remained on the bases grocery stores he had managed to visit and acquire goods from. That this hard earned stash was put on display for them danged Russian security guards as well as this wealth of now irreplaceable goods was still half ass secured and tarped down in the back of his truck vexed him no end. A few favors from old comrades in arms and a couple well placed bribes at the emergency gas dispensaries' and he was home with his double tanked pickup truck about two thirds full.

Telling David of this glorious accumulated bounty was not something neither he nor Ray wanted to do at all at the moment but they had many concerns that David might be able to advise them on concerning the alleged "hoarding laws" they had been hearing and being warned so much about on the radio. Those Russkies at the plant must have certainly got themselves more than an eye full of alleged prosperity when they pulled that tarp back on Ray's truck and they had both bet that cagy old Prepper David most likely had some thoughts or advice about the situation and how to maybe make it disappear.

"It sort of can't wait on inspiration or desperation Ray, see I am going to have to be leaving out in a day or so to parts unknown and we need to get around to discussing about having you and your cousin looking out after my place when I am gone. I could come on over and put this drink down now to help you with whatever it is you are needing to do at this time and then we could talk some more, that is if that would be alright." David said wondering what the big mystery was that was so pressing and diverting their attention to a street level problem.

"Hell them boys come down here and drop a bomb shell on me about foreign troops just up the road and now them so and so`s don't have the time of day to finish a conversation about me leaving out! What the friggin hell is so important it can't wait on another drink or a few more words?" David thought to himself angrily wondering if his trust was misplaced in Michael and for that matter should he might should be considering Ray as some kind of foreign mercenary collaborator he needed to be watching closer than he wished to.

A momentary long drawn out silence occurred as the group eyed each other suspiciously before Ray spoke up.

"I can go on by myself to tend to what needs doing and you can stay here and talk to David awhile Michael. No disrespect Julie, soldier David. I will come back over here in a bit and we can evaluate things better later when I am done." Ray said, anxious to get his hoarded and somewhat hidden food stuffs out of the hot Alabama sun and he was no way no how particularly wanting to divulge anything to the stranger David without further conversation and clarifications with his cousin Michael about the man and woman's true character.

Michael and Ray looked grimly at each other for a moment and then some unspoken agreement between the two was made before Michael said that he thought that it would be alright for Ray to go take care of business and to excuse him from helping because what David needed to tell him seemed to be very important to them all and settled back down to talk to Julie and David at the picnic table.

After Ray left, a very curious David waited impatiently for Michael to say the first word and break the strained silence.

"I will tell you what that was all about later David; meantime explain to me about where you are going and how long you will be gone if you can. You are picking a hell of a time to be traveling anywhere, I don't get it." Michael said confused and frustrated at his supposed alliance.

" Damn, it's not like I want to be leaving more than a few steps from here anywhere Michael, but my presence is requested by an old friend to help out with some kind of disaster and I got to go. You know how it is I just got to. Just what exactly the emergency is or what I am able to do is not clear to me so be patient and bear with me the best that you can." David said before recounting how an established trust must be maintained with his prepper buddy Crick who had managed to get a call into him on the telephone to ask for his assistance had come in but it had been cut short before any further communications had been possible.

AUTHOR NOTE: (Complete background conversation is included in book one of the series a Prepper is Cast Adrift (The Preppers Lament).

"Wow, David, you sure must be some kind of a great friend to basically say that you are going to drop everything and task yourself to go charging off halfcocked on a rescue mission not even knowing if you can do any good or not once you get there. Have you even considered for a moment that you might not be even able to get there to where they are stranded at, now that you have heard for yourself that we got foreign troops on the road and securing assets from Ray? And while you're at it old man, you ever think that if you do some how get there intact and in one piece that you might not be able to get back home ever again? Where's your mind at man? You got some crazy ass idea that you are going to try to drag all of them preps you got stashed to save the day for them in your own obscure fantasy world or are you thinking about something sensible like maybe leaving them for me to try and protect on the dubious off chance this little adventure you're going on isn't just a suicide mission." Michael said pretty pissed off at the whole notion of it and David considering any of the above.

"What I take or leave is my business and my decision to make!" David warned in response to this outburst with a very dangerous narrowing of his eyes that most folks could not have missed.

" Hell it hadn't been but a few days since they had both shared a deer together and that riff raff bunch of neighbors that had headed out for a relocation camp or wherever still played heavy on their minds. Wasn't it David who had been preaching mutual assistance and defense amongst the remaining neighbors on this dead end road and now this fool was just going to pull up stakes and expect his shit to remain untouched and unmolested if the dumb ass somehow made it back? Shit, let him go; he

would watch his crap and keep it safe for him for a little while, a damn little while at that! He was curious as hell just what exactly that prepper survivalist had in his old storage sheds anyway. If David didn't come back well then it served him right and David's preps would soon be his." Michael decided thinking that as far as he was concerned David had already somehow reneged and broken their pact on mutual trapping and hunting and jeopardized him and his family's survival with his absence and lack of efforts on their part to carry on here.

"Now don't you be getting all pissed off about anything before hearing me out Michael? I know its risky business going on this road trip and it is probably pretty dang bone headed of me to even be thinking about going to Deer Lick creek but you got to look at the bigger picture here. For one thing I can't just up and ignore a call of honor from a friend to come to his aid and help him when he is in need and at the most trying time in his life. For another thing, I want you to consider that area as my highly considered backup or secret bug out location and what with what Ray just told us about the proximity of them goons from some kind of a foreign security personnel force that are enforcing martial law or continuity of government mandates hanging around, I need to go check it out. Besides, if you would open your eyes and engage that brain of yours, you might consider that your ass might just want to possibly be moving in that direction yourself sometime in the future if it got too crazy around here. Think about it, there is no way in holy hell that I can leave that many fellow preppers in a lurch and dire straits if it's just something I can man up and do. I couldn't live with myself the rest of my life if I tried to weasel out. A lot of them folks are personal friends of mine and I would like to think that if the roles were reversed that they would come answer the bugle call for action and assistance themselves to come help my own sorry ass out if I truly needed it." David reasoned, trying to describe how he felt that he was duty bound and honor tied to go help out anyway possible, if nothing else more than him making a concerted effort and an appearance at the boat landing to try something or anything to get them out of the mess they were in." David said watching the furrows in Michael's brow lessen while his own set of stress wrinkles deepened.

"David now you know that I am all about lending a hand and helping folks out when we can, you know that of me. I still say that you need to really think this thing you are proposing over some more. You ain't going to be doing anybody any good if you end up robbed, killed or incarcerated in a FEMA camp for some bull shit you can't control or have thought of yet. It ain't like you're going to be the last chance first responder or soldier to go rescue an orphanage or free a P.O.W, camp or something. Think of all the obstacles, hell think of your age or any infirmities you have these days to slow you down. You said all them folks stranded up there are preppers, don't they stand a good chance to get by on their own somehow?" Michael said inquiringly with a raised eyebrow and a caution to himself what he had just said might make David cuss a might at him loudly and strongly.

David sighed, then grasped Michaels shoulder for a moment in comradely playfulness and explained that just because somebody labeled themselves as a "prepper" didn't mean that they could survive anything or everything life threw their way. It just meant they were better prepared than most folks to face a disaster and try to persevere regardless. Preppers, he reminded Michael, came in all shapes, sizes and attitudes in regards to the level of preps they had stored personally or in regards to the survival knowledge they had attained from their efforts or others to spread the word of prepperdom and it was almost a sacred thing to consider that it was totally unfair to consider them as some kind of backwoods survivalists that could live off the land indefinitely by themselves without community let alone last for weeks without equipment and supplies in the wilds on average. Most preppers realized the futility in even considering such a notion of long term self-reliant living and prepared themselves and their families to just maintain a somewhat normal existence for a small period of time in a shortfall of goods and services after a catastrophe. Military and Bush craft schools taught the basics of survival for days before you are rescued when lost in the woods or shot down behind enemy lines, not the attainment of a Mother Earth News type self-reliant lifestyle that would take you a decade or more of failures to prepare for and attain if you had any chances of becoming self-sufficient in an off grid lifestyle means of truly feeding yourself past eating grubs. Besides a lot of the folks attending Prepper Stock only planned on being there at the camp grounds with city goods access for only a few days, a week at most if they had somehow managed to use up or save some of their precious vacation time in anticipation of, or got a few days off from work to attend the event and were now far away from whatever they had stored back at home they had by hook or crook they had somehow managed to put back to help them and their loved ones survive such a calamity.

"Well ok, I got to say that I am sorry and I wasn't being very realistic or truly caring about your friend's needs, I guess. I doubt most of the country boys around here could even last that long out in the woods living under the conditions you have described. You never said how long you had planned on being gone, David. I guess it's sort of hard for to say how long that mission will take but you must have considered some kind of estimate time wise." Michael said still perplexed about what David thought he could possibly do other than somehow assist in getting that group of people off that island. That was enough he guessed, but he still wasn't in the least bit convinced that David was somehow uniquely capable of achieving that task to be called upon and risk leaving the area. Maybe he knew somebody in Emergency Management that he was going to call on to help him out somehow. David had said he once had lots of contacts in that service and knowing him had a supply sergeant or two in mind to throw a bit extra gear or assistance his way if he asked for a favor.

David soon answered that question by stressing the fact that all first responders and relief services were surely overwhelmed and anyway he had no way of contacting anyone anywhere unless he showed up at their offices front or back doorsteps if the guards would let him.

"Well, don't think of me as trying to be a smartass or anything David, but just what in the fields of god's green earth is it that you think you can accomplish that 70 or so of your fellow brethren prepper minded people haven't already thought of or come up with for themselves?" Michael asked, waiting patiently for whatever it was that David convinced himself that he alone had dreamed up in some way to save the day.

"That's a good question, Mike; it took me awhile and then some to come up with that answer for myself. I couldn't for the life of me come up with an answer why Crick called upon me for anything else but moral support, then I decided to try and think like him and act like him in that sort of a situation. The biggest worry I can think of that he has other than getting everyone off that island ASAP is evidently how to try to feed all those people once he does manage to extricate them. Everyone including him is already going to be pretty weak and weary by now from lack of food and the elements. That's the particular problem I think that he wants me to personally come down for and help him out with. You know that Michael, I constantly explore and wrestle mentally with all kinds of disaster scenarios and try to find corporate supporters to demonstrate their products as a possible solution to make life easier should I need to survive such situations. Well, back in the day sometime or another I came up this notion of creating for myself something I call a "Lake Living Bag". What I mean by that concept is designing a bug out bag specifically designed for surviving by any type of a waterway. Makes perfect sense to me and maybe you might also agree if you think about it in the context that I am trying to explain it as. I don't know why a large majority of preppers don't already try to specialize or focus their own personal preps and bug out bags based on their needs in a specific geographic area or anticipated future bug out location should the need arise. I have had visions of a separate food procurement bag for years designed to assist in gaining some kind of sustenance for long-term possible living arrangement in a woodland environment. Anyway, I have had the opportunity to play with all kinds of various gill nets, crawdad and fish traps etc. and I hadn't made any recommendations or done a giveaway of extra or endorsed tackle I had acquired to the prepper community and me and Crick compared notes on that and I asked him about fishing conditions and recommendations specific to the area that he lives around. He knows I have that kind of equipment ready at hand at the moment and as far as I know that's what it is he wants of me.

255

He has no other way to access that kind of fish catching stuff and as far as I know that's the only way you can feed that mass of people utilizing natural resources readily available. You need someone that can understand commercial fishing and trapping and I happen to be the only candidate for that job at the moment, I reckon." David said pleased with himself that he had puzzled out Crick's riddle and inspiration.

"Well, I will be damned; I could have never come up with that solution. Now that makes sense! Hell yea, I will support you in that endeavor and rest assured I will try and protect your stuff while you are gone but there is no way I can be everywhere at once no matter how close we live to each other, which brings me back to another point." Michael said as David motioned for him and Julie to come on back in the house and fix them another drink before he had another problem to deal with.

On the way to the house Michael mentioned his and Ray's fears that the possibility of confiscation of "hoarded food" existed under the emergency powers acts that might be enforced by unscrupulous authorities and what did David think about that scary subject and the suppression of the Second amendment to the Constitution regarding firearms.

"I knew I was getting me another drink for some reason." David grumbled and made a motion to Julie who was playing bartender in his small ships galley of a kitchen to add another finger measure worth of brown liquor to the already potent drinks they were consuming.

"That thorny question has been echoing in the back of my mind ever since you brought Ray by with that bucket full of bad news. When is he coming back over here anyway? I think he rather needs to be in on this conversation." David asked Michael, still wondering about the man's odd disappearance and thinking enough time had passed for him to reappear and explain himself.

"Maybe he will be back in a half hour so. I agree he needs to get in on this conversation but we will discuss that more later. He is probably jawing with the wife and getting reacquainted with the kids. Now then, David, try and answer my question if you will, more directly. Do you think we need to worry about either one of those situations I mentioned?" Michael said altering the conversation back to the matters at hand and still keeping David in the dark about Ray's stash of goods that he was putting up unbeknownst to him.

David eyed him for a minute and then went back to the conversation of the subjugation of the constitution and personal liberties and his thoughts on such encroachments.

"Look Michael, neither one of us needs any kind of further education about how foreign soldiers or rogue law enforcement acts in times of disaster or war. We both have plenty of history lessons and real life experience's to clue us in on the highly probable occurrence of that shit occurring if you start getting treated as a peasant or undesirable when the chips are down and they think nobody's watching. Are you asking me do I think they will go door to door trying to enforce it? Hell no! There are not enough soldiers or crazy enough Law enforcement types to even attempt that and they know the citizenry will not stand for it and revolt. Some might be opportunistic S.O.B.s given the smallest chance but I have heard a many police officer or sheriff say that for one I wouldn't enforce such crap because of strong personal liberty belief and secondly I am not going to go get shot at every time I pull in a driveway. Just not going to happen. Do the new world order types want us to revolt so they can call in more foreign soldiers and draconian measures? Sure, that's a possibility but they will only do it to take control of certain areas at first close to their base of operations or as a distraction far away they can extend so called authority to. Hotspots as they like to call them, mass surge reactionary forces and then you will see the alphabet agency's trying to call in civilian mercenary operators to assassinate or imprison whoever they consider resistance leaders so they can quell an uprising without getting their hands directly dirty. The government has already has dumbed down schools, prescribed massive amounts of psychotropic drugs to adolescents, brainwashed kids to snitch on their parents etc. and it will be jealous vindictive neighbor against neighbor and spoiled state owned brats acting like the secret police for the bastards to point accusing fingers at those they feel are holding on to more goods than they deserve. What people can't take by force in time of need will be done by lies and treachery that won't enrich their bellies much before some other asshole does it to them. Just remember the majority of the fore fathers that signed the constitution died impoverished and without thanks or charity from their neighbors that benefited from their sacrifices for pledging their lives and fortunes to the cause of freedom in this once great Nation. Patriots will all always remain the minority while the cowardly self-serving minions of greedy evil humanity serves their own devils messiah and forget what it is, or for what actions they will be judged by a higher power for when their day of reckoning comes around. Oh, the Oath keepers as a majority can be depended on, some of the folks in militias will hold true, many common men and women will remain faithful to their vows but I think the majority of so called citizens will not stand up to this oppression but instead try to profit by it, not take a stand." David ranted thinking disgustedly that schools probably didn't even teach anymore how we could learn from history about what it meant to have foreign troops on our soil and how the colonists fought back against this tyranny so hard that the British hired professional soldiers from Germany called the Prussians to try and suppress us. Would anyone still know or remember about the French Indian wars anymore when a bounty was placed on American settler's scalps and the most horrific attacks came from Canada for any number of political or economic reasons? History repeats itself, our job of living in the present and remembering it is to never allow such tragedies and miseries like the holocaust, wounded knee, the Bataan death march, Stalin, Mao, Poppa Doc, and a million other things and atrocities that have happened to allow man's inhumanity to man to ever repeat itself again. However we are a fickle and unworthy benefactor of these lessons from time and forget all too easily how the progression of events that allowed such terrible things to happen is complicity and lack of preparedness. I don't mean preparing for a disaster like prepping food and ammunition for the day you see coming, I mean preparing the hearts and minds of others not to turn a blind eye to such events occurring in their lifetimes. When any dictator or mad man or woman anywhere wants you to lose a right or liberty they are patient at first while they deviously deceive and distort facts that first rewrite and influence history to subjugate your mind, then affirm it through the kids in order to create a false reality.

"So you think it might happen then?" Michael said with an over mine and a lot of other cold dead bodies look.

"Always consider it will happen and can happen. Look to history and lessons learned and try to plan accordingly is about the best advice I can tell you. Let me explain that little zinger for a moment, Julie and I have been having a similar discussion on the same subject concerning this trip we are about to undertake. For example Mike, I explained to her that if we got stopped at a road block somewhere we need to try and look as uninteresting as we can, no frills and no obvious party affiliation like a screw the prez or legalize cannabis t shirt let alone a prepared prepper bugging out crazy pocketed or military surplus looking thing which is going to be difficult without some thought and planning. It's not an insurmountable task to go gray wolf or man, plenty of folks I am sure are loading up their possessions and heading for parts unknown these days, we just got to be careful with our stories and what kind of goods we are carrying so we can Gray Man our way out of possible situations. That's why I like being southern and picking my duds accordingly. Take for example my choice of weaponry for this road trip we are about to venture out on. On the one hand, I already know folks are awfully desperate these days and might not hesitate to shoot me over a can of beans, that makes me want to go full battle rattle and carry my AR or AK rifle openly and wear my army crap I am used to in such a situation. However, I don't need to be looking like I am a militia member going to form up to engage or homegrown terrorist in the light of day that needs to be tagged and bagged if the National Guard, Homeland Security or lord knows who stops me for a ID check and don't like my appearance or firepower. I also ain't going to have a pickup truck load full of food going anywhere or at any time unless I can disguise it because law enforcement would declare I must of stole it from somewhere and lock me up so they could consume it on their own or let some Army commander appropriate it for his troops." David said wondering why Michael flinched on the last statement and waiting for him to question him further or carry on the conversation.

"If you leaving you are thinking about leaving your AK and AR behind then let's talk about can I borrow them until you get back?" Michael said coveting his weapons of war craft.

"I didn't say I wasn't taking them with me; better yet let us just say that I didn't want them on my front seat if I got pulled over." David said narrowly taking a sip of his barter or bomb elixir he had managed to distill with much afore thought and generally not liking how this conversation was going so far.

"I didn't mean nothing by asking you to lend me your guns there, David, I just meant for you to consider if you were not carrying them with you on your road trip then you could lend them to me. You know, so I could better help guard your house and your stuff while you were gone." Michael said grinning sheepishly and not liking how David was adjusting his bowie knife at the moment.

"Yea, right Michael, you get that brainiac mind of yours. I haven't decided on what to do with guns at the moment. I had thought to leave the few extras I got in my gun safe until I got back but you and that damned Ray got me to thinking that might not be the best option. If we are in what might be considered a zone of resistance or perhaps a security force pursues somebody into our area, then a search of my premises might be in order and I am liable to lose my crap. On the other hand like you said, I might never be able to make it back and I would feel terrible that you or any other worthy soul didn't have access to a bit of extra firepower I could have provided. Let me think on that one awhile further and we come back to that point. I also got a pretty decent stash of freeze dried and dehydrated food I haven't clued you in on that we might as well start discussing. I will tell you up front that discussing those preps in detail as we are about to do goes against everything I feel and sort of believe in. You know most preppers are obsessed with OPSEC (Operational security) and rightly so. I have always been open about my prepping because I was seeking input and alliances from our community but now that also makes me a target for some. Hopefully, the alliances I have made will help me defend my goods instead of tempting them to also become my enemy. I feel like I am walking a tight rope at times showing a bit of my preps to people to learn from and enjoy while also trying to maintain some secrecy about what I actually got which is not only prudent but necessary. Many folks around here know I have several guns and a pretty good amount of ammo. That acts as my deterrent to someone thinking it would be easy to take something from me. That I would have no problem shooting someone if need be, is also known. People know I have food put back and I am sure that in their imagination it is much more and much better than I actually have. People will come asking for food, some already have come begging as you know." David said a bit sadly but also with warning and resolve that his and Julies possessions were their own and remained so even if someone was aware of them and the couples normal caring and sharing nature refused any pleas to share.

"You are going to have to move most of your stuff David before you go. I can't guard this place; take care of my family and run trap line and hunt, you know." Michael said while thinking *"Oh hell, cat will be out of the bag soon. If I got to move in God knows how much preps from David's to my house then we all get to see exactly how much food we all actually have. Damn and David and the rest of the clan will want it stored like they keep gold in banks. That piles yours, that belongs to somebody else etc. That is not going to work. I don't know what David's got but I am sure his pile is going to be bigger than anyone else's and that will end up causing problems out in plain sight. Hell, I best bring up the hoarding confiscation crap again and remind him of the Russians. If them son of a bitches run low on supplies or get tired of eating the same old thing over there at the plant you can pretty much take it to the bank that they would be coming to visit Ray if he didn't take that job and most likely someone might try to black mail him if he did.*

"Yea I am considering that, I want to move a bit of to your house and introduce you to my house sitter, Ross. He can watch my house, do some garden work and help you on the trap line." David said half smirking at the surprised look on Michaels face.

"Who is Ross? Where did he come from?" Michael asked disarmed at the notion David had some kind of hired help about to move into his home.

"He is a local boy, lives just up the road. He is a member of the mole boy gang I borrow once in a while to help out with some landscaping work. Basically I just group them four or five young men that range from 14-20 under the title mole boys and share some wood lore and youthful exuberance with them upon occasion. They have been half ass prepping by themselves and a little help from me for years. Anyway, Ross is the youngest and lives the farthest but he would be perfect for this little job. He also has the most woods sense of them all. Why that boy could track an ant through a cornfield I bet!" David said chuckling.

"Well I guess you know what you're doing but opening your house and your preps to a gang of kids sounds dumb as hell to me. What about their parents?" Michael asked concerned that David seemed to be losing his mind.

"Oh they belong to two single lady parents. I figure left to their own devices they probably couldn't scrape by except for a hit and miss long starvation but with a little organization they are going to be exactly what we need for this little apocalypse." David said, bemused at Michael trying to figure out what David was going to do with a bunch of "mole boys"

"Look here, Michael, and try not to laugh because I am serious, as crazy as this is going to sound. I am starting a free lunch program around here," David said smiling before Michael spluttered out an objection that basically said now he knew David had lost his mind and he wanted no part of it.

"Calm down Michael this will make perfect sense once you grasp how ingenious my little plan is." David said chuckling before carrying on and giving Michael a brief outline.

"Ok, all of them live over by the church about 4 or 5 miles from here. They have been tromping them woods and the road to this house for years so they know the territory better than both of us. They also had various uncles and aunts of the years teach them some country living so the majority of our work advising them is already done. They just need a little supervision and coordination to all pull in one direction and tribe up with us somewhat for mutual survival." David said seeing he was losing his audience.

"Now in ordinary times I would say have at it and let you play scoutmaster or whatever the hell it is that you think you're doing but now it's time to quit playing and be serious. You said you didn't have that much food stored already and now you're considering, what the hell was that you said? A free lunch program? We need that food David, if you're just going to give it away, give it to me. I will keep it safe and you will have a lot more left when you get back to eat yourself and hopefully your house will be still standing." Michael said exasperated at the notion of David doing handouts to protect his crap. It was ludicrous he objected.

"I am not opening my pantry to them; I am forming a hunting gathering community that has enough folks to succeed." David said sternly.

"Look, Michael, they all have gardens but probably few seeds for spring planting. They have some old fruit and nut trees we don't have on our properties. Everyone needs to survive until the gardens produce and you need help with the hunting and trapping as well as security. The idea is to let Ross move in here for a bit and swap out assistants to help him here and there. His buddy Charles for example can help set traps between my house and their house through the woods. While they are getting proficient at that survival skill I will feed them lunch. Ross gets dinner with you for watching the house, garden etc. and can help you tend my modern traps. Pretty soon on alternating days the rest of the mole boys can come back and forth through the woods and check the trap lines or set new snares coming and going to visit Ross and bring whatever game they manage to catch. I figure the free lunch program will have a good meal day and an iron ration day, That is something good and recognizable from my stores, a suck ass meal of wheat porridge, maybe a half ass day of beans and rice, etc. That's the pay and it spreads the food out a couple survivors at a time. Game meat is shared as a community endeavor and is the bond of our little tribe. All them boys have got guns but are very short on ammo because they tended to shoot it up like kids will do and the shit is expensive and hard to find in the best of times. I don't have a ton extra but I got enough to equip our little army. Their homes act like little outposts for listening and observing for dangers, our end of the road acts like a last stand bastion if they need to beat feet through the woods and take a stand to fend off any gangs or whatever." David said letting the wisdom of his suggestion sink in.

"I see, that would add considerably to our range and foraging but we would need that with the extra mouths to feed. How much food are you thinking this little endeavor going to cost you? I mean in food stores, not money." Michael asked speculating just how much stuff David might have stored.

"Well considering you got to know what we are working with I will tell you. It has taken me about 7 years to accumulate about a year and a half worth of food for me and Julie in Mountain

House, Provident pantry, etc. freeze dried. I got a years' worth of the basics like wheat, beans, rice and legumes for one person that I call iron rations. There are 7 new mouths to feed in this little endeavor, let's call it six for math's sake and not doing full adult recommendations for calorie counts. That means two months at best if I gave them nothing but iron rations. Six people dividing up food for twelve months meant for one equals out to two months. That calculation doesn't really work because I want to plant some of that wheat and beans for next year but it also don't take into account that a handful of rice, some wild Oxalis or whatever else they can gather in the fields and woods can make a hearty stew and stretch the hell out of the stores. Like I said I will share some of the good shit, hell I got like a few cans of sweet and sour pork for a treat all of us could sit down to. Says 18 servings in a can, a one day a week feast maybe, anyway you get the picture and you will be in charge of rationing while I am gone." David said wondering how long it was going to be before the bickering and cajoling would begin to get into his stores further and diversify the diets.

Michael did a bit of mental calculations on his own and appeared to be disturbed.

"What is the matter buddy? You don't like my ideas?" David said mentally searching for more flaws that might have been included in his planning than had been discussed thus far

"You didn't really add my end of the road into those calculations you were using. You did mention a weekly possible eating the good stuff in some kind of communal meal but you're going to be out of that kind of food very quickly if you are spreading yourself that thin and not holding some reserve back for yourselves. Not that it isn't appreciated mind you but I doubt your planning on letting us eat all that chow up until it finally all runs out. How much food are you devoting to that endeavor and how much of that stash is taboo and for just yours and Julies use?" Michael said trying to evaluate David's line of thinking and any shortfalls or implications it might indicate.

"I hadn't even thought of Ray until now, I guess you're already going to be hard pressed to feed him. He is committed to our community food procurement deal me and you agreed on, isn't he? I mean did you stress to him we were going to be having to do one pot suppers for all of us unless there was a bigger catch than we expected? I mean if all we get is one turtle or snake in a day's food procurement it goes in the pot to be shared by all?" David said wondering further about the man he just met demeanor.

"I didn't go into great detail with him but he gets the general idea. What we can hunt, trap, forage or catch is to be shared like one big family whether a lot or a little. Yea, he gets that. David he brought his own food with him, actually he probably has more than me." Michael said and went on to tell David about how smart he had been in collecting groceries from every military base he managed to stop by. Michael then went on to explain the concerns Ray and him held regarding the discovery of all the food stuffs Ray had transported in the back of his pickup.

"I see why he was in such a big hurry to get home and unloaded now. I also see he might have brought the wolf to our door inadvertently. Do you know which way he is leaning regarding that missile plant job?" David asked speculating and a bit alarmed a contingency had come up he hadn't planned for.

"No, he didn't say for sure one way or the other which way he would go. He is pretty mad about it all at the moment and his first inclination is to tell them all "take this job and shove it" but he didn't burn any bridges. I imagine he will think it over and end up taking it because he has no other options. Man's got to eat you know." Michael said wondering if he shouldn't for his family's sake try to get on that plant also. A wave of conflicting emotions came over him to even consider such an idea but feeding his children came foremost in his mind.

"I guess we best think about cashing and stashing some stuff off property but I will be danged if I know where off hand. Damn, Michael it seems I no more start dealing with one problem than another one crops up that needs my immediate attention." David said feeling like he was up against insurmountable odds.

"I doubt we have anything to worry about for a while but it is a lot to consider. Figure out how you want to divide up your stuff and we will figure out where and how to store it later. I tell you what, I am going to walk back up to the house and talk to Ray a bit. We can come back this evening or if you want we will come by in the morning around nine." Michael said, getting ready to leave.

"Let's do it in the morning, I am still packing for my trip and right now I am just going sit, sip and ponder awhile before going back to work deciding what gear goes and what stays. Thanks for updating me so quick on the Russkies, take care." David said looking over at Julie who had been following the conversations closely.

"Bye Julie, see ya David." Michael said and then proceeded walking down the driveway.

3

Plotting And Scheming

"So Julie, what kind of thoughts are you thinking over there? "David asked noticing that Julie was staring confusedly at her 3 bug out bags she was trying to organize into one.

"Oh David, I was just thinking how mentally tiring it is to try to organize these things. I just know if I leave something I will need it later but there is no way if we have to leave the van for some reason I could carry even a quarter of this gear very far." Julie said dismayed.

"I know what you mean, I have to dive into mine later but my get home bag is small already and I just need to arrange some basic items in my backpack and a few changes of clothes. Pack as light as you can. Wow I can't believe I said that, never mind I will show you what to take later when I do mine." David said chuckling thinking about all the trips he had been on with her where he used to pack everything but the kitchen sink and she would sneak that in somewhere when he wasn't looking and maybe a couple bags of other things he hadn't thought of or was planning on leaving behind.

"Hey Julie, have you figured out what you think we should be taking food wise yet?" David said dragging a couple of duffle bags full of gear he had put together to go on this crazy rescue mission to Deer Lick Lake that he still had no idea what exactly was expected out of him attempting it. It had been about three days ago when his prepper buddy Crick had managed to get his call through to him asking for some help and David remained flummoxed as to what exactly was expected of him. Julie and he had gone back over what little conversation there was with Crick a hundred times trying to see if they had overlooked any kind of clues but to no avail. All he knew at the moment was somehow the men and women attending Prepper Stock got themselves stranded after a dam got blown and needed some help. David could understand that outside help was needed because government services were pretty much nonexistent now that society was collapsing but he still had a lot of reservations about going anywhere and particularly so now that Ray had informed him that foreign troops were being implemented..

"I have gotten a few things together like a weeks' worth of food for us in MRE packages but you are going to have to give me some more insights into how long we are going to be gone before I can figure out anything else. What's in those bags? They look heavy." Julie said arranging things for packing and watching David drag two bags into the living room.

"Yea, they are pretty heavy. I guess you would call them my squad level lake living kits. As you know, I got to thinking about why Crick most likely wanted me to come help him out. We figured it out when I was gathering supplies in the prep shed the first go round. Pretty simple actually to come up with fish nets! He wants me to bring him a couple of those military surplus gill nets he knows I have. If you got a bunch of folks trying to find food around a lake or river, that's the simplest and most effective solution I can think of and the hardest thing to find if you don't already have one. That's got to be it, he wouldn't be asking me to take this kind of risk without a damn good reason and we are going to get him his fish net and a few other things come hell or high water. That is of course unless I can talk you into staying here while I go." David said knowing there was no chance Julie would consent to staying behind.

"We already had this conversation, David, and you already know my answer. You can rest assured that there is no way I am staying here while you go off on some mission or adventure into the great unknown leaving me here by my lonesome to fend for myself until you get back. I know you have taught me enough to do it if I ever had the need to, but we both know that we need each other to lighten the load, give moral support and to watch each other's backs. Now then, I didn't think about that big net you had collecting dust on the shelves. I thought you had it around for dragging a farm pond if we ever had to. On that note you also have a regular trotline or two sitting in a box next to it don't you?" Julie asked.

Trotlines worked well under the right conditions but they took bait and a lot of it. Net fishing made sense but she wasn't very familiar with all the ins and outs of the process let alone all the different types manufactured for different types of fish or the techniques fishermen used to deploy them.

"I only have that one commercial trotline setup to donate to the Crick cause but I have the makings for another one or two in my preps we can reserve for us. I have that big heavy duty military grade green 50 ft. net, a couple of those light weight small white survival gill nets and several food procurement devices you probably have never seen that I am bringing with me to augment the big net, though. For example, check this cool gizz wiz out." David said, rummaging in one of the duffle bags and then handing her a package with what looked like some kind of light weight folded up net.

Julie looked at the picture on the packaging and instantly recognized it for what it was. "A dip net! Way cool, I didn't know they manufactured these commercially, looks like that survival trick you taught me using a nylon net hammock. "She said studying the advertising picture.

"Well it is mostly, but like anything else purpose made beats survival improvised any day. This is only a small one for crawdads and minnows and such, but with a bit of tweaking I could catch a turtle." David said starting to point at the picture to expound upon the concept.

"I can see that, this one has a skirt to keep the catch in and a cool net lifting rig already built in." Julie said excitedly tracing the diagram of the nets attributes with her finger and clarifying it also had a small zippered mesh pouch in the center to add bait.

"Yea, it's lighter and better than anything I can field construct or convert another type of net for the purpose. Just a lightweight survival tool to tip some odds in my favor. I could catch minnows to bait my hook or trot line, go after crawdads if I checked it regular, etc." David began explaining before Julie began quizzing him again on its use and functionality.

"I can see how we can use this kind of net on the creeks and streams around here but I don't really see it being used on a lake." Julie said looking at him questionably.

"Well I admit it has its limitations, particularly in its small size but just like any net that is purpose built for a certain type of fishing there are adaptations and tweaks that can be done and most folks won't think of them unless they understand both the fish they are after and the other creatures and bait fish sharing the same waters.

"Let me give you an example of how I would fish a lake with this particular net if it was all I had to survive with." David said as he look bemused at the "let me settle in" look Julie gave him knowing he was going to expound upon one of his prepper or survival theories to the inth degree and she might as well get comfortable. David had a penchant for playing games with folks when it came to piece of survival gear or a common household item that became a game of sorts to him and whoever liked to participate in it to see how many uses an item could be used for or had as to extend ones survival. The survival game he played with others was simple, he would spiel off 10 common or odd uses for whatever it was they were discussing from a lawn mower blade to lip balm and then challenge whoever he had cornered and was chattering at to come up with just one more thing it might be useful for. He and his captive audience would go back and forth until all ideas were exhausted or until a later date when for whatever reason one or the other, (usually David") would come up with another obscure but useful application for the object of his or others imagination. Julie found David's odd preparedness and survival game of wits amusing as well as aggravating, as he would often times come out of the blue with some obscure application of prepper knowledge to an event that hadn't happened yet and ask you how would you fix something or say " You know what you might need?" To which Julie started answering with a grin his favorite catchall piece of survival gear "a poncho?" which seemed to be his current obsession in usefulness and he was working on answer number 38 for that so she offered it for his current query.

"No but I think I already used that one regarding fishing." David said looking up towards the sky as he was apt to when contemplating or devising something.

"Earth to David! Come in, David! Get back to the subject of this net in a lake." Julie said with some exasperation shaking it at him.

"No, not yet." David said with a sly smile in her direction.

"Number 39!" David exclaimed pointing one finger up in the air and grinning like a Cheshire cat to Julie's obvious discomfort his mind was wandering off stage again.

"Ok, David what the hell is number 39?" She said patting his leg playfully and playing along.

"Well I ought to get a two for one for this idea. Humm maybe a three for this idea! David said exuberantly as he searched his brain for a third application but her groan of discontent brought him back to just stating the first two new ones he had wrapped his prepper brain around.

"Hey you know I used to live in Fairhope Alabama we did the jubilee fishing thing when the waters oxygen content went down enough to drive the fish to shore. Sometimes those damn jellyfish would be the first to arrive with the current and we held off any ocean activities. Sort of like down there in Panama City when the jelly fish would do that "bloom" thing and just be all over the place and if you were thinking about wading out and using a cast net for mullet you best keep to the shore line. I know it would look funny for me to be wading around in the surf with a poncho on but it would work to keep them stingers off me." David said drifting off once again into his survivalist daydreaming about weird ways of overcoming obstacles with common items.

"That's good." Julie said "but how can you get around to declaring that trick number 39 and 40? I know you busting your britches to make 40 uses for a poncho but remember I still want to talk about how to use this dip net." Julie said waving the crackling plastic package of the net that had started David's favorite game once again.

"Ok, I officially declare I got number 40 regardless of where you are wading in the water with a poncho, Hey I might have even thought of 41 and 42 in the process!" David began dreamily.

"PLEASE! One more only or am going to whomp you on the head with this! "Julie said slapping the packages against his leg to bring him back to reality.

Ok! Ok! You know I don't understand why this might not be a an advisory or state prescribed precaution already, but you remember all those folks wading around in that toxic mess of flood waters during Hurricane Katrina?" David asked arching one eyebrow at her for confirmation.

"Well yea?" she began before David grabbed his center stage back again as an experienced emergency manager.

"Look, oil and water don't mix as you well know and if you are slopping around walking in the shit and chemicals that the oil refinery's spewed up and the chemical factory's leaked, you get a top surface layer on water that is best not to be accumulating around your thighs if you get my drift. Wading floodwaters under those conditions in a poncho would also make sense and hey by the way, those Czech ponchos were made by the damn cheap ass Soviets to serve double duty as rain wear and chemical protection suits. That damn cheap ass appearing PVC material has got god knows what in it to protect against U.V. Light, acid rain, chemical attack, storage in unheated warehouses, the test of time and about a dozen other things I haven't thought about yet!" David said looking pleased with himself for winning this game of preps and preppers once more.

"Damn David, you are good! I hadn't thought of that one or the other but could you quit drifting off the subject of nets, please?" Julie said coddling his ego to get back on point as to what to do with the fish trap she was about to whomp him with.

"Oh yea, of course Julie." A very slightly subdued David said.

"You see Julie, most folks never consider that crawdads live in every stream and creek emptying into every lake or river the same as they do in the shallower waters. Good anglers know this and generally use some kind of artificial crawdad looking bait to try and catch the larger game fish that live in these environs but it's rare to see anyone selling these types of critters as strictly live fish bait. Crawdads are for fish boils, crabs in

saltwater or brackish back bayous are for dinner and people
don't think about them just screaming "hey fishy fishy" for bait!
So most folks look at this kind of net as a shrimp, lobster,
crawdad, crab, etc. trap for a very small dinner table, but let us
not forget that a gathering of any kind of game be it bait or
predator produces the same results. When you set one of these
kinds of dip nets down on the bottom of a waterway you are
creating your own eco system that rings the dinner bell for
everyone. Now I ain`t going to catch me a mess of crawdads by
sinking what you might consider a crayfish net next to the bank
of a lake or river like I could in a feeder stream or slough but I
am setting up a stocked picnic table. The net could collect me
minnows, crawdads, water bugs, tadpoles etc. to use for fish
hook bait because that zippered bait pocket in the middle puts
scent and attraction for everyone but with a bit of skill I can use
it unbaited. If you stand at the side of a lake or pond you can see
the minnows in the shallows along the edges and just set it down
in a likely place and wait for them to return swimming over it.

Minnows also think the edge of the net affords them
some protection like weeds so they have no problem wriggling
over it if you set it in the water that shallow. You can also set it
deep like chumming with a can of cheap cat food for catfish but
instead you put a tiny amount in that zippered mesh bag at the
center of the net, hell you can even use minnows you trapped
without bait to do it. It's like sprinkling flaky fish food that is
their mouth size in a fish tank. The minnows will come from the
shallows they are normally hiding in to steal a bite from your
feed station while them big carnivore fish that cruise the
shallows waiting on a stray minnow to feed on take notice. Bait
your line with a live or dead minnow, fish a little deeper near the
darting minnow trap and wait on your bobber to high tail it

away. People that think fish ain`t smart are stupid because they don't watch how nature feeds or teaches her own. Young boys or girls can tell you where a likely spot is to try to do this trick because they watch what happens at water's edge during the day and observe when they are on the docks watching what the fish do or an old fisherman points out.

I always like to start any of my newbie or youngster fishermen out by telling them that every fishing hole is different and that it requires getting your "fish face" on and sitting back and watching them for a second or two if they are going to recognize my next words. This pause to observe nature and my reflections on life in general pretty much describes how this fine fishing day is going to turn out.

If someone is open for suggestions or has some grandiose notions of just sinking a baited line in any body of water anywhere and coming up with a stringer of fish because they are "special" is soon dispensed with as the lore and experiences is told of fishing salt, fresh, murky etc. waters becomes apparent. The greatest Salmon fisherman from Alaska or the top dog of Southern bass tournaments soon can become outclassed by a 6 yr. old with luck and grand pappy's patience, advice and wisdom as the day goes on. All fishermen are equal if you know what works in your local waters and it's a matter of timing, location and luck. What you know from your home waters probably doesn't work as well in someone else's and your fish brain needs tweaking with a trick or two from a local sportsman to be truly successful. Thoughts of going alone to a new Mecca for fisherman and holding your own soon becomes a lesson in humility as familiarity overcomes contempt for new experiences and knowledge learned the hard way. Kids are different, children don't carry the baggage of adult anglers and just want to catch fish. They think any angler with the time to take them fishing must know some special secret to some lost art of fish calling and will jealously defend their matriarchs or patriarchs that bought them a fish pole or said come on boy or girl lets go fishing with that special gleam in their eye regardless if they catch anything. You see Kids, those special beings some of us are blessed with and or those of us adults that are blessed to borrow one occasionally know that they are what fishing is all about. It's the hundred and one things an adult might know to put a fish on that little girls or that boys line for the first time and get bragging rights with the other adults in the community we tend to compete for, but really it is so much more than that. David would rather he never caught a fish himself all day or ever for that matter as long as he could teach the patience needed to sit and talk quietly or not at all and see the joy in some child's eye to be a part of the sport and survival skill of catching one of these finned wonders.

All kids must go fishing at least once in their lives and if he had to hock the farm to do it for him or her to buy the first fish rod and put gas in the car he would do it! Now he was beside himself with excitement as he had the opportunity to not just teach kids but adults as well the fine art of fish poaching with no worries of a game warden or someone's jaded notion of sport fishing interfering with him. The rule of the day was catching, not hunting or fishing for something and he had a whole bag full of tricks he had tried, wanted to try or had heard about that were about to be tested to the limit.

"This wasn't going to be just a rescue trip to drop off some survival gear. No this was going to be the biggest funfest of

hunting and fishing ever! He just hoped he was up for the task and the game cooperated long enough for him to get some meat back on the starving castaways bones before he had to say farewell to them. If the dams were broken and the rivers were trying to regain their course, he was reasonably sure that the fish were disturbed enough to be highly unpredictable let alone try to locate them in silt and debris laden water." David mused losing a lot of his enthusiasm.

"Why are these bags so danged heavy, David?" Julie said dragging one duffel bag out of the center of the floor.

"You probably grabbed the one with the cans of cat food in it; I also have about 10lbs of fish meal cakes in there to attract things. We best keep an eye on the cat food, folks probably will want to eat that when get there." David said making a bad joke.

"That wasn't funny David. What else you got in there? Hopefully no dynamite!" Julie said making her own more appropriate joke.

"Ha! You have been listening! I can do something like fishing with grenades with MRE heaters and pop bottles but no I don't have any explosives." David said smiling and remembering how he had answered a question of hers once. "David what works best to hunt game with?" His answer was pretty simple. "Just get you a list of fish and game laws and whatever is illegal is what works best!" had been his serious but humorous reply.

"Thanks for reminding me though of nefarious ways to catch things. How many of those cheap floating LED lanterns we got?" David asked.

"The ones with those square batteries? We can spare a few. You going to use them for fishing?" Julie asked, thinking David might make a lighted fish buoy to use with a cast net.

"No, that's a thought though. Never tried that on freshwater fish, hum should work. No they are for doing the deer in the headlights routine or shining up some raccoons or possums in the trees." David said opening a duffle bag to once again review the contents and try to figure out what else he might be able to add if he had it around the house and had enough to spare.

4

STRANDED

The narrow paved road leading up to the parks pavilion climbed up a steep hill winding through the woods towards the facility's entrance and restrooms. This was the official assembly area for the guests of this Corp of Engineers campground. To continue to call them guests of a federal reserve was a bad joke now as the residents of the campground usually referred to themselves with any number of more appropriate names like, survivor, refugee or even castaways. No matter what an outside observer might call the mix of people already waiting at the large wooden pavilion or trudging towards it for a meeting, they all shared the same plight of being stranded on the peninsula and surrounded by water. Having the water round no matter how murky or questionable it was, was regarded a blessing. Problem was it also kept them from accessing any food or escape to the mainland.

The campground used to sit on a large wooded bluff situated between two dammed rivers that formed a lake but after a terrorist attack destroyed parts of the dams, the reservoir overflowed and the rivers returned to their natural courses. This event flooded much of the lower elevation land that was subject to the rivers whims before the dams had been built and currently held second growth pine plantations.

No one really knew how much damage was caused by the attack upriver from them, because the roads leading out of the campgrounds and the dam crossings were now all submerged. Crick Miller (Crick as in Creek, you know kind of how some of us good old boys in Alabama and elsewhere pronounce the name of a small stream) remembered the night the seventy or so park guests heard two gigantic earth shaking explosions and then about an hour later were further jolted and confused by the sound of rushing water and cracking trees as the water that was formerly held back by dam flood gates was suddenly released in an onslaught spilling tons of earth, concrete and swirled debris and smashed boats by them in the river channel at the bottom of the bluff.

Crick still couldn't for the life of him ever forget the eerie but awesome specter of a huge white tug boat and a steely black coal barge being swept by his vantage point overlooking the lakes impoundment late one evening. The tug had all its bright running lights still on, the crew on the deck was hanging on for dear life dressed in their red life jackets and it's captain was blaring its shrill horn in a panic of long and short roaring bursts. The boat was being dragged sideways by the twisted steel cables attaching it to the barge and it looked like it would have been swamped and sunk momentarily until all of the sudden a cable broke loose and the boat started to spin and flounder in the opposite direction while still being dragged by the ferocious current caused by the hydroelectric dam failure.

Crick didn't know if the courageous captain or crew ever regained control of their boat but the next morning when he and the other campsites awoke after a fearful night spent on higher ground for safety's sake they saw a tragic sight. The disheveled and bedraggled campers came down slowly but methodically in a group to the main campgrounds to survey the carnage and gauge the flooding rivers rise or fall and after poking around his own trailer for a bit, he looked upstream from an observation deck and spied the coal barge about a mile down river, run hard aground on the opposite shore. All through the long dark night before this sighting, people had tuned to their radios listening for some news on what might have caused this catastrophe but heard nothing. The local radio stations were silent but the larger transmitters elsewhere only said two power stations had unexplained explosions and were being investigated by the authorities.

Refugees are people who have crossed an international frontier and are at risk or have been victims of persecution in their country of origin. Internally displaced persons (IDPs), on the other hand, have not crossed an international frontier, but have, for whatever reason, also fled their homes. Folks stuck at Prepper Stock just decided to call themselves homeless for the moment.

The next morning's radio news was even sparser and much more disturbing. News of a cyber-attack of unknown origin had taken down the electrical grid on most of the eastern seaboard and California's grid was faltering. That bad day had occurred three weeks ago and things had just gotten worse from then on. Tents were struck, trailers were hitched as everyone scurried to break camp and get the hell out of dodge and head home to ride the disaster out. Everyone knew why they didn't have power at the campground and was nonplussed about it. After all, they were here to be camping anyway so most people barely missed it's convenience. Not having water for the campgrounds restrooms and showers was missed rather quickly night one when the toilets didn't flush. The explosions they all heard happened about 1:30 in the morning and had rousted everyone to action and bleary eyed sleepers and late night revelers both wandered from campsite to campsite checking on friends and questioning others as to what the hell had just happened.

LowBuck had been up at settlers' camp having himself a well-deserved drink with Pop and his crew who were supervising the all-night vigil of cooking a whole hog by slowly feeding seasoned hardwood split logs into a stainless steel commercial smoker. His wife, Cat, had gone back to their campsite previously to go to bed earlier and let LowBuck play with his buddies and get herself some much needed rest.

LowBuck heard the explosions echoing off the lake and being misguided from the woods playing with the sounds couldn't quite place from which direction they came from.

"Ramro! What the hell was that? Where in the world did that sound come from?" LowBuck said looking in the direction of the shoreline campsites where his wife lay sleeping.

"Man I have got no freaking idea what that was. Gave me a hell of a start I thought I saw a big blue white flash off to our right but we were all staring into that cooker with our flashlights blazing at and admiring that hog when it happened. Let me turn this lantern off and see if we can see any fire." Ramro said after he turned off the Coleman lamp and then eight or so people tried to scrutinize the dark woods with night blindness as their eyes tried to adjust to and make out objects in the darkness.

"I can't see a damn thing." LowBuck grumbled as various voices declared their assent and lack of vision in this pitch black woods.

"I am going to go check on my wife and make sure that she is alright." LowBuck said turning on his flashlight and blinding everyone after they stood listening and trying to get their night vision working.

"I got to go see about and check on mine also." Ramro said, helping LowBuck round up the small blue and white cooler they were sharing and the rest of the adult beverage supplies.

"It could have been a couple of them gas wells you seen coming in from the main road or it might be something to do with the dam's electrical substation." Morgan said walking over to the pair.

"I didn't know what those things were pumping. Looks like those rigs you see in Texas pumping oil, so they're for natural gas then?" Ramro asked clutching the cooler and a brown paper bag.

"Yea, those things are all over the place around here. I never heard of one blowing up or a gas fire before, but I would say that is a likely possibility or could be something happened over by the main dam." Morgan said clutching his own bar supplies.

"Where is Crick at?" LowBuck asked about Morgan's sidekick and long-term friend.

"I don't know off hand. Him and BcTruck were talking about those rocket stoves of his when I left the campsite to come down here for a bit and see what was happening. He said he was going to be coming down here most likely about now but as you know he ain't here.' Morgan said as Modoc and SoCal joined the conversation with Pops and, RCchop following them over.

"So Morgan, you think that loud noise was caused by a couple of gas well pumps going off?" SoCal asked trying to fathom what the risk of them setting national forests on fire was.

"I said that was one possibility. Those explosions were not like any I have ever heard before, dang sure were loud enough. They were like Da Dump, one went off to our right and a second or two after the first I heard one off to our left. There are two power stations in both directions but there is also those rocker pumps pumping gas everywhere and on whose ever land has a lease. Those big bangs sounded pretty damn close though but the woods and lake can amplify or muffle things. I will tell you one thing; it was a hell of a lot louder set of booms than a couple big transformers make normally blowing out in a thunderstorm." Morgan said taking a nervous sip from a red solo cup while fidgeting with his unlit flashlight and grocery bag in his other hand trying to decide whether to put it down or not.

Morgan and Crick were everyone's go to guys for all things concerning local information. The pair had grown up together and still lived in the general area so their advice was sought after by all, regarding where liquor and grocery stores were, road access, camp rules etc.

"I know that you and Crick got your shit together but did you all actually physically inspect all those ammo cans you got stacked up at your camp?" SoCal said flashing his Hollywood smile at Morgan.

"What do you mean? Oh, I got it. Funny, no it wasn't us that made anything go boom. I mean all me and Crick did was just enjoy buying a government military surplus deal on a pallet of cans was all. Empty ammo cans for caches or stashes was the order of the day. Those things are dear in price if you try buying them one at a time," Morgan said for SoCals edification.

"Tell me about it brother. Government castoffs ain`t what they used to be price wise. By the way, I am still laughing like hell you got that Taj Mahal of a trailer you are staying in propped up by 50 cal ammo cans." Socal said laughing and reviving the mental picture he got when first observing things.

"Hey, they are great items and most preppers don't really know how functional or versatile and durable they are without a demonstration." Morgan said grinning.

"Well, you got me sold on durability, I never seen that done before. I just remembered that you had a stack of 120 millimeter mortar cans off to the side and I considered you might have had an oversight." SoCal said, not sure if LowBuck knew he was just joking about the possibility of loose mortar rounds going off.

"I got to go check on the wife, I am sure your government surplus booty is ok. Those inspectors for that crap got checklists out the wazoo to assure its safety before you buy and I was just joking that a round might of went off. Still and all though those inspectors are human and can still make mistakes."

"Are you all about ready?" Morgan asked.

" Downhill always beats uphill, let's get going and go check on folks." LowBuck said leading the way back down the trail to their prepper community campsites.

It was a community, a community of like, minded souls that had gathered under his banner and YouTube channel of what was referred by one and all as Prepper Stock 2014. This was the biggest congregation of preppers in one location under that black and yellow banner that had occurred to date and everyone was having great fun.

Preppers had streamed in to Alabama to attend the gathering from as far as northern California and as close as across the river for folks like Crick and Morgan. It had been a magical and mystical assemblage of like minds that couldn't be more different in geographic, racial, economic or otherwise ties. Many hours and days had passed for those who had counted the months to attend this prestigious celebration of preparedness from the last great meet up. Many of the participants had been on the LowBuck bandwagon from day one and could say they had attended every Prepper Stock to date from the first originating one.

Many folks like LowBuck's friend David couldn't afford to go to every one of the Prepper Stock assemblies due to mileage but had evidenced support in a myriad of other ways to the events they missed in presence but not in spirit. David had pledged what little bit of treasure he had as well as his full faith and support to Lowbuck from the first conception of the event by the man over the years. David wrote about him and shared supporters the same as if they were both neighbors working on a block party but their allegiance to each other went much farther than that.

Times had changed for everyone in the ever evolving internet and changing prepper community to the point of who used to be on top of YouTube channels had faded away and the books David had written including them as characters were passé to a new generation. Didn't matter too much on the surface to LowBuck and David that fame was but a fleeting image. Neither had joined the prepper community or advocated for Tea Party views because they had some prior views that their acceptance as a voice of the community could do anything other than inform and help prepare others. You know what preppers are? They all start humble with but one hope. Every single blogger, youtuber, author, follower, subscriber, participant etc. had only one goal in life that they somehow grew into. We all agonized, we all questioned ourselves and dealt with the same rejections to a preparedness message we were not quite sure why we were so vociferously declaring.

The other blocks of campsites next to the prepper community were sparsely occupied by the regular RV type travelers and campers. The lights were on their camps also and people looked anxiously out into the night towards the lakes shore.

LowBuck and Ramro checked on their wives and then they all gathered on a campsites deck looking over the moon lit lake. They stood talking about what might have occurred and it took them a bit to notice that the dam lights off in the distance were no longer visible.

"I guess something happened to that power station over there…" LowBuck began before the dull roar of rushing water gave them all cause for alarm.

"That doesn't sound good, look over there at the shoreline! They must have opened the floodgates." Ramro declared as water started to wildly splash and lap the shore.

"Hey what's up guys?" Crick said as he and Morgan joined he group.

"Ramro said they must have released the floodgates." Cat said staring out at the dimly moon lit turbulent waters.

"I dunno, I been around when they have done that before and it don't sound nothing like that. They usually also sound a warning siren." Crick said studying the turbulent churning waters.

5

CALLED TO ORDER

LowBuck looked around at the assembled crowd and told Crick they might as well get the meeting started for today as it looked like everyone that was coming was now here. Earlier today he, Crick and Morgan made the rounds to all the campsites and left word they were having assembly at 2 Pm today. Assembly was called pretty regularly as desperation and realizations became apparent from their plight of being stranded on what was now essentially an island.

There were no real cadre or leadership designations amongst the community. The preppers had organized themselves into "solution groups" to think tank out or implement measures to try to survive this disaster as best they could. Groups were pretty much organized around skill sets and natural leaders or highly skilled individuals naturally filled necessary spokesperson roles or task foreman jobs.

LowBuck, as the organizer and originator of Prepper Stock, basically retained his role to act as chairman for all meetings and general organization. There were tons of things that needed organizing and discussion. The community had to be mobilized to address the issues of sanitation, food procurement, how the hell to get off this island, etc.

Previous assemblies had been held for all sorts of things. The community needed to assess who had fishing equipment and who didn't. Who had trapping and snaring knowledge, who was marksman enough to think they could possibly take a deer with a pistol, did anyone have any better idea to collect water than to try and fill a container after navigating the steep slopes down to the river.

A myriad of things all the sudden needed to be discussed and haggled over. Fishing sucked because all the campground fishing piers had been washed away and the water had only now calmed down. Deciding how 50 or so individuals should confine their foraging and hunting areas soon became apparent. Getting the agreements from the 20 or so non-prepper campers required some parlaying and diplomacy.

At first everyone was very helpful and much more sharing with each other. As time progressed, people changed and became less helpful and more resentful. Sharing survival skills like edible plant identification became something to regret because now everyone competed for the same sparse resources. An empty trap or a sprung snare allowed creeping suspicion and jealously to cause discord and false accusations to surface.

When the disaster had hit three weeks ago, the community was on its last day of Prepper Stock and the preppers had only whatever left over food they had brought for the event and their 72 hour kits to nourish themselves with. Everyone ate well that first day of the disaster as Pop Preppers' smoked hog was shared around. Half of the hog and all of the bones, fat, skin etc. was saved in ice chests and shared out over the next couple days and a watery bone soup was cooked up in one of Crick's steel 120mm ammo cans because no other pot could be had that was big enough for the last community supper.

During this communal affair the somber conversations and lack of alcoholic beverages made for rather a sad meeting. This was the last of the available food in open evidence. Not being a prayerful group it was unusual on this day to start a meal with a prayer of Thanksgiving but it was expected, no demanded by many, for this day of reckoning. The prepper encampment had suffered no deaths or injuries; they were to be spared from the wildfires raging somewhere far off but still noticeable by the haze and smoke on the horizon.

Their position in the unfolding calamity had a cynical gallows humor about it. For several of the confined campers, the irony of having already packed up all their gear and be camping at a bug out location seemed like some kind of miracle and if a disaster happened with a bunch of fellow preppers gathered around them well then so much the better!

The older hands of prepperdom and woodland survival considered such an outlook delusional but still got a kick out of the mirth of it. Bugging out in an unorganized herd of preppers with no plan for community survival creates its own sets of unique problems. Oh, they were way ahead when the poo hit the fan in resources and knowledge and with this group of preppers cooperation was freely and smilingly given. Like I have said before, there was not any formal leadership structure and it was interesting to watch how people related to each other when it came to making suggestions on how to get off this damn island or how to try and survive upon it.

It was surreal to not watch or hear the normal internet forum bickering about what's in your bug out bag or what type of gun they should be carrying to survive such a fictional disaster. They were in it, it wasn't a game anymore and they were adapting quickly.

People related to each other with patience and understanding for the most part just like they did before they lost about 30 foot of shoreline.

"Ok guys, the first order of business for today is that we think the river has calmed down and fallen enough for Crick to attempt a crossing. Now we have been over this before but let me reiterate what this means again because we all got ourselves some hard decisions to make. The first one that should be on everybody's mind is what we are going to do if he finds some official help to get us off here and what we think the chances of that occurring are. We know from the radio that all river traffic is closed on the Tombigbee and Black Warrior rivers. We also know that the majority of all Fish and Game and other boats were severely damaged from the flooding and were also possibly attacked or arsoned in some way because of the way some marina locations were burned to the waterline. We know we got wild fires in the National Forests north of us that are considered acts of terrorism." LowBuck said checking over his list of news and developments.

The radio was manned 24/7 and all updates were posted on a community board and a separate list was given to LowBuck to chair community meetings with. Unexplained wildfires had broken out nationwide as well as the cities themselves had many uncontrolled fires raging. The civilian radio stations which were still broadcasting were distant and they only got bits and pieces of local news when the hourly recap of National news was covered by these stations. The emergency broadcast system was overwhelmed with having to allocate frequencies relevant to so many locales.

"I am going to turn the meeting over to Crick now." LowBuck declared and Crick took the podium.

"I have heard talk from a lot of you about thinking about staying on where we are at. I can understand this line of thinking but I think we all know this would be futile unless we make some major changes and a lot of people need to make some promises they will find they can't possibly keep. We know that there are just too many of us here and too many mouths to feed to survive much longer the way we are going. That little problem hopefully I will soon alleviate and evacuate some of you..." Crick said before happy voices of assent rose expressing that "hell yea" rescue couldn't happen fast enough and that Crick was a hell of a man to undertake such service.

"Quieten down you all! You know that don't apply to everybody! We got folks here that got nowhere to go and no hopes of getting anywhere once they do get off of here!" LowBuck said with a scowl and the former joyous audience became a bit ashamed of their outbursts and settled down.

"Yea, getting back to those who might be staying or going elsewhere. What we all got in common as a primary problem is none of us has a working vehicle on the other side of this river to even drive 10 miles home let alone the distances most of you all need to be traveling. I am lucky enough to only live about 15 miles from here. That's 15 miles I will most likely be walking unless some passing stranger has mercy on me and gives me a ride home." Crick said pausing and letting the momentous task he had of forging a flood blown river safely and then hoofing it home past Lord knows what kind of conditions and people he might meet to a possibly already raided house and then somehow miraculously come back and rescue them all.

"You can do it, Crick!" Morgan cheered and his wife affirmed their faith in him.

Normally Crick and Morgan would have both undertaken this heroic effort of crossing the river and trekking to their homes and the pair would have looked at the task as just one more big adventure to share. However, Morgan had his wife with him and risking his life and leaving her alone on a castaway island was not something to be considered. Besides that, LowBuck and crew couldn't risk both their local guys on one singular dangerous mission. The President and the Vice President don't ride on the same airplane, right? This reasoning was more than logical and reasonable so no further discussion of Morgan going at this time was to be considered.

Crick was all for going it alone rather than traveling with a non-local or untried stranger as a partner but pretty much everyone agreed that at least two people had to undertake this "Preppers Road March" versus just one person for survivability and defense reasons.

Some folks argued three people would have been even better but Crick had argued that with limited resources across the land that two people would be better received and more apt to receive help than three and that in his mind he would still like to go it alone.

"That isn't going to happen, Crick, you don't face danger in anything other than a two man foxhole if you get my drift." The old retired Marine campground volunteer had told him.

"You know better than that man! The Army didn't teach you to build no one man foxhole, it was always a two person affair. What if you got hurt? Who is going to watch your back and drag your sorry ass back to safety? We got too much riding on this rescue effort of yours. You are our best hope and if you do something dumb like twist your ankle or don't see a water moccasin somebody else could of seen for you, we would all be screwed. How about anything that will take an extra pair of strong arms or alert eyes once you get home and that's if you get home. Why it would take weeks for us to give up hope of rescue because something happened to you that we won't know about before we send Morgan and his wife down the same trail we lost you on somehow." Mack the jarhead said.

Crick flinched at the thought of his friend and his wife trying to make the crossing and journey together alone. For one thing she would have to agree to it and for another thing who would they have to depend on if not him to insure their safety?

"How about if me and Morgan and his wife tried to make the initial crossing together? Oh hell no!" Crick thought thinking about such a journey. Physically the lady was more than capable of it, but mentally that was another story. Oh, she could be more than brave enough to attempt it but she wasn't an advocate of the prepper mindset and her mind was more attuned to the social niceties of life. There wasn't going to be anything nice about this little raft and hike trip and the dangers of having such a beautiful woman along such a trip through the backwoods of a chaotic land could not be discounted or denied.

Better she and Morgan stay safe and sound in the known than venture out in the great unknown." Crick admonished himself.

"I see your meaning Sarge, you are kind of stove up in body to make this kind of trip, you got any suggestions on who I might take?" Crick said hoping the man might have a Game Warden or some other kind of official stuck on the island with them that he hadn't thought about and that this federal Parks and Recreation notable volunteer might know about.

"No Man, I want to think I could make that long march with you but I know better. I am medically disabled and would give out on you and need a rest after a few hours. You got a ton of good folks down here at your little prepper whoop de doo and I am sure you can find someone to go with you that can support you better than me or anybody else on staff at this campground. I would have said the Game warden but I haven't seen him since the dams were blown. I tell you what though Son, grab one of the old military guys to go with you, if they are fit enough. Get you somebody that's been tried and true and knows how to overcome adversity and having grit thrown in their gears. I don't need to lecture you Crick, you already are considering what troops you got to deal with ain`t you?" Mack said staring at the younger man intently.

"That I do Mack, you're right I need find me a swimming buddy it's just a matter of choosing who. Thanks for the advice man!" Crick said, extending his hand for a shake.

"Ok Prepper group, as I was saying I will attempt the crossing tomorrow about 8:30 in the morning if the weather and the river appear to be cooperating. LowBuck and I talked to a bunch of you all informally yesterday regarding what we foresaw the other side of this river being like and we all came to several conclusions no one liked. For one thing, I think my chances of finding you an official rescue vessel to come get you off here are slim to none but I am going to try. We all know if I do find any official help then official rules apply. That means no evacuating with guns, knives or bazookas or anything else on a contraband list they going to search you for before you board a boat or a bus to the FEMA camps." Crick said before a chorus of boos and hisses in regard to the word "FEMA Camps" was expressed.

"Shit! You all listen up or we will be here all day! Now if you all pay attention to Crick he might have the educated solution most of you all need!" Morgan groused surprising everyone with the normally taciturn and reserved man's outburst and bringing everyone's attention back to studying every one of Crick's further foreboding words.

"Excuse me folks, but I personally didn't see the value in decamping in mass until Crick brought up one of David's studies and I see the sense in it now. Crick, gimme a minute to explain something if you don't mind." LowBuck said, looking towards Crick for approval.

"Go ahead man, there is a lot to consider and they need to know." Crick said settling in to allow the chairman to have his say.

"Thanks, Crick brought something to my attention yesterday that I hadn't considered. He called it "Cohesiveness. Is that the right word, buddy?" LowBuck said looking to Crick and Morgan for agreement.

"That's right, everybody stay in a group and stick like glue, if we can." Morgan said before Crick could give his affirmation.

"Well, Morgan let me explain it differently since I had to listen to David rattle on about the importance of that word in this instance and never realized how valuable that advice was until now. You all know David was an emergency manager and he is the only one that I know is both a prepper and a professional master of mitigating disasters. He told me last year how he would handle a predicament like we are in now in an official capacity of a government relief force and made some good points to consider." Crick stated eying his deeply attuned audience.

"Well, what did he say?" Rod wanted to know, unsure if a government ride to his house 75 miles away beat even considering trying to hike that far regardless of the circumstances he found himself in.

Prepper Stock, well this year's prepper stock anyway was sort of an eye-opener if you looked at our partial group photo. The graying heavy set participants were more represented than the younger more fit 30 something's. No bunch of weight lifting or exercising health nuts here, just a general slice of America that laughed that we were not the men or women that we used to be. At least we knew our limitations and had no fantasies about our youth as age and physical capabilities had been tried over the last 3 ½ grueling weeks of just plain trying to live on this becoming desolate island.

"Anyway, folks," Crick said taking center stage in front of the speaker's podium, "What David related to me was his experience and studies of Hurricane Katrina on how they bussed out the refugees and how the cops dealt with the hold-out "I ain`t moving types." Crick said wishing he had had an alcoholic beverage to sip on before carrying on.

"David said if for some reason we found ourselves in a situation like we are in now and we were participating in a government mandated evacuation would be what we all know as an enforced disarmament and baggage minimization effort. The crux to all that, is you can't get on a bus or boat without possibly being searched and joining a herd of sheeple and lot of those people will be without honor or morals. That means no guns, no knives and if you don't take advantage of the amnesty to turn your shit in willingly before you get on the bus the guards give you to give up contraband under emergency powers acts, you will be classified a criminal offender and processed accordingly. I asked him what that meant but he said he didn't know the outcome of those yanked out of line with undeclared found contraband and put in handcuffs but it couldn't be good, as enhanced mandatory sentences had been pre legislatively passed for such events just like they had been for merchant price gouging. On the upside of this law enacted meant a bus load of preppers could stick together on the same evacuation bus if they were willing to comply." Crick stated observing the conflicting emotions of his audience.

" If I somehow find you a government assisted relief effort to come get everyone, you are going to have to leave your shit behind and take your chances of riding a bus or being forced marched to a camp without your protections or most of your supplies. However, for some that is not a bad thing and I am not pointing fingers at those that might be physically less capable than your neighbors to not take advantage of the governments' offer of assistance. I am just saying LowBuck and I unfortunately had to consider what we call the "Give up the Gun and Knife" club should some of you choose this as your best option. If this route sounds like your best option to consider and you are comfortable with it, don't get stupid and try to smuggle shit on a bus or a boat. It is martial law now and there is no telling where or what kind of internment camp or jail you will most likely find yourself in. There is no escape or sneakiness you can come up with as they are going to metallic detector wand you coming and going. Now, we have possibly come up with a way for those who choose this route of getting back to their support communities that might make sense to some. Either give your weapons and tools up to someone you like or LowBuck is going to come around with a box you can dispose of your property in for the common good to be distributed later. That means you leave without your pistol or anything with a sharp edge and we give options to those "bugging out" on their own or for whatever reason chooses to remain here." Crick said causing a great deal of consternation and personal self-reflection on the assemblage.

"You all don't start no shit but LowBuck you take this pocket rocket and maybe my fingernail clippers for your collection box." Rod said, surprising everyone to be the first volunteer for the dreaded conspiracy theories of the camps most were aware of.

" Hey Boys and Girls I am a HAM radio operator without his commo gear, my place is at my radio in Millbrook and I got to open lines of communication and touch base with the rest of my fellow operators as soon as I can. Give me a bus ride home and I am in your debt, the hell with thinking I am going to some kind of gulag, folks need us ham operators during disasters and the government already knows this and appreciates us." Said Rod adamantly.

"That's the ticket!" LowBuck said jubilantly putting a check next to his name on a roster he was making.

"I got a question though, LowBuck, you ready for it?" Rod asked, hesitantly.

"That is?" LowBuck inquired.

"Yea, if home is not like I think it's going to be can have my stuff back?" Rod said seriously scrutinizing everyone before he released claim to his goods.

"Most assuredly, are we all in agreement that anyone surrendering pistols and knives and such can get them back if they ever happen to return back to this place?" LowBuck said looking around at everyone who thought it was easy to give assent to such an impossibility.

"I mean it now! If you throw in this box your wares and I lend you another man's or woman's personal protection you have to give it back based on personal demand, am I clear?" LowBuck said studying the faces around him.

"Sure, Sure!" Was the response by most in the crowd and the motion was carried.

"Now, another thing has to be considered." Crick said sternly looking all around.

"In order for those that choose a different course of action like bugging home under their own foot power or deciding to stay on this island, "mums" the word as to our armament or numbers. Let those that desire some anonymity or OPSEC remain obscure from the government numbering and decision making processes. We live free or are indentured based upon those of us that by fate or fortune choose the government path to possibly easier living or further hardship. You know what treason is gentleman and ladies and the penalty for such based upon your own morals and what history predicates. We have no formal rules or even talk of something that might indicate a death penalty but such an infraction of the rule I propose should occur be forewarned and be deathly afraid because there are willing enforcers present." Crick said, letting this message of warning not be dismissed casually.

"I for one have no problem exercising a final option on those that don't heed his words." Many preppers were heard to mumble before going back to rapt attention to such words of wisdom.

LowBuck decided he would take back over the show at this point and either diffuse, reiterate or further explain the ramifications of such a declaration.

"What it all boils down to is we have several groups of people bent on their own survival and even though their paths are quite divergent they all depend on one thing and one thing only." LowBuck said and a restless and confused audience conferred.

"You know I am too far from home to consider bugging back and if one of you Yahoos tells the FEMA man I am holed up on this island with a pistol and an attitude, it won't go well for you if I have to give up and end up in the same camp as you." LowBuck said glaring.

"Enough said LowBuck and I will back that statement up. Do what you want for you and your families but everything that goes on at this island stays on this island. Now, we got basically the following classifications of would be rescues if I can somehow bring some realization to these plans we are discussing. Our first group of folks are those willing to depend on government help if I can find it and I assure you I will do my utmost to try and get it for you. If you are part of that group keep in mind we got us a passel of preppers trying to hide in the background waiting for those FEMA buses to leave that ain't giving up our weapons and plan on trying to walk to home. Then we got whoever is left for whatever reason chooses to remain here and try to start a new life while we carry on with an existence. A lot of people are just too geographically far from home to ever consider getting back... These folks are strangers in a strange land and never considered getting stuck in Alabama and let alone on a desolate island to even consider what the hell they going to do next. I for one am going to give my commitment if I can keep it to getting some supplies back and making their life easier. Hell, I could drown tomorrow or get shot trying to make it home and some of these damn naysayers would think I might be being selfish by never returning to help in their rescue. It's not a game guys, I said I would be back and carry what I can. However, if only one person impeded this effort by saying something stupid like I was bringing guns and ammunition back to my prepper buddies, I would have no problem tacking your hide to my barn." Crick said in a final warning.

He couldn't stomach anyone breaking the codes of honor he and LowBuck prescribed as necessary.

6

TASKS AT HAND

"Ok, this is the plan folks." Crick said leaning on the table that was serving as his podium as everyone quieted down and listened intently.

"I don't have us a chalkboard and I am no artist but if you will all bear with me, I think you will understand the principles of this river crossing we are going to do." Crick said going to a makeshift board which consisted of a desk calendar blotter from the registration station tacked to one of the pavilions support beams.

"The idea is that we will construct two rafts and initially keep them connected with these two litters that Ben the bondsman donated for the giveaway drawing. Think of these two rafts being rigged like a catamaran or out rigger canoe and you will get my meaning." Crick said, doodling two square rafts connected by the two military stretchers forming a platform between them on his makeshift blackboard with a blue sharpie marker.

"Ok, so basically we have us a 4 man boat with two people per raft. Me and Cowboy Prepper will be on one side of the boat and Country Boy prepper and whoever he picks as a volunteer will be on the other side." Crick explained before his sidekick Morgan chimed in.

"No need for a volunteer, I told you this morning that since the rafts were separating midstream and you were going on a mission I would be on the other one and not going far from shore." Morgan said miffed that all his talking to Crick and LowBuck hadn't changed their minds about letting him attempt the crossing.

The idea that the rafts would be somehow disconnected midstream hadn't been brought up yet caused the audience to chatter and question the concept and interfered with Crick's briefing.

"Thanks for the spoiler, Morgan! Settle down you all and listen to Crick." LowBuck growled, taking on the added role of Sergeant at Arms for the meeting.

"Thanks LowBuck, now if Morgan could of waited for a second, I was getting to who was going to be the other rider on the raft and why we were building the rafts this way." Crick said looking meaningfully at Morgan to stay hushed for the moment so the rest of the gathering could understand the plan they had come up with.

Morgan still looked like he had more to say but allowed that this was a good idea and that he would wait on Crick to finish before he had his say.

"Hey by the way Crick it ain't him but me going." LowBuck said confusing the issue even further once more.

"Damn it! Not you too, LowBuck? Not by the Sargeant At Arms at that?" Crick said, exasperated that he had another voice of discontent to deal with.

"Just saying." LowBuck declared before sitting down to let Crick carry on with the meeting.

"Well you ain`t going either and we will get to those reasons later." Crick declared wishing it didn't take so many confounded explanations to just tell folks what he was going to do just to cross the river.

"I am quiet!" Both detractors said almost at once and looked around the assembly for salvation and affirmation.

"Back to business then folks, this joined raft or out rigger idea we have is based on some pretty sound logic that you all need to understand before I explain further the why fors and wherefores of this for lack of a better word disjoinment of rafts later. One of the main points of contention as you all have probably figured out by now is who gets to ride on that other side of the boat and why. Now, LowBuck and Morgan both want to claim that extra spot but if they would think community versus personal ambitions for a moment, they wouldn't even consider it." Crick said trying to chastise the pair into further silence but it didn't look like they were going to have any part of it.

LowBuck and Ben were evidently comparing notes on how they thought the rafts should be joined with the stretchers that served as Crick's backdrop as a speaker and Morgan was just staring bullet holes at him waiting for a chance to speak again.

Crick considered both men's situation for the moment before continuing on a different tack.

"I don't need to tell you all how important a successful crossing of this river, lake or whatever you want to call it as it exists now, is for all of us. We got to be successful and we got to do this by thinking outside the box with safety and comfort for all. I told you all earlier that LowBuck and Morgan were disqualified for this task but because we couldn't get in agreement about it we all gave our solemn promise that we would abide by whatever vote the community supported..." Crick said letting his words weigh heavy on the gathered preppers and outsiders that they themselves would influence the outcomes of whatever the proposed plan might be.

"Back to the drawing board, boys and girls! As my crude drawing here depicts we plan on having two self-autonomous rafts joined at the hip as it were until we hit midstream. There is method in this madness and you need to concentrate on what I am saying to fully understand the principle." Crick said using a hefty Damascus knife his buddy David had given him as a pointer.

The knife he was carrying was not something he would have normally chosen for himself but David had gifted it to him and its beauty and functionality of it had grown on him as he carried it in support of David's Damascus steel promotional efforts. It was far from being cheap steel but it wasn't extravagant, it was more form function and artistic expression to Crick to value and carry the blade with a bit of reverence.

"Ok, we have two 100 yard rolls of paracord that was slotted for the giveaway and donated back to the cause. That river still has a pretty good current to it and we don't want the boat getting too far downstream before Crick and Cowboy can get to the other side. He knows the roads and what's across from us here but not further downstream. The general idea is for everyone to paddle out as far as they can to the middle of the channel while we pay line out and try to keep them from drifting so far. When we get to the end of the line, we will throw it in for them to retrieve. Our end is attached to a buoy of sorts and they have another buoy on the other side of the raft to tie a line on when they disconnect. This is where it gets interesting so bear with me. We originally thought the rafts sailors would retrieve the line and buoy and throw it out in front of them and eventually it will entangle some of that debris on the other side and guide them in but we come up with a different plan. What we are going to do is disconnect the two rafts and let Country boys raft float ahead of Cricks on a hundred yards of line for a bit. Crick can sort of hold position for a while by sea anchoring in the channel using some of them crazy bucket boots that came with those crazy ponchos Julie donated for the giveaway.

"You mean pickle suits, don't ya?" LowBuck said laughing taking a playful poke at Neil who had been the impromptu model for one.

"You never did put the boots on!" Crick said joining in the fun playing with Neil.

"I was saving them for LowBuck to wear next time it rained so he could leave some tracks and give everybody a Sasquatch scare." Neil retorted back amusing everyone.

The Czech ponchos had a pocket inside the skirt of them that contained the damndest piece of military gear anyone had ever seen. It was basically a PVC and rubberized bucket like bootie with tie strings on it that seemed more fitting for an elephant's foot than a human. It had draw strings and ties to secure above your knees and well, was just Soviet bloc crazy in its construction and materials but still served a purpose well.

"Well we are going to secure a couple sets on a paracord dragline and basically try to hold position with them. That could back fire and the current grab them and pull us along but we are thinking they will work well enough to be able to guide us some by letting out line or pulling against them. Anyway, the idea is try to be floating along in two rafts in sort of a C pattern dragging two buoys to snag some debris and make landing on the far shore. I am guessing worst case scenario we hook on to that tugboat washed up on the other side if we miss them logs or that runabout smashed on the remains of that dock over there." Crick said referring to what flotsam and jetsam they could see from their camp sites on this side of the river.

"Can I hold onto your hat for you, Cowboy?" Morgan asked like it was an innocent question knowing it was sure to get a rise out of the old wagon train scout. Yea, Cowboy was actually a wagon train scout with many years' experience scouting for the Alabama Wagon train. That was the reason he was chosen to make the crossing with Crick because it was his job to round up the cavalry if needed but more on that later.

"You ain't wearing my hat, boy!" Cowboy Prepper said playfully holding on to his Stetson like he was trying to keep it on in a hurricane.

"That's right!" SoCal prepper added to the conversation's levity. "I bet he already knows how to turn that

314

Stetson into some kind of personal flotation device!" SoCal said chuckling.

RC Chop reminded everyone not to get Cowboy Prepper going or the next thing we would hear about was how he might try to swim a herd of horses across the river.

Not put off a bit, Cowboy told him he probably could and nobody knew if he was serious or not as he eyed the river and appeared to be doing some mental calculations.

"Hey, not to be joking around but Country Boy, you ain`t going to try to make that crossing in them Carharts are you?" Rod said referring to the large pair of cotton duck overalls he was normally seen in.

"You fall in you are going to sink like a rock." Rod said expressing some good advice.

" No, I got me some blue jeans but them overalls are going with me, it's still cold out here and no telling how long I am going to have to stay on that other shore before I find me a way back over here." Country Boy said with a smile.

"I was wondering did you have any regular pants or not. I thought you and Texas Two-step would have to maybe share wardrobe or you were crossing in your skivvies!" BC truck said laughing and grabbing the straps of his own pair of denim hog washers for effect.

"Hey, I was going to ask to borrow a pair of your skivvies for a sail but I wasn't sure you wore any." Country boy chortled back at the big man.

"Hey, in all seriousness that's a point. Why aren't you all going to try using a sail instead of all that paddling and letting out lines you talking about?" BC Truck, the Rocket stove engineer and metal fabrication specialist, asked.

"Well, they did think of that!" Pop prepper said drawing everyone's attention his way.

" I took a door hinge off each one of the men's and ladies restroom doors and attached it to a two by four to make a collapsible mast but since we don't have the time or materials to make it pivot, it may or may not work. You see them rafts don't have a keel and then there is a matter of creating a usable rudder, etc. and I told Crick if he gives me a day or so I could create something more sea worthy but you all know we are in a hurry." Pop Prepper the master cabinet maker said, miffed that he couldn't use his skills to play boat Wright but people were starving now and there were no electric saws, drills or anything else for manufacturing except axes and large knives.

"Now given time Pops we know you could have built us a grand piano or a giant butcher blocks to float across on." LowBuck said grinning at the old woodworker.

" But Pops, as you know, just making that makeshift crap we got took us two days and if Crick hadn't donated that tool set we would have been hard pressed to just get them deck railings off to make the rafts."

All the camp sites on the bluff had nice wooden decks for the enjoyment of the campers but the railings were bolted on and it took a socket set and a piece of pipe to break the rusted bolts off for removal. Hell, we didn't have one single carpenters hammer or axe amongst us for nail removal and just that fact vexed us immensely.

The rafts that were constructed from makeshift materials and ingenuity wouldn't win any prizes in looks or draft but they seemed functional and practical never the less. Who the hell knew that a simple prep and a good deal on a dozen Czechoslovakian ponchos would save their asses so much. Everyone had tolerated and been bemused by David reciting 28 uses he could think of for them off the top of his head for the cheap Cold war things but no one had even considered what a life saver they turned out to be. Regular military ponchos of this modern era were designed for but one thing, to be light weight and keep a soldier dry. Cost effectiveness, ergonomics, bullshit about the performance of miracle applications of fabric treatments like Gore-Tex had influenced modern preppers and armies not to consider breathable and waterproof didn't equal hard use and replace- by dates under extended harsh conditions with no chance of resupply. Waterproof was waterproof, as simple as that. Yes it wasn't as comfortable but truly waterproof materials that did not depend on an impervious spray-on coating that could wear off, get UV breakdown or deteriorate with age or dumbass factory worker applications was being evidenced everyday as this flock of preppers was finding out for themselves. Yea, it was funnier than hell that all us "prepared preppers" tents leaked first good downfall of rain that sent us scurrying to our vehicles and spending the better part of the day drying our gear out the next, but now no one was laughing at this problematic doubts on our gear. Like it has been said before there was no hierarchy to our encampment when we first got here but times now were changed.

Failure to heed warnings or participate towards mutual efficiency was no longer tolerated and this created opportunities and challenges no one could foresee. Too many people wanted to go hunting or fishing at the same time, too many folks were collecting every edible woodland plant in sight, hoarding them for another day's meal. There just had to be a consistency and a methodology of so many folks trying to live together with these limited resources available and meetings were held to try and contain the misguided exuberance of some to survive over the ignorant actions of others.

The very first meeting Crick and LowBuck called for the community was about a funny or necessity minded thing they had both experienced that had explained to them the hazards of close living with humans that haven't experienced the woods as a sustainable habit that must be nurtured.

Crick walked away from his camp for a call of nature and accidentally stepped in someone's poo and had himself a conniption fit that some A-hole hadn't buried their crap and now he had it on his shoes. Generally speaking, in his days of camping, a shovel with a roll of toilet paper shoved down the handle was an indication and the tool to go take care of your business off in the woods when there were no crappers available.

Apparently someone thought shitting in the woods was a squat and forget but with 75 folks in the area of operations that dog would never hunt. LowBuck had grabbed his shovel and his wiping gear one day headed towards a likely spot when he came across a buzz fly smoking heap of somebody's excrement uphill from him that would have washed over his campsite next rain that also set him off.

Ramro was pissed because whatever kid had crapped close to his muskrat hole he was attempting a trap at evidently looked like there was a grizzly bear in the area and had run them off and it was decided that sanitation was equal to salvation and we must do something about establishing a general sanitation order for the camps.

Latrine duty was not a subject or duty any one was willing to undertake outside of the military-minded experienced boys and girls trained in the protocol with it but all the campers acknowledged the need. Digging a slit trench is easy, getting everyone to use it with the stench and the bugs was another thing, so as we say in the military, being a screw up was punished with duty to maintain them things but such discipline needed to be enforced with logic, reasoning and a bit of attitude adjustment and a hierarchy was formed.

Somebody needed to enforce rules and a prescribed penalty needed to be stated. Weird how crap got everyone together to enforce rules and choose leadership but it happened. Caught pooping in a non-designated area would give you shit detail of throwing extra wood ash from the campfires onto the sewage pits. Collecting ashes for the task was considered a minor reminder of what was in store for you for a minor infraction of the rules of this community they seemed to need to enforce daily.

People just don't tend to think outside the box daily unless there is a penalty and shit was getting out of control as folks scented a trap or walked a trail that would discourage game being taken daily. A bunch of preppers with survival on their minds would transgress on other people's efforts inadvertently as they learned distance and recognition meant more than an apology when all the chips were down.

The only solution to so many prepper efforts they thought could assuage their hunger or anyone else's, was to get organized and try the community effort thing Crick and LowBuck had said.

The two men and many others in this community of castaways advocated was a joint effort of getting things done by allocating duties to the best prepared to undertake the tasks at hand. Of course, personalities came in to play but it was decided that it was best man or woman to do it and no complaints would be broached unless simple reasoning could tell you different.

A man like Neil or his wife who could hit that target with that 22 Rough Rider pistol of his consistently, was on squirrel detail. He would wander the camps, question occupants to the mannerisms and habits of the observed wildlife in the area and move on or take shot. The 'hey asshole don't shoot a squirrel with a 9mm that would vaporize a squirrel' when his 22 was best suited for the task went unsaid.

7

ANCHORS AWAY

"Hey Crick! You about ready to shove off?" LowBuck bellowed from the shore where he and most of the prepper community had gathered to see the wayfarers off.

"Just about. Let me make sure these things are going to hang together first!" Crick yelled back about 50 ft. from shore and proceeded to gingerly bounce the questionable wood frame up and down on his side of the raft.

"Dang boy, don't swamp us!" Cowboy prepper groused while holding onto the wood slats that were already sloshing far more water over them than expected.

"Yea settle down Crick, I ain't trusting that outrigger not to let go before it's supposed to anyway." The bondsman complained but was still grinning as he held on to his makeshift sail mast trying to keep his balance.

"Better to get dunked out here than when we get to the middle of the river." Beauregard aka "One Ugly Guy" on YouTube declared bouncing his butt up and down while holding the makeshift tiller.

"Holy Crap! Stop that Beauregard, you are going to bust the slats out of the decking." Ben said watching his rudder man now doing a walrus rocking motion to the rig that caused everyone to hang on for dear life.

"Don't be trying any of that shit midstream you all! I saw your centerboard come out of the water and if that is all it takes to do that then both of us ought to think twice before trying set a sail." Crick said pondering the usefulness of the improvised dagger boards they had just recently affixed to their rigs to try and add some stability to the rickety rafts.

A couple of doors had been sawn in half with a bow saw and had been shoved down the slots in the rafts once they cleared the shallows to reduce the lean of the rafts and keep them from tipping if the sails caught a strong wind. Since the rafts were basically not much more than floating wooden squares, sailing or steering them was doubtful and the sailors depended more on the current like the old flat bottom river trading barges of old to arrive at their destinations.

The use of sails on the tiny craft was hotly debated, because most folks saw no problem giving them a try but those that had some experience from their childhood remembered all too vividly how easy it was to tip a purpose built sailboat let alone something that resembled a wooden pallet with a log attached. The naysayers offered some half remembered sailor tips and tricks to avoid such a catastrophe and the centerboard addition was their inspired idea.

"Let's get this rodeo on the road, Crick. You about ready?" Loomis said impatiently.

"I am ready, how about you all?" Crick said to the other rafts' occupants.

"Anchors away!" Ben declared and smiled as Loomis gave his 'wagons ho' signal to LowBuck and Morgan to payout line and let the rafts drift into the channel.

The first 50 or so yards was pretty uneventful but as soon as the makeshift craft started to enter the deeper channel, it picked up momentum and water sloshed across the flat decks of the somewhat unstable craft.

LowBuck end Morgan quickly wrapped the line around a tree to relive the strain of holding the line and keep it from burning their fingers as they paid out line much faster than they had anticipated.

"This thin line ain`t going to hold." Morgan said worriedly and then started laughing with the rest of the group as Crick struck a comical Captain Morgan pose on his raft and Loomis and the rest pretended to be galley slaves rowing with their improvised 2x4 paddles.

""Well, looks like they are having fun anyway," LowBuck chuckled before calling out to the raft they were getting ready to let go the line because it wasn't going to hold.

Crick quit his clowning and told them to heave the line as he made ready to pull it and the buoy in.

"So much for their lifeline." Crick mused and told Loomis to throw the sea anchors out to try to slow their downstream progress.

"Make ready to separate." Crick called over to Ben and Beauregard on the other raft as he and Loomis started to loosen the knots on their side that would allow the two rafts to split and become autonomous.

"All set! You all be careful and good luck there, Captain Crick!" Ben yelled back smiling.

"See you when you get back!" Beauregard said waving farewell and throwing out his snag line buoy into the river far to their front.

When the rafts separated, the unburdened raft of Ben and Beauregard picked up speed heading further downstream.

§

LANDFALL

Crick and Loomis finally poled their raft to a likely landing point and surveyed the steep slope up from the river.

"This is about as good as it gets I guess." Crick stated flatly surveying the steep wooded incline.

"I guess you're right, let's land this thing and get going then." Loomis said pushing along the bottom with his makeshift 2x4 oar.

They tied off the raft to a tree to keep it from drifting and began their steep ascent, grabbing branches and bushes for handholds to assist their progress up the slippery slope.

"Any idea where we are at?" Loomis asked puffing along climbing up after Crick.

"That's kind of a yes and kind of a no. What I mean is, I know what general direction to go but I have no idea how deep these woods are until we get to a paved road and figure out exactly where we are at." Crick said unsure of what lay in front of them.

They had drifted a couple miles from where he hoped to have landed at and the terrain they were surveying looked pretty primitive. There was no telling whether or not they were on private land or they were in part of lakes adjoining the National Forest.

Crick and Loomis had created for themselves sort of a hybrid overboard and get home bag for this little jaunt they found themselves on and neither one of their kits contained any food. Well that wasn't exactly true, they both had two MRE foil pouches of fortified Cocoa scrounged from the starving prepper community that were wistfully donated to their important cause.

These would give them some much needed energy and help assuage some of the hunger pains they already felt. Double portions of food had been allotted for them to have a bit of an edge in escaping from castaway island but the days foraging for the community hadn't produced anything more than some oxalis leaves and green briar roots flavored with a couple fish in a watery stew.

Fifty people and two fish doesn't divide well and the lucky fisherman who had caught the two small pan fish had announced that at the next meeting this policy of community sharing had to be adjusted or no one was going to be strong enough to perform any of the tasks needed to survive around here.

Besides they loudly declared that it was just plain unfair to expect them to always donate their hard won bounty when sharing was so useless in the long run. There were just too many people and several folks proposed going to more of a squad support system where members of a squad were depended on to support the individuals it contained.

Small groups that were codependent made more sense
and had evolved and been depended upon historically under the
direst conditions. From Civil war prisons, Japanese and
Vietnamese prisoner of war camps to the Death camps of the
holocaust, men and women's ultimate individual survival relied
on the camaraderie and support of small close knit groups to
separate them from those less resourceful or resilient than
themselves.

Daily tasks of cooking, cleaning, nursing the sick etc.
could be shared and free up others to scrounge or defend what
meager foodstuffs were brought back under mutual survival
pacts that somehow seemed to endure the worst that man and
nature could throw at them. Many of the preppers of the
community had already formed loosely allied groups while
others had decided they would share with no one and thought
their chances were better playing lone wolf survivor far distant
from the main group.

As the disaster progressed, many others thoughts drifted
to taking such a course of action but reason and caution overrode
such divisive and ill-informed moves. Better shelter, more
resources and survival knowledge was present here and like all
indigenous peoples of old they knew that safety and survival
relied on community and not outcast individual efforts.

"Loomis, I figure we got about 4 days hard walking if we
can make about 5 miles a day and don't run into any trouble or
can't talk someone into giving us a ride." Crick said getting a
compass bearing and trying to guesstimate where they were at
the moment.

"Speaking of trouble, you keep your eyes peeled for hunters and any dumbass playing bug out survivalist." Loomis said scanning the woods that seemed to go on forever.

"Yea, the brim on that Stetson of yours does kind of look like a deer's antlers in this light." Crick quipped back.

"You and everybody else's damn hat jokes. I tell you what, wait till it rains or we get back out in the hot sun and you will wish you had such a fine bit of hat haberdashery such as this." Loomis retorted.

"I know man; I am just funning with you. I like that hat but seriously, I guess we need to think about how loud we are talking. On the one hand it allows the snakes to get off the trail or warn hunters of our approach; on the other hand I don't want to be alerting anyone that might think we got food with us or admire that .45 you got on your hip too much." Crick said pondering their dilemma.

"I don't plan on talking too much anyway but you got a point. Hey other than me maybe concealing my pistol, what kind of suggestions you got about approaching somebody's house when we see one?" Loomis said calling for a break so they could rest for a moment and strategize.

"Man, that's a hard one to consider. It's been weeks since this crap happened and folks will be desperate and more fearful of strangers than normal. Outside of hollering at the house when we approach and not looking like we are sneaking about or reaching for a weapon, I don't have too many other, ideas." Crick said adjusting his belt.

"I see you got the same problem I do, my belts on its last factory notch now and I will probably be boring me another hole in the morning." Loomis said observing his traveling companion.

"I ain't going to say a damn thing about folks that carry extra weight after this shit. At least you got a ways to go before you can fit into my pants." Crick said only half joking.

"I don't know there is something to be said about being a bit lean already. I tell you what, all joking aside about my hat, let me approach whatever house we find alone and you hang back and watch. A cowboy hat says something about the man or woman wearing it these days and it beats that ball cap you're wearing." Loomis said pondering his Marlboro man caricature and full mustache.

"I hadn't thought about that point but whoever answers the door around here is likely to have a hat similar to mine on." Crick advised.

"Exactly! All kinds of southern country folks wear various kinds of ball caps but this fedora of mine says I am stockman, kind of like a straw farmers hat identifies them and that creates a mental picture of a man's work ethics and honesty in people when they first meet. An expectation, you might say." Loomis offered.

"Well, at least you ain't wearing a sombrero but I get your point. It's an odd one, mind you but we will play the game that way." Crick said with a smile and stood up and reached down to pull the bigger man to his feet and resume the trail.

Loomis regained his feet chuckling and Crick asked him what he was laughing about.

"I was just thinking about them two heathens Beauregard and Ben having this same conversation, who you think is going to go first or are they going together? Loomis said non chalantly.

"Damn boy, I thought we were going to be quiet! That's funnier than hell to think about. You know what kind of shirt Ben was wearing today?" Crick said laughing.

"No I didn't notice, some kind of black pull over thing, oh I got ya! Damn thing had a bail bondsman's sheriff star and company logo on it!" Loomis said guffawing.

"Man I hope he thinks about that before he knocks on a door for a social visit, I know he will but it's still funnier than hell to think about a down and out bail bondsman knocking on some fugitive from justices door these days asking for a ride or a food handout." Crick said following a deer trail through the briars and bushes that formed the under story of this section of rivers normal hardwoods and pines.

"This has been clear cut not too long ago." Loomis observed.

"I been noticing that and it gives me some hope civilization is not too far off but the park service and power company land tends to do that building firebreaks or conservation projects. Hard to say, lots of land holders sell off wood and don't replant after cashing their timber in at tax time. It's too early in the season for me to get any kind of read on the vegetation how long it's been since somebody thinned the woods around here but I am guessing it was done by one of those wild cat pulp wood operators and that means private landowner." Crick said, surveying the blazed clearing they were approaching.

"That could mean we are approaching someone's backyard unannounced instead of politely approaching their front door with a country holler to announce ourselves." Loomis said grimly.

"Yea, some folks got some funny notions about how they view trespassing. I ain`t worried about it though, no fencing in sight, look for deer stands might be hunting property but most likely someone just sold off the wood to pay on mortgages or taxes." Crick said, feeling uneasy stepping off into the clearing and looking around for any structures to indicate the lands purpose.

"I say we follow the wood piles and overgrown truck ruts back to whatever road they came in on rather than trying to blaze through. What do you want to do Crick?" Loomis said looking first left then right and back to the woodland on the far side of the field they were traversing.

"Let me get a compass read and I will give you an opinion. Scout around a bit and figure out which direction looks like had the most traffic meantime and we will make a decision." Crick said trying to make sense of a compass bearing and dead reckoning towards remembered landmarks he hoped he would eventually trip over.

"Ok I will head towards the wood line and most likely swing left, you go the same way once you done with your calculations and look to the right. I'll meet you back in the center over by where the forest starts again in about 15 or 20 minutes, ok?" Loomis said as Crick started digging out a basically useless map until they found a marked road.

"Sounds good to me." Crick said looking down at the map pondering and trying to get some kind of read off the little button compass they were using.

The field was covered in scrub oak and bushes and it was easy to lose sight of each other as they undertook their explorations.

Crick eyed the worn trails and tire and tractor tread tracks that dotted his side of the field. It looked like the majority of the traffic followed a trail down the center of the property but were they hauling wood out to the left or to the right? He pondered.

"Hey, that looks like a vehicle or trailer assembly area farther down to his right. That needs closer inspection, Crick considered, and headed down that way to try to make some meaning out of the signs.

Loomis trudged along a caterpillar track that had truck tire prints running parallel towards it looking for wherever they had a skidder yard or loader imprint when he spied an area that had a bunch of turned up red clay weathering under the sun. He was dismayed when he finally got there to find the cat tracks he had been following appeared to end in a boggy marshy area that seemed to have had equipment at one time bogging down coming and going.

"Well this must be an off shoot logging road from the main line. Damn sure wasn't an entry point off the main road or they would have log road bedded it." Loomis thought

considering the practice of timber crews to use logs and branches to make a more permanent road to a logging area. Well, he and Crick could puzzle it out later, meantime it was time for him to backtrack and tell his buddy what he had found out so far. Loomis thought to himself sweating bullets from his hurried excursion and headed back in the general direction of their rally point.

Crick arrived at what he thought was a truckers rally point or a loading zone and tried to make heads or tails out of the aged and rain deteriorated signs in the dirt. Lots of traffic had been here at some time or another but what it all meant was quite a puzzle. Evidently who ever had been cutting trees out here had themselves some lunch and serviced some equipment he observed from the empty oil and hydraulic cans as well as an occasional sandwich baggie or fast food bag from Mc Donald's but as to which way the road they came from to the right or left was a mystery. Even though the amount of litter left around by the work crews disturbed him immensely as uncaring lazy fools blight on the land he was glad to see it because it told volumes as to what it was he was trying to discern. The fast food bags were particularly intriguing as those items could only mean one thing. Civilization and town was closer than he expected and this was reassuring. No one sack lunches from happy meal land and because this type of work was normally done on a very brief lunch break, that meant he was within 10 minutes or so from a major thorough fare by car. Most roads around here run anywhere from 55 to 45 mph from the interstate so that put him how far by foot, he began to ponder before a voice startled him.

"What are you doing boy? Up to no good I bet." A blue plaid shirted grizzled old man called at him from the wood line with a casually held shotgun pointing off handily in his direction.

"Uh, nothing sir. Got myself a bit lost and trying to find my way back home." Crick said trying to sound friendly but not quite carrying it off with the sudden frog in his throat trying to strangle his voice.

"You lose something? What are you doing poking about on Mc Cloud land son? This land is posted boy." The old man said slowly walking out of the wood line in his direction.

"I ain't lost nothing my friend, I was just poking about in all this trash trying to figure out where the hell somebody got them a Mc Donald burger in this god forsaken place and how far it was to go get me one." Crick said, trying to add some levity to the situation but not impressing the old cuss a damn bit.

"Damn pulp wooders got no respect for nobody leaving all that trash lying around and neither do you either by sneaking about in my woods. You some kind of hobo or backpacker or something looking for a place to crash?'" the old geezer said lowering his weapon a bit under one arm and touching one shoulder indicating Crick's sling pack he had on.

"Neither, like I said I am just lost and needing directions to the main road. Highway, I mean, you mind doing me a favor and pointing that scattergun of yours in a different direction." Crick said a bit imploringly.

"I might, just as soon as I find out what it is you're actually doing poking around here." The old goomer said covering the distance between them much quicker than Crick thought the gangly old sod buster could.

"Seriously, man I am lost. I ain't doing shit but walking in the woods trying to find my home, if you would be kind enough to point me in the right , I would be much obliged." Crick said nervously wondering where the hell Loomis was at the moment.

"Gave you a scare didn't I? You were so damn intent on poking around in that trash you didn't see me standing out here in plain sight ready to say how do you do. What are you doing out here, poaching? We don't allow any poachers around here even though I know that times are hard." The old man told him halting about 15 feet from him and still keeping the shotgun at the ready even though it wasn't pointed in Crick's direction.

"No I ain't poaching, I am just passing through. I will be happy to get the hell out of here if you just let me and my friend pass..." Crick began before the old man instantly brought the shotgun back to bear on him.

"Friend! Whose with you and where is he at?" the old man said looking in back of Crick and then quickly looking to the right and left.

"If you just let me explain." Crick began before Loomis called out from the same place the old man had come from.

"He is over here."Loomis declared standing next to a knarled old oak with his 45 pistol leveled in a gunner's stance in the old man's direction.

"Now ain't you a sneaky bastard! Come on over here cowboy and let's parley a mite before we both do something we might regret." The aged veteran said looking over his shoulder but not lowering his shotgun aimed at Crick an inch.

"I might, put up that old coach gun first, we mean no harm." Loomis called out still in his 4 point stance with 45 auto cocked and locked on the center of a pair of patched overalls that looked as threadbare as the wrinkled old gnomes pate.

"I dunno Cowboy, seems we got us what used to be called back in Roy Rogers day a Mexican standoff. If you pull that trigger I am going pull mine and your friend here is history. Now seeing you ain`t got nothing but that pistol you are liable to miss my skinny ass and I might manage to get a   shot off at you too and let me tell you Pa Pa don't miss when he aims his gun !" The old codger said belligerently and went back to watching Crick's every move because he was the closest.

"Come on old man, this ain`t necessary." Loomis began before a gravelly sweet voice in back of him advised him to be still.

"I don't like me no cowboys." An old black woman said with a leveled 30-30 Marlin from the Muscadine grape patch off to his left.

"Oh Shit" Loomis said to the large white haired cotton dressed black woman looking at him with murder in her bloodshot eyes.

"HA! Sneaky Pete you just thought you had the drop on old Bowman, Bertha you ventilate his liver if he don't put that pistol down nice and smooth. Now then, what's your name son and you best really tell me this time what has got you traipsing around with the sheriff on Mr. Mc Clouds property." Bowman demanded.

"Do what he says, Loomis." Crick said trying to figure out how to get to his 40 cal pistol and save the day but soon giving up that notion.

"Look here, Bowman is it? My names Crick and that's Loomis and like we said we don't mean no harm. Our raft washed up on the shore about a mile and a half from here and we ain't doing nothing but trying to make our way through these woods to get to a main road and bring some help back to our friends stranded at Deer Lick creek." Crick said huffily.

"Caught you in another bald-faced lie you damn revenuer, what kind of song and dance you think I am going to believe about you and that damned sheriff riding a raft over here? Check his credentials, Bertha! Is he a state or Fed ABC man?" Bowman called back as Bertha secured Loomis's pistol and removed his wallet from his back pocket.

"He ain't got no badge of any sort, Clem, he just got a picture of himself and them credit card things you told me about." Bertha bellowed back.

"Bring him up here and shoot him if he gets froggy, Bertha, might be one of them undercover types." Clem aka Bowman said motioning for him to get to his knees before forcing Loomis to do the same before he examined everyone's ID's.

"They look ok, Bertha one of these days you got to get around to learning to read, comes in handy sometimes. Ok boys, you can stand up but keep your distance as we sort things out. Now what possessed you to get on a raft and sail the river?"

Clem said laughing and then asked them and informed Bertha about his favorite book he once read called Huckleberry Finn.

"I remembers that Book Clem you told it to my sister's son Jeremiah before but it makes no sense a fat cowboy and a country redneck decide to take them a ride on a homemade raft." The old stand in dress silhouette sizer for a bottle of Aunt Jemima`s syrup said.

"We sort it out, let's take them to the house and hear the rest of this tall story." Clem said motioning for them to grab their gear and walk in front of them.

"You take them to your house, Clem. I don't want no cowboys in mine." Bertha said poking at Loomis with the barrel of her rifle.

"What's up with the not liking cowboy shit" Loomis complained being guided down a hidden trail.

"Oh don't mind her, you see living this far back in the woods we never got movin' pictures and the one time I decided to show her the town and carried her to the motion picture show a movie called Blazing Saddles was on and she thinks cowboys are more prejudiced than rednecks."

"Want to make him sing?" Clem said laughing at Bertha who still eyed Loomis warily, referring to one of the more memorable parts of that particular movie.

"Doo Dah! "Doo Dah!"" Loomis sang hoping Clem was joking with a disarming smile that Bertha seemed to enjoy and his antics the sound of his voice singing the chorus of the song

"The Camptown Ladies Sing This Song" cracked Crick and
Clem up, laughing.

"I suppose it be alright to go to my place first but it don't
seem fittin that he got that hat on iffin it means he has got it in
for black folks." Bertha commented unsure as to the mans'
beliefs and intentions.

"Bertha, I done told you there has been many a black
cowboy ain`t that right loonyness? I mean er excuse me fella,
Loomis. Damn boy, you can't sing worth a damn." Clem said
still having fun but humorously relaxing with his two captives.

"Oh yea, they even had buffalo soldiers in the Cavalry.
The Indians called them buffalo soldiers because the hair on
their heads reminded them of the revered animals." Loomis said
with a friendly smile.

"Did he just say I look like some kind of a reverted
buffalo animal? Why I will shoot that pot belly right off him!"
the 73 year old grandmother that probably outweighed him by
60 pounds protested while shaking a finger in his direction.

"No he did nothing of the kind Bertha, calm down old
girl. He just sort of gave you a backward compliment but we talk
about that later.. Now back to business, boys ain`t nobody run
shine here since my pappy and her husband got busted for doing
it back in the 60`s and them folks all are dead and gone and long
buried. Me and Bertha live back in a couple old sharecropper
shacks and watch over this land. 5 generations of share cropper
and slave been through here and we are all that's left to tell the
tale and when we gone so is the memory of it all, bad and good
times." Clem Bowman declared, poking Crick in the side with

his shotgun barrel and immediately calling a halt to the procession as it clinked the metal of his concealed pistol.

"Damn you trying to be some kind of a tricky Dick, search them better, Bertha!" Clem declared and both men endured a much more intimate search by the old black woman who pretty much seemed to enjoy her task more than either one wanted to recognize or acknowledge, although she did get a muffled protest out of Loomis.

"They didn't have nothing more on them except for a couple of fancy pocket knives. The fat one had some chewing tobacco though," Bertha said stealing her a chaw and offering Clem one.

"Fat one? Why you big walrus." Loomis started to exclaim before Bertha's rifle barrel reminded him he shouldn't try insulting her further.

"I still want to know why you dumbasses decided to get on a raft what with all them rich folks riding power boats everywhere up and down the river. I would reckon that one of them would of gave you a ride if you asked them nice." Clem said trying to wrap his head around this strange encounter.

"Damn Clem I been trying to tell you since we first met that we had no choice but to ride a raft over here after them f-wording terrorists blew the dams" Crick protested before getting a shotgun barrel poke from Clem.

"Look here sonny, she might be a white haired old mammy but that old mammy was my sons old mammy and her old mammy raised me and her mammy raised my Pa so you best be respectful and watch your language in her presence." The old caretaker said of the old custom in some parts of the south to have a black dearly beloved maid raise many a white boy or girl as a nanny to the family and be protected like a bulldog guarding its bone while keeping those lucky children out of all kinds of mischief from cradle to sometimes grave.

"I meant no disrespect. I am sorry, Maam" Crick said apologetically. I had a wonderful mammy myself help raise me when I was young, rest her soul but I couldn't think of a more descriptive word for whoever caused the chaos that sent us on this trip. By the way what have you heard about them terrorists country of origin?" Crick said marching along with his fellow prisoner Loomis.

"What they mean country? Nothing wrong with being country or from the county." Bertha protested.

"You need to get out more, Bertha. Country as in foreigners." Clem suggested to the beetle browed old woman.

"I think they saying somebody from another country exploded a dam. Was it the Russkies?" Clem asked, pausing their walk down the trail.

"I don't know who the hell it was, all I know is the roads got cut to Deer Lick campgrounds and I am supposed to carry back a rescue party before they all starve to death." Crick said ominously.

"Do what? Boy make some sense,. Some yahoo tried to blow up the dams? Why didn't you just wait for the police or the Army? Now tell me what it is exactly you thought you were going to accomplish with all this rafting and hiking and mighty concrete dams blowing up and such." Clem said rubbing his noggin in dismay and confusion.

"We been trying!" Loomis protested.

"I want to listen to this one here" Bertha said indicating Crick and motioning for Loomis to sit down on a fallen log on the trail.

"Ok it's like this. You know them two dams they built that closed the rivers off and formed the lake? Well they are gone and that camp ground that was up on the bluff between the two rivers is now an island and it has a bunch of our friends stranded on it." Crick said so Bertha and Clem could follow his story so far.

"And you rafted ya'll selves over to here from that there island, didn't you." Bertha said knowingly, catching on and looking to Clem for approval, beaming her 'I can be smart too' look.

"And Al Quida terrorists blew up the dams." Clem said knowingly, nodding at Bertha like he knew all about such things already.

Crick started to correct him and tell him it was pronounced Al Qaeda and he didn't know if it was them or not but he decided that would only confuse the issue even more, so he carried on.

"Yea, terrorist criminals blew up the dams and we had to raft over to escape from the island. Then when we got to the shore on this side we walked several miles through the woods and bumped into you all and here we sit like bumps on a log." Crick said watching Clem and Bertha glancing back and forth at each other and trying to form words to carry on further.

"Well you ain`t said what you planned on doing once you got over here yet. We already know you're here and how you got here." Clem said with feigned exasperation for Crick to get to the point.

"Yea we already knows why you here, we wants to know what is you doing next." Bertha said scooting Loomis over and having a seat beside him on the log to listen better in the shade.

Loomis didn`t know what to do when the large women's ample bottom started rolling in his direction and his first reaction was to try and stand up and make space for the lady. Well he got his butt about one inch over the log about the same time she put a little hip action into her scoot and Loomis and Crick ended up hugging and hanging on to each other in order to not go airborne off the end of it which tickled the hell out of Clem who was standing there watching the spectacle.

"Ha! Bertha, I ain`t had so much fun in a coons age. Crick I am going to sit down with you all; I believe your story but you got to finish it before me and Bertha feed you supper and send you on your way." Clem said sitting down but still retaining Crick`s pistol in his belt.

"Well I am happy to hear that, Clem." Crick said.

"Me too!" Loomis echoed before turning quickly to see Bertha appearing to be sneaking up on him if that was possible with her close proximity and rather wide girth.

"Now that we all friends, can I touch it?" Bertha said somehow managing to get her head half way over her shoulder and starting to reach with her far hand.

"Touch WHAT!" Loomis sort of shriek croaked while sliding Crick into Clem with his own bit of butt weight.

"Now Bertha, you know you can never touch a man's cowboy hat!" Clem said, regaining his seat and straightening it.

"Well, I asked him politely first real nicely, didn't even touch when I had a gun on him. Did I Loomis? We friends now, Clem said so. Can I touch it?" Bertha pleaded.

"Now, Bertha, I told you when we was growing up that it was the code of the west never to touch another man's cowboy hat." Clem said reverently placing his hand over his heart.

Crick and Loomis both suppressed grins as Bertha acted like a child being scolded for approaching a hot stove and Clem acted like he had just said the most profound thing that had ever been said.

"She can touch it, it's a special day, Clem." Loomis said and doffed his Stetson and handed it to Bertha who received it like it was the holy grail itself.

"Wow, it's kind of heavy and stiff!" she said examining it further. "Look here, it's got a bow on its underwear!" she said peering inside of it.

"A hat has a liner, not underwear." Loomis said wresting his hat back from the woman to Clem and Cricks hoots of laughter.

"Dang, you all are fun!" Clem said chuckling and motioning for them all to come on and follow him down the trail.

"Get back to your story Crick and leave Loomis alone Bertha." Clem said as he led the way.

"I ain`t bothering him none," Bertha called back from the rear of the column.

"His haid ain't near as big as I thought it was." Bertha commented which made Crick have to choke back a laugh.

"Wait a minute, wait a minute." Clem said chuckling and calling a halt to the hike.

""Bertha you get up here and lead the way home. We ain`t going to make no progress with you talking to Loomis all the way home." Clem said grinning at Bertha`s Aahwwww! look she couldn't play with Loomis any more.

"Thanks buddy!" a relieved Loomis said.

"Watch out for the barn," Clem whispered back to a "Oh shit" look from Loomis before telling Crick to carry on with what his rescue plan was supposed to be.

"Ok Clem, Bertha, on with the story. I only live about 15 miles from here I think and the idea was we basically find help and notify someone to get them folks off that castaway island. I don't know whether or not phones work or not around here after that cyber-attack on the country's grid." Crick said starting to explain.

"Them Al Quidey used swords? Hear that Bertha they was toting sabers. Them are crazy bastards Bertha, kind of like them stories Uncle Willie told how he got that samurai sword off that Jap officer. They promote the craziest dumbest one to carry a big pig sticker and charge the enemy while they carry guns and run after him to make sure that he does it. I guess they think if we watching that crazy bastard hollering he is going to kill us and were waiting for one of his own men to shoot him and save us the trouble we won't think about shooting at them running behind until they get too close. Doesn't work though, Uncle Willie just said shoot the crazy bastard in the lead first or whoever is hollering loudest with the most stripes. Go ahead Crick resume your story." Clem said hollering at Bertha to be thinking about what they were having for supper since they had company today.

Loomis started to interject something snide but Crick laughingly cleared his throat and said to let it ride.

"Anyway, I don't know who I can find in charge of anything to help get them folks off the island but once we do and we get them off there safely they are going to need some help getting home. You know the gas pumps aren't working a thousand miles in either direction now that the powers been cut, don't you Clem?" Crick asked.

"See, I told you to fill up 3 weeks ago, but nooooooooooo. Then you had to get drunk in the truck and run the battery down listening to the radio!" Bertha complained.

"Hey you were in on that, we had to listen to that school station that has gotta tell you everything about a jazz song or big band hit before they play it for ya." Clem complained.

"Well who the hell listens to race cars on the radio? You never even seen a race car let alone been to one of them racetracks you listening to. Besides, how you tell the race cars from the static on there without an announcer, anyway?" Bertha fired back.

"Don't mind us, bickering is one of the things we do to pass the time around here. Truck won't start until we get a jump so we can't help you out none with a ride to town. Got an old bicycle if you can ride it. Slim Furlong lives about 6 miles yonder way, he give you a ride if you tell him I told you to." Clem said as they walked out into a field across from 10 cinderblock and wood ramshackle shacks. You could see which ones might be still serviceable and not collapsing and one had an old blue and white pickup truck sitting in front that had seen its better days.

"That's my truck over there in front of Berthas, told you she was in on that hoot nanny the other night. I live over there on the other end of the field." Clem said pointing at another assemblage of tin roofed shanties and a few big wooden barns.

"This here is what we call the bottoms. Used to be reserved for colored folks. Still is, I reckon." Bertha said with a giggle, smiling mischieviously at Clem.

"They called it the bottoms because it's at the bottom of the hill. I told her to move up to one of the houses up by me years ago but she is stubborn and won't do it." Clem said complaining.

"Don't listen to that crazy old white man. Them houses up by the barn yard ain't no better than what we has in the bottoms excepting his house which was reserved for the foreman. I keep telling him he ain`t no foreman anymore but you should hear how he tries to boss me around. Least ways down here in the bottoms I ain`t so accessible for him to holler at me to help him do something." Bertha replied with a shame on you look towards Clem.

"Now Bertha you know I don't boss you as much as you nag me. It ain`t fittin that we still got us a black and white section on this plantation. Told you back in the 90`s we should integrate the place just like the schools are now and invited you to my neighborhood." Clem said protesting.

"Don't listen to that old fish eyed fool. He just don't like having to walk down to my house every day for breakfast and wants me closer to cook and clean for him." Bertha said fussing but with a slight smile.

"Now I tell you what Loomis, you ain`t going to believe this but she is the most contrary and most prejudiced one on this place. Her chickens lay brown eggs, she's got Black Nubian goats, raises black magic zucchini, why the only thing integrated down here is that black and white jersey milk cow she has got that is more cantankerous than that world's oldest black mule she keeps around for no other reason than he don't like me." Clem advised stopping momentarily to wipe his brow with an old blue bandanna.

"That's another thing, every Christmas she gives me a blue bandanna and I give her a red one. Told her we ought to swap one time and she gave me a look and a talking to like you wouldn't believe mister. I am telling you I ain`t seen her so riled since that social worker offered to exchange her white picture of

Jesus for a black one." Clem said about to carry on with his tirade further but Bertha pointed her weapon at him and advised him there were places for people who blaspheme like him and told a bit of that story.

"Now, I don't know what color that man might have been and it don't matter to me as long as somebody don't tell me he is red like the devil. That was my mammy's picture and I like it. Besides Jesus is always white now my grandma says, he is the Holy Ghost now right? She tell me not to worry about folks saying they seen a ghost around the old cemetery. Might have been Jesus or Saint Peter coming to lead somebody up the golden staircase to heaven." Bertha declared in a don't- mess-with-me admonishment.

"See what I mean? You just can't talk to her about modernization, religion, politics or them critters she keeps." Clem said sulking.

"I got mines and you got yours. You move up to the big house if you want to put on airs. You as poor as any field hand that ever worked this place being white and living in the foreman's house don't mean nothing around here." Bertha said with a bit of fire none of the guests had seen out of her yet.

"She's talking about the old Mc Cloud plantation house up on the hill a mile from here. Hell, them Mc Clouds were poor as far as plantation owners went and if it wasn't for the slaves staying on after the Civil war and the share croppers moving in, they would of lost everything they had. I just hope that old bastard Talmadge stays alive long enough to keep paying us a pittance to look out after the place before that scurvy son of his Earl sells the place off piecemeal to pay the taxes. Ain`t no Mc

Clouds living on Mc Cloud property for nigh on 40 years I would say unless you might count Bertha." Clem said with a "Oh shit" look that he had said something he shouldn't have.

"Clement K. Bowman! You ain`t to big or too old for me to find me a hickory switch to dust your britches with. It's true I might have more than a drop or two of white blood in me but it's not your place to be telling folks such. And it's damn sure it's not fitting to be washing our laundry around city guests." Bertha scolded a much apologetic Clem.

"Here we be, you all come in side. Its lots cooler than on that little porch." Bertha said escorting every one into the darkened main room of the old shotgun style house.

"Have a seat, boys." Clem said indicating an old 1960 style gray couch that Bertha had festooned with what appeared to be handmade starched white doilies.

The house was spare but immaculate and had homemade braided rag throw rugs of every color imaginable placed strategically throughout. Loomis sat uncomfortably for a moment and then advised Clem he needed to use the bathroom to which he was advised that there was an outhouse out back and bushes aplenty if he didn't need to utilize a seat.

Loomis walked out back after excusing himself and Bertha hollered at him to go use the backdoor because it was closer and to mind the mule if he had a notion to go see it. He had no sooner got out the door and they heard the screen door slam when Clem jumped up and Bertha bustled herself back into the living room following Clem in a rush out the front door. Crick just sort of followed along out the front door trying to keep up with the animated giggling pair wondering what was going on but not going to miss whatever it was when the procession came to a halt next to a bush by the front fence that they all peered from in anticipation. The back of the sharecropper compound had three venerable old blued with age wooden barns of which only one seemed to be in repair and holding its roof up without leaks with a small split-rail corral that a milk cow and a mule were sharing and peering at Loomis with interest.

Various breeds of chickens were scratching around in the sand and weeds in back of the house and Loomis was trying to whizz on a big honeysuckle bush when the cow and the mule commenced to talk about him.

"E ah! E ah! Moo Moo! Commenced to echo around the chicken yard and small garden area as Loomis tried to look over his shoulder without getting his feet wet as to what the animals were complaining about.

The mule was having himself a complete fit and it looked like the way he stretched his head out every time he brayed that someone must be pulling his tail to help him out. The cow was a bit more reserved in her vocalizations but she was damn sure fertilizing more ground than what was normal.

"Easy! Easy!" Loomis crooned in their direction as he finished his business and zipped up and went to see about the animals.

"What's got you so riled up? Settle down mule! You need water? Is there a snake in your pen?" Loomis said approaching the old split oak rail corral.

"Get out of my road chickens I ain`t got no grain for you. You all hungry? Miss Bertha not fed you yet today?" Loomis said trying to figure out how to cow and mule whisper while watching a giant black multi colored rooster fighting chicken with spurs an inch and a half long start towards him.

"Surely the house hears this commotion going on.' Loomis said to himself looking towards the backdoor and then noticing Crick and crew were grinning at him in the front yard watching the show.

"What's the matter with these damn beasts? I ain`t done nothing to them, I just watered that bush a little and all hell broke loose." Loomis called up to them pointing a don't even think about it finger at the rooster who had decided to back off, just for the moment.

"I told you to mind the mule, Loomis! He is a nice old cuss once you get to know him but he don't take to strangers." Bertha said smiling a brilliant white but gap tooth grin at him.

"I told you to quit picking on him, Bertha." Clem said with a laugh and smacking Crick on the back of the shoulders with a lets go see thump much harder than Crick thought the old geezer could produce.

"It's the hat, boy! Talk your hat off, Loomis!." Bertha declared and gathered up her dresses to hurry his way with a bemused Crick and Clem whispering and grinning to each other.

"Now Toby, Bessie, you all settle down. This here is Loomis and he is a friend." Bertha said taking Loomis by the hand for an introduction.

Loomis wasn't sure what to do, he had his hat half off and was holding it about shoulder length not knowing whether to put it back on and run or keep it handy for beating off that damn foghorn leghorn looking rooster that seemed like he was trying to sneak up on him once he looked the other way.

Clem and Crick caught up to the pair and Crick was trying his damndest to keep a straight face as Bertha and Loomis seemed to be using his arm as a tug of war rope to keep him moving towards the corral when a shot rang out.

"Ah hell, Katy bar the door!" was all Clem managed to get out before the already disturbed Barn yard erupted into even more pandemonium. All the chickens made a beeline for Bertha like they were going to hide under her dress and that great big rooster must of thought hiding in back of Loomis`s knees must be the safest place around as the mule started spinning and kicking and Bessie the cow high tailed it back in the barn a pooping and a sliding.

"What the F-word!" Crick said reaching over and grabbing his pistol out of Clem's waist band and trying to figure out where the shot had come from.

Clem and Bertha somehow managed to remain calm as a cucumber and told Crick to put up his pistol that everything was alright and for Loomis to lower his cowboy hat further.

"I told that damn Rossi Ross not to hunt so close to our houses but she don't listen. Could be too she is watching us and up to no good." Clem said spitting out the last of the chewing tobacco he and Bertha had "borrowed" under threat of guns from Loomis.

"Rossi Ross! You out here?" Bertha bellowed in a voice that would have probably carried to the county line.

Silence. Nothing but silence was heard as Crick and Loomis nervously looked around for indications of where the shot had been fired from before Clem started yelling that Loomis wasn't the sheriff and to come on out of the woods and be sociable if she was near.

"I am here! Who are they then?" a voice not too far from Loomis's watering bush called back.

"Told ya! They are friends, we is just fine! Now get your little hiney over here and quit acting like a wild Indian." Bertha called back.

After a minute or two a non-descript rag clad form toting a single shot 20 gauge shotgun emerged from the woods and hollered "howdy" to the group.

It was hard to tell between the ill-fitting clothes and the ragged cap if this youngster was male or female until she got closer. A wisp of dishwater blond curls managed to poke their way out of what was once was a brown stylish slouch hat from the disco era. The kind that looked like a beret with a brim you could see in a fat Albert cartoon or JJ had on the TV show Good Times.

Crick still had his pistol out but he had it pointed down to his side as he watched this creature of the fields and forests approach carrying the old single hammered shotgun easily in one hand without a care in the world.

Loomis on the other hand was considering just how much what he knew now to be a teen age girl had seen as he took a nature break and remained kind of freaked that someone with a gun could of got the drop on him so easy.

"It's ok, babies" Bertha cried to which the cow poked its head through a window to reassure itself and the mule snorted like he knew that already but calmed down and quit his incessant braying.

"Shit fire! Is everyone around here crazy or do you all just wait in the woods all day hoping to get the drop on somebody when they got their guard down?" Loomis complained looking around and listening to the woods to be sure nobody else was going to join this carnival of peepers and creepers that he had got stuck in somehow.

"My names Rossi Ross!" The boy now known to be a developing girl thrusting a grimy callused hand out to Loomis declared with a bright smile.

"Uh, I am Loomis. How long you been over there?" Loomis started to question.

"Long enough, but no worries I got a little brother. Miz Bertha! Uncle Clem! I am sorry to scare your guests but I was just beside myself seeing this here sheriff taking a pee on old Marmies grave." The 13 or 14 year old gushed.

"Marmie was an old Blue Tick hound Bertha used to have that that child played with when she was young. Unfortunately for all, Loomis didn't know that Marmie's buried under that old honeysuckle and I reckon that old' cow and mule remember too, the way they's protesting." Clem advised everyone.

"Well I just couldn't let that happen and I got riled. I figured maybe if it was the sheriff trying to throw you off the land I would distract them and give you a chance to escape his deputy. Who is that anyway?" the little hellion said pointing at Crick.

"Why don't he have on a cowboy hat?" the little darling declared.

"They don't fit my head.." Crick started to say before Clem bumped him and explained they were not police and that it was best to explain things nicely to the girl because she was going to repeat everything word for word that transpired to everyone in a 50 mile radius.

"I like him Bertha, he got them Jesus blue eyes just like the picture you keep on your mantle." Rossi said walking up to Crick and starting to hold hands like he was her new Beau and looking up at him adoringly.

"Uh.. pleasure to meet you Rossi, thanks for giving me my gun back Clem." Crick began, trying to get his hand back before the mule started braying again because Loomis had put his hat back on and the cow uttered one long moo out the barn window and disappeared.

"What is wrong with this friggin hat and you people?" Loomis began, taking the hat back off and examining it for a second, trying to find the flaw or 'kick me' sign Crick mighta put on it.

"Nothing at all, go ask him nice Rossi to see the inside of it. It has a pretty blue bow to size the underwear inside of it just like a pair of bloomers." Bertha advised.

Well at this point Crick didn't know who spluttered worse, him trying to hold in the laughter, Loomis telling everyone he didn't wear underwear on his head, Clem doing his code of the old west lines or Bertha trying to understand it all and why Loomis left the packing labels on it like Minnie pearl with her price tags on hats at the grand ol opry.

Once the levity and confusion had died down, Bertha apologized once again and told Loomis to take off his hat to meet the mule.

"Damn it Crick, I ain't took my hat off so many times since my military days." Loomis said as Crick took his own off to go greet the livestock with his fellow rafter.

"Yea, I know, Uncover! Recover! Hats on, hats off. Still in all this shit is kind of fun. Maybe I need me a Cowboy hat?" Crick said not letting a chance go by to needle his buddy a bit.

Clem enjoyed the hell out of two good ol boys to share the fun times with but with livestock and dogs and such it was a matter of safety or serenity to take them hats off to make everyone comfortable.

"You see boys, and I am sorry Bertha but its funnier than hell. These folks around here mule included never seen a cowboy hat mean anything other than the law and that one non gentile veterinarian we once had around this place, so they sound the alarm. Be glad we ain't got no geese to goose you any more, why if I remember right this black gander one time Bertha had.." Clem began before Bertha indicated enough said.

"Well anyway, animals don't see faces like we do, they see hats, whether or not you got something in your hand etc. and you got to well for lack of a better word get naked for them so you and they can see your inner being. Kind of like don't stare a bad dog in the eyes or forget to get down on your knees to greet a smaller animal so you're less threatening." Loomis left them for consideration.

"Now here is where it gets weird, some folks like or love their animals so much they humanize them in their outlooks and the danged things think they are human too and act like their masters. Bertha's daughter died when she was six and at that time Bertha would take all them cast off clothes she got from the big house and the hill top and make dress up dolls and Sunday best for the kids around here. Well, she takes care of me and darns my socks, etc. and that little demon of a boy-girl wears what she decides she wants to regardless what Bertha fixes for her, so she got nothing but the animals to fix for once in a while. She makes fancy hats for the mule, the goat and the cow. You might say she is a bit "tetched" in the head. Now mind you, you are allowed to laugh at them things, that's part of the fun. But you must never allow Bertha or the animals to think you are laughing at them. You got to tell Bertha what a fine job she did making them. Tell the mule how handsome he is, how pretty the cow is how admirable that goat looks. For some reason, I guess it's the horns she tries to make him look like some kind of general or king. Don't say shit about the chickens, she tried dressing them once you know. And hey Crick, find you something to hang on to or you going to fall over, you going to like this, I'm gonna tell you something funnier than hell! She does put underwear in them hats so they don't get dirty stretching them over those animals heads. She told me one day after putting a purple and green crushed velvet Easter bonnet on that dang cow of hers upon it's bovine head and it coming off dirty and smelling like cow, something needed to be done and said, "Why hell, Clem, folks wear underwear to keep their clothes clean so they can wear them again another time, why not put some johnny jump ups inside the hats? Clem said looking solemn at first and regaining his humor as he had to wipe a tear of laughter out of his eyes as Crick tried to hold himself up on a fence post as they both began to hysterically point at Loomis and his trademark cowboy hat.

"So that's why that danged woman is so fascinated with my hats lining. Dang! I don't believe this. You mean to tell me that that old woman makes frilly hats and something called hat underwear for her livestock!" Loomis said grinning and shaking his head.

"Yea, she probably never seen no store bought hat underwear~" Crick quipped as Clem slapped his knee with mirth and looked at Loomis once seriously and then went back to laughing once again.

"Oh my word, you all stop now. We really got to get ourselves to going back to being serious again." Clem said trying to regain his composure.

"We just one big family out here by ourselves, everybody from the goats to the chickens, from the mule to Rossi`s insane momma is included and we sometimes play a game of sorts of putting on airs and dressing up for Sunday services. There ain`t been a congregation gathered at the old church on this property for nigh on 30 years. We used to go to the end times Baptist church over in the squalls until about 7 years ago occasionally, but we never really fit in. Now every Sunday we gather and dress up, mind our P`s and Q's and let Bertha recite a memorized passage from the bible and sing an old timey church song together. Service is done and we picnic and share a covered dish and go home. It's like the tides in the ocean boys, that's the flow and no need to try to fight it, just go with the flow." Clem said looking like he was going to tear up once again from the memories but it soon changed to laughter as he turned and repeated "Store bought hat underwear?" to Crick who beamed a smile at him and Loomis, as the two snickered with each other.

"That's nice, thank you for sharing the story, Clem.." Crick answered before a waggling finger by Clem asked for his silent indulgence a bit further.

"Hey you boys are going to like this if she will allow it. Bertha, let's call it Sunday today if that be alright." Clem said attempting to influence his friendly fight-over-everything nemesis.

"Oh we shouldn't, the Lords day is his and shouldn't be taken in vain. You know when spring comes I place some flowers on my Rachel's grave and give thanks we made it another winter. Oh no, wouldn't be fittin." Bertha said wringing her hands.

"Miss Bertha, wouldn't be anything wrong in showing Mr. Crick and Mr. Loomis how we are preparing for that fine day now would there? I know you ain`t got my dress finished yet but I would sure like to show it off before we got to alter it again." The blooming young lady cajoled the grandmotherly matriarch of the blessed spot on this earth that time had passed by.

"Well, I would like to see if that gingham is fitting your ankles or your knees. I swear child you growing like a colt. Ok, you go round up Sophie and Clem, you take them men back up to your house to clean up and lend them some bib and tucker and come back here in two hours. I am telling you now, Clem, I will take a frying pan to ya if you bunch of heathens get into that apple jack I know you're hiding and don't make it back here on time with clean smiles and clean collars, ready to sit down to what we're declaring Sunday supper. I'll butcher us a couple chickens and make it official." Bertha said hustling Rossi back to the house for a wash and a scrub before trying on the party dress she had started making and lengthening for god knows how long.

"We will be here with bells on." Clem said checking his watch and led Crick and Loomis back towards his house a comfortable walk distant.

"Hey, when do we get our guns back?" Loomis protested on the way to Clem's.

"You ain't getting your picture taken today boy, don't worry about it. Your partner got his pistol back and I got enough lead in this here double barrel to take care of anything that might bother you, so be still. I will tell Bertha to give you yours back before supper. Matter of fact, this whole party we are going to be having is cause of you." Clem said taking Loomis's tin of chewing tobacco out of his pocket.

"Guess this here is rightly yours, but with everything we going to do for you, you should be more sharing and grateful." Clem said slapping it back into his hand.

"Well what exactly is it I am supposed to be grateful for?" Loomis said relishing the thought that he got his chaw back and could have some now.

"Well, first off be grateful you could offer me some more chewing tabbacy, next would be I got an ice cream suit that would fit you just fine and ain't charging you for it by doing so." Clem said snatching back the tin and helping himself before returning it to an astonished Loomis.

"I got to ask, what the hell is an "Ice Cream suit"? Crick said grinning at Loomis's discomfort.

"Oh, you know back in the day some folks used to look like Colonel Sanders of the fried chicken franchise fame and when me and Bertha went through them trunks in the attic of the big house I told her them suits were too fine cut up and make pillow shams out of. Don't worry you just need to wear the jacket not the whole suit unless you just want to." Clem said before they arrived at his house.

"Hey, I appreciate the hospitality and you offering us dinner and all but we need to talk about leaving out soon after and getting on the road." Loomis said.

"Why? You got a fire to go to or something? We due at Bertha's in a couple hours, takes time to kill and cook a couple chickens. You boys haven't been eating regular and time you eat that feast Bertha is fixing you won't be fit for nothing but sitting on the porch and having a sip of apple jack with me. Leave out in the morning. I will get Bertha to fix you a breakfast of grits and gravy and some scrambled eggs. You never did tell me what it was you had planned now that you managed to get over to this side of the river." Clem said looking over at Crick

"Well like I said it all depends on what kind of help I can round up and if the phones are working. When I get home I am going to lend Loomis a horse so he can make his way back to his place. There is no gas to be had as I explained to you so that's the best transport for him to have. Loomis here rode scout for the Alabama wagon train for many years so a couple days hard riding won't bother him a bit." Crick explained.

"What is the Alabama Wagon Train?" Clem asked and motioned for them to walk over to a barn off to the left.

"That used to be an event where people rode old-timey covered wagons and carts down at the historic reenactments.

"So you are a real cowboy then? Ha, wait until I tell Bertha. There's that bike I told you about. My son sort of customized it after seeing' an old James Dean motorcycle greaser movie and made it up as his very own imaginary custom-built chopper. There is a hand pump over there. I know them tires probably need airing up." Clem said pointing at a rusty old banana seated Stingray bicycle.

"Let see what we got here." Crick said examining the bike. Evidently someone had taken the forks off one bike and added them to the existing forks of this one to extend it out a foot or so. It had playing cards stuck in the spokes that Crick would remove the first chance he had.

"Ha! Ha! You going to look pretty riding that thing Crick!" Loomis said imagining a funny mental picture of Crick peddling along holding onto those ape hanger handle bars and looking like Easy Rider.

"What the hell is that over there?" Crick said ignoring the jibe and looking back at the end of the barn at what appeared to be a very old tractor with paddle wheels like you would see on an old steam boat attached to its wheels.

"That there boys is a product of some more redneck ingenuity. It's a swamp logger. Made it myself. Me and the boys around here used to take that thing out to Foleys swamp to cut Cyprus trees to carry down to the mill. I used a couple of them steel hay cages you see in cow pastures sometimes for the rings and them boards came off of the teeter totter set at the old school house. It don't run no more though or I would lend it to you." Clem said as he proudly walked over to it to show off his back woods craftsmanship.

"Now that's cool as hell! And it floats?" Crick said momentarily forgetting the bike and studying the contraption while a plan started to formulate in his mind.

"You could run that contraption either way but yea, it floats. I put-putted it and paddled it across many a pond. Steering it around is slow and clumsy and takes a dang football field of water to turn it around but it got me where I needed to go." Clem said watching Crick climb up on the seat to get a feel for the thing.

"Are you thinking what I am thinking Loomis?" Crick said, grasping the tractors steering wheel and jiggling himself back and forth side to side as if he was driving.

"Yea, I am but Clem said that paddle wheel tractor don't run. It sure would have been cool to drive that across the river and surprise everyone. Wouldn't that be a sight!" Loomis said, patting the big tractor tire.

"Oh yea, you talking about rescuing your friends. That old tractor would of done it back in its day. Heads blown and won't crank up no more so it won't do you no good. We could of gone down to the old crossing and towed that pontoon barge they used all the way across and loaded them folks up and brought them back." Clem said, wishing he could have gone on that adventure.

"I got a tractor!" Crick said scrambling off the tractor and studying the wheel wells on the tires to see how Clem had attached the paddles on.

"Well they just bolt on, don't know if your tractors bolt pattern would match but I could probably alter it a mite to make them fit if need be. You thinking about driving your tractor back over here and giving what I said a try?" Clem said looking like Popeye excitedly chewing spinach as he wore out the chewing tobacco puffing out his cheek thinking about all the possibilities of going on a great and glorious adventure.

" Hell yea! How much you want for these paddle wheels?" Crick said looking at Clem excitedly as Loomis also studied him in anticipation.

"Now that's a million dollar question. Just kidding, guys. What would I take for them? Can me and Bertha go and watch you drive that thing?" Clem asked slyly.

"Well uh, I guess you could. I can jump start your truck when I get back. I can also bring you a little gas to make the trip with. Sure why not, it's only fitting that the inventor gets to see his creations in motion." Crick said shaking hands with Clem and making him preen like a peacock at the praise for him.

"Hot Damn! Let's hurry up and get dressed for supper. Bertha is going to bust her bonnet when she finds out what we're fixing to do. By the way, Bertha's bonnets tend to be more fancy than anybody else's, we're supposed to notice that. Ya'll remember that, you hear? We going to go down early for dinner but not until I know she got everything on the stovetop. That damn Rossi Ross can kill and pluck them chickens. Oh hell, we can't say nothing around that girl. She would tell that bat brained mother of hers and lord knows who else. Even if I swore her to secrecy on a stack of bibles she would still want to come along." Clem said beside himself with wanting to run down and tell Bertha immediately the great news and frustrated beyond belief because he couldn't.

"Rescuing folks ain't no spectator sport but we might could use some help." Loomis said speculating.

"Oh you don't want none them riff raff river rat trash that lives around here helping you with nothing unless you want your pockets lightened. Hey you said you were going to go try to get the authorities to help you. Does that mean I might not get to see my invention in action?" Clem said, crestfallen at the notion.

"Well not necessarily. Like I said, I don't know if there are still any authorities to call upon. I am certainly going to try and find some professional rescuers or responders available but I have my doubts." Crick advised.

"Whew! Still a chance then. Hey I got an old hay wagon that's still serviceable. Is that horse of yours broke to traces? You are going to have to transport them people somehow once you get them over to this other side of the waterway if you can't find no authorities to do it for you. We could go get the benches out of the old church and put them in the wagon to tote a bunch of folks at once. Don't tell Bertha I said this but I have my doubts if that mule of hers could pull that wagon all the way out of the half-mile to the driveway without falling out." Clem said grinning. Clem hadn't bothered to mention to Crick that it was about a half-mile up to the driveway the way country folks measured and 'bout another mile up to the main road.

"Now that sounds like a great idea. You know Clem, Crick didn't get a chance to tell you this but I had planned on rounding up as many of the drivers of the Alabama Wagon train as I could and doing the state run one more big time. Several of those people stuck out on the island are members of the wagon train so finding folks to volunteer to help get them home shouldn't be a problem." Loomis told him as Clem fidgeted around wanting to go get dressed for dinner but needing to hear more about this magnificent adventure unfolding in his mind.

"I told him that a wagon train was a cool idea to transport folks home without the need for gas but it wouldn't be a good idea for him to want to scout for it again like he used to. He might be liable to come under Indian attack the way things are now a days." Crick said looking over at Loomis.

"Indians? What kind of Indians? You mean like the ones that rode around in a circle attacking the settlers on the old Saturday afternoon western movies?" Clem said confused.

"Yea but these Indians are liable to have AK 47 rifles. Times are crazy out there even if I haven't seen it firsthand myself yet. You and Bertha are danged lucky to be living on this old plantation and having livestock. People in the cities won't be able to get food or heat without electricity." Crick informed him.

"Imagine that? Me and Bertha are lucky to be nothing more than caretaking poor dirt farmers these days. Times are indeed strange. Hey Crick if you do need to buy my paddle wheels you can have them for whatever food you can find to trade. You set the price. We do pretty good out here without much store bought goods but we still need them things." Clem said hopeful he could at least get some coffee, flour and sugar out of the trade.

"I can fix you up a bit of supplies, Clem. I have a pretty good size pantry stocked for hurricanes and such." Crick advised.

"Thanks, don't have to be a lot. What are you going to feed them folks on the island when they get off?" Clem said looking off towards the direction of the river.

"Good question. I have a few sacks of feed corn and barley. Maybe a hundred pounds of beans. Other than that I really don't know. There is no food on that island, folks will be better off on the mainland no matter what we do. That's the whole idea of running the Alabama Wagon train and getting the authority's involved. We need to get most of them folks back home where they got some supplies and friends to help them out. The ones who can't get home for whatever reason are going to have to depend on the kindness of others or the government to help them." Crick said lamenting the fact that he didn't have an answer for that question.

"I thought you said nobody could get food out of the grocery store anymore? Even if some of them folks do get home, what are they going to do in a week or two when they run out of vittles and can goods?" Clem asked trying to understand the current state of the world.

"I did say most folks would perish because they couldn't buy food or get clean water anymore but this group of friends is different than most people. A lot of them planned for a disaster like this and have anywhere from two weeks to two years food and supplies put back to see them through the trials and tribulations of these hard times. The ones with less food have camping supplies and plan on trying their hand at living off the land some until they can get someplace better." Crick advised.

"You must have a farm yourself Crick, what with having a horse and a tractor and all. Are you going to take some of those rich folks home with you so they can have a better place to live?" Clem asked studying him

"What makes you think they are rich folks, Clem?" Loomis asked already knowing the answer.

"Well you said some of them had a whole bunch of food and tents and such looking for a better place to live and I can't think of nowhere better than a working farm to be staying at if the grocery stores are all closed." Clem reasoned.

"Smarter words were never said. Yea I might take in a couple people temporarily but my acreage is really small and it's more of a hobby farm than anything else." Crick said wistfully.

"Is that feed corn you got cracked or whole?" Clem said drawing a circle with his boot in the dirt in front of the barn.

"It's whole. I have a mill though." Crick answered watching Clem start to pace going deep in thought about something.

"Them poorer folks that are going to be moving to the woods when their food runs out. Are they uppity city folks that are scared to get their hands dirty or are they just plain people down on their luck?" Clem asked speculatively.

"No they understand how much hard work is required to just survive. I bet anyone on that island now has lost any fool notions they had of bugging out after the first week of getting stuck there. Bugging out is just a slang word for having to leave somewhere and having to go somewhere else to live and camping if you have to." Loomis said watching how the word confused Clem.

"I got ya, we called that riding the rails or going hobo back in my day. So where do these people plan on "bugging out"

370

to? A hobo goes city to city looking for work or a hand out. If nobody wants to live in the cities no more where are they all going to go? Campground to camp ground looking for work like migrant farm workers?" Clem said looking over hundreds of acres of unworked fields.

"I doubt most of them have any real idea where they are bugging out to or how long they could last once they got there." Crick said wondering how many people had already found out going to a national forest somewhere and trying to survive off just the land was slow suicide at best.

"If they ain`t been raised in around the woods they are not going to find much but bugs and misery." Loomis said backing Cricks appraisal up.

"Now used to be when a man and his family were down on their luck a body would seek out a likely landowner to grub stake him and do a bit of sharecropping or hire on as a farm hand. Do you reckon that there might be a few people on your island looking for work like that?" Clem said letting the idea develop.

"I bet some of the survivors would be up for the idea of maybe hiring out for terms on this place. Is that what you got in mind, Clem?" Crick said brightening at the notion.

"I would have to talk it over with Bertha but this spread could be made to produce again. Now to be honest it would be a hard go to even put in much of a crop of anything even if we had the seeds and the equipment to do it. Those fields are all played out from years of raising cotton and peanuts. It would take a lot of fertilizer to even raise a fuss on it and we ain`t got any money or any place to buy some iffin we did. I guess it's just an old man's fancy to even think we could raise a vegetable truck farm let alone get them shacks back to being habitable once more." Clem sighed.,

"Now I don't think that is something that is a totally insurmountable problem Clem. Let's talk this notion of yours over some more and come up with a couple solutions if we can." Loomis said eying the fields as dreamily as Crick and Clem were doing.

"First thing to consider is seed. I got enough spare seed stored to put in an acre or so of assorted vegetables when I come back with the wagon train if I am able to round up enough folks to make it safe and worthwhile." Loomis declared.

"I got that or more extra I can bring with me when I bring the tractor back. You talking about long term canned storage seeds or something else Loomis?" Crick asked while pondering the fertilizer problem.

"I got both, I don't really like the selection in that vacuum sealed stuff and have some fresh packets saved from last year that is more suitable for this climate and my farming style." Loomis declared.

"I don't know nothing about vacuum seeds but old seed don't sprout. Me and Bertha save enough seed every year to plant some things but we usually go to the feed and seed once a year to get some new fresh seeds of some vegetables. Seems some of that seed we save just don't produce right the second or third year." Clem said not understanding the intricacies of Heirloom versus hybrid seeds.

"That leaves fertilizer a problem. Now every one of those shacks used to have a kitchen garden or a little plot to sell extra vegetables to the general store or the restaurants around here but they ain't been turned over in years. Soil should still be good though, lots of manure and sweat been dug into that soil over a hundred years of hoeing and planting." Clem said perking up at the possibilities of raising food this year and all the seed they needed for next regardless if they could no longer buy any.

"Well there you go! How many shacks and little garden areas you got around here?" Crick asked with enthusiasm and interest.

"On this end of the plantation we got 20 but I would say maybe only 10 or so of them shanty's are fixable as they stand. The big house had a big kitchen garden but weeds and little pine trees taken it over and the place is a mess. Been vandalized once or twice, age time and general disrepair been eating away at it for years but there is lots of good wood still left in it and a few usable items but nobody would want to be around it. It's hainted don't you know? Them ghosts don't bother me and Bertha none because we belong here but strange lights and noises been known to go on." Clem said looking like he was about to tell a ghost story before reminding everyone they needed to be washing up and heading down to the bottoms for supper pretty soon.

Clem led the way to the plantation foreman's house he had taken up residence in years ago when the former tenant had passed away. He happily babbled about what a great lunch they were going to have when they got to Bertha's and apologized that he hadn't had the time or money to paint anything around the place in oh so many years.

"Now then boys you got several ways to wash up around here. We got the hand pump on the well, a 55 gallon barrel shower, wash basin in the bathroom. Oh yea, I got indoor plumbing but it don't work cause I don't have the gas to run that hit or miss motor on the well pump. Runs off electricity too if we had some. We ain't as backwards as you all might think. We even run power down to the bottoms in the early sixties. Anyway if you use the shitter in the house you got to haul water in buckets right after you use it for the next person. I don't care if it's night or day you do it then and not wait. I don't want nobody leaving their business in the toilet bowl any longer than they have too. There is three outhouses in the back. Use the one on the right. The one on the far left used to be for colored folks back in the day and the center one is for ladies. Me and Bertha dispensed with all those formalities long ago and just use the one on the right." Clem said bustling around the house and opening a big armoire and taking out three what he called dinner jackets for his house guests.

"Now Crick you can be staying in Arbuckle's room, that was Cletus's eldest boys room that used to be foreman around here and cowboy you can stay in his youngest boy Jeb's room. The beds a bit smaller in there than you might be used to but you will like the décor." Clem said pointing out a boys room still decorated with what looked like every Hopalong Cassidy and Lone Ranger paraphernalia ever made for kids.

Crick was happily poking and grinning at Loomis behind Clem's back that his room was specially chosen for him because he was the cowboy before he got a load of where he was going to be spending the night.

The walls were festooned with posters of some of the ugliest women he had ever seen in his life and a big four poster bed with a flowered canopy sat in the middle of the floor with what appeared to be ropes from a boxing ring half way around it.

"Now let me explain the odd decorations in this room." Clem said with a wry smile as Loomis busted out laughing and slapped Crick on the back.

"That boy Arbuckle was just crazy about going to see the professional wrestling shows and had a thing for them lady wrestlers. That's the Fabulous Moolah over there the champion in the day." Clem said indicating a scowling woman dressed in white tights portrait and she actually at one time slept in that bed that he somehow acquired and managed to move in here. The ring ropes came from the National Guard armory where he used to go watch the matches and I don't want to even know what he was thinking about when he decided to attach them to his bed. He was a bit different, you might say. You can take the ring ropes down if you want, I just sort of leave everything like a museum because I never use these rooms except to entertain company and that has been many a year since I had any. That's a picture of his mom over there and not a wrestler by the way, even though she favors one. She died when he was about 12 and his old man let them two kids do pretty much what they wanted too. Looks like he had a thing for that style of women, too. Bertha made that canopy on the bed best she could using the old one for a pattern. Seems he got a bit rambunctious one day jumping on the bed or using it for a wrestling ring with his brother and managed to tear the old one up." Clem said to the incredulous Crick who was trying to take in this bizarre household while Loomis looked at the picture of Mad Moolah and tried to imitate her face with his tongue hanging out comically when Clem wasn't looking to bedevil Crick that her ugly mug would be disturbing his sleep the rest of the night as well as the look he was going to give him every chance he got.

"I stay right down the hall here if you need anything but I warn you I sleep light, so no tricks." Clem said pushing open the half closed door and disappointing or relieving them that the room's contents only held what once was probably fine Victorian furniture dragged down or donated from the big house.

"Ok, this is home guys. I show you the livestock barn later. I only got a few hogs and a couple of piglets down there as well as some guinea hens who will scream bloody murder at any stranger cowboy hat or not ." Clem said with a playful smile and a light elbow poke to the ribs of Loomis in the close confines of the hallway leading to what he called his parlor. .

9

DINNER PARTY

Crick stood impatiently and uncomfortably as Loomis adjusted the string tie that Clem had forced him to wear. It was that or a very ugly bow tie so he opted for the lesser of two evils.

"You know I am going to get you for this if you ever repeat a word of it." Crick said as Loomis affirmed he would do the same thing if they ever made it back around civilized and sane people.

"Why you boys look right nice. Loosen up them ties, this is an informal affair and you need some swallowing room to eat up all that good food Rossi and Bertha are fixing for us." Clem said as he just clipped what looked like a boys tie onto his T shirt and stuffed the rest of it down the front of a newer pair of overalls. A pair of polished dress shoes and an old timey straw hat with a red and blue band completed his ensemble.

"Before you two start braying like a pair of matched mules I will have you know that this here hat aint got no underwear in it. I convinced Martha this style of hat needed to breathe because of my bald spot and it was specially made to show the vote for Ike label inside. Here watch this!" Clem said as he grabbed a cattleman's cane out of the umbrella stand and did an impromptu doffing of his hat and a little dance like an old song and dance vaudeville act.

"Hot cha cha!" Clem declared finishing his brief exhibition looking amazingly like the actor Jimmy Durante with that nose of his held up for comparison.

"Damn Clem, you just full of surprises." Loomis said laughing as he and Crick adjusted their ties for comfort.

"Well if your all set and don't need to use the facilities let's get on down to Bertha's and tie on the feed bag. Oh, wait a minute now,I aint told you all this yet but Bertha also would of insisted you wear a bib to keep your ties and shirts clean if you had of left them that tight. Let me clue you in on a few more rules of etiquette for that house so I can save you some discomfort and embarrassment. I should of got you all stuck with the bibs but then you would of told on me for some of the fun I have had with Bertha over the years and that might of spoiled the party. When you get there, gush and fuss over how nice the women look of course and how nice the side board and table are decorated. Now Bertha didn't get up to the big house very often around dinner time and the two times she did to assist with a big party the menus were put on the dog fancy affairs that she took a notion of that was how fine people generally ate. The first go round she got a peek at all them rich folks both men and women wearing lobster bibs so no matter what we will be doing with our napkins her and Rossi Ross will be wearing a set of them." Clem said with a twinkle in his eye and a grin.

"I take it you never explained to her about lobster dinners?" Crick said raising a bemused eyebrow in his direction.

"Well I sorta did, we weren't but about 13 years old and you see being a mischievous boy back then I had to fun her a bit. Hell, I didn't know what them Lobster things were until me and Grand Pa unloaded a couple crates of them preserved with dry ice and seaweed. Old Man Mc Cloud had some Yankee investor fly in to maybe invest in cotton for his textile mills so the old bastard was putting on airs pretending like he was a rich landowner and that throwing such an extravagant party was just par for the course around here. I tell you what it took 3 weeks to just even get ready for that shindig what with everyone polishing what silverware was still left from selling it off to pay bills and manicuring the lawns and fields around here to look like a golf course or something. Them Mc Clouds pretty well wore everybody in the bottoms and the sharecroppers out. Anyway, my Pappy decided that he would tell me that those things were not giant crawdads and more akin to armored cockroaches that lived in Asia somewhere so I wouldn't be begging a taste or stealing one out of the pot if I got a chance. Well young folks listen to the adults in secret all the time so I soon caught onto that yarn and commenced to plotting and scheming how to get me one for myself if

I thought nobody would miss it. I mean they had a fine mess of them things and a croaker sack full of Apalachicola oysters on ice my daddy went down to Florida to get to really put the icing on the cake. Speaking of cake, there were all kinds of cakes and pies set out that the best bakers in the bottoms had been fixing and picking fruits and berries to make them treats for days also. Anyway, the centerpiece for the table was going to be this gargantuan 15 pound lobster they had bought special and it was sitting off in the shade next to the kitchen back door in a split birch basket of its own. Wasn't unusual back then to have a crate of chickens or rabbits around the back door waiting for the cook's approval and whoever was tasked with doing the first stage of butchering back then? Well me and Bertha were carrying us a bushel basket full of sweet corn up from the field and she had been asking me why old Ms. Mc Cloud had made us string them Chinese lanterns from the last party out on the veranda if the white folks were not going to eat any of that "Japans" food they had at their last whoop de do. Bertha had always been fascinated by the little oriental chef and his crew that had been borrowed from a restaurant in Birmingham to fix that supper and cook in their pajamas. Clem had told her that their eyes were slanted that way because they had a lot to think about with them dragons like pictured on the lanterns in their home country lurking about. Bertha for some reason thought that was pretty cool and would take one hand and place it on her forehead while slanting her eyes if she needed to go deep in thought and think about something. She still does it to this day! If you see Bertha slanting her eyes and hunching herself down small, well then she had some mighty troubling and scary thoughts she needed to think about." Clem said, as Crick and Loomis turned around and slant-eyed him like he was some kind of scary and troubling notion to carry the joke on even further as this crazy eye adjustment must be performed as if Bertha probably did to him, to observe him!

"See, I told you that you boys ain't right." Clem said chuckling before continuing his story and doing the same slant-eyed motion back to them!

"Anyway there was this giant lobster in the crate that I had already done peeked at and weren't nothing but a little bitty piece of wire holding the lid down that I must of not fixed tight enough. Now wait boys, quit your chuckling for a minute, it gets better! We aint loosening that monster Lobster on the world just yet. See we been back and forth about did dragons like on the Chinese menu and lanterns actually exist and how the bible said there used to be giants and such back in the old days so she always been naïve about what did or could actually exist in these backwoods around here to give her fears and that sort of been my thing to play and scare her with. Well on the way up from the corn field I had been scaring her with the story of Medusa; you know that Greek mythology story about the snake haired woman that could turn you to stone if you looked at her? I told her about how the hero used a polished shield to look at her and wasn't affected by the magic and had sort of wondered out loud if them dragon creatures that lived in China needed to be looked at special with some kind of protections like slanty-eyes so they couldn't put their MoJo on you." Clem said grinning and pulling on the end of that Durante nose of his like it was lucky.

"You got you a mean streak in you, Clem!' Crick said smiling at Loomis and waiting on the rest of the story.

"I'm not mean, it's just that there ain't a whole lot to do around here. Anyway, somehow or another that big old lobster managed to knock the lid loose off that crate and swing that big nipper of his out which caused Bertha to freak and scream and squeal. I said "Go get the spatula Bertha!" to which she said was "Are ya sure you don't want a shovel?" to get that thing back in there. I told her no my Pappy had already told me what to do in this kind of emergency and did the China man routine with both my hands and that I was going to use its shiny surface to look at it like in a mirror so it couldn't do no magic on me and to fix her own eyes." Clem said beside himself giggling at his own mental picture of that fine day.

"Damn and we got to sleep in the same house as him?"
Loomis said trying to hold his gut and sitting down on the old
gray sofa which Crick soon joined him on quietly laughing at
how strange the world he had found himself in actually was.

"Now then, Bertha who was beside herself with fear of
the unknown the way that only a backwoods black girl of her
age can be, commenced to slant her eyes and try not to look over
her shoulder at that giant lobster claw waving around sticking
out of that box and bumped into the screen door jam as she run
to get the utensil I had requested to deal with this critter. Beulah,
that was the house maid and cook as well as Bertha's Auntie,
was in there in the kitchen cooking bacon for the salads and
boiling a pot of kale and collards when Bertha ran in with her
eyes squinted with both hands and grabbed the spatula out of her
hands hollering it was an emergency and she needed it. Having
one eye unslanted and not having an extra hand to fix it she
remembered my story about that Greek soldier using a shield as
a looking glass so she grabbed the pot lid off them boiling
greens and carried back the whole shooting match to me to fight
the lobster with. Now watching all this and the confusion of the
Auntie was funnier than hell and I didn't think twice about
taking my lobster armaments from her as she turned back to the
door slanting her eyes but there was a problem. Both them damn
things she handed me were hotter than hell so I hollered and
dropped them both on the floor and Bertha thought the lobster
had gotten me and commenced to wailing like a banshee getting
spanked. All this madness and confusion soon had the Auntie
heading our way and because she didn't have a clue what was
going on or was after us she figured she better grab a rolling pin
and come see about it. By that time the lobster had managed to
get both his claws and head out of that damned crate and I guess

seeing Beulah with that rolling pin and me and Bertha screaming bloody murder decided it was time to make good on its escape and did one of those tail flip things crawdads are known to do and launched itself between us all on the porch. Well, Beulah, who had not seen this sea creature in all its glory yet, gave out a yell thinking it was going to eat her children, Bertha turned around doing the slanty-eyed thing, I was busy sucking on my burned fingers while getting out of the road and that mad black woman, Beulah, commenced to lay waste to that poor lobster with that rolling pin. Now I guess you would say big bottoms run in that family because a Big Beulah butt chasing that lobster commenced to clear that back porch of me and Bertha trying to get out of the way when old Lady Mc Cloud come out to see what the hell was going on as the field hands and the rest of The Mc Cloud clan came to see what kind of ruckus was going on. When the dust, water, seaweed, ice and bits of shell cleared and the pitch forks and guns were put up, you had one very sorry young man standing there that everyone seemed to be looking at and that was me. Thankfully, folks saw the humor in it and had mercy on me for my burned hands or I think they would have taken turns smoking my britches.

Loomis and Crick eyed Clem with derision and sparkling eyes, enjoying the old man's tales and faraway memories that brought laughter to them all.

"So you never got around to telling us how not to wear them lobster bibs! Crick said, making Loomis look like he was going to count Clem's ribs.

"Oh yeah, yal'll made me forget that for a minute! Look here, there's three different napkins you going to have laid out for you: there's the white one's that's under your silverware that you probably know what to do with, that's for wiping your face and to lay on your lap; there's a stack of colored ones that you're supposed to pick from to match the color of the suit you got on and stuff down your collar, that's why we wear loose collars if'n you don't want to wear no bib! If everyone wore tight collars like ya'll had them fixed before, you'd have to wear one of them lobster bibs with the little lobster printed on the front of it like the rich folks wearing tuxedos had on the day she saw 'em.

"Of course, you told her dragons aren't real." Loomis said grinning.

"Well, I kinda did tell her lobsters weren't dragon babies!" Clem said with a laugh.

"You should seen her oh well I guess when we were eight or nine, about sprinkling salt on a bird's tail to keep them from flying!" Clem said.

"You just ain't right, Clem" Crick said. "How long has it been you been bedeviling that old woman?"

"Aw hell, it's been nigh on fifty or sixty years I guess, it's just too much damn fun!" Clem said, unapologetically.

Loomis and Crick followed Clem down the red dusty clay road to Bertha's house, shaking their heads, not quite sure what was going to be happening once they had arrived but they hoped Clem didn't have anything cooking up in his mind to get them with.

Bertha and Rossi stood out on the front porch as prim as the ladies at the big house watching their approach. Loomis and Crick reviewed exactly what it was they were supposed to be doing at this time to greet these special ladies as the fragrance of a home cooked meal and something that smelled like lavender or honeysuckle greeted their noses.

"We're here, Bertha!" Clem called out. "Them boys dress up nice don't they, Bertha!" Clem stated as the two well-dressed men came up.

"Oh they look fine, fine! Never seen any two better dressed boys coming to Sunday dinner! Ain't they a handsome sight, Rossi?" Bertha said as a blue checkered gingham dressed Rossi peeped out the front door, ready to meet the guests and flicked her Spanish lace collar flirtatiously at them.

"Adieu! Adieu!" Loomis said, doffing his hat in a gentlemanly bow, nudging Crick to do the same.

"Boy, you look nice, Loomis! You and Crick sure decorated up well!" Bertha said, with a whisper to Rossi did she see the pretty blue bow on Loomis' hat underwear?

"Ya'll come on in! We got you all a fine supper fixed up!" Rossi said, flouncing her gingham dress fishing for more compliments.

"Well I declare, aren't you two the most charming ladies I ever seen!" Crick said, remembering everything Clem had said about entering the home of this one Bertha Bartholomew.

"Shitfire, I told you they'd pretty up nice!" Clem declared. "Smells awful good around here! But you won't believe the great news I got for you! Now you been telling me, Bertha, for a hundred years that all my ideas ain't worth nothing! Crick here has been telling me I'm going to be the Master of Disaster! I'm telling you, and you are not going to believe it! He wants them paddle wheels off that old swamp logger I used to run down here. We are going to save the day, Bertha! Why he is going to attach them paddles to his own tractor and ride that damn thing of mine all the way over there and rescue them folks! Me and you get to go along and watch too! Rossi can also, if she behaves her damn self. Now listen up, that is I mean, if we don't have to first go see how those old animals got fixed up pretty for the day!"

"Well you can tell me your story on the way to the corral. The animals been waiting to show off their finery and you know how impatient that mule gets." Bertha said as she led the way to te barn.

The Mule, the goat and the cow were lined up together at the corral rail like they were patiently ready to stand inspection for a military parade.

Everyone ooohed and awed appropriately over the animals and told them how fine they looked and they seemed to eat up all the attention and compliments until Bertha gave them their Sunday dinner treat of oats and molasses.

Clem chattered all the way back to the house and all through dinner and into the night telling Bertha about the big plans to try and fix up the old share cropper shacks and get a crop in the field. Bertha couldn't really wrap her head around the fact that the power was out all over the United States and probably wouldn't be back on for several years, if ever. She agreed that some of the preppers could stay and work the land on shares but worried about how they were going to feed that many extra folks until harvest time came around. Clem explained that Crick and Loomis had some ideas about that and that if they could find a boat somewhere, Crick had a friend that might be bringing them some commercial fishing nets if he could get in touch with him.

"Well if he can't, Clem, we could build some split oak catfish traps, come to think of it I think we still got a few stored up in the top of the barn. Oh, it will be so nice to have folks working the old place again. Clem you best look around up in the attic at the big house and see if there is any serviceable clothes left and bring them down for me and Rossi-girl to wash and mend." Bertha said.

"Sure Bertha, Loomis can help me with that. He is sticking around for a few days until Crick gets back. He might be back sooner if he can get Slim to give him a ride home." Clem said speaking of his neighbor about 5 miles away.

"I been by his place twice last couple weeks and didn't see hide nor hair of him. House is locked up, driveway don't have no tire tracks in it after that rain we had a week ago." Rossi said referring to her wide ranging hunting and wanderings through the fields and woods around the area.

"Sounds like he has gone off somewhere, Crick. Might take you a lot longer than you expected to get home." Bertha said worrying about him.

"How long you reckon it will take you to pedal all the way home?" Clem asked Crick.

"Oh, I should be able to make it in a day if I don't run into any trouble. No one hardly lives on the road to the house so I am not expecting any trouble.' Crick advised.

"Well, come by early for breakfast and I will fix you a sack lunch to take with you." Bertha advised as she bid everyone good night.

.

10

CRICK'S RIDE

Crick peddled the old chopped bicycle down the two lane county road leading to the main highway and cussed its wobbly front wheel for the millionth time today. It was hot as hell riding out on this asphalt and it was impossible to go more than a moderate speed before the rickety thing tried to rattle his fillings out. Going downhill was really interesting and a bitch because this part of the country was filled with hills. If you didn't have enough speed at the bottom of a hill you might as well walk and push the bike up the next hill. If you were not real careful with the front hand caliper brake, you could lose control very easily and end up in a ditch. Problem was, it didn't have no coaster brake for the back wheel and that caliper front wheel brake was all he had. Crick already found out how persnickety a front brake on a chopper is and was probably only good for performing backward wheelies.

Crick hadn't seen a single car or person his entire way home and he was glad he lived a bit remotely. He hoped his home was in the same condition he had left it in and mulled over what he was going to do if it wasn't. His guns were locked up in a safe so he wasn't sweating that. His preps were pretty well secured but if someone had broken in and found them, then 10 to 1 they were still there chowing down on his food. That scenario was scarier than he cared to dwell on and instead he focused on what Loomis and Clem were going to be doing today.

They were going to going to get the paddle wheels off the old tractor and that was no small feat because they looked like they weighed a ton. Once they got that done Bertha had said they could use the mule to plow up some of the sharecropper house garden plots if they took it real slow. "Mind you, Loomis, neither that mule, that plow or them worn leather traces with the rusty buckles been worked in a while and any one of them things are liable to give out when they aren't supposed to." Bertha said.

Bertha had really taken a liking to Loomis and thought it was hilarious that he was going to try his hand at handling the mule and the old offset plow.

Clem told him that mule was mighty cantankerous but Loomis had assured him he had handled mules before as well as plows and could do the job if the mule could do his.

Bertha explained to Loomis that the mule might be old but it was strong and could do the job. Whether or not Loomis could get Toby the mule to do it or not remained to be seen.

Crick had a full tank of gas in the tractor and he could get all he wanted once he got back to all the stranded vehicles at Prepper Stock. He chuckled to himself thinking about arriving on a paddle wheeled tractor towing a barge and how surprised everyone would be.

He was going to find out what was going on with the authorities when he got home if the phones were working. If they were not, he had a lot of thinking to do about whether or not he was going to ride his tractor in to town to seek any out.

Crick figured doing that would be futile and time consuming but it had to be considered. He had debated that with himself and Loomis and it basically had all boiled down to what kind of news and insights he could get once he arrived at his destination. If the phones worked, he could check in with some friends and try to get the lay of the land before contacting the fire department or somebody to advise them of the people stranded on the island.

The prospect of possibly being able to actually get back to Bertha`s and Clem`s place on the Mc Cloud plantation tomorrow, attach the paddle wheels and do a test run over to the island without the barge was just too much for him. First thing in the morning whether he got in touch with any rescuers or not he was heading back to Prepperstock.

The barge had to be checked out but Clem said it was still attached at the ferry crossing landing and wouldn't be anything to get it loose and hook it to the tractor for towing or pushing.

Crick hadn't thought about just pushing the barge which was described as basically a platform on pontoons. It was strong enough to transport 1 car across the river, had a railing around it and was occasionally rented out as a party boat tow for them spring breakers and tourists.

Clem had said if they could figure out how to attach the front wheel or forks of the tractor to the barge like an outboard motor, they would basically have themselves a pretty good paddleboat. The boat would steer just like the tractor did with the wheel but in their case it would cause the back paddle wheels to pivot in the direction they wanted to go. Basically, what you were doing is turning the whole body of the tractor to swing the two paddle wheels and keeping the singular tire in the front stable someway if you were attached to the barge deck.

Crick would look at what Clem had in mind later. His tractor had to stay mobile and unencumbered right now, it was his only transport and there were plenty of fields that needed tending. Once he got Morgan and his wife back over here they would have the use of another car and tractor and having that extra transport was a game changer.

The curve of the road marking the property line of Crick`s Farmstead came up and Crick stopped pedaling and just rested and listened for a moment on the side of the road. It was all quiet and his nose couldn't tell if it was fresh wood smoke he was smelling or the forests burning miles from here that had filled his senses all day with acrid smells.

He peddled down to his driveway and viewed his house from a distance. Everything looked all right from this perspective but caution was still called for. Crick laid the bike down at the edge of the woods and cautiously made his way to the house. A slow walk around it eying windows for damage or forced entry and finding the back door still secured put a big smile on his face as he realized nobody had messed with his stuff.

He opened his door and a deep sense of relief came over him as he went in and viewed his familiar surroundings. He then rushed over to the wall and removed the handset of the kitchen phone from it's cradle and listened. Yes! He had dial tone, Crick thought excitedly and then spied the half bottle of whiskey sitting on the counter next to the sink.

"Oh yea, that's for me!" Crick said to himself while hanging the phone back up and heading to the cupboard to get a glass. He then opened his refrigerator to get a Coke and was taken aback by the smell.

"Whew! That is bad funky! I must of not cleaned that thing out as much as I thought I had of perishable food before I left for Prepper Stock. Damn, I aint worrying about that rotten garbage now." Crick thought and just grabbed a partial liter of coke to fix himself a drink. Ice Machine! Got to remember to hook up my ice machine here in a bit." He mused while pouring flat coke into a glass containing a shot of whiskey.

"Ah Ambrosia!" Crick declared after taking a long swig out of it. Horses! How are the horses? He hadn't seen them on his way in. Probably hanging out in the shade over by the barn." Crick mused and went to look out his bedroom window.

"There they are." He rejoiced to himself after spotting the pair. He was supposed to carry Loomis one back but figured it would be best to just bring him back to the house to get it. No sense trying to lead a horse with a tractor all the way back to Clem`s. I wonder if Loomis is actually going to try that wagon train thing he keeps talking about? Oh yea, speaking of which he had phone calls to make. Who was he going to call first?" Crick pondered before the name David instantly came to mind.

Crick went back over to the phone, his mind whirling with ten thousand things that needed to be done or said today and dialed David`s number.

The phone was ringing, "Hello?" Julie`s voice came crackling over the receiver.

11

A WAITING AND A WISHING

"Damn Clem, these bolt nuts are rusted on here pretty good." Loomis fussed as he added a length of pipe to the wrench he was using to get some better leverage.

"I told you we should of let that penetrating oil work on them some before trying to take them off. Hell, they been drove in a swamp and parked here about 15 years." Clem groused.

"Yea I know, I just wanted to get this chore out of the way. I wonder how Crick is making out?" Loomis said getting some satisfaction as the nut he was working on began to loosen.

"Oh he be fine. I hope Slim got back from where ever he went to, could be he went and gave Crick a ride home but I told him that if there was enough gas in Slim's truck to come back over here first and jump my truck off." Clem said looking out the barn door hoping he would see a cloud of red dust coming down the driveway.

"If Slim was coming, I imagine they would have already gotten here by now. Most likely Crick is halfway home and thinking about breaking for lunch. What the hell is a 'corn dodger' anyway, Clem? I saw Bertha give him a small bag of them this morning." Loomis said finally getting the nut off the rusted threads of the tractors' wheel.

"They are kind of like fried corn nuggets or hushpuppies. Traveling food, Bertha calls them. Basically they are made with sugar, salt, cornmeal, flour and lard. They will fill you up and last a longtime without refrigeration. I like mine's with Tobasco sauce." Clem advised and changed the subject to inquire about the other two men that were sent out rafting from the castaway's campgrounds.

"Well, like I told you, Crick and I went right and they went left a bit upstream to look for a usable boat or get some help. They are supposed to stay near the shoreline and backtrack this way if they can't find anything useful or any help. What's down that way anyway, Clem?" Loomis asked trying to wrestle another nut off the wheels.

"Not much as far as I know, haven't been down that way in years. Used to be a couple fish camps scattered about, a boat landing and a wooden cabin or two. Rich folks been buying up plots and building lake houses on this end of the lake, I don't know if they have been doing the same down that way. Most of it is paper company land or National forest. Maybe when Crick gets back we can take my truck and go looking for your friends." Clem said mulling the situation over.

"That would be most appreciated; let's get that chain hoist hooked to this paddle wheel, Clem. I only have 3 bolts left on this side and one
I already got loosened." Loomis said wiping the sweat off his face with a bandana.

THE END BOOK TWO OF THE PREPPER ADRIFT SERIES

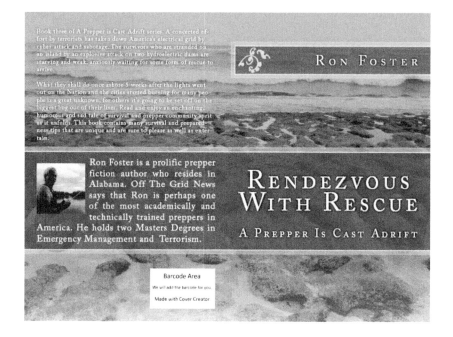

1

MAKING READY

"Bertha is you about ready to go down to the landing? Crick and Loomis have finished putting them paddle wheels on his tractor and are just cleaning up." Clem asked through the screen door on the front of Bertha's porch.

"In just a minute Clem, I just got to finish putting our lunch together. Rossy Ross brought me three rabbits just after breakfast I fried up. Told her you would replace the shotgun shells for them and that she could come along for the trip. Did you fuel the truck up yet with that gas Crick brought you?" Bertha said bustling back to the kitchen to get a jar of her homemade sweet bread and butter pickles to add to her grapevine basket full of lunch fixings.

"That sounds good! We sure have been putting on a nice spread and eating well since we got visitors down this way. I hope they don't come to expect such fine meals out of us all the time though." Clem said only half joking and not voicing all his concerns for the future state of affairs of their dinner table.

"Yes we sure enough have! I wouldn't worry yourself none though Clem. Them boys has got lots of common sense and no city folk airs or misconceptions about them concerning what it takes to live through hard times..." Bertha began before Clem started to object and came on into the house.

"Wipe your feet first Clem! Land sakes you can keep a body busy! Your boots are dusty and me and Rossy got my place all swept up and clean to receive company." Bertha scolded and then handed him the wicker basket holding their picnic lunch for the day and then began to sort of push and herd him back out the door.

"Dang it, now Bertha I ain`t dirtying nothing up in here. Besides old woman, I done told you that we aren't going to get no newcomers today. We are just going to be going to the river and trying out one of my inventions to see how good it does." Clem complained looking around for Crick and Loomis to see if they were within ear shot so he could finish what it was he wanted to talk to Bertha about.

"Now Clem, what's got you so antsy and looking like your boots are pinching' at your toes? You look like you going to bust at the seams. Bertha asked, adjusting her little house on the prairie looking bonnet instead of her normal red bandana on her head.

"What's got a hold of me? Girl what's got a hold of you today? What's got you wearing that Sunnybrook farm bonnet anyway; you decide we are going to have Sunday go to meeting service today? What are you thinking over there? You too good for your regular old bandana now that we got ourselves some new city folk visitors here abouts? Land sakes old women, you putting on your Sunday best for folks we don't even know yet that will probably be all looking like death warmed over and not caring a hoot if you were even bald headed. Now Loomis and Crick we already seen they's are nothing more than some down to earth good ol country boys at heart and what do we care anyway if half them other folks on that island they have been talking about are the city slicker types coming over here? No need to put on airs for none of them neither I say! They going to have to learn to be farmers now and the closet thing they going to see to a office cubicle is cleaning out a horse stall around here. Why Bertha, You the one that said yourself that you only wanted certain types of people allowed in your house and now you want to get all duded and frilled up and let just any kind of folks come sit on your front porch and access your kitchen? Hell you don't want even me coming in here half the time. I am telling you, you might want to look the bunch over real good before you get too friendly with any of them." Clem said, grabbing one side of his overall suspenders and holding the basket on the other side body in a casual but aggressive stance, wanting to have this argument out and over here and now.

"What you talking about, Clem? You said they's going to be sharecropping over here, is there something you need to be tellingly me about them people from that island? You tell that Crick to leave any of them bad type boys over there far away from the shacks or we ain`t got no room for none of them! You tell him that good now you hear?" Bertha said, loosening the tie downs on her bonnet so she could hear Clem`s response better and probably also to let the steam of her anger out from under it.

"Now Bertha, you silly old thing, you know that there are all kinds of people in this here world and in the worst of times the bad often times comes out in people as you well know! What might be your friends today could be your enemy tomorrow when you get down to the last pickle in the barrel, if you know what I mean?" Clem said, trying to warn the old woman about having too much of an open door and faith policy for the unknown guests that were soon to be arriving.

"I knows that Clem! I still want to know if they told you 'bout anybody particular to look out for, they can leave them over on that there island till later, you know?" Bertha said, opening the screen door reaching around into her umbrella stand to get what she called her pokey stick.

Pokey sticks are any kind of strong wooden stick or sometimes vine curled canes or staffs country folks use to go investigate something they don't know too much about what it might be that drew their attention.

Before diving into a blackberry patch to do some picking, you poke around to make sure there isn't a snake or some kind of snarly creature in there to mess with you first. If

Clem hollers, then you had better grab your pokey stick to come help him cause you never know what it is you might be up against, could be a fox, snake, possum or other country critter you might need to help him poke at. Also it is a point of conversation of many a kid, you got to go poke something creepy with a stick and talk about it! I don't know why poking things with a stick becomes the point of conversation, but that's the way it is, if you don't know what it is, poke it with a stick and then talk about it later!

Clem eyed Bertha studiously for a moment and then thought about just what her getting out a pokey stick meant and that he hoped she wouldn't be poking at him with it today. Clem reckoned that like with the old family and the lobster she mistook for a dragon once that they might be needing them a pokey stick for defense. And if Clem didn't calm her down some and quit funning her he might get her all spooked like when she was a girl and then she might end up just starting to spin around and start whomping everything in sight like that danged old mule of hers did when it had a fit!

As Bertha raised her pokey stick like she was going to do an attitude adjustment on someone or something, Clem raised a hand and soothingly said, "Bertha, as far as I know there ain`t nobody in particular at all in that bunch we got to worry about. But then again they's starving folks just the same. They are just like starving dogs that wouldn't normally bite you on a better day but those folks are starving and bone tired weary by now and ain`t got their good sense or wits and manners about them. I just as soon you leave that stick at home today Bertha, but we's going to be around the river and weeds. You remember now, you don't be going whopping no two-legged critters, you hear me? I promise I won't fun you or try to scare you with no dead snakes neither and upset you. What I'm trying to tell you is sort of like when I tried to teach you playing poker one time, you got to keep your poker face on and not show your hand to people! We don't want to be showing them everything we got at first and they're going to be trying to figure out what we might have put

back anyway. There's fifty or more of them folks that we ain't
never met yet and from what Crick and Loomis been telling us
they all got guns or knives they are going to be toting', and they
could take anything we got if they wanted to I reckon." Clem
said.

"Oh so I should go get my gun instead Clem?" Bertha
turning toward the door to head for her rifle instead of her pokey
stick.

"No Bertha I ain't saying that at all, you just leave your
rifle home where its at and take your stick, Knowing you. You
got yourself a straight razor in your garter belt as backup
anyway!" Clem said making her uncomfortable, underwear in
her opinion was only supposed to be referred to in a hat and not
on your person in polite conversation.

"Look here Bertha; I see that Loomis and Crick are
heading down here now so we got to cut this conversation a
might short. I'm only just advising you that we only tell them
folks everything they know, not everything that we know about
the goings on at this place. We are just a pair of old dirt farmers
but we got more cards than they do for winning this here
survival game we find ourselves in." Clem said letting the
warning sink in.

"I ain't never understood all the rules 'bout them poker
games of yours, you always seems to be changing the rules on
me! I am going to have to get Crick to pull out that Holt's book
of rules while he is here so's I can keep up with you and your
shenagins. Every time we're disagreeing about them rules, you
pull out that durn book and read off sometimes a sentence or two
in your favor that just sounds different from what you told me
before and I think you might have been pulling my leg so you
could win!" Bertha said to try to see if Clem had been up to
something sneaky or not.

"Have them check those dice your Uncle Luke left you
Bertha while you're at it. Them's loaded dice, I swear Bertha
and you knows it!" Clem reminded her

Thankfully Crick and Loomis came up the red dusty clay dirt road within what was considered earshot by the pair of old porch-sitters and ended their little fray they were about to have over who's more apt to be cheating who.

"Hi Bertha, that's is a fine bonnet you got on today! Very pretty!" Loomis said remembering his manners and what to say to get on the old girls good side.

"Fine indeed Miss Bertha! You're looking well today!" Crick said wondering if she had just changed the underwear recently in that hat and if it might have been the mule's bonnet at one time or another and stifling a grin at the thought.

"Hey Crick, Loomis, Ya'll ready to fire everything up and go on down to the landing now? I can't wait for you to see my invention in all its glory a paddling along" Clem said with his eyes sparkling and boots twitching to get on down to the river and let the show and fun begin.

"Now Clem, you said we were going to discuss this first even though we are going down there to the river bank directly. What about those boys Ben and Beauregard you looking for, that Ben feller is, what did you call him, a bonding man?" Bertha said.

"No, a bondsman, you know the guy that puts up money when you got to get out of jail! A bonded man is kinda like a slave or indentured servant." Loomis began before Bertha said "I'm taking my gun with me now instead of this stick, there ain't nobody making no slave out of me, bonded with dentures or not!" Bertha exclaimed and hustled to go get her gun before Crick put a calming hand on her shoulder and slowed her down before things got out of hand with her ideas about bonded and unbonded dentures.

About that time Rossy Ross rounded the corner with her venerable old single shot 20 gauge shotgun, declaring she ain't going to be no dentures servant either and that them city folks could stay on that island whether she had herself a sore tooth or not!

"Now ya'll settle down, ain`t nobody talking anything about indentured servants or slaves! All we got here to be concerned with is to go out and look for this Ben the Bondsman and a fellow they call Beauregard that took themselves a raft ride over here to also escape that island and find some help who we ain`t seen hide nor hair from yet. They are supposed to be somewhere downstream as far as Crick and Loomis knows. But Crick said if they didn't find any help down that way they're supposed to be coming back up this way." Clem explained.

"Them bondsmen, are they like them slave hunters of old like my Grandmamma told me about?" Bertha said looking around worriedly.

"No Bertha they the money guys you got to go see like when we had to get Jebediah out of the cross bar motel. Course if they gets you out of jail, they also make sure that you show up at court whether you want to or not so they don't lose no money." Clem said jogging her memory.

"Oh yeah, I know what they talking about Miss Bertha! My Momma has to get one of them fellas once in a while, but they always seem to want something more than money when they come around!" Rossy said scowling and holding her gun a little tighter.

"Now there are good ones and bad ones just like in everything. Think about them like money changers in the Bible, Bertha. They exchange a little bit of money for freedom, you don't have the money then they share it with you but you beholding, it's more like sharecropping: you ain`t got it, I lend it to you then you got to work it off till you pay it back with interest." Clem said.

"Oh we going to be like bail bondsman's now then!" Bertha said puffing out her ample bosom a bit, imagining something new.

"Well I understand sharecroppers foreman gets a piece of the crop you make, but the bail bondsmen they get you out of jail it's like they own a piece of your body!" Rossy said remembering her Momma's experiences.

"That not what it is at all, the worlds full of haves and have nots and people that profit from saying that they're helping somebody out but sometimes abusing others by overcharging for the right to do so. Might be what you call a necessary evil. Now you remember Bertha around here, payment for shares of the crop were always fair, nobody had their finger on the scales to cheat you of money so you could afford to take your young un to the doctor, The McCloud plantation always been fair, we going to carry on that tradition! We don't need no bondsmen no more, according to Crick there ain`t no jails around here, no more bonds, no fines, no rich folks trying to get no richer, it's just us and the little bit we have and those less fortunate we trying to help to replace what's lost, ain`t that right Crick?" Clem said.

"Well yeah, but we need to talk about that a bit more. I would like to find my two friends first before going to the river, like Crick said he's one of the good ones, have no fears about him!" Loomis declared.

"I know me and ma needed a hand out or help up sometime. If someone wanted to help us out they wasn't always in it for the profit. We used to call that being a good Christian, guess they got names for it all nowadays what with no government food stamps nor such things anymore. I don't know about being Christian all the time though, that holier than thou preacher down at the four lane there got kinda handsy with me and my Ma when we needed some donated clothes from down there once." Rossy said not sure about what intentions were sometimes represented as always.

"I fixed him good for you Rossy. I don't think anybody's heard about him in five counties have they?" Clem said before spitting on the ground.

Loomis and Crick eyed each other with a bit of sorrow over the ways of the world and how these families had survived so long without society around to help them for so long and now these good souls were going to be the salvation for so many.

"Now when the hell do I get to go see my brainy contraption work? I'll explain everything later about how to find your friends, do we have to go gallivanting off to find your two friends first or can we go ahead on down to the landing? Hey Crick, you better keep that tractor close to the shore, that paddle wheeler thing is older than the hills; keep you and it close to shore in case it decides to show its age and come apart at a seam! Why don't we honk our horns along the way to the landing and maybe them two will hear and come see what all the commotion's about!" Clem said not to be put off any longer than necessary today, from what he called 'floating the boat"

"How about me and you Clem just take ourselves a run up and down the highway a mile or two in each direction and see if those two made it up here that far? If they made it past this access road then they might be trying their hand at hitch hiking, you know, we will just take us a quick little look see around the general area before we take off and test the machine! I gave you enough gas for that little jaunt, didn't I? I might be able to spare a bit more if not"" Crick said thinking about what was best thing to do at the moment.

Well I suppose we could, but it's gonna cost you a tiny might though. If I agree that we are gonna ride a few miles up and down the road looking for your lost friends Frick and Frack the Fresno twins first, then we gotta come to some terms, do you agree?" Clem said speculatively.

"I dunno, what's it gonna cost me then?" Crick said confused.

"Oh not much at all, the deal is, that iffin that thing floats the first go round and you don't drown or sink it in the mud, then I get me a turn at driving it Ok? I sure would like to spin them old paddle wheels around one more time by myself." Clem said clapping and rubbing his hands together with glee while looking dreamily off into the distance thinking about all the fine tales he could tell afterwards for years.

"Daaamn! Well sure, why not? I guess you can have your turn then Clem, I was going to let you give her a try anyway but if you want to call it a deal, then it's a deal!" Crick said looking to Loomis for confirmation that they were going to let this crazy old race car loving country plough boy play with their one piece of equipment for survival.

"Hey Bertha, how would you like a ride on the lake with me up in the cab? That tractor of Cricks is so damn fancy it's even got speakers in the wheels that plays radio that you can hear more of if you leave the doors open to listen!" Clem said grinning at Crick about his modern conveyance.

"I ain`t going to be thinking about listening to no damn music coming out of any of them wheels while you try driving it Clem! I ain`t even considering listening to no more of your craziness neither, so don't even try it Clem Bowman. There is no way that you are getting me to ride that darn thing off with you out into that muddy river water. You knows I can't swim! And don't you even think about asking Rossy Ross neither just so's you can have a passenger to bedevil along the way. She is going to be standing right here by me on the shore and if you swamp that thing or try splashing us with it I am going whomp you with my pokey stick when you get back ashore!" Bertha said only half serious and wanting to see how good of a job Clem did driving it in the river before maybe she would think about letting Rossy Ross have a turn at being part of such a spectacular thing. *Imagine that she mused to herself, a tractor boat! Oh Clem is going to be hard to live with after this adventure; he would talk them to death.*

"Are you really going to let him drive that thing?" You think it's safe?" Loomis whispered to Crick.

"I got no choice Crick; he traded us for the wheels." David whispered back listening to the animated threesome chatting excitedly in front of them.

No, hell no, I done told you a dozen times already Bertha them boys we are looking for ain`t got nothing to do with no dentures or bonding servants if we find them. The word was *indentured* and I don't have time to explain to you what it means again. Just treat them folks when we find them the same as you did when we found Crick and Loomis and everything will be alright." Crick overheard Clem to say.

"Now then Mister Crick do I get to ride the tractor some if it works?" Clem questioned wandering away from Bertha and Rossy.

"Sure no problem, I told you so already!" Crick answered before Loomis poked him in the ribs to ask when was it going to be his turn to try it.

"Dammit, we can't be riding all the gas out the tractor and spend a ton of time playing with it. You know Ben and Beauregard didn't even have those packets of hot chocolate MREs like we did and they will be in far worse shape than when we were when we arrived here. Sorry for the fussing guys. I just figured that we needed to hurry up and go out and look for them boys as quick as we can, course they might be doing fine up river somewhere working on a rescue plan of their own. I just don't know. Anyway I need to get back over to the island and tell them folks about how we are planning on getting them off there and what our plans are after we get them back to this side. Hell I ain`t going to look for them two river rats that long anyway. Shoot if we did find them I bet they probably would ask a turn to drive that dang tractor thing around themselves some also" Crick said still smiling and laughing at the strange company he found himself keeping these days.

"Loomis! You get your cotton picking fingers outta there, I done fed you once already this morning!" Bertha said as Loomis peeked under the cover on the wicker basket in order to see what there might be available for lunch later.

Aw hell Bertha, I just thought you might need some help carrying it and wanted to make sure it wasn't stone soup or something and it be too heavy for you to tote all by yourself!" Loomis declared smiling at the old woman.

"What's stone soup Clem? Never heard of such before, oh maybe I do know what it is. Did you show them that there patch of wacky weeds where those hippie boys you run off had all that rabbit tobacco growing? Loomis you have had my wild weed gathering and cooking before, you know I ain`t got you neither stoned nor made nobody sick yet when I fix it! I only use a little Sherry in it once in awhile if it's available" Bertha declared thinking Loomis had broken her taboo about saying anything derogatory about her cooking.

"Now Bertha, he didn't mean anything. He has just got himself a healthy appetite for your good cooking and wanted to see what kind of vittles you got fixed up for us. I don't know nothing about no stone soup though, but it sure sounds awful interesting. Can you eat that shit too, Loomis?" Clem asked.

"Eat what? Uh, what is it your talking about Clem?" Loomis exclaimed, totally confused as to what it was the old man was exactly referring to.

"The stoner soup we was talking about, is it made out of that stuff that some folks call wildwood weed or Mary Jane that people say they get stoned off of? Is that why the dish you is talking about called stone soup?" Clem said as Loomis looked like he caught on to what it was they were talking about.

"No not that stuff at all, He wasn't referring to marijuana. What he was talking about is an old story about a hungry soldier that got a village to all add to the pot to make soup. You never heard that one before? Stone Soup is an old folk story in which hungry strangers persuade local people of a town to give them hidden food. It is usually told as a lesson to children in cooperation and community sharing." Crick declared laughing at the confusion.

"What kind of stone do you use Crick? Has it got salt in it or did he get the villagers stoned to get them to donate?" Bertha asked more confused than ever as Loomis groaned and shook his head.

"No its well, its well what you might say is a fable sort of thing with a moral at the end to teach people something. I ain't going to try to explain it to you right now, Crick you want to take over here and explain it?" Loomis asked as Clem and Bertha waited for more information on this mysterious culinary dish.

"Me or Loomis will tell you all about that story later on; meantime, right now we got to be getting this show on the road folks! OK, now then, I tell you all what I think we should be doing. I don't know my way to get down to the landing so I am going to follow Clem's truck down there later on so what I suggest we do now is we all load up on that pickup truck and we spend a little time running the roads around here a couple miles up and down have ourselves a look see around the area outside this plantation. Could be we see a sign of Beauregard and Ben. We get done with that and then we can all come back here and start up on seeing if that tractor will float. Do we all agree?" Crick said looking at the group.

Nodding heads of assent for the plan occurred but soon an argument ensued about where the picnic basket was going to be transported at and the seating order for everyone. Bertha said she didn't care as long as the basket was away from Loomis which created even more confusion and hub bub.

Crick and Loomis were all for riding in the back of the pickup and stuffing Rossy Ross in between Bertha and Clem inside the pickup.

Bertha wanted Loomis in the middle of her and Clem in the trucks cab for whatever reason, and Rossy could ride in back to advise Crick of the local sights. Scientifically, there was no way in hell Loomis could fit in between Bertha and Clem in that truck and there weren't no way he was sitting in her lap so somehow it ended up with Rossy Ross, Loomis and Crick all riding in the back of the truck as Bertha hung out the window trying to talk to Loomis all the way!

That conversation wasn't going well what with the sound of the wind and the engine and every time that conversation got going good Clem would honk that "AH-OOOO_Ga" horn Loomis decided was sometimes like a model T and other times like the old General Lee's horn in a TV sitcom as Clem seemed to hit a electronic switch or something to cause the first verses of Dixie to start playing right after it made its first strange sound. Neither Crick nor Loomis had heard the damn horn before but memories of the movie Deliverance played in their heads as they were rolling down the country road.

Clem had an old can type boat air horn that he put Rossy Ross in charge of to help raise a ruckus with as they progressed along hoping that the survivors they were hunting would hear it.

Problem being she like to point it playfully towards Loomis's hat to see if she could get a rise out of the hat or him when she blew it and that didn't go over well with him at all! Crick knew there wasn't a house for miles around here so creating such a commotion seemed like good sense in this situation and Loomis's blustering just added to the noise.

Well after about 15 or 20 minutes of raising a racket along that old country road trying to alert anyone who might be listening for help coming all the while scaring all kinds of critters along the way and no luck finding the other rafters, they finally got back to the mission at hand of going down to the river landing and the group turned back toward the house to pick up the tractor.

2

LOST FRIENDS FOUND

"What in the hell is all that noise going on? Do you reckon that it is somehow meant for us specifically? Could be rescuers or Crick trying to find us" Ben said cocking his head towards it and listening.

The last fifteen minutes or so they'd been hearing the sounds of Dukes of Hazard meets McHale's navy or something and evidently somebody had an old Model T around here or something similar with a klaxon horn and somebody else had some kind of musical horn. Ben and Beauregard figured someone must be trying awful hard to alert someone around here or draw attention to themselves but it was awful hard to figure out exactly where all that noise was coming from.

Then everything kind of went quiet up on the bluff for a while so they kept trudging along hoping it was probably Crick looking for them and eventually they would all meet up soon.

It had been three long days since they had washed up on the shore after leaving Castaway Island as they'd been referring to the place after Crick and Loomis had separated those rafts and sent them on their different ways.

The coal barge they had checked out soon after landing upon the opposite shore where it was washed up at but a brief examination showed it held nothing useable for them and where the tugboat was that had once pulled it had ended up at, nobody knows.

Ben and Beauregard hoped to find a boat or some house with some people willing to come help out but there was nothing along the area that they had been assigned to scout that offered anything useful for a rescue or a refuge.

It had taken them upwards of a half a day and then some to figure that out and then slowly begin backtracking while stopping occasionally along the way to fish and hunt blackberries in a vain attempt to get some sustenance and they were in a sorry state as they headed back to where they figured Crick and Loomis had gone ashore at.

They had seen the raft Crick and Loomis had used tied up in the weeds yesterday on the shore and the trail they had left leading up to the woods away from the raft but they didn't follow that path and instead tried to stick to the shoreline like they were supposed too still doing their boat and house hunting. Then they had heard the crazy truck and horn sounds and decided to turn inland.

"Something is definitely going on up there, Beauregard! We are heading that way the very first clearer patch of woods and vines that we can find and go see about what and who that is!" Ben said.

"Yeah, but what if it's not Crick? I bet it is, but you never know, maybe someone wants somebody else besides us to come out of the woods for another reason?" Beauregard speculated.

"I don't know, I do know at least if we keep on going along this way, everyone at Prepper Stock can see us going up the shore line soon and know that we are working on something to get them off that damn island, though I don't know what that something might be right at the moment!" Ben said wearily trudging along.

"There's those damn sounds again! Listen, now there's a 'beep beep' sound like a truck backing up warning I am hearing not too far off." Beauregard said as they listened to the sounds in the woods.

"I got no idea, doesn't' that look like smoke across the river from the campground?" Beauregard said, pointing in the general direction of the campground where they had first left on this excursion in to muck and mire.

"We got to go inland and upwards now regardless; there is a big ass ditch up ahead in front of us. Shit, lets sit down a second; I'm too totally worn out!" Beauregard declared.

"Look man, we got to be going on inland and up this hill now while we got plenty of noise to follow. We will take a break in a little bit ok? I am wore out to but we can wait on a rest. Somebody's is riding around on what has to be some kind of a road nearby with all them car horns blaring." Ben said eyeing the shore around them.

"Yee Haw!" A voice not too far away called. And all of the sudden they heard a big motor gun followed with the sound of a big splash.

Beauregard and Ben looked at each other trying to figure out what that might mean.

"EEe Hee Hee!" The sound like a female Earnest T Bass rang out not too far distant from their position on this side of the ravine.

"That's close, what is it they could possibly be doing? Don't sound like no rescue party to me." Ben said checking his holstered pistol.

"Dang close, I say it sounds like a bunch of kids having fun at the beach." Beauregard said, doing the same.

"They must have got themselves some kind of a boat! We need us a boat lets get hurrying along." Beauregard said, pushing by Ben to get down to the pencil thin shoreline.

"Not so fast, we watch and wait! No telling who that might be, or for that matter how they will be acting after all these weeks without power! Hell they might be the superstitious type and be doing something crazy like drowning a witch or something." Ben said thinking about how strange folks could get and who they might blame after a disaster or some odd religious belief they had influenced them.

"They are having fun with something though and it doesn't sound much like anything bad offhand I would say."

413

Beauregard complained thinking that caution wasn't that necessary now.

Two worn weary dirt smudged faces peered out of the bushes of the shoreline and they heard the putt-putting Lap-Lapping sound of some kind of boat coming around the bend.

"What do you think it is? Damn sure is a weird sounding boat motor" Beauregard said.

"Damned if I know, but keep quiet, that sounded kind of close and it will be here soon enough for us to get a look at it." Ben said.

"Look sees I told you it would be here in a minute. Whatever it is coming this way it's sure got dang big headlights!" Ben declared

"Headlights! What kind of headlights? How close are they together? You got a guess on its size?" Beauregard said sticking his head out from around the bushes to get a better look.

"What in the hell is that contraption?" Ben said, doing the same maneuver to get a better view.

The pair looked like Heckle and Jekyll sticking their heads out of the bushes on the very narrow shore with their bodies remaining hidden behind a bush as Crick rounded the corner riding that paddlewheel looking gizmo they had created.

"Do what???" The pair both exclaimed at once in astonishment at the spectacle.

"Aw shit!" Crick declared seeing two dirty ugly wall trophy mount looking heads poking pistols out of a bush with there free hands while rubberneck looking his way and he started laying on his horn and creating a lot more noise that the shore party of Clem and crew took as a excuse to raise another ruckus of their own with hoots and horn blares in response.

Well, what with the sparkling sun lit water reflecting off the windshield and everything else awash in white foam from the paddle wheels and the odd crafts progress through the water, neither Ben nor Beauregard could see who was driving this odd looking contraption that looked like it had came out of the back swamps of Louisiana. Not that they were worried so much about a strange apparition in these times, but this one kind of took them aback and left them speechless as to what it was and what it was doing there.

What made it worse for them was whatever or whoever was driving the thing climbed halfway out the door and started yelling 'Hey! Hey! I found them!" loudly as the driver hit a submerged log that nearly threw him out into the river before they got a good look at him.

"Found what, did what?" Beauregard said stepping out into the open for a better look. no longer worried about remaining behind cover anymore..

"You son of a bitches, you darn near scared me to death with those pistols poking out of the bushes towards me. Your surprising me like that nearly broke my rig!" Crick shouted not knowing whether he should go into reverse or go forward with this weird contraption he was traversing these waterways with to get off of whatever it was he had hit.

"Crick is that you?" Beauregard shouted.

"Well who the hell else would it be? You expect anyone else to come save your sorry hides today?" Crick hollered back jubilant and blessedly happy at finding his friends safe today.

"Damn man, just what in the hell is that thing you're riding on and where did you find it?" Ben called out.

"Don't be talking about my puddle jumper like that! I will have you know that one Clement T Bowman designed and engineered this for me special. You might have messed it up distracting me like that with your ugly mugs and uglier guns suddenly appearing in the bushes like that though, give me just a minute to assess some damage here." Crick said as he checked out the paddlewheels and jumped up on the hood of the tractor for a better look.

"Let me get myself clear of this log and you all walk your pretty selves just about a hundred yards or so up the shore from here and through the woods apiece and we got friends waiting to meet you! Never seen crazy guys like you two poking their heads and guns out the bushes like that except in a bean the clown tent at the carnival show!" Crick said celebrating by fussing at them playfully and laughing as the pair came out of the thicket to stand on a clearer piece of shoreline.

"Can't do it man, there is a bitch of a ditch over here full of mud and water that looks dang near impassable. We'll try to go around Crick and meet you up their somewhere when we can get a clean path!" Ben hollered back.

"Who yare you talking to Crick? Who's that? Is that them damn prisoner catcher releasers you been talking about?" Bertha bellowed in her strong voice out from the other farthest side of the ravine.

"They are our friends Bertha! Told you that already! You are going to like them just fine." Crick said over the noise of the engines and all the crowing going on about all the confusion.

"Tell them to come on over here and get acquainted! I can keep Bertha in check," Clem called out trying to get a glimpse at where the other voices were coming from.

"They can't cross over from where they are at Clem, they're stymied by a ditch that is between ya'll!" Crick called back

"What the hell's a 'stymie'? Just float them on back on the tractor. Never mind I'll come down there and get them myself, tell them to stay put David!" Rossy called.

"No you stay right there yourself Rossy where you're at and don't be pointing no guns at them when you do see them. They are our friends! Let me see if I can idle the engine here in front of them for a second and figure things out." Crick said, deciding if it would be better than to shut the tractor down out here in the water or try to let it idle. *Damn thing should start back up .He had enough experience with amphibious vehicles in the Army that he figured it should start as long a s the exhaust pipe and anything that made it go bang like the air scoop also* stayed above the waterline.'

Crick finally decided what to do and with an 'Oh Hell' this might hurt pause gingerly turned the key off to tractor in order make conversation possible over the noise of the engine and the lapping of the water from his wake.

"What's up boys? You don't look too bad considering the trip you been on." Crick said swinging open the door of the tractor to greet his fellow rafters and figure out just what he'd hit in the shallows to stop him and figure out how best to get off of it.

"Well ain't you a damn sight for sore eyes man! You couldn't find anything better to captain than whatever that is you're riding on? And who the hell are all these folks who keep yelling back at us?" Ben called back having some fun for the fist time in a month and curious as hell about what he would get back for an explanation...

"They're some new friends we met! Awful good people actually, that believe it or not knows more about how to survive this disaster than the whole bunch of us preppers put together. I don't know how you're going to get over there but find your way best you can and I will see you over there." Crick called looking at the ravine leading up to a bluff.

"Don't worry about us; we will get our butts in gear and get there eventually. Have you been over to the Prepper camp yet?" Beauregard called out to him concerned about those they had left behind.

"No not yet, this is our very first maiden voyage if you want to call it that. I think they might can hear us over there but unless someone is fishing that steep slope at the far end away from camp they can't see us this far away. "Crick said sitting down on the front end of the floating tractor boat and hiking his boots up on the bumper so he didn't get his feet wet as the unwieldy craft rocked up and down in the rivers current.

"Got anything to eat?" Beauregard called out.

"Got something for you all good to eat already fixed, but you got to get back around that way somehow. Hey boys, this currents picking up, I got to fire this thing up!" Crick said as he started drifting down river some.

Crick climbed back into the cab and attempted to restart the old beast. RRR, RRRR the thing grumbled before its engine finally caught again and rumbled to life in a billow of smoke and diesel belching. Crick managed to pull out of the shallows and off the log he had hit and get in the main channel a bit more as he started to throttle down to make it back to the landing where Clem and Bertha stood waving at him at the other end of the bend.

"Now what we are going to do, Ben? Do you have a course of action you prefer?" Beauregard said.

"I guess we are going to walk it uphill and around unless you want to try swimming it." Ben said.

"Seems like us swimming would get us there a lot better and faster than crawling up that ravine, but this pistol don't swim so well. I say we walk" Beauregard replied.

Crick idled the tractor's engine down and reduced the white froth coming off the paddlewheels and hollered at them while bobbing along more midstream in the river.

"We' will keep honking the horns on and off down at the boat landing and you can find your way to us easier!" David called out

"Follow that redneck reveille and we'll finally find who's making all that noise and what it is they are driving!" Ben said to Beauregard and they set off on the rest of their trip.

It was roughly about 45 minutes later that Ben and Beauregard who had probably walked a little further than they had to all the while cussing the briars, the heat, the mud and life in general while figuring out the way until they came upon the faded peeling white paint signs pointing to the boat landing.

"That's got to be where they all are!" Beauregard said with a renewed spring in his step.

"Head that way then, don't worry about me, I can keep up just fine." Ben said as they trudged up to a small paved road coming up on the clearing where they observed a unique heart warming sight.

An old blue and white pickup with Loomis sitting on top of the cab in that old cowboy hat of his looking like a cop siren, Crick hollering at them from the paddlewheel tractor parked off to the right, an old country man in worn overalls happily cavorting about everywhere pointing in their direction making exclamations and an old black woman with a bonnet on waving welcome to beat the band when all of the sudden a gangly figure popped up out of the woods in front of them hollering "Howdy ya'll"   as Rossy Ross came out of the edge of the woods to greet them personally with a childlike glee and a smile that would be forever be remembered.

"You let them men folks hands go and quit hugging them and come on down here Rossy!" Bertha said as everyone came up to greet the lost rafters.

"Introductions are in order! " Crick declared and set about restoring order while grinning like a possum eating honeysuckle.

"Well I already know which one Ben is; he got that sheriffs badge on!" Bertha said, to which Crick and Clem started chuckling about it and Loomis took control of the situation by doing the intros and reliving the men of their burdens by taking their packs.

"I can't tell." Rossy said puzzled

"Tell what, darling?" Bertha said, talking to Rossy as everyone started greetings and shaking hands once more firing questions at one another.

"If he has got the badge on, does that mean the other one's the dentist?" Rossy asked, poking a finger in her mouth and not quite wanting to talk about what it was paining her.

"I am not any dentist, who told you that? What is she talking about?" Beauregard said complaining. "You got a tooth hurting honey?" Beauregard said starting to reach a caring hand over at the child as she caught sight of his pistol and started to hide behind Bertha.

"I ain`t no dentist I said!" Beauregard exclaimed and wondered what his pistol she had observed had to do with that obscure fact.

"Well we don't need to get out of jail but we do need teethies fixed around here. So are you the dentist or do you just know about dentures if someone needed some bonded?" Bertha declared.

"Just what is it that we are talking about? Stupid shirt, I didn't even think anything about wearing it to be honest. I ain`t no sheriff or dentist neither. I am a bail bondsman." Ben protested.

Crick said he would tell them later and not to worry about it.

"There he said it, just what kind of men is it you put bonds on if it ain`t for teeth Ben? We don't needs no indenturing or getting out of jails" Bertha complained.

"You boys got to eat something regardless I guess! Crick said you wouldn't bother us none and I believes him" Bertha said going to get her picnic basket of goodies.

"Ha! I tell you who the denture man is now!" Rossy whispered to Crick watching the boys salivating over the rabbit and goodies in the basket that Bertha took the cover off and shoved it their way for further inspection.

"She got pickles and other fixings in there too Gents, we ain`t going to make you sing for your supper boys, no worries, just eat real slow ands save us some. We will let you eat first in peace before we start into telling our stories and asking for yours." Clem said, shaking a rabbit haunch at Beauregard who only took about one second to make it disappear out of his hand and headed towards his mouth.

"Now ya'll munch munch" Loomis began, trying to talk with a mouthful of rabbit and reaching over towards Bertha's pickles before they went too far away as his audience reached over carefully to get their own foods away from the ravenous heathen who had been waiting on that picnic basket lid to be opened and lunch to be called all day.

"Loomis! Where is your manners at son, the guests eat first and they gets the first choice!" Bertha scolded him but still enjoying how that country boy loved eating her vittles. Then Bertha snatched the pickles back and said "Here get you some." as Ben and Beauregard's eyes popped at the feast set out before them.

There was a momentary pause and Crick said "Get you some corn dodgers also and dip them in the syrup." Before Ben and Beauregard fought each other to be first to get some of that good eating out of the basket Clem started taking care of the distribution in a more orderly fashion.

"I'll get mine in a minute that is if you three leave me anything." Crick said joking.

Well if you didn't know anything about two ravenous dogs eyeing each other before chowing down you could have used old Ben and Beauregard as an example. Took a second or two of them wolfing down ravenous bites of country fried rabbit and corn dodgers before Beauregard finally felt sated enough to have surfaced for air and say something.

"This is the best, munch munch, food, munch, I ever tasted! This is wonderful! Thank you, Miss Bertha." Beauregard declared, Ben agreed, eating with two hands and seeing how much he could fit in his mouth at once with a playful poke at Loomis who acted like he was going to steal a bone from a starving dog as he reached past them for some more hot sauce.

"Settle down boys; eat slowly now it's better on your gizzards. It's kind of like drinking water after being in the desert; you can't wolf it down all at once! I know you got spider webs in your assholes from not eating for a while, but you got to settle down and pace yourselves better!" Clem said looking at the two gluttons consuming even the sweat off the pickles on a napkin.

"That's right; don't be saying you got sick off my cooking or anything crazy like that. Ya'll can't be punishing yourselves that way or I'll have to give you my old cure and dose you some later!" Bertha declared sternly. To which Crick and Loomis declared "Oh hell no", because Clem had clued them in as to what the "Bertha cure" was that included some turpentine in it and the gamut of medicinal meadow weeds she knew that said you sure didn't want to go there! Bertha believed in expectorants and purges to get the poisons out of you as she put it and the cure was as about as bad as the cause and they had seen she also kept asafetida and castor oil about for the occasion.

"You will end up puking or shitting your guts out either way oh believes me you don't want to try or need the cure." Rossy advised making a face.

"Bertha had this thing about turpentine." Clem said. "It goes in everything she makes from horse and mule liniment to cough medicine and you didn't want Bertha dosing you with none of her concoctions or it'll be coming out one end or the other or both!" He declared slowing down eating himself.

Needless to say the chomping fest stopped when Bertha started fishing around in that big old purse of hers for her 'medicine' and the boys slowed down to a almost comical pace so they wouldn't get that dose of medicine!

"If you don't take a dose, you know she's going to snatch hold of you and sit on you!" Rossy Ross said in a whisper.

"That's the secret to good health my friends, don't tell her you got anything wrong with you!" Clem said;

"Bertha used to chase me around when I was a boy and sit on me to dose me with that medicine of her and her maws and you don't know which way it's going to come out, but one good thing about it, she will wash your drawers afterwards!" Clem exclaimed. "You better leave her a clean pair of drawers on laundry day too or you are going to get dosed again!" Clem guffawed and everyone took note to be wary.

3

THE CAVALRY ARRIVES

Julie and David were traveling down a winding country road about thirty miles from Crick's house watching the road and the horizon for any telltale signs of smoke or danger ahead.

For the last two and half hours they had been listening to the emergency broadcast channels giving directions to the FEMA relocation centers and warning of wild fires and traffic hazards. The trip had been pretty much uneventful except for a wildfire detour of a national forest that had got them lost for a while until they could make heads or tails on a map where exactly they were at.

David didn't know if GPS was working or not and that fact bugged him a lot. GPS was relatively easy to bring down if you were a foreign power with satellite killer technology but he wondered also what a dedicated hacker could do to the system if they had a mind to.

The military as well as many other commercial ventures relied entirely too much on that navigation system in his opinion and he had been aware for years how fragile and how dependent they were on the technology. Well maybe they will say something about it on the radio or he could ask Crick if he had heard anything when they met up.

"Julie it won't be long until we get to Crick's place, I guess we sort of over worried ourselves about this trip in some ways, but don't let your guard down just yet. I don't know if it's just my nerves being jittery from the ride or knowing the lack of us seeing very many people means bad things about them holding up in their houses, but its downright creepy thinking about rolling up on any house I don't know well right now." David said carefully watching anything and everything with a detached curiosity that hoped to gain answers from the most obscure things.

The muddy river banks that looked like they would soon cave in they had seen along the way didn't really tell him much about the hazards of the waterways. He already knew a dam was blown around here, but it also appeared there had been a great deal of rain fall around the area recently. That was a good thing. Maybe it would help knock out some of those wild fires.

Good thing the damned terrorists had not included weather in their plans or had they? Now that was a confusing thought. It would make sense for them to blow a dam right before a deluge to magnify the effects of an attack but on the other hand if you planned on doing some economic damage as well as hamper and exasperate recovery efforts with a firestorm you don't want a rainstorm reducing your efforts.

"I know what you mean David about feeling apprehensive and emotionally drained. Heading out on this trip I didn't know if we were going to see the apocalypse or get pulled over by some kind of military storm troopers wanting to take some of our stuff." Julie replied.

"Except for that congregation of military police in Montgomery, I guess we we're very lucky not to see anyone. They sure are warning the public a lot on the radio about what martial law is these days." David said slowing down and observing the woods ahead.

"Why are you slowing down David? You see something?" Julie asked looking ahead to see what was up.

"I'm trying to decide if we need to go ahead and get the long arms out of hiding and make them more available." David replied, still scanning the area.

"You expect trouble, David? Do you think that their might be something wrong at Crick's house?" Julie asked looking across the car seat at David carefully.

"No, but forearmed is forewarned or some shit like that, I'd just as soon have my shotgun handy driving up on that house. You get that Keltec 9mm carbine out and that bag of clips in the duffel bag when I pull over." David said staring over toward the road's shoulder.

David had his 7 plus 1 shot Sig 45 pistol handy as well his .380 Keltec pistol in his pocket. Julie had a 17 plus one shot 9mm Astra A100 and a 9mm Keltec pistol in her Thunderwear holster and extra clips. Both had relied on these armaments on the trip so far and in no way felt under or over gunned in anyway..

A carry pistol and a backup pistol, David advised should be the same caliber if possible. Everything Julie carried for this trip was 9mm caliber, two pistols and a thirty shot carbine. David didn't have another 9mm pistol or he would have matched her. The 380 was his daily carry pistol, he was known to say if he had his pants on he had his pistol on.

The 45 pistol of his required some thought from him as one of his carry choices. But he did not consider this dilemma of choosing a weapon for long. His other option was the .357 single action Ruger pistol or a CZ52 semi auto pistol which shot 7.62 x 25mm Tokarev ammunition.

The CZ was a hotly debated item between him and Julie because David knew it was a vest buster with a standard load up to and a bit past a level one ballistic vest and with the hand loads he had it could surpass a level two bullet resistant vest. In a martial law situation, that was a serious thing to consider. However, after much thought and soul searching, David had opted for the 45 because of dependability and availability of ammunition over the more exotic round in the CZ52 pistol.

A CZ52 which is Czechoslovakian made version of Tokarov famous Russian pistol of the cold war era. The Czechs didn't like the crudely made pistol of the Soviet bloc and decide to make one themselves with precision engineering with better fit and polish as well as dependability under certain circumstances.

A normal Tokarov pistol round comes out at about 1500 fps (feet per second) but many hand loaders load the more sturdy CZ with hotter powder that pushes the 7.62 x 25 pistol bullet at a screaming rate of 1950 f.p.s. You're not going to buy these rounds at your local department store, especially not Wally World. They are however easily purchased on the internet as there are hundreds of thousands of imported pistols that shoot this round. The key to the CZ52 being able to be loaded so hotly is it's rolling block mechanism versus the traditional blowback design of the Tokarov. This is what gives a CZ52 phenomenal strength of what can be loaded into it. however it has its shortfalls.

ONE THING TO NEVER DO WITH A CZ52 IS DRY FIRE IT! It has a very brittle firing pin and it will break!

After market strong firing pins are readily available on the market for $15.95 or less and is a must purchase if you own one of these weapons. Some folks call these guns ugly, but to David they were beautiful. It looked like a James Bond gun and fit his hand well. He was lucky enough to get a hand-picked factory refurbished one that looked like it had never been shot before with a holster and an extra clip at one time when they were plentiful. They are hard to find now but not uncommon .David had told her his doubts regarding the ammunition situation. Now finding ammunition for that particular type of pistol or if you needed parts, was assuredly impossible these days.

He had left the pistol with Michael and advised him of its vest buster capabilities if he needed such with those foreign troops at the missile plant, but warned him of marginal results.

David also warned him about a can of ammo he had, a whole ammo can that you have to watch out for it because it's old military Soviet bloc issue. The thing is, Russia has plenty of submachine guns that were made in the caliber of 7.62 by 25. Those rounds are too hot to shoot in a regular Tokarov pistol but some of that stuff you don't even want to shoot out of a CZ52 with its short barrel.

426

Unless you read Russian or know what to look for you can make a serious mistake because it all fits in any gun of the same caliber. David got a case of it fixed from the Mole Boys and hadn't gone through it to separate the pistol and submachine rounds but he had gotten a good deal on it because he basically got into impasse on who got the cool pistol or the ammo for the right price.

David told them not everyone wanted that old kind of caliber and they might have trouble getting rid of it when they wanted to buy David's pistol. David told them he didn't really want to sell the pistol anymore but if he could get that much ammo at a decent price he wanted to keep it even more. The debate was resolved when David told them about that machine gun bullet issue and that he was not about to teach them Russian to keep them from blowing the barrel off. So they opted to sell the ammo to David cheap and try to get him on another deal another day.

David had settled on the 45 which to him was a no-brainer over the .357 just because it was semi-auto. David had also been highly impressed with the weapons record in battle as well as Sig Sauer's infomercials of being thrown in a muddy truck tire rut, run over by a tank, caught on fire and picked up and shooting a perfect group there after.

What is weird in the gun world is that everyone agrees straight out of the box, the Sig Sauer 220 is the most accurate 45 caliber pistol made out there. Countless people spend countless dollars on modifying Colt 1911 pistols to the nth degree with very satisfactory results. But a stock Sig beats them out of the box hands down every time. The venerated 45 caliber is a celebrated and known man-stopper. No hollow points or miracle rounds are needed for it as even a standard 230 grain military issue ball round has proven its lethality time after time. As for bullet speed and weight, big and slow is sometimes the best way to go

"OK, Julie, here's the game plan when we arrive at Crick's place. I know that we've been over this more than once or twice but let's do it again. When we get to Crick's house, I will honk my horn just like I do with every country place I pull up at. We know Crick and the rest of the preppers over on the island don't have cars, so the property should be pretty much abandoned looking. We will wait a minute or so to see if he answers the door and then I'll get out with the shotgun. You release your door but don't open it and you have your carbine at the ready and be glancing to the front of the house and out the rear view mirror occasionally as well so as to try and be aware of what is going on to the side of you. If I have to blow that shotgun off, get out of the car and lay down covering fire with that carbine of yours while I'm retreating. That reminds me, let me change out the first shell in the shotgun, give me a second while I unload this thing." David said ejecting a couple shells. "OK Julie, what I'm putting in here is 3 inch number 4 buck shot, that's 42 pellets of about 25 calibers going downrange. Poor man's response to a machine gun, I suppose." David said with a sly grin.

42 pellets of number 4 plated buckshot from his approach distance if someone was fool enough to take a shot at him out a window or from around on the porch and miss him would likely to be ended with about a 3 foot swath of hot lead by him depending on distance flying back in their direction. David always said the point man in an infantry patrol in Vietnam that was ambushed in the jungle should have had number one shot instead of military issue buckshot. Its suppressive fire going down range in ambush situation you need. You want to make the other guy miss or duck; you don't want to allow him to have an easy follow up shot and you want to and keep his head down. If you have 42 zinger pellets ventilating the leaves while breaking twigs, snapping branches, whizzing by your ears etc., then that sort of thing tends to spoil your opponents aim.

That was the basis of David's tactics should they be fired upon from the house. David would try to respond towards aggressor and mark the position of the enemy while heavy suppressive fire was laid down by Julie with her more automatic weapon. David told her that we were lucky to have so much extra ammo that every shot didn't have to count and don't waste time aiming at an antagonist, you more wanted to spray and pray in his direction while you found cover.

David had not had too much opportunity for range time with her to teach her accuracy in engaging targets nor had she ever had a target that shot back at her. The number one thing that you have to instill in everybody the first time you hand them an automatic weapon is to control and cycle their fire. The old M-16's that David was used to could be emptied in two or three seconds if you had your finger on the trigger. The Army taught him two to three round bursts to conserve ammunition and make your fire more accurate was the thing to do.

Some time or another after he got out of the service, they put a regulator on full auto to only make the guns shoot two to three round bursts regardless of operator intent and this was implemented because in the field of battle many trainees will panic and just hold the trigger down emptying their weapon of ammo all at once.

Julie was thankful that she had taken the time to sew the elastic cartridge holders tighter on the shotgun bandoliers. They had been so loose that not only were they not in position to grab and go but shells would often fall out of the holders. Those cheap shotgun bandoliers and slings get all stretched out with age and become a liability rather than an asset.

4

CRICK`S HOUSE

This sure is one crazy note he left for us Julie" David said handing it to her.

David,

Glad you made it here safe; sorry I couldn't be here to welcome you. Make yourself to home but we need to meet up as soon as we can. Rescue efforts by me and Loomis are taking place at the Mc Cloud Plantation about 20 miles from here. Be sure to announce yourself loudly when you enter the property. The property caretakers Clem and Bertha carry guns and are very suspicious of strangers but I have warned them that you might be coming. I drew you a map on the back of this note. No problems to report, thanks for coming. Be safe.

Regards,

Crick

"Well he certainly didn't tell you much or why you are here" Julie said handing it back to him after a quick look at the map.

"I could have used a bit more info but I guess what could he really say? He and Loomis are conducting the rescue effort so that means no official efforts underway or offered. I sure would like to know what he plans on doing with all them folks once they get off that island. I guess it doesn't matter much at the moment, just getting them off there is an undertaking in itself." David said looking in Cricks kitchen pantry out of curiosity.

430

"Well he said meet him at a plantation so maybe they have lots of food for the survivors." Julie guessed.

"I hope they do but he didn't make mention of it so I have my doubts. That could be a pine plantation, cotton or peanut plantations etc. so your guess is about as good as mine. It doesn't look like he has depleted his pantry by a whole lot though whatever that means. Hang on a minute, ah hell yea! His liquor cabinet is still full, hot damn! Want a drink Julie? Crick won't mind and I will let him sample my moonshine when we hook up." David said picking up an open liter of coke and shaking it to see if it still had some fizz left in it.

"I would love one, sounds good. What is our schedule today David?' 'Julie asked as David played bartender.

'I guess we have ourselves a few drinks, relax from the trip for a short bit and head on over to the plantation. I figure we can stay here for about an hour and make it over to meet Crick at about 3.30 or so this afternoon. Plenty of daylight will still be left "David said relishing the taste of his adult beverage.

"Sounds good to me, that trip was nerve wracking and tiring." Julie said settling down into a comfortable chair with a sigh.

"I want to check on Crick's horses before we leave. I don't guess he wants me to bring anything from here or feed them or he would have put it in his note. David said sitting down upon the couch.

"Well it's not that far to the plantation so I guess if he needs it he can come back himself and get it. Hey I haven't tried his phone for service yet." Julie said going over to it and picking up the receiver.

"Well it's not dead but there is nothing but static on the line. " Julie said pushing the button to hang it up several times and listening for any kind of dial tone.

"That's something anyway; some signal beats no signal I guess. Maybe they will get it fixed soon if they got power on the line." David responded.

"You never realize how much you miss having communication until you lose it." Julie said while going to the window to look at the horses grazing.

"Normal conversations and touching base with others is reassuring, but what is heart rending is the number of people wanting to, or needing to call for help and that are cutoff. That kind of misery is only amplified and exasperated by the feeling of forlornness those people will be feeling now as they attempt to reach out to unknown neighbors and struggling friends that have no choice but to distance themselves from the chaos and dependency of others." David said putting his arm around Julie and looking out the window with her.

"David I have a question for you. Do people you have known just all of the sudden pop into your mind and make you wonder how they are doing?" Julie said looking up at him.

"Yea that happens more often than I care to think about. Damn depressing. I try not to think too much on that subject though; their futility tends to fuel my own self-doubts about self-preservation and how hard my heart might need to be getting in order to survive myself." David sighed.

"I kind of figured that, when this crap first hit it was more of an adventure even though we were pretty well prepped for it. I still get satisfaction out of how well we were able to respond to the loss of power and grocery stores etc. but it scares me to death how fast we are going through preps and energy and this apocalypse is now only beginning to get crazier. You said a huge amount of people are already evidencing dark and animalistic behaviors, will we get that way too David?" Julie said with a shudder.

"No sweetie, well not like others anyway. We have hope, knowledge, skills and tools to see us through when the last crumb of food preps is used up and that's why we will retain much of our humanity. I haven't brought this up yet but there are a few things we need to go over before we join in on Crick and Loomis's rescue efforts." David said and told her they needed to sit down and have another drink and talk a few things out further.

David poured them two more drinks a bit stiffer than the last and settled down at the dining room table across from Julie and studied her a moment before telling her what needed to be said.

"Julie we were very lucky indeed not to run into too many people on the way here but there are a few reasons for that which we need to discuss. Now I know we went over a little bit about what we would do if we saw a family with kids stranded on the side of the road and how we might handle someone trying a road block to rob us, but shit is actually much more worse than that and I need to make you even more cautious and aware." David said taking a big swig of his drink and deciding it was going to take more than two drinks before they were ready to face what was coming next.

"The main reason we didn't see very many folks out on the road is that they are sick or they are trying to tend to those sicker or weaker than themselves or already dead. Much of the populace is already dead or dying from medical issues and the living are in fear of their own shadows at the moment. If you have water but no food you can still be wandering around after 30 days searching for or sustaining yourself with practically anything for food. People will be eating grass, bugs, pets, maybe even thinking about eating each other about now if they haven't lost the will to live and committed suicide and that's a funny thing. Mental illness will come to those who have never experienced it in some cases; it will be enhanced in those that lack the medication for preexisting conditions. The weak minded, acutely depressed or desperate might choose suicide; the criminally intent will increase their level of violence and discard for the physically weaker, the unprepared and unaware will seek the security and sanctity of their homes and mentally shutoff and play hermit awhile, most folks will think they have to do something but not knowing what exactly that something is, will venture out into a world that is unrecognizable and not governed by the rule of law or mercy and they will soon expire or become as lawless as the rest.

Good people are at an extreme disadvantage under such dire conditions, the law of the jungle is an obscure thought to them at first. They will form bad alliances, make stupid mistakes, wait too long, surrender too much and be absorbed into the dust of the earth eventually as just one more statistic as the cruel and the strong war on others. Then when the wolf packs start forming up, at first the packs are large and the prey is easy. As the prey lessens internal strife, disputes with other packs, leadership role challenges and a host of other influences will lessen their numbers. The hunter and the hunted change roles daily, the people in Law enforcement that supposedly are there to protect and serve quit their official duties and become a force of oppression to be dealt with as they try to wield their power to support their own and their families. Soldiers and police officers desert their posts, the populace revolts and follows the first charismatic leader that steps up as the religious minded does the same with prophecies of the end times causing more insanity and bloodshed.

This holocaust of humanity is just now starting to gain momentum however and the dark ages haven't even begun yet in totality. People with power, governments and state agencies never relinquish control without a fight and they have been planning on events such as these because they fear the populace ever finding out that they were the actual ones that created such mayhem and plan accordingly to brutally suppress any threat to their seats of power and control. Throughout history they have wielded their armies and the best minds they can find to advise them how to both appease as well as how to subjugate the common man to their maniacal intents.

"Julie, we met a lot of folks at Prepper Stock last year and they all were the best of the best in my opinion. You know I have been playing with preppers and either teaching them or learning from them before the name was even being coined by the major media. At first it was like hippie days of an awakening of millions to go back to living off the earth and regaining personal freedoms. They changed a lot but those idealistic thoughts hit reality's and now the majority leading the country has short hair and different values and won't even admit to being one at one time in their life in order to chase the all mighty dollar.

5

CHICKEN THIEVES

David and Julie approached what they thought was the entrance to the McCloud plantation and turned on to a red clay rutted weed overgrown road.

"David, are you sure this is the right turnoff? Doesn't look like any plantation I ever saw." Julie questioned.

"You're the one navigating and reading Crick's directions. We'll travel down this road a bit and see where it's goes." David said eyeing the scrub oak and pine woods on both side s of the road.

"David he didn't say what kind of plantation it was." Julie said looking at the edge of the second growth fields.

""Looks like we got some cleared land coming up." Davis said as they rounded a curve and saw what appeared to be fields that had not been worked in years.

For as far as the eye could see in several directions, a rolling plain of pasture grass, scrub oaks, bushes and fences in general neglect met their eyes.

"What's that over there by that old barn looking thing? Looks like there might be some more old buildings or something." Julie said pointing off in the distance at a rickety array of outbuildings and a few old whitewashed shacks.

"I don't know. I guess we head over there first; it's the closest thing that looks like civilization back there. This might be a plantation but I'll be damned if anybody's worked this part of it in years." David said looking at fresh tire tracks in the red clay soil.

CHICKEN THIEVES

"Someone has been down here recently. A truck and a tractor have been through this way not too long ago it appears." David said as they made their way down to the farm buildings.

"Look David, that one house over there with the porch on it looks like it has a bit of fresh paint on it compared to the others. The rest of them places look like they will be falling down pretty soon. Maybe that's the one where Clem and Bertha live." Julie said looking around at the ramshackle buildings.

"Shit, Julie, Crick should have said we were going to tobacco road! These damn places look like old sharecropper shacks or slave quarters from a bygone era. But evidently someone's painted that one house in the last ten years or so." David said looking at the disarray of buildings in front of him.

"Damn sure smells like they got farm animals around here." Julie said testing the breeze out of the rolled down windows of the vehicle they were riding in.

"Yea, it smells like a working farm to me." David said grinning and honking the horn to alert the people who lived there that somebody was coming for a visit.

David and Julie pulled up in front of the old wood frame tiny shotgun style house and honked the horn again looking around for any signs of its occupant's whereabouts. They looked and listened some more and heard nothing more than a jackass braying and what sounded like a cow having itself a conniption fit about something.

"Well, they definitely got farm critters but I don't see any vehicles around here. Doesn't look to me like anybody's at home at the moment Julie." David said opening up his door and pointing his shotgun at the ready and looking around further for any signs of life at the place.

"They might be in the back. Sounds like some kind of commotion going on in that barnyard." Julie said opening her door and holding her 20 gauge single shot shotgun in a one-handed position.

"Julie I'm going to walk around to the backyard and see if anyone's about. You stay up here and see if anyone comes up.

437

I'm going to walk carefully around the house and see what all that commotion is in the barnyard and you be on your guard and haul ass out of here if you have to. Now before you say it, just back the van out and haul ass out of here if you have to because I have no idea what's going on back there." David said admonishing her not to hang around to back him up and him having to be worried about her instead of hauling ass himself or engaging a target if he needed to.

Understanding David's warning and his nagging at her to escape in the van if need be, warred with her own desire to want to back him up anyway, Julie agreed to stay where she was at in order to placate David and watched as he made his way surreptitiously moving from cover to cover towards the backyard to see what had riled the animals back there.

"HEY! COME HERE! I DON'T MEAN YOU ANY HARM!" David yelled when he was half way around the building after he spied a blur of faded blue jeans with holes and a worn-out blue cotton shirt running from the chicken coop.

"David are you all right?" Julie called to David's back observing whatever it was he was hollering at.

"I'm fine! Hey, come on back here buddy! We don't mean no harm! Are you Clem? Are you Bertha? Crick sent us!" David yelled confused as to the gender of the disappearing shadow in the woods.

David surveyed the old barn and corral that had a mule defiantly braying at him and eyeing wherever the other person had left to while a skittish cow poked her head out of the barn and occasionally mooed her dismay. A giant African fighting rooster was strutting his stuff backwards and forwards by the barn while the hens and biddies alternately pecked the ground while occasionally cocking their heads to look around nervously.

David stood up tall and watched the wood line looking for the apparition he had seen leaving the chicken coop running while he glanced around the barnyard to see what had the animals still upset.

"Hey you crazy old ana-mule, be you a Jack or Jenny to be making such a fuss? Hush now you mule! Mooo to you to cow! You need hush yourself also so I can hear what's going on! Get back over there you danged old ugly rooster." David was saying before a quick glance over his shoulder showed him that Julie was creeping up in back of him.

"I thought we agreed that you were supposed to stay in the car and leave out of here post haste if there was any trouble." David said halfheartedly as Julie carefully approached his position with her gun at the ready all the while looking about and listening to the farm creatures complaining about something.

"I don't know what these animals are complaining so much about yet, but whoever was here a few minutes ago has hightailed it for the woods and I can't tell you very much about them except they move awful dang quick." David said still looking in the general direction towards the area that he had seen they had disappeared to.

"I caught a glimpse of a leg going into that thicket of bushes but that's about all David." Julie said not letting her guard or her weapon down.

"So what should we do now David? Who do you think that it was anyway?" Julie asked glancing at David nervously.

"I guess it was whoever owns the damn place or whoever lives here. I know they should have heard my horn as we were coming in earlier, why they didn't stand their ground and holler back to us I have no idea. I don't even know if we're on the right piece of land or not. This looks like it was some kind of old timey plantation or sharecropper set up in the past I guess. Damn Crick was kind of sparse on his description of the place he wanted to meet us at. Let's go back up to the front porch and check the house and I guess we sit around and wait until whoever that was gets their nerve up and comes back or decides we're safe and hollers up to us from the woods." David said turning and walking back towards the front of the house with Julie.

"That road keeps going a ways it looks like David. Do you think that Crick might be staying further down this road and we haven't arrived at where we're supposed to be at yet? "Julie questioned looking at the well-worn tire ruts in the red clay and gray gravel road leading away.

"Hell I don't know. That idea does make some sense though I think, not much we can do sitting around here but wait on who knows what. Yea come on Julie let's go ahead and ride on up there and check out what we find at its end, we can always comeback here. We definitely scared off whoever that was from this place. I still can't figure it out. Crick said Clem and Bertha would be expecting us, just for us to be aware of them toting guns so we didn't scare them or ourselves I guess. But whoever that was didn't even take any time to stop and be sociable or look like they had a mind to be defending their property for that matter." David said still narrowly all the while eyeing the fringes of the woods for any kind of suggestion of movement.

David and Julie got back in the van with several wary looks around and then slowly backed out to proceed on down the road towards a hill that looked like it had other outbuildings and structures on it.

David stopped the car on the top of the hill and eyed a dilapidated couple of houses with one more recently painted one that looked a lot more habitable than the rest.

"Same thing here for a lay out, just one house a little better than the rest and the others looking like they're about to fall down. Somebody's is definitely living over here however; the same as the last place but this house looks a lot bigger. Hopefully they're not as skittish about receiving guests." David said once more honking his horn in announcement of his pending arrival as he headed toward the larger house with a big wrap around rail sided porch with a huge old weathered barn in the back.

"Doesn't appear to be anybody at home at this place either, this is kind of freaky to me David." Julie said looking for any movement or signs of life around the place.

"I am thinking the same thing Julie. I'll go to the door and knock first this time and you can hang back and go back to the barn with me later." David said shrugging and wondering exactly what was going on and where in the hell exactly was everybody at that lived around here.

A firmly locked and unanswered door greeted him and his quick perusal of the property gave him no more indications than some tire tracks coming and going in the direction they had already traveled.

Julie and he went back to the porch and sat down on two old white steel garden chairs in silence for a moment, occasionally glancing around curiously at the untilled and overgrown pastures and row crop fields.

"Well Julie I have no idea where Crick and crew are at, I guess we just sit here and wait until someone makes an appearance. Maybe who ever that was I glimpsed at that other house will go find the residents around here and come to greet us as a group eventually." David said pondering the odd disappearance of the raggedy figure he had seen running for the woods.

"Yea that was pretty strange of whoever that was just to up and disappearing like that without a word. You would think if it was someone who was expecting us that they wouldn't have got scared off like that." Julie said speculatively.

"That's just what I am thinking. Crick's note warned us to expect the residents of this place to maybe be pointing a gun in our direction and whoever that was just beat feet and didn't even bother to look back over their shoulder. Evidently they just had nothing but escape on their minds, might even have been a prowler or a thief you think Julie?" David said evidencing his concerns and probably wanting to go back to the other house for a further look see.

"That thought had crossed my mind David, but do you think maybe that it could be that they were just either plain scared, or possibly they could have been rushing to go inform somebody that strangers were about the place. What do you want to do now David? Stay here or should we go on back to the other house?" Julie said anticipating David's decision to return to the other house and try to solve the mystery in order to look around the grounds and barnyard a bit more for signs of mischief or a break in at the main residence.

"Let's just sit ourselves down here for a bit longer Julie and wait awhile to talk things out a bit more before we start heading back down there so soon. It's so weird operating under these conditions, I am dying to try all the doorknobs and windows to see if any of these houses are open or not and get a quick look around to see if I can see any signs of Crick or Loomis but on the same note I don't want to start out on the wrong foot with anyone around here by assuming I can just walk in a door or climb in a window without a proper invitation. Folks could be sitting off in the woods right now watching us and seeing how we act with other folk's property when no one else is present you know.' David said warningly and then began once again carefully scanning the wood line in front and to the sides of him as well as keeping an eye on the road leading here.

"Shit David, I see your point of caution but you didn't have to go and give me the hebee jeebies now about worrying about the idea that their maybe watchers in the woods. Crick said we were invited to this place and that we would be expected by its residents so I was happy that we had finally arrived and I could relax some and quit being so much on edge with all you're reminding me of a battle drill we needed to be thinking on. I am tired David, damn tired and more than a bit afraid of all this unknown we are living through. I know why we came here and I totally agree with you that we needed to come to this place, but I can't help thinking for the life of me that we should of never left our home to begin with and stayed at home where it was safer." Julie said a bit emotionally and welcomed David's hug of reassurance and love that things would turn out all right somehow.

"It will be alright Julie, we just got to hang in here and wait. I am guessing Crick and his friends are down by the river somewhere working on a rescue of some kind but I will be danged if I know what he might have dreamed up to accomplish one or what his plans are after he gets done doing it. I know I shouldn't, but I can't think of anything better to do than kickback and have myself a drink while waiting on him to show up. You want one Julie, a little toddy for the body darlin?" David said rising and heading for the van and supplies to make one.

"No, not for me David, you go ahead, it's still a bit early in the day and the very thought of that batch of shine you cooked up doesn't sound so good to me at this particular moment. I might take you up on one later though to help maybe settle my nerves a bit however." Julie said as she watched David fix himself some shine and coke and remembering that this stuff was more potent than normal as he had redistilled the batch many times to up its alcohol content and make it the equivalent of gasohol if he ever needed to pour it in the gas tank to get home instead of drinking it.

A 50/50 mixture of ethanol alcohol or in David's case, what he had made which was some basically home brewed triple distilled top shelf vodka run back through the still and taken to the state that it could be mixed with gasoline to run any vehicle built after 1983. It was also good for dewatering fuels in gas tanks or making a maltov cocktail should some obscure need arise.

"Whoo! Hoo! This stuff sure isn't Ancient age sipping whiskey. It has a pretty good bite to it I mean to tell you." David said grimacing as the raw alcohol concoction hit his throat and had him exhaling as loudly as he could with pursed lips.

Julie didn't scold him or giggle too much at him for his antics and his indulgence. That was just David's way sometimes, he was going to do it regardless and she had seen him take one drink and put it down to handle a task and never finish it as well as have many more after the first until the sun come down and was working on coming up again to party with an old friend. . It was his crutch to lean upon to ponder upon a point until inspiration or a answer was decided upon at other times. Dumbed him down and let him think he was quoted to say. He could not drink anything alcoholic for a month if he was busy on a project that had his interest or he might arbitrarily decide that this was a party month and he would just think on something. You never could tell what he had decided on when he hollered that it was " Five o'clock somewhere! He even had a big clock on his wall that was stopped a few minutes after 5 to evidence that fact if it needed pointing to.

"That's better I think, but next one is coming out of Crick's whiskey I brought with me. As for what I am going to do at the moment is I am just going to sit right here and pretend that I am having another one just like the other one in a honky-tonk bar somewhere with Crick sitting alongside and figure out what he might be thinking about this situation if I can." David said adding more coke to dilute the fire and take the edge off his 16 ounce drink and then he settled back in his chair with a satisfied smile. He and Crick had pondered the problems of the world and prepping in general over such libations a many a time and he sort of knew how the man's head worked.

"Now then Mr. Crick you old prepper we have had this little conversation before , what do you think I am going to do in this situation and what do I think you might do." David mused before Julie reminded him to watch his drinking and pay more attention to the present.

"Watch out that extra strong stuff doesn't sneak up on you David. I take it that you're not too worried about who ever that was you were hollering at earlier?" Julie said warning David not to get too buzzed off the over potent joy juice and wondering if she should be looking out more for whoever that might of been if David seemed to be getting too unduly distracted or possibly a bit drunker than he imagined he was later.

"Nah darling, I am not too worried much about that raggedy scoundrel much at all at the moment. Who ever that was is probably still running. But, don't you worry; I AM still thinking about them. The back of that khaki kind of floppy fishing hat of theirs and the white fluff from the holes in the jeans was about all I saw in a blur as for any details that I can remember. I can't even tell you what color their skin was or how much they weighed exactly. It was just whoosh, zip and a glimpse of them going around the corner of the chicken coop and off into the woods. I am assuming by the way that they were dressed that they got to be a local person and not to well off at that. Or for that matter they were not any kind of a hunter or woodsman just happening by because of the choice of clothes they had on to be out tromping in the woods. Otherwise we would have seen a bit of camouflage. Maybe it was a neighbor from around here somewhere that came to see Clem and Bertha to borrow some eggs or something?" David said and then made exaggerated head shaking motions and squinchy eyes after another sip of his drink that he hadn't quite put enough coke in yet to tone down the fiery fumes of the white liquor in his red solo cup.

"I didn't even see half that much of them David so I really can't help you form any kind of a true description for them, about all I saw were a leg and a shoe going around a tree and that was it." Julie declared.

"You didn't happen to notice what kind of shoes they had on or the type of tread on them did you? Slick bottoms, tennis shoe soles or hiking boot treads would be a good thing to know." David said looking at her intently hoping she had noticed some detail to give him another definitive clue.

"Well no, not really I am sorry to say. I couldn't tell you if they were wearing boots or regular shoes, seems to me about all that I saw a wisp of faded brown. I don't think I would say they had on tennis shoes over wearing leather ones, no it was just too quick to say what I saw." Julie said searching her memory of the brief mental image she tried to pull up in her head.

"Well they certainly appeared scared enough whatever it was they were wearing and that is worrisome, because scared people don't think straight and you never know there real motives or reasoning sometimes until it's too late. If someone was messing around out stealing eggs or a chicken then they would have certainly hightailed it out of here like that. I tell you what, oh well, damn it never mind, we may as well go back there. Darn it, I thought I was going to be able to sit here for a bit and enjoy this drink in peace for a moment but it appears now we need to go on a mission. The answer to this little quandary we are discussing is probably as simple as just going back and looking into that chicken coop a bit closer. I should have taken the time and done it while I was all ready there. If we found a forgotten or discarded wicker basket or maybe a gunny sack left on the floor that could have told me a lot. This ain`t the kind of drink I want to hurry up chug on down if I can help it and I think it might still be best to wait a bit before going back so if you don't mind indulge me in some more conversation before we go back there and play detective." David said knowing Julie would be mentally evaluating his decision and reasoning to wait something out instead of charging over to check it out might mean something other than he just wanted to sit around and finish his booze.

She remembered his instructions about the need for patience with certain situations because it was just wise to do and particularly remembered the example of it he had taught her about deer hunting. David had explained to her not to let her exuberance of wanting to check out a freshly shot deer for example override the wisdom he had taught her about the nature of such game and the need to wait sometimes. A deer David had told her was first to be respected as a dangerous animal, more than one unwary hunter had had his ass kicked or even been killed by messing with what they thought was a dead deer.

At first Julie thought when David started to relate his hunting stories that he was trying to play a prank or joke on her in some kind of way as to how such a beautiful and docile looking creature could ever be aggressive towards a human let alone kill someone unless it was in pain and got a lucky antler stab in.

David had however changed any misguided notions she might of still had of Bambi cuteness when he explained the deer's fighting style to her and even provided a YouTube video of a 265lb misguided photographer who ended up in the hospital from messing with one when it was rutting season. Dumbass had sprayed himself with deer attractant.

Julie had always thought that a deer's horns were its primary weapon but David quickly corrected her and explained the creatures knew boxing like a kangaroo and those hooves could be razor sharp.

Another favorite thing of a deer in a fight was the two front hooves at once mustang stallion style stomp on you from the rearing back on its hind legs position. What's odd about a deer is that they can stand on two legs and go backwards and forwards in their Chinese Kung Fu fighting Mantis stance and stay up in that position much longer than you would think. It appeared to be their favorite style of engaging taller humans in a game of fisti cuffs that the human was likely to lose.

When David had showed her the first YouTube outdoor amateur video of someone actually engaged in a battle with a deer and the statistics about how many people nationwide in the media had actually been attacked by deer her opinion of the sweet lovable creatures had changed.

They were indeed deadly and were not going to necessarily run at you like a bull or a goat and use their horns. They would rear on their back feet like a bear and say bring it to them or they were going to carry it to you like a bar fight with a redneck in some backwoods saloon and you better be ready for it.

Although deer generally are docile and timid animals that do not attack humans, the deer population explosion, due to human activity, has greatly increased deer-human contact. In addition deer have been forced to live in close proximity to humans and as a result they have lost their fear and become more aggressive toward humans, especially when feeling they themselves or their young might be threatened.

With the ubiquity of phone cameras, the Internet abounds with disturbing video of deer violently attacking people and pets.

The next thing David told her to admire and respect was that a deer when shot was often able to run 50 to a hundred yards or more on pure adrenalin alone whether they were just wounded or already dead away from the threat or attacker and then they would stop. If you pursued a wounded deer and they thought danger was after them they could start back up and run for miles before they expired.

If you were sitting up in your deer stand or hunkered down in a hide or blind and you just shot a deer, wait even if you saw the perfect shot take the beastie down. If he runs he will pause and if no pursuit is noted he will stay in one place and bleed out and you will have less of a chase or distance to pack out the meat. Give the animal a chance to die in peace and the meat tastes better. David told her that those that hunt with dogs find out that animals that are chased taste different than those that can expire without relentless fear or anger driving blood to the surface of the skin etc.

Poke the son of a bitch with your gun barrel at a distance before inspecting it in case life remains was also a caution he had given.

Your attitude can provoke a deer in rut or a doe with fawns. Deer are territorial during these times. If you turn away and retreat, an attack is much less likely than if you stand your ground or move toward the deer. If all else fails you can puff yourself up to look bigger and shout and raise hell waving your hands and arms.

Surviving a *Deer Attack*

If you still are attacked, try and protect your head and face. If possible grab the antlers or front legs.

In the case of whoever that was had run from them, David was probably waiting until they got far away or if they were going to get help or others to wait for them to approach him so he could watch them carefully at a distance he chose.

David and Julie sat on the porch and watched the road leading towards them for about 15 minutes before loading up everything and going back to the first house. Nothing untoward was evident in the chicken coop or around the house so once again there was nothing to do but watch and wait. The hours passed slowly as they talked about setting out off the plantation to try and find a road to the river and try and locate Crick or attempt to see what was going on over at the island.

"Julie do you want something to eat? You got a choice of MRE`s or some of that Wild Mushroom Risotto you like so much we got from survivalbased.com (10% off foodstuffs coupon code Prepper1). David asked looking around for a suitable spot to set up his Silverfire Scout stove. (Coupon code Prepper1 for a few bucks off and free shipping)

David had his big Silverfire Hunter model rocket stove with him for cooking the big meals but the small lightweight scout couldn't be beat for a quick dish or heating water to reconstitute dehydrated or freeze dried food.

Just gather up a few thumb size sticks. Throw in a cotton ball dunked in a bit of Vaseline and that's pretty much it to make a fuel efficient basically smokeless fire.

"I am not all that hungry at the moment but I could eat if you want to now or we can keep waiting for a bit longer. I hate just sitting here; I am up for going scouting for that river road we were talking about. There has to be some access to a boat launch or a landing around here somewhere close." Julie said standing up and stretching after sitting in one place so long.

I agree, hey hang on a minute I think I hear something." David said looking towards the long driveway into the plantation and listening intently.

"Sounds like a tractor or something heading our way." Julie said looking off in the distance and then pointing off in the distance as a dust cloud appeared and pickup truck leading a tractor began to appear in the distance.

"Well lookie here, the cavalry has finally arrived! Glad we sat here and waited so long." David said as he and Julie walked towards the driveway waving a hand in greeting.

"Somebody's parked over there at my house Clem. That must be that feller David that Crick said was coming. "Bertha said pointing towards the two waving figures.

"I reckon it is; now we get to finally meet that feller." Clem said honking his horn and waving his arm out the window at the couple.

"What in the hell kind of tractor is that?" David said as the odd paddle wheeled tractor came into view and began honking its own horn.

"I bet it's some kind of Crick contraption he built specific for the rescue but I never seen one like it before. Do you think it is steam powered?" Julie said trying to get a better look at it by walking off to the side a little and thinking it resembled a old paddle wheel boat on the Mississippi river.

"No its gas or diesel powered. I think that's what they used to call a swamp tractor or a rice field tractor. I have seen something similar to it working in a rice paddy in Louisiana one time. Some folks use them on farms and other people use something similar to go after Cyprus logs in the bayous." David said as he got a better look at it as it got closer.

"Hot damn there is Loomis; I recognize that cowboy hat of his. Hey Loomis!" Julie called looking at the packed cab of the truck as it turned into the driveway. Loomis was squished up against the passenger side, Bertha was in the middle and poor skinny Clem looked like he would ooze out the driver side window with all that weight leaning against him.

The vehicles pulled in the driveway and parked and everybody bailed out all at once in happy meet and greet,

"Hot damn David you made it! Hey Julie girl, it is great to see you!" Crick said getting ahead of the pack to shake hands with David and hug Julie.

"Mr. Loomis I presume?" David said with a laugh doing a Stanley Livingston in Africa interpretation as he greeted the familiar horseman.

"Look who we got with us Loomis said indicating --- Beauregard and Ben who beamed smiles and said their greetings ecstatically that the prepper clan was shaping up well for the rescue.

"This here is Clem, Bertha and Rossy Ross." Crick said introducing the plantations caretakers.

After a brief conversation about how was David and Julie's trip down here and that Cricks house was still standing last time they saw it, Bertha finally invited everyone to move inside her home to get out of the noon day sun.

"Hey Crick does anyone else live here? Me and Julie saw someone running out of the chicken coop a few hours ago." David said as he followed Bertha and Clem into the house.

A puzzled look came over Crick as he looked toward an equally puzzled Clem and Bertha frowned.

"You think your Maw snuck back here Rossy?" Bertha inquired.

"What did they look like?" Clem asked and shook his head in bewilderment who that might have been after the sparse description that Julie and David gave in response.

"Don't sound nothing like my Maw but I will go see if I can spot them here about." Rossy Ross said

"I will go check on my chickens. You all excuse me. You can entertain the guests for a might Clem, I can't imagine who that might have been if they just run off like that." Bertha said skeptically and headed towards the backdoor with Rossy following

"You be careful now Rossy Ross, you don't take no unnecessary risks now you here me?" Clem called after them.

"I won't, I got my 20 gauge handy if the varmint wants to object about me following them and asking what it was they were doing here abouts." Rossy called back and then followed Bertha out the rusty screen door.

"That girl could probably track a possum up a tree but she sometimes doesn't have too much walking around sense when it comes to dealing with strangers in the modern world." Clem said and then asked if anyone wanted some cool tea from the stoneware crock Martha had sitting on the kitchen counter wrapped in a damp cloth.

452

After everyone settled into their seats, talk soon turned to what survival gear David had brought with him and how the people on the island were faring with their various kits and gear they had been using.

David explained about his fish nets and trot lines he had brought with him and his thoughts on how they needed to basically set up a commercial fishing venture to try and sustain the prepper survivors. Everyone thought the plan would work because we were not dealing with your normal group of refugees. As a whole the preppers had the number one skill they needed to survive and that was the willingness to face adversity and persevere. They were alive because they had the will to live and had the spirit and skills to see themselves through this disaster as a capable and pretty cohesive community.

The conversation paused abruptly as the voice of Rossy was heard calling from behind the house and for everyone to come a running.

.

6

CAPTIVE AUDIENCE

"Hey Bertha I need some help here! Hey Clem you all come outside right now and see! I got myself a prisoner out here!" Rossy Ross yelled out.

"What the hell? Who you think she has out their Bertha?" Clem said rising and hurrying towards the backdoor shotgun in hand. It only took but a moment of confusion for everyone to start tripping over each other all hurrying after him and trying to get out the backdoor all at the same time to see what in the world was going on.

The spectacle they beheld was very strange one indeed. Rossy had some poor disheveled and dirty skinny middle aged man that looked the worst for wear backed up against the barn and looking at them fearfully as Rossy Ross kept her .shotgun trained on him.

"Who you got over there as a prisoner Rossy Ross? Who in the world are you stranger?" Clem said eying the grimy bearded fellow in threadbare clothes.

"He says his name is Will Perkins but you ought to just call him plain old thief. Do you know that son of a bitch broke into my house and tore up my door? I tracked his sorry ass from your chicken coop and when I noticed he was heading towards my house I took the shortcut and cut him off trying to leave my driveway. Evidently he had already broken into my place before he found his way over here. Ain`t that right Piss Willie?" Rossy snarled at him.

454

Evidently the new nickname Ross had pot on him was pretty apt as the poor soul evidently had peed his pants by the wet spot that appeared on the front of his jeans.

"Don't eat me!" the pitiful soul squeaked.

"I done told you ain`t nobody eating anybody a hundred times you crazy old coot!" Rossy scolded in his direction.

"That don't mean we won't hang you for being a dirty lowdown burglar though". Rossy snarled.

"Now child quit scaring that man. He looks like he is scared of his own shadow and probably just wanted something to eat. Lower your gun a bit Rossy Ross and let's hear his story before we decides what to do with him," Bertha advised.

"I kind of like the hanging suggestion." Clem said wanting to bedevil the man further for his alleged crimes and misdemeanors.

"Now you hush yourself too Clem. It seems to me that you have been caught with your hand in the cookie jar before after thinking foolishly that you just couldn't live without something." Bertha chided.

"Now Mr. Will you need to explain yourself better and I don't want to be hearing no lies. You tell me the truth now, what were you doing sneaking around my chickens and breaking in Rossy Ross's house?" Bertha said scrutinizing the man further.

"I am sorry, please folks believe me I am very very sorry. I told Rossy how sorry I was, I didn't know anyone was living in that old house I broke in to and I didn't even steal anything but a few cans of food. I wouldn't even have done that if I hadn't been starving to death. I ain`t ate nothing in three days and the last thing I had before that was a can of carrots." Will said like he was about to cry.

"Well son I guess we can overlook a whole bunch of misguided judgments maybe if you are actually in such dire straits but what are you doing around here on Mc Cloud property anyway? You don't look like you are from any parts around here" Bertha declared.

"Can I have some water? I am about to fall out." Will pleaded.

"Sure. One of you all goes get the man a drink of water. Better yet, stranger you go sit up on the back porch stoop and finish telling your story. My mule doesn't take to strangers and its best for all of us if we move away from the barn. Bertha said and waved the interloper along towards the house.

Will drank a glass of water down so fast he had to get rid of a coughing fit before he could carry on with the rest of his story. Julie handed him another glass of water and cautioned him to take it easy and sip this one or he would make himself sick.

"Ah yes, thank you for your kindness. Like I said I am terribly sorry to have caused so much trouble for you all. I am basically what I used to call an honest man but these troubling times have me doing things I thought I would never consider." Will began before Rossy reminded him the worst thing he could have possibly considered was breaking into her house.

She just fumed a bit when Clem told her to hush up and let the man get on with his story about what he was doing around these parts.

"That's a tale of woe and misery my friend that I hate to repeat seeing how you all think so badly of me already." Will said.

"I can't see myself thinking any worse of you than I already do!" Rossy said before a warning look from Bertha quelled any further out bursts from her until Will finished his story.

A greatly deflated and miserable Will carried on with his story and told them that he was living in an apartment outside of Birmingham when all the trouble started and after about three days had gone by he went out looking for water and food.

The military and police he said were riding around telling everyone they needed to stay in their homes and observe the curfew imposed by the governor and that he had heeded that advice as long as he could. He explained that was all well and good that they were telling him to stay at home but he didn't have the means to stay in his place and not venture out because he was already out of water and the few liters of soda he had been drinking off of were about gone. He had to have him some supplies so he ventured out.

The pool in the apartment complex had been drained for the winter and now only contained some greenish slime laden dubious water so he was in a quandary as to what to do before he was blessed by a rainstorm and he and the other residents in the community spread out every pot, pan and container they had out to catch the bounty. That thunderstorm had helped out immensely and he had gathered several gallons of water and stored it as best he could.

Stores all had been emptied seemingly overnight when the power was still on in the beginning of the disaster and the promised water tankers from the National Guard never materialized at what was supposed to be the distribution point at an old strip mall in his area.

He like so many others had showed up early on their appointed day before the designated time and waited uncomfortably for hours waiting on a relief convoy that never came. A pair of police squad cars had arrived about an hour after the designated time and made a brief announcement that he said infuriated and incited the assembled crowd to take violent actions.

"Go back to your homes; all of you go back to your homes now peacefully. There will be no deliveries today. You are instructed to come back here two days time." An officer said over his cars public address system.

He said more but whatever it was he was saying couldn't be heard legibly as an overwhelming sigh of distress was put forward by all the hungry and thirsty folks of the assembled mob which soon turned to shouts of anger and a general move of the crowd in the police cars direction.

The cops immediately aggravated the situation further by turning up the mike and announcing that the crowd was ordered to disperse immediately or they were subject to arrest under the emergency powers act. It didn't take long before the sea of desperate humanity began to surge forward shouting questions and indignation at the officers before they retreated back to their cars with guns drawn and left the parking lot in a hurry leaving the milling crowd to their own devices.

The more uncaring or radically minded people soon began to take out their anger and needs on the strip mall as garbage cans, paper stands and the like were used to bust out the store fronts and batter down doors as an orgy of looting began in earnest.

Will said his first instinct was to leave the area as fast as possible but any thoughts of returning home without anything to sustain himself in the coming days soon lead to him jostling his way into a broken window of a Dollar store with the thugs and common folk all just wanting something, anything they could grab and carry off.

People were shouting, threatening each other, crashing about and generally just mindless as they swarmed the stores aisles snatching whatever they could grab and hold on to. Will grabbed a cardboard case of sweet peas and managed to make it mostly out the door without too many hands trying to steal cans of his hard won goods from him.

Other people didn't fair so lucky as fights, strong arm robberies of the weaker and accidents took their toll. Will said he didn't wait around to find out what was next or try for any more goods and instead got in his car and hurried home before the mayhem of the crowd or police reinforcements to suppress it caught up with him.

The strip mall wasn't far from his house so about two days later he decided to walk up there and see what was going on. The batteries in his weather radio had gone dead the day before and when he started his car to listen to its radio he noted he only had only a little under a half of a tank of gas. Travel restrictions were in force but the radio said FEMA was mobilizing and assembling relief supplies in the city of

Montgomery about 80 miles away just like they did to respond to hurricanes along the Gulf Coast after Katrina.

Will had a good life long friend named Ned who lived in that town and figured that if he could make it down there that his chances of receiving some help were much better in the less populated city. He decided that he would leave out in morning after he ascertained just what was going on in and around his neighborhood and he figured he should have just enough gas to make it.

Will was no stranger to power outages and the aftermath of storms spawned by hurricanes that made their way far inland to his area and was not worried much about any dangers of walking around his neighborhood despite the lawlessness he had participated in the other day. That was a fluke he thought, a momentary misjudgment as he got caught up in the desperation of the moment.

People in his community normally all pulled together and grew closer as a community after a disaster and looting was a rare occurrence mostly brought on by greed and opportunistic criminals looking for whatever goods they could steal like electronics and not out of necessity to obtain food and water.

His conscience had plagued him for days after participating in the Dollar store fiasco and his curiosity and need overcame his fears of returning to what was supposed to be his relief distribution point. Maybe today there would be some emergency supplies he could get. The only neighbor he knew in his apartment complex was out of town and he desired news and human interaction after being held up in his apartment for these long weeks. Getting out in the light of day and fresh air and possibly running into somebody to talk to was exactly what he needed to clear his mind and help him to figure out what he needed to do he had decided.

There were very few cars traveling out on the street and except for a few furtive worried faces peering out from behind the curtains of their homes windows Will said that he saw no one else until he got near the shopping center where he spied a military vehicle with its two Guardsmen occupants.

Will wandered over to the vehicle and one of the soldiers asked him what it was he wanted. Will asked if this place was still a disaster relief distribution site and was informed that no, this place wasn't designated as one anymore and that the new site for his zip code area was a local school building about 3 blocks away. The guardsman advised however that there were no real supplies available to give out to the public there and that the only service he could get at the location was when they fire department turned on one of the hydrants every few days to allow who ever brought a container to draw some water.

The soldier also further advised him that the highways leading out of Birmingham south were pretty much impassable at the moment because of stalled or disabled cars and was pretty much a mess because of the mass exodus that was going on in the city and that it would be best for him to try an alternate route if he was going to try reaching Montgomery.

On his way home to his apartment he started thinking about somehow making his way over to Tuscaloosa and then heading south but he really didn't have the gas for that. He had a business associate that he was on friendly terms with that lived in that town and he had been invited over to his house for dinner a few times but that didn't mean his friend would have any precious gas to spare or for that matter be inclined to give it to him if he made it that far and asked for it. However this still seemed his best option, it sure beat staying around here he considered.

Will told everyone that once he used to walk the streets in his neighborhood with money and friends but in a blink of an eye or the flick of a switch his world had ended and he soon ended up pretty much as destitute as if he had always been homeless.

He had finally decided to try for Tuscaloosa and deal with whatever fate or luck brought his way when he got there. He certainly couldn't stay around where he was at much longer.

He had barely any food of any kind whatsoever left and there was the water shortage to contend with. He knew from past experience that the technologically prehistoric water system for the city wouldn't last more than a day or two, hell the sewage system that the city had over spent on and mismanaged and had almost bankrupted the city and was far from complete was backed up already. He hadn't had a flushing toilet in days if you had water to pour in it and that fact alone told him he had to leave. People in the complex of 150 or so apartments had resorted to whatever means necessary to dispose of their waste and the funk and the stench from the areas where the dumpsters were parked would have gagged a maggot.

Will had simply peed in the sink and thanked his male plumbing for the ability to do so until the pipes in the apartment began to backup. He used a garbage bag lining his toilet bowl for his other business but disposing of a sack of turds was problematic at best because it seems that everyone in the complex thought of using the dumpsters for the same purpose as he did and rotting garbage bags of filth appeared to be just casually tossed in the general direction of the receptacles without any regard for the consequences of the bag bursting open when hitting the pavement. Will said he couldn't really blame folks for this much as he was guilty himself of getting in smelling and throwing distance from the dump sites and let fly of a garbage bag before quickly hurrying away gagging.

Will gathered up what few cans of food he had left, poured what little bit of water he had into empty soda bottles and precariously balanced an open boiler pot full of rain water on his cars floorboards and headed out one fine morning without a plan or much hopes for his future.

As he drove to Tuscaloosa he was amazed by the number of cars that were stuck on the sides of the road as well as the number of people trying to hitch a ride or walking along the highway aimlessly. Will wasn't one to pick up hitch hikers but a couple and their 4 or 5 year old child pulled his heartstrings and he decided he had to stop and give them a ride.

461

Will was scared to death after picking them up though because the man kept referring to the gun he had in his pocket and how they would be ok if anyone messed with them while traveling on this road. Will had never been an advocate for guns and had never been around anyone that talked so much about shooting someone let alone allegedly having one in their pocket and he feared what at first appeared to be such a nice looking couple might turn out to be not so nice and rob him of his car or worse.

The couple had a plastic bag full of bottled water and a couple suitcases with them and upon seeing his pot full of water sort of obliged him to give them all a drink of the precious commodity. The couple explained they had left out from their home under similar circumstances such as his but were forced to leave what they had behind when their car ran out of gas miles down the road.

Talk turned to where everyone was going and why and apparently they didn't have much of any real plan either and they were just seeking shelter and sustenance like Will was. The couple's ultimate goal was to try to get to some relatives country property somewhere on the Georgia border but how they would eventually get there they had no idea about now that they didn't have a car or any money.

Will took this news in with suspicion and apprehension but he tried to assure them and offer hope that the government was setting up camps to help folks like them and maybe they could get a ride of some sorts from FEMA or some other relief agency. The man was not so sure of the fact that the government could mount such a huge response but his wife was adamant that help must be locatable somewhere in the city ahead and they would be all right somehow soon.

Will mentally went over his route to his friend's house and then eventually told them he would have to turn off before the city proper and that he was sorry he couldn't carry them all the way into town but he didn't have the gas or the time to do so. This bit of news didn't go over well and the couple tried to cajole and beseech him to please not put them out and to take them on into the city proper but Will told them that the best he could do was slightly go out of his way and drop them off at the first highway exit they came upon before he had to turn around and go back towards his friend's house in the suburbs.

Will got a niggling uneasy feeling as the man and woman riding with him became more silent and argumentative with each other and him. The child sensing his parents aggression soon began fussing and caterwauling and Will suggested they pull off at the next exit and stretch their legs some and let the kid wander around a bit.

The couple agreed and in a mile or two he pulled into the rest area in front of the restroom. Will got the map out and showed the man where they were at and that his turn off was about 8 miles away but the city exit was another 20 or so.

Will asked them "What do you think about me maybe leaving you all right here? You can have the rest of the water in the pot to see you through until the next ride comes long and they could rest under a picnic shelter?"

The man didn't like the idea much but Will was adamant that this was the best idea and they could stay here or get out where he had to turn off at the highway junction up the road and the man scowled at him and went to talk to his wife who was over in the shade of a tree at a picnic table next to the non-functioning bathroom facilities.

A lot of what seemed to be hushed talk and a thumb gesture towards the woman that indicated Will who was back at the car made his mind up and Will got out of the car and opened the rear passenger door to remove their luggage. The women pointed at him and yelled and the man turned and hollered at Will to wait but he just dropped the suitcases and jumped into the driver's seat and started up the car with the backdoor still open and the man starting to run toward him and he sped off towards the ramp.

"You know what that man did next?" Will told the assembled crowd of Clem, Bertha and others listening to him intently.

"The son of a bitch pulled his gun out and started shooting at me! Blam! ..Blam! Blam! Well at that point I just floored it and got the hell out of dodge. Can you imagine? I was helping them folks; I wasn't taking their stuff that was obvious to see. I can't believe he decided to fire at me not once but three damn times, I tell you what, I sincerely believe that man was going to try and take my car and maybe my life if I had not of got that weird feeling about them and left them there. I swear people are just not right and I vowed then not to trust another soul but that's not the worst of it or the only person that threatened me with a gun before I got here." Will said still visibly shaken from his encounters.

"He had this here knife on him." Rossy Ross said producing a smallish kitchen butcher knife from her kit bag slung over her shoulder. Then she stared at the man like it was the only righteous thing to do in her opinion to a chicken thief armed with a knife was to keep threatening him to outright shoot him he moved in her direction.

"A man needs some protection and that was all I had. I didn't try to pull it on you or nothing I just had it stuck in my belt." Will complained.

"Yea this dumbass had it shoved into a piece of cardboard I guess thinking it was safer to carry that away." Rossy said tilting the barrel of her rifle in his direction.

"Nothing wrong with someone trying to protect themselves Rossi, knife is just a tool unless it's used otherwise." David admonished before telling Will to carry on with his story.

"Well that asshole actually hit my car's trunk with one of those wild shots he sprayed in my direction and as my sorry luck would have it, it hit right where I had my water bottles stored so he really screwed me up beyond giving me the first biggest scare of my life." Will said somewhat visibly relaxing as everyone commiserated with him by saying how wrong it was for the couple to attack him for no reason or for that matter even if he wanted to leave them and they couldn't understand it wasn't his fault they had a predicament.

"Wait folks this story gets better!" Will exclaimed and proceeded to tell them that when he finally got to his friend's house all he had was six cans of sweet peas, a can of chili and a box of minute rice that was wet along with his clothes from the hole getting punched in his trunk and the guy he had come to see wasn't at home. Will said he waited around in the driveway for about 4 hours and decided that maybe he should go on into town and see if any aid was about because he was already spooked about being shot at once today and a neighbor had come by asking what he was doing in Mr. Neil's driveway and was sporting a revolver on his hip.

The man was nice enough but somewhat threatening to him none the less and inquired of Will's further plans. Will told him about the only thing he could think of was to keep hanging out and hoping Neil would come home eventually to which the man raised his eyebrow and asked Will what he had planned if he didn't. Will tried to explain to him about his horrendous journey to get here and the horrible scare he had earlier today but the man just said "Not my business and said that he thought it would be best that if Neil didn't show up this evening it might be best for everyone if Will kept moving on in the morning. Will explained to him he was light on gas and had little to no water so the man said he could remedy that situation with a gallon of gas and 2 liters of water for 20 bucks.

Will explained that he only thought about the outrageous prices for a second before readily agreeing he would clear out tomorrow and sleep in his car tonight if that would be ok. Will said he had a fitful sleep for a few hours going to bed about ten for lack of anything better to do and cranked up his car about 4 am the next day and was surprised to see the same neighbor out on his front lawn now carrying a shotgun and waving goodbye to him with a smile before he went back in his house.

Will drove into town the next morning distraught and currently not having a friend in the world. He had no idea where his next drink of water or food was coming from or even where he was going to lay his head down tonight. He had about a 1/8th of a tank of gas left and no options. What to do? What to do? This question had been rolling over and over in his mind as he headed towards the towns center knowing no other options other than to seek someone, anyone to give him a clue about how to get out of this predicament. Smoke hung on the horizon like a curtain on the stage for the big last show on earth. A black man running from his attackers scared the hell out of him as he outran his pursuers at a stop light intersection Will had luckily observed. All the traffic signals were out, wrecks littered the intersections as the unwary or impatient made up their own set of driving rules. Will was a stranger in a strange apocalyptic world. Where were all the people at he wondered as he proceeded carefully through a city of locked doors and shade drawn windows? What the hell was that? A body? A mannequin from Halloween Will thought looking at a bloody carcass lying on the side of the road. No that was real, Will thought with a shudder and decided he should try to stop at the first police station he could find in order to get some help and report the body. Weren't cops the people who you needed to be talking to in such a situation he advised himself? But he had no idea where a police station was at and since you never knew what kind of militarized yahoo officer these days you might meet who just wanted to arrest someone, anyone for that matter regardless of the situation, he decided to think better on the notion but didn't see too many other choices.

Will saw a couple squad cars parked in front of a Piggly Wiggly supermarket off to his left and pulled in apprehensively. They must be guarding against looters he reassured himself and drove slowly straight toward the cruisers.

"Halt! Move no further!" A young cop brandishing a shotgun called to him as he approached while his partner took a pistol stance behind the passenger car door and a AR 15 wielding smartass balding Sergeant exited the obviously crowbar pried doors of the establishment leveling his weapon art him and bellowing several orders all at once.

Will said he had his hands up in the air quicker than his foot fully applied the brake which caused his slowly moving vehicle to swerve and he almost damn near hit an overturned grocery cart.

"What do you want?" a scowling sergeant called with weapon leveled at his windshield.

"I managed to stammer out nothing and that I just needed some information with my hands raised and sticking out my open window before that asshole of a sergeant told me to just keep it moving, that I was in some kind of a police powers zone before I guess a lieutenant or a captain or something exited the same store with a full grocery cart and told the guy "At ease" and walked over to me. He said that all grocery stores and warehouses were under the emergency command powers act and that any foodstuffs they contained were under the auspices of provisions for first responders like police, fire departments and medical first and that Homeland Security would advise how excess was to be distributed to the civilians.

"Let me tell you now folks he no sooner got that out of his mouth than the fourth of July started or World War 3 or something as a bunch of camouflage wearing men started shooting at them from the edge of the parking lot and I burned rubber the hell out of there without a backward glance and kept heading down the road until my gas run out not far from here. I tell you I shook and shaked for about 15 minutes wondering just what the hell had just happened to me and then started crying like only a man that has lost it all can before finally stopping sniveling and began studying my surroundings." Will said looking at his audience to see if they were sympathetic with him or not before carrying on with his story further.

"There was this place, an old beat up trailer just setup and stuck out on the side of the road in the middle of no where I guess you would call it and I walked towards it thinking I am

soon gonna die but surely somebody would still have some
compassion or mercy on me because I didn't know what else to
do. Now I didn't throw caution to the wind and go beating on the
door, no I sat there for a while peeking out through the woods at
it then eventually found myself sitting my sorry ass down in the
middle of the driveway leading up to it for some time just
waiting. I eventually found my courage to approach it directly
and hollered out my intentions but there didn't appear to be
nobody to home. I hung around the outside of that place for
hours waiting on its residents to get home before eventually I got
balls enough to just break into the dang place and that was where
my thievery and callousness got born. I had to look around the
property to find me an odd bit of metal that I used to pry the
door open and I came upon an awful sight upon entry. An old
women and I swear she was blue as a Smurf sat in a chair deader
than hell and looked like she might have been possibly chewed
upon by the cats that hightailed it out of the house once I began
looking around. I don't know what the old lady died from,
couldn't of been more than a few days I am guessing but I still
get the creeps imagining her bluer than that weird old folks
southern hairdo she was wearing. Lacking any supplies or any
other options I stayed. I ain`t proud to say it but I grabbed the
quilt off her bed and drug her out and left her about 50 yards
from the place at the edge of the woods. At this point I neither
had the energy or inclination to find a spade to bury her with so
instead I then went through her kitchen trying to find myself a
meal. There was lots of flour and baking supplies but little else
and I just sort of camped out there for a few days in her place
hoping that no relatives of hers would come by to check on her. I
was out of gas, out of luck and had no other options than to eat
what was there and move on. I ain`t no country boy, wouldn't
know a edible weed from poison ivy and when I got done with
what she in her cupboards then I sometimes became a thief in
the night to survive.

    I had my suitcase. A pot to boil water in, a couple liter
bottles to carry water in and not much else. I tried eating clover

but couldn't stomach it. I used to stop at houses to ask for help but folks just mostly run me off after saying sorry they couldn't help me, more than one threatened me with violence if I didn't hurry up and get off their property. I found another house after awhile that was unoccupied; guess who ever owned it didn't make it back from where ever they were. That one had about a weeks' worth of can goods in it that I stretched out for a couple weeks rations before moving on once again.

I did get a handout or two along the road, people ain't all bad or just plain crazy or mean, well I used to think that. I won't go near an occupied house anymore. I was watching a house from the woods one day for any signs of life in order to get a clue as to who the occupants were and I was just about to approach it when I saw two men coming back from the road leading a man with his hands tied like a prisoner. That scared the hell out of me, maybe they had caught a thief like me or he had done something particularly bad. I was curious though why anyone would take a prisoner these days? Were they maybe holding him for the police? If they were holding him for the police that meant maybe the government had regained control of the cities and things might be getting back to normal again. I decided to stay in the woods and watch for a while to find out what they were going to do with him. I sure wish I hadn't, they killed him but that wasn't what bothered me so much. I thought maybe he had done something really bad and maybe he deserved it. I was waiting for them to go dispose of the body somehow so I could sneak away. But they didn't dispose of the body, they started cutting him up! That when I realized those evil men were cannibals!" Will said looking at everyone anxiously and shuddering.

"So that's why you were scared we were going to eat you. Nothing to worry about here boy, you tell me exactly where them folks live and I will go put them out of their misery myself." Clem said disgusted at the notion of how anyone could eat another human.

"Yes, that's why. I have been trying to stay off the main road and travel around at night and early mornings. I saw the trail leading to Rossy`s house over here and followed it to see where it went and that's when I tried to steal me some eggs from your chickens. You can see why I wanted just a few eggs to eat; I wasn't going to harm any of your chickens, just take a few eggs. They would produce more and you wouldn't miss them I figured." Will pleaded wondering what they were going to do with him now.

"Bertha looked at him intently for the moment and then said "you poor man! All is forgiven. I will fry you up some eggs myself in a few minutes." She declared and then squished him with a big hug.

"Hey what about my door?" Rossy said, touched by the man's story but still miffed that her house was now wide open for Lord knows who ever came by the place next.

"Don't worry about your old door; Clem will fix it for you Rossy." Bertha said and Clem agreed.

"Well you can stay for a bit but if you cause any trouble or try to steal anything else around here you just think you been living in hard times, I will personally show you what hard times are all about if you cause any mischief. Do we have an understanding? Clem said warning the stranger.

"Oh thank you sir, thank you all! I will be good rest assured!" Will said greatly relived he had found some kind of friends in this world gone mad for no matter how short of time they might let him stay.

"You said you were trying to make it to Montgomery? I could drop you off on my way back to my house but I can't tell you what you may find when you get there, might be more of the same or maybe worse." David said ominously.

"Hey I would really appreciate it. I will take my chances in the city. I guess I am more suited for that than trying to survive on the road way out here." A grateful Will replied.

"Perhaps there is another solution; we will speak of that in the coming days as you get your strength back." Clem said wanting to study the man's character more before speaking further.

7

SURVIVAL MUSINGS

David had been prepping and studying survival for years and had watched the debates in the survivalist and prepper forums speculate on what was needed in a bug out bag without too much interjection and greatly waning interest mostly because by now it seemed he had pretty much seen it, done it, been there many times over..

The majority of the discussions in the prepper forums and blogs centered on packing far too much gear for everything imaginable except for what people would actually be facing in those circumstances. The thousands of lists of items to put in your bug out bag, get home bag, long term survival packs etc. were usually predicated upon unrealistic scenarios and expectations.

Countless hours are spent every day by people with good intentions to disseminate preparedness information, debate contents of bug out bags etc. and further research the same tired old knowledge bases for further info thinking it would increase theirs and others chances of survival and often times it is all for naught.

When someone first starts prepping for a disaster and joins the prepper community, they are besieged with all kinds of advice both good and bad about what they need that ultimately begins draining their pocket books and psyches before they come to profound realization that they can neither carry all the crap they have bought nor is it as useful as they once thought.

Oh David himself had tons of survival and outdoor gear stored in boxes or collecting dust on shelves and much of it came from dinking around trying to create the ever elusive all-purpose world-class bug out gear setup. It had caused him various degrees of anxiety, pleasure, financial hardship and hard won knowledge to finally say enough and accept the fact that he had approached his own survival in a bug out situation all wrong in some ways.

Situational awareness is what is needed before anyone packs their first bag. Sit back and mentally envision your route and its conditions. Where are you going? Why are you going? Are you going to return home someday? Is there anyway you could just stay where you are at?

Normal survival kits are small and designed to keep you going long enough to get rescued. Larger survival kits such as those required by aviation rules for bush pilots in Alaska or nautical overboard bags for life boats are larger and both are specific for certain survival in particular environments. The larger kits still are designed to be lighter weight than most of the bug out bags this author has seen but usually contain an item or two specific for food procurement in a certain environment like a gill net to take advantage of the abundance of fish in streams in Alaska, or larger hooks and heavier lines for saltwater fishing.

Before the reader goes charging out to the internet searching for such large premade kits and examining the content lists to the inth degree, let me tell you this, they are mostly overpriced, expensive, often contain cheaply made goods in them and the stuff you already have around your house or that you can procure cheaply from the dollar store will serve you much better. People will still believe they wire.

Don't get me wrong, there is definitely a place for ready made kits, particularly if you buy one such as the Henry Repeating Survival Kit which is one of the most complete, and high quality compact survival kits made. The only items missing are food and water. The tools for getting and carrying these are in the kit. I have made up and carried similar kits over the years but this a great all in one pre made item for you to add to your gear that is well thought out. I could live for a long time with one of these and a Henry rifle.

These are assembled in the USA specifically to save lives; many included items are U.S. Military Issue and/or NATO Issue. I carry one of these in my cargo pants.

SURVIVAL MUSINGS

The Survival Kit contains:

- Basic Survival Instruction Sheet
- Aloksak Water Tight Bag
- Personal Use Fishing Kit
- Mini Map Compass
- Mini Rescue Flash Signal Mirror
- Beeswax Tea Light Survival Candle
- Tinder Quick (10)
- Type 1A Utility Cord (20 ft)
- Photon Micro Light
- Sewing Kit
- Spiral Wire Survival Saw
- 1 ft flexible latex tubing
- Trauma Bandage and Gauze Roll
- Adventurer Compact Repair Tape
- Adventurer Compact Fire Starter
- Rapid Rescue Survival Whistle
- Snare Wire (20 ft)
- Adventure All Weather Matches (10)
- Utica Kutmaster Mini Multi Tool
- Flat Coffee Filter
- Water Bag
- MicroPur Water Tablets (05)
- 12 Hour Light Stick
- Space Survival Blanket
- Compact Signal Panel
- Silica Gel
- Fresnel Lens Fire Starter
- Derma Safe Razor Knife

The Survival Kit Box

- Hard Anodized Aluminum
- Size: Appx 7.3″ x 4.6″ x 2.3″ (including clasps)
- Weight: 6.2 oz
- Fire and Water Resistant
- Extremely Durable
- Not recommended for cooking
- Color: Dark Gray

Don't forget to add some gun food in there, it will fit! Add a condom to put inside of a sock to make yourself another canteen.

I have written many books and articles on survival and have furnished old common survival knowledge refreshers as well as some new insights and tips but as a prepper and survivor I remain selfish and reluctant to reveal all my personal tricks.

My selfishness to disseminate some information is based upon my own desire for self-preservation because if everyone plans on surviving the same way I do, then competition for resources increases and reduces my chances. It took a bit of soul searching on this authors desire to help others yet be ahead of the pack if the worst comes to teach you the following, but maybe by me doing so I will create a lot more sane survivors on the road I might have to travel down with hope versus a bunch of wore out, disillusioned desperate preppers with too much ammo and the wrong resources to rely on.

I kind of feel like I am giving up family secrets or something like the talking dog in the bean commercial giving up the secret recipe, but I like many of my fellow preppers and their family members are getting older and passing on all their experience and survival information to future generations and by remaining silent I feel I am might be needlessly condemning others to unnecessary suffering that I could of prevented by not trying to selfishly give myself a few small advantages for whatever reason.

Ok, enough pontificating, here is the simplest survival plan I can give you that makes practical sense and is also one of my most effective solutions to a long evasion and escape situation. The application of such a scheme will depend on your own circumstances but I hope my advisements will get you thinking in the right direction what might be needed for your own personal situation. Whether or not you share this with others someday is your own personal decision but a kind word about who you got it from and my books would be appreciated.

It is said that the majority of the population in the United States lives within 100 miles of the coastlines and that means there are rivers, streams and ponds around the areas many people will be traveling through or towards. Civilization has always started and located around waterways. Where are you bugging out to? It better have water and you need to travel as close to water as you can depending on your mode of transportation or ability to haul supplies. Let's look at a worst case scenario, say for whatever reason I am forced to be on foot in bug out situation heading 50 or more miles away to a destination.

I live in the Deep South and farm ponds, creeks, rivers, lakes etc. are abundant. I can see them from the highway, the back roads etc., and every 10 miles or so it seems. Let's say you have your bug out bag of 40 plus pounds or so and I have my backpack weighing much less and a lightweight shoulder bag, ready set go, let's begin this fictional preppers road march.

I won't get into road conditions at this stage, it all depends on how many people are fleeing their homes and why, which is something else to contend with. For conversations sake let us be hiking on the roads less traveled and come up on our separate ponds in a pasture. You have your handy dandy survival fishing kit and I have mine.

While you start hunting for bait in the form of bugs or worms that you may or may not find burning calories I am one step ahead of you because I am already carrying bait in my survival fishing kit as well as my food procurement shoulder bag. There are tons of different commercial marshmallow baits containing fish attractants as well as various preserved natural baits you can choose from and purchase to add to your gear. You can also make your own dough bait with a little flour, salt and water and the variations of recipes for it are endless, thing is I grew up using dough bait successfully on all kinds of pan fish and catfish so I just carry the makings of it to be mixed as needed instead of investing in commercial stuff, well I take that back, I do like the crappie nibble baits like many companies make.

They are light weight and I carry a jar of them in my food procurement bag as well as a few vials I filled with the little bits of play dough like substance that I added to my survival fishing kit that always remains on my person.

These kinds of baits come in a galaxy of colors, try to find out what works best in your area but be aware different conditions have differing success results from season to season and water conditions.

Ok so while you are probably resting up from your long hike before you starting wandering around looking for bait , I can already be fishing if I want to so I head over to the pond to check it out.

While you're resting you are probably pondering where the most likely spot is to cut yourself a good stick for a fishing pole. I may or may not be thinking the same thing for a variety of reasons. One is that I often carry a walking staff. I have a bunch of those cheap cane pole fishing set ups in my bug out gear that already have your hook, line sinker and bobber attached so it's a simple matter for me to just tie a line onto my stick and start fishing if I want. The end of my staff is also carved down and narrows enough to attach my frog gig to it should I need to get that adventurous and need a spear. Keep in mind that when you first walk up on a pond your more apt to see a turtle or frog or some such so be alert for any wildlife and particularly alert in the south for poisonous snakes.

Now while you're trimming branches off your fishing pole, tying the line on the hook and the weight etc you start to cuss the fishing kit because it has no bobber in it and set about to fashion one of those also before you get serious about hunting bait.

Me I have finished my scout of the pond and decide I want multiple lines out for more chances of success and reach in my food procurement bag for a bit of automated fish catching assistance.

Basic rig
(3) Yo-Yo automatic fish reels
This automatic fishing reel is great for docks, boats, or bank lines because the hook is set without you being there. Galvanized reel features stainless steel springs. This reel comes with 60 lb. test line and a brass swivel.

As you see from the pictures you can set it from over hanging limbs etc or use it on a rod if you desire. While you're not doing anything now, you see that little whole on top of the reel? Go ahead and run about a foot of line through it so it leaves you two loose ends, this reduces the need too perform this task later I the field so you can attach it to something. Go ahead and buy you some pre-snelled hooks also, you can just attach them directly to the swivel.

Now while your doing all that wandering around high profile bait hunting, fishing pole making, sitting on the side of the pond fishing waiting on farmer john or another survivor to wander by and come ask you what it is your doing, I got better things to do.

I can move back in the woods to make camp, gather firewood, recon the area, go hunting etc and check my luck at the fishing hole later or just keep an eye on my automatic fishing reels from the obscurity of some cover while I rest.

Hey by the way when you decide to break camp and dismantle your fishing pole, do yourself a favor and make your self a simple bottle reel.

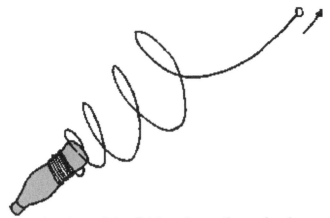

The simplest of the fishing rigs: a line, a hook, a weight, some bait, and a can or coke bottle. Variations of this arrangement are used all over the world by local fishermen for whom owning a fishing rod and reel would be considered very much a luxury. It works on the same principle as the basic spinning reel. The line is secured to and wrapped around the can or bottle, while the weighted and baited end is swung overhead generating speed, and released toward the water. The line then peels off the bottle or can with as little friction as possible. I am always amazed at what a considerable distance can be achieved by fisherman tossing a weighted hook by hand.

I have no idea how the fishing is in that pond is going to be and neither do you so I decide to hunt and trap some small game while waiting for the fish to bite.

What kind of a gun are you carrying? Humm now well that's a good question. If we were say traveling in our cars and got busted down out here because a Coronal Mass Ejection from the sun fried the computer circuits in our cars then chances are we only have our concealed carry pistols with us. Some of us more prepper oriented or outdoor types might have a truck rifle or something but what caliber is yours and mine? Now we get to see if you are a "gun prepper" or a practical prepper. My backpack contains a U.S. Survival AR-7 Rifle made by Henry Repeating Arms.

Yes I said my backpack. The entire rifle breaks down and fits in the stock. Worth mentioning is the entire gun will float when stored away – especially meaningful to boaters. Since 1959 the venerable AR-7 has been the choice of U.S. Air Force pilots who need a small-caliber rifle they can count on should they have to punch out over a remote area. Through the years the AR-7's reputation for portability, ease of operation and reliability has carried over to the civilian world. Today it's a favorite of bush pilots, backpackers and backcountry adventurers who, like their Air Force counterparts, need a rifle that's easy to carry yet has the accuracy to reliably take down small game.

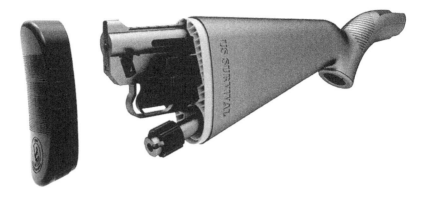

Like the barrel, the receiver is also coated with a layer of waterproof Teflon for superior weatherproofing, waterproof protection, even in harsh salt water environments. The .22LR chambering provides the ability to carry lots of ammunition with little bulk and weight. The .22LR is also one of the most versatile rounds affording the user to dispatch a variety sizes of game and if need be can be used for self defense. CCI Mini-Mag's is a great ammunition diet for these fine rifles. Its tack-driving accuracy, its light weight and compactness make it ideal where other firearms just can't fill the niche

So perhaps you have a truck gun in some kind of pistol caliber carbine. Good choice, I won't fault you for it as long as the caliber matches your carry pistol. Those types of weapons are very expensive often times and not something I could afford to be leaving in my vehicle all the time. Gun laws in how you have to transport them can be kind of funky also but hey we are not worried about that here. You get the thing out, load it, hopefully its not to rusty or oily from storage and you are going hunting. What are you going hunting for? You probably got that thing loaded with the baddest, hottest, heaviest miracle hollow point bullet man stopper you could find so deer is your likely target. Problem is you know deer hunting ain`t that easy you are going to spend more calories hunting one than it would be worth to get a lucky shot so you decide to try your hand at trapping and snaring instead.

Well you got lots of brass wire and read lots of books on trapping and snaring go try your luck. Me I have different plans. I have me some rat traps put away in my food procurement bag that need to come out and play and that grove of oaks over there looks like a likely place to start setting up. Course if I see squirrel while setting a trap for one I could just shoot them with my .22, I hope you don't decide to do the same with a 9mm or better. Which reminds me, when I go back to check my fish lines I hope them turtles I saw basking on a log are back, maybe I can get a shot off at one with my survival rifle.

The new rat and mouse traps they have got out nowadays that have a little cup in them to hold the bait are so much easier to bait and use but they don't pack down good. I have both anyway and I strategically put six of them out baited with MRE peanut butter for this set. Ok I have at least 3 fishing lines in the water, six squirrel traps (oh yea tie those squirrel traps off something bigger might get in the trap and then carry or drag it off) now for bigger game. A few commercial premade rabbit snares on the edge of this pasture should do the trick and I have only spent about an hour out here so far. How are you doing? Are you still looking for fish bait or building your first snare?

I could go sit off in the woods or rig up a shelter with my poncho and wait but I think I will go back to the fish pond and see if I caught anything yet. If I did get my a fish, I got plans for its head and Mr. snapping turtle that cost me the loss or the noise of a bullet.

Trying to keep a low profile and stay in the shadows is a important part of survival evasion and escape. I want to limit my exposure in this open field around the pond as much as I can.

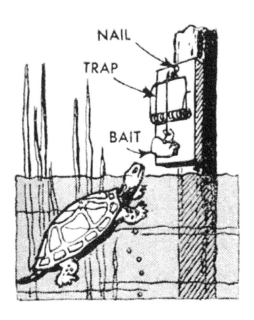

Ok back to the story at hand, you needed to know a bit about how David thinks about his own bug out scenario so you can try to guess how he is planning to overcome other people's different levels of preparedness or gear in a community prepper scenario.

"What's in the grenade box David?" Crick said watching David carrying a small wooden crate with tarred rope handles in his and Loomis's direction while wearing a sly knowing smile.

"Guess! Come on now you two, I will give you three guesses" David said chuckling as he set it down on the porch with a mischievous grin in the two men's direction.

"Looks like it might have some weight to it" Crick said skeptically nudging the crate with the toe of his boot to test its weight and raising one eyebrow in David's direction as the crate didn't yield or slide across the deck boards when a bit of pressure was put upon it.

"You don't really have hand grenades in there do you?" Loomis said thinking it might not be out of the question for

David to have some strange notion of doing a bit of dynamite style fishing.

"Nope, you got two more guesses." David said with his eyes a twinkle and hugging a bemused Julie who was watching the pair studying the box like they had x-ray eyes.

"Can I pick it up?" Crick asked trying to figure out what it was David had called his "Nuclear Option".

"Oh I suppose you can and you can shake it some also if you like, nothing breakable in there, but I am not answering any questions on its contents like the possibilities of "animal, vegetable or mineral." David declared looking over in Loomis's direction who was studying the box intently and reading the military stencils painted on it like they would give him some clue to the contents.

Crick picked up the small crate and hefted it a few times, gave it a shake, studied it at every angle and then set it down for Loomis to do the same with it. Both men looked puzzled and alternately eyed the box and David for further clues while pondering its contents.

"Its dang sure heavy enough. Crate says a box of grenades weighs 24 lbs. so you got me stymied. Did you fill it full of lead? Lead huh? I bet it has a shitload of 12 gauge birdshot and you're going to organize a Dove hunt!" Crick said thinking he had figured out the mystery boxes contents.

"Nope wrong again! One more guesses left." David said delighted at playing his game.

"We better be careful and discuss this next guess." Loomis said picking the box back up and shaking it again.

"Hey no peeking you bunch of cheaters!' David said laughing as Crick tried to lift the little bit of slack the lid had up to get a quick look through the crack..

'Humm heavier than hell, let's see Loomis do you think it might be a bunch of steel arrow points? Maybe David here has been out in the sun too long and fancies himself William Tell or something and is going to teach us all how to be English

Bowmen?" Crick said with a snide look at David to which Loomis guffawed.

"Hey rattling my cage isn't going to help you out none, let's put a little wager on you all guessing right to make this more interesting." David said looking at Julie who beamed a smile at David's two guessing game contestants like they were in for it now.

"Like what? I don't like to bet on another man's game and particularly not so when it comes to anything David dreams up." Loomis said frowning.

"Oh let's see, Crick you had a half gallon of Ancient Age whiskey on your kitchen counter, if you lose its mine. Thanks for leaving it out by the way. Now then Loomis, if you lose, I like nothing better than a big roaring campfire to sit around and drink that bottle at. You have to gather the wood and tend it until that Jug is gone." David said studying them with a poker face at first and then lost it and was back to being all smiles.

'What do we get if you lose?" Crick said speculatively looking over at Loomis to see if he was going to play along.

"I got a couple pints of that jet fuel I have been known to occasionally conjure up. Got myself a couple liters of real Coca Cola also to mix it with also so that's a pretty sweet deal I am offering." David said ready to parlay.

"That sounds to me to be a bit one sided, are you saying that you are going to tend your own fire while we all sit around and drink up your libations if you lose?" Loomis said looking for any hidden glitches in David's favor he was sure were built into this deal somehow.

"Well yea, don't you think that is fair man? Seems to me the only one sidedness about the bet is that it is all in your favor because you get to have a drink either way." David said winking at Crick.

Crick didn't know what David was up to but on the surface the deal sounded fair to him. What did he have to lose anyway? David probably had put a hell of a dent in the bottle of whiskey before he had even left his house and knowing him had most likely brought it along with him anyway for safekeeping or some other made up excuse. David would probably tell him he had brought what was left in the bottle with him as a favor to Crick because he just knew he had inadvertently forgot to bring it with him himself so that he and David could share it as a celebration of rescuing the survivors.

"Ok I am in, how about you Loomis? We got one more guess but David has to agree we are guessing what the majority of that box is, not every item. Seems like there is some light stuff sliding around over the heavy crap at the bottom of it.' Crick said tapping on the lid of the crate like the sound it was giving off was giving him some kind of sonar indication.

"I guess so, are you sure Crick? David doesn't always play nice you know and he tends to try for an advantage." Loomis said grinning at David who feigned indignation that he would make anything other than an honest bet.

"So it's a deal then?" David said offering his hand to both man to seal the bet.

"I guess so." They both chorused and went back to speculating after shaking hands.

Loomis and Crick conferred for a while in private trying to deduce just what in the hell David had stored in the mysterious wooden crate. Loomis thought it must be books, books that held knowledge that could solve their problems. Crick thought that was a good angle but since David was a writer that had authored a few books of his own on preparedness skills he couldn't see David hauling around the extra weight of what he already carried in his head. No, David would have that box full of whatever parts he needed for whatever scheme he dreamed up.

" I say you got a box full of them heavy duty conibear style traps." Crick finally said.

"Nope! But there is a couple in there I am donating to the cause." David said grinning.

"Ok so what's in the box?" Crick asked

"Well you know how build a squirrel trap with picture hanging wire? Well I brought along the nuclear option for that task. We going to have us a rodent rodeo, Check it out. I got 1550 feet of that picture wire stuff stored for an occasion such as this. Yea I know, I am a prepper nerd, but be glad I plan for strange stuff like this." David said proudly opening the box and pointing at a whole big industrial size spool of it.

"We need to organize the preppers to building traps all along the pasture line. I mean atomic Annie the hell out of it and put squirrel traps out like telegraph poles in every direction. Use the brush they will create or accumulate making squirrel poles and use it to make V shaped funnels on the edge of the woods to channel rabbits and other critters into more snares we can construct.

I don't know how such a drastic move will affect the game population but it should take care of the food problem for several days and the excess can be smoked and cured for use later or as traveling rations for those that are going to try to bug back home. Leave a few 50 ft. wide or so clear pathways in between the long stretches of traps and snares for me though.

Quail snare

Small game noose

The other end of the pasture leading in leave alone
entirely and I will show you how to rig some deer snares if you
don't already know how. You got to be careful where you place
them and how many we set or you will screw up the deer herd
and hunting around here for years. I have some commercial
grade aircraft cable snares with cam locks for that. That kind of

lock will choke them out quick; they use them for wolves in Alaska. Even though those things are strong they will be tore up and kinked beyond use after a few catches. I have ways of minimizing that snarling as well as releasing snare locks meant to just hold the animal until I get there to dispatch the animal also that have their purposes. For example in the summer time if it's going to be awhile until I can get back to a set, keeping the animal alive will keep the meat from spoiling.

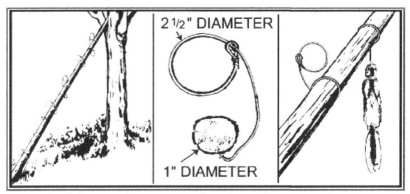

Several of these pole traps can be placed in areas where there are active squirrel signs or sightings, other places guesstimate about.

Refer to the diagrams above to see how a squirrel pole is made. The loops for the snare should be approximately three fingers in diameter. The wire length should be approximately 4 inches long after being tied off to the pole. This is to allow the squirrel to dangle far enough away from the pole when it falls so that it cannot reach the pole with its feet. If it is able to reach the pole, the squirrel can actually chew through the wire and escape.

The loops should be placed at different intervals around the pole. One pole can actually catch more than one squirrel. The poles should be placed at an angle propped up against a tree that shows signs of squirrel usage. Squirrels are prone to take the easiest path up a tree, which would be the pole trap.

Traps should be checked at regular intervals so as not to leave a dead squirrel for too long of a period making it useless as food.

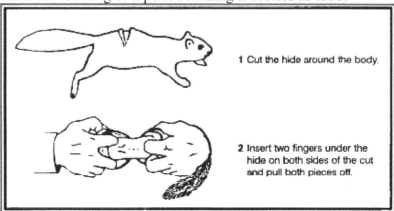

1 Cut the hide around the body.

2 Insert two fingers under the hide on both sides of the cut and pull both pieces off.

Cleaning a squirrel after you have trapped or shot it is a very simple process. Prior to cleaning any animal, ensure that you have any open cuts on your hands covered so that you don't get an infection of some type.

First thing to do is to cut the feet off at the first joint from the toes upward toward the body. Then remove the head.

Next, cut around the mid-section of the hide around the diameter of the body as shown in the diagram. Place two fingers under each side of the cut and pull the hide outward toward both ends of the body. This should remove the outer hide like pulling off a glove.

Next, cut down the center of the belly side from groin to neck. Remove the innards. You can eat the heart and liver. Ensure the liver has a smooth wet deep red appearance. Any other color may mean the animal is diseased and should be used as bait for larger prey or discarded.

Next, wash the carcass if water is available. When eating meat in a survival situation, it is important that you have water to help digest the meal.

You can then cut the meat into large chunks to make a soup or stew or you can cook it over an open fire like a shish kabob.

It takes about three squirrels to make a full meal with addition to whatever plant food you can find.

I know that all those preppers are probably collectively carrying a mile or so of 550 Paracord in packs and bug out bags and that's a good thing. Later on I will break my rule about teaching people how to use that stuff to catch deer and teach them a few snare sets and triggers but not for a while yet. How many long guns do they have amongst them Crick?" David asked

Cut notch in trigger bar (a) to fit notch in upright (b). Drive upright into ground. Attach snare to trigger bar and use cord to sapling to keep tension.

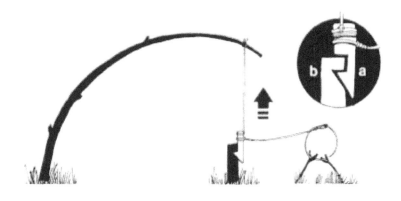

Simple Small Game Twitch Up Snare

" None that I know of, there was a lot of confusion as to the gun laws, concealed carry permits etc. on a federal reservation so some people don't even have their pistols with them. I have a spare rifle or two at the house and maybe a couple single shot shotguns I will lend to the cause however and I have plenty of ammo put back to supply the weapons for a good bit." Crick responded.

"David I sort of had my doubts about the wisdom of Crick making you come all the way up here on that dangerous trip to just bring some fish traps and some of that survival knowledge of yours to this little party but I must say you are awfully handy to have around sometimes. That spool of picture wire trick for your atomic rodent rodeo that you brought was brilliant." Loomis said thumping David on the back in a comradely fashion.

"Thanks buddy, but I got to hand it to you and Crick for finding this place, that great tractor giz whiz and organizing this rescue. Man just keeping them folks from killing themselves or each other over on that island must have been a chore and a half already." David responded with his own compliment.

"We had ourselves a few hiccups in the beginning but that's a great bunch of survival like minded people. Once we got organized they basically just further bonded together and pitched in on surviving as a community versus a bunch of individuals." Loomis said proud of the folks at Prepper Stock.

"Now we got to get them same people into a sharecropper frame of mind and that may cause us a little friction. Everyone right now is pulling for the moment as one thinking they just needed to hold out until rescued, now that they are out of the confines of the encampment and have the option of bugging out on their own and hitting the open road I think they are going to be harder to direct and less compromising in their outlooks." Crick said wisely.

"That fact opens up a whole another can of worms but this subject needs to be discussed further and in depth. I haven't had much of a chance to bring up road conditions to you yet and that might influence them to want to stay as close to this place as they can. The radio probably has left out several things of importance no one has considered as of yet.' David said ominously.

"I thought you said it was all clear roads and no problems getting down here?" Loomis objected.

"I did, but I didn't tell you what was occurring on my own home front that causes me some major concerns. Hell I might even want to move back down here with you all myself." David said and told them what he knew about the foreign troops manning security checkpoints at strategic factories and facilities.

David told them that he hadn't had for himself any firsthand experience or even seen such forces in action but related his neighbor's observations and experience with the surprise of seeing allegedly Russian troops guarding the missile plant not far from his house.

"There goes your wagon train plan Loomis. There is going to be absolutely no telling who you are going to run into trying to cross the state now. My offer of a horse to get you home still stands but maybe you might want to rethink on whether or not you're getting home in a hurry getting beats staying here." Crick advised.

"Oh I am going home one way or another my friend. But I might could see myself sticking around for awhile to help you with this little rodeo you got getting cranked up here. I am thinking that is the best thing that I can do at the moment for the both of us. I can help you with some of the administration around here but at the same time borrow that horse of yours that you are offering and use it to do a scout around the area and see what exactly are the conditions in the near proximity of this place. I mean this place is pretty well off the beaten path as far as the highways and byways leading here to it but if the government is augmenting its security forces with friggin Russian paratroopers we might just have a bunch of them foreign troops camped out over at those blown dams and power stations that got destroyed. If we are somehow in it now for the long dark and are only focusing all our efforts on just to surviving, then we might be missing the bigger picture that we should be observing if the business and government continuity plans actually are being implemented and if they are they going to have a chance to work." Loomis offered for consideration.

"You got a point there Loomis, now if there is actually construction or repairs going on over at the Dams then things might not be near as bad as we think that they are. On the other hand, who is to say at this particular moment in this disaster that some desperate backwoods hick doesn't shoot you for your rifle or wanting to eat your horse? You might just be riding along down the road without a care in the world one day and some starving yahoo or highwayman wants to take advantage of the situation to see if you got any interesting morsels in your saddlebags or bullets that fits his gun. I don't think the lone Ranger approach is as cool as it sounds or might be considered to have any merit at the moment." Crick said and Loomis immediately and loudly told Crick what he thought of the term "Lone Ranger."

"Hey settle down you two, I can see both of your points but we got to expound upon the pros and cons about them and not argue so much about doing something exactly one way or another. Maybe as just a suggestion mind you, if you got enough horses to do it Crick a larger show of force might work, or as Loomis probably can already do, take a swamp fox commando approach with a lone rider to send out scouts. Either way I can see the necessity in both ideas but right now we need a cohesive front for all those preppers coming over here from Castaway Island that might help keep anyone from straying off property too soon until we actually know how dark those woods in front of us are. The preppers are basically a unit now from living and surviving together, lets remind them to remain so for awhile longer and that any losses to our little ad hoc community lessens the chances of the others no matter how good their own homes and preps look at the moment. We need to stress safety and success in numbers and appeal to their desires to strengthen the weakest links instead of break the chain. As a group or a tribe we are a force to be reckoned with be it from nature or from aggressors. As individuals we are subject to the whims and chances that nature and other groups or tribes wish to subject us to." David said seeing that this was no time to lose the chain of command or let everyone's personal individuality takeover.

"Point taken David and it's a good one, but let me remind you that probably over half of them preppers have misguided notions of bugging out or have just given up to the realities of hard living and are hoping deep down in their hearts that a bunch of FEMA buses are waiting on this side of the river to take them to a camp somewhere with a real bed and a warm meal, if such still exists. It's hard to say right now, what with such an overwhelming need for services and supplies if it's even possible the government resources can be up to the task at any level. There are over three hundred million people in this country facing dire straits and there's no way in hell the government can possibly have that many stores in hand let alone available in every location that they might be needed in. Many folks won't be contained here longer than it takes for them to eat a bit, regain their strength and carry on with whatever mythical or real road trip they envision going on with or without our blessings." Crick said advising David of the true nature of the spirits and mentalities of those people they were trying to rescue.

"I know one or two folks over there that it would be particularly merciful to just go ahead and shoot them but they are plain people and part of us in a predicament all the same. We have been discussing in several group meetings and in private who wants to get on the bus, who wants to get home by bugging out and who sees no other recourse other than just trying their hand at staying over there and attempting some more woods living. It didn't take long for even some of the more hardcore types to say the hell with trying to eat the cambium or the soft inner layer of bark on a pine tree as a get by method of food procurement. David you seem to have come up with the new glue that binds by providing the means for ready food and hope for all and to me with all my survival knowledge that seems pretty amazing, but like you said that ain`t going to last for long. Hell I still can't wrap my mind around that nuclear squirrel and rabbit option you dreamed up. Them little goomers are smart and that trick might not work for long as they see their buddies strangle and dangle and will avoid those areas soon enough if you don't wipe out the majority of that kind of game the first go round. Now hear me out! It is a great idea but not the solution for the long-term benefit of providing for these folks and they are going to see it as clear as me eventually. They will realize you are depleting and educating the game around here to human hunting and trapping tricks thus making the surviving animals harder to catch and more wary. We need to start planning other options to leave this area if need be before the inevitable starvation starts again." Loomis predicated in a condescending tone to David's exuberance he had somehow miraculously provided a solution to their woes.

SURVIVAL MUSINGS

Crick eyed David how he was going to respond to this accusation and alleged lack of planning with great interest. He knew David had specifically said he didn't know what that atomic option of his was going to do to the squirrel and rabbit population close to the sharecropper shacks that would soon be occupied by destitute and perhaps somewhat deranged from starvation people they had taken under their wings to give them a better chance of surviving this apocalypse. He saw the method to David's so called madness in providing such a solution but he didn't think that such an extreme affair was necessarily that great of an idea now.

David had not seen how weak and pitiful looking many of those poor souls were already. Weeks of lacking good food, the strain of wondering how loved ones were getting by and how they themselves could possibly go see about them to help out played heavy on his mind. The hell with zombie preparedness movies, some folks were already walking around like the shambling dead from infected mosquito bites, red bugs, poison ivy, oak, untreated minor cuts etc. plaguing the survivors came to mind and the first prep he remembered when coming to his home to bring back preps and relief was various medications like Calamine lotion. Zinc oxide, clear nail polish, rubbing alcohol and peroxide etc. to give some relief to the debilitating maladies that most everybody had some experience at this date and time. A thousand and one "got cha`s" lived in the woods to make a strong man weak and great woman cry. A basic lesson of outdoor skills in the flora and fauna of this neck of the woods was not only necessary but had to be done before the strongest and bravest of the lot were disabled beyond helping others in something as basic as identifying poison ivy before butts were wiped or trees climbed as nature said you just think you can survive here.

I always used poison ivy mnemonics to remember what the plant looked like in nature and to teach others like Leaves of three leave them be."

The Wikipedia article on Poison Ivy ends with a list of traditional mnemonics to help people identify Poison Ivy. I thought it would be fun to re-print a few of them here along with a photo illustrating the saying.

1. *Leaves of three; let it be.*

The catch is that there are plenty of plants with three leaves that are safe to touch, such as wild strawberry vines. *Blue Jay Barrens* blogged about safe, three-leaved plants in a post called *Three-Parted Leaves*. But if you have difficulty telling one three-leaved plant from another, it's probably best to avoid them.

2. *Side leaflets like mittens, will itch like the dickens.*

3. Unfortunately the side leaflets on poison ivy don't always have these mitten thumbs. If you look at the "leaves of three" photo shown in the previous item, you'll note that it lacks these mitten thumbs.

4. *Longer middle stem; stay away from them.*

5. *Red leaflets in the spring, it's a dangerous thing.*
PLUS
Hairy vine, no friend of mine.

This was photographed April 23rd. It is unusual to see red leaves in the spring.

6. *Raggy rope, don't be a dope! Another one is Hairy vine no friend of mine!*

This was taken January 13th after all the leaves were gone. The vine is still poisonous.

7. *Berries white, run in fright!*

This was photographed on December 8th, also after the leaves had dropped.

This mnemonic kind of goes with my edible berries one
White and yellow, kill a fellow.
Purple and blue, good for you.
Red ... could be good, could be dead.
If [red berries are] growing in little clusters, they're probably not good. If they're growing in little singletons, they probably are good.

People's brains changed when subject to the stressors of deprivation and disease. They are sometimes liable to try to eat anything. What was unthinkable before became nagging thoughts of "don't think about that" as weird cannibalistic or aggressive thoughts of theft or violence occurred. Just that little bit of knowledge about edible berries goes a long way. **Avoid ever having to use this method without careful planning.** Some plants can be deadly, and even if you follow these guidelines perfectly, there is always a chance that a plant will make you seriously ill.

- Prepare yourself for wilderness outings by learning about the local flora and fauna, and carry a guidebook or taxonomic key to help you identify plants.
- Even if you are unprepared and cannot find food you know to be safe remember that, depending on your activity level, the human body can go for days without food, and you're better off being hungry than being poisoned.

Find a plant that is plentiful. You don't want to go through the rigorous process of testing a plant if there's not a lot of it to eat.

The Universal Edibility Test is a series of tests you can use to determine if a plant is safe to consume. At the site

HowStuffWorks they've outlined the prongs of the test and how you can apply it safely in the field. The initial part of the test is to separate the item into its parts like leaves, stems, roots, buds, and flowers—many plants have edible and inedible portions. The first actual experiment is the contact test:

First you need to perform a contact test. If it's not good for your skin, it's not good for your belly. Crush only one of the plant parts and rub it on the inside of your wrist or elbow for 15 minutes. Now wait for eight hours. If you have a reaction at the point of contact, then you don't want to continue with this part of the plant. A burning sensation, redness, welts and bumps are all bad signs. While you wait, you can drink water, but don't eat anything. If there is no topical reaction after eight hours, move along to the next step.

Some plants have edible parts and poisonous parts. In order to test if a plant is edible, you must separate it into the leaf, stem and root and test each part separately for edibility.

- After you have separated the plant into parts, inspect each part you are preparing for parasites. If you encounter worms or small insects inside the plant, discontinue the test with that sample and consider seeking a different sample of the same plant. Evidence of worms, parasites or insects indicates that the plant is rotten, especially if the organism has vacated the plant.
- Many parts of plants are only edible during certain seasons (for example, acorns collected after the fall are usually rotten). If you find grubs inside the plant, the plant is rotting, but the grubs are edible and contain high amounts of protein (although they taste sour and are gritty).

1	Test only one part of a potential food plant at a time.
2	Separate the plant into its basic components—leaves, stems, roots, buds, and flowers.
3	Smell the food for strong or acid odors. Remember, smell alone does not indicate a plant is edible or inedible.
4	Do not eat for 8 hours before starting the test.
5	During the 8 hours you abstain from eating, test for contact poisoning by placing a piece of the plant part you are testing on the inside of your elbow or wrist. Usually 15 minutes is enough time to allow for a reaction.
6	During the test period, take nothing by mouth except purified water and the plant part you are testing.
7	Select a small portion of a single part and prepare it the way you plan to eat it.
8	Before placing the prepared plant part in your mouth, touch a small portion (a pinch) to the outer surface of your lip to test for burning or itching.
9	If after 3 minutes there is no reaction on your lip, place the plant part on your tongue, holding it there for 15 minutes.
10	If there is no reaction, thoroughly chew a pinch and hold it in your mouth for 15 minutes. **Do not swallow.**
11	If no burning, itching, numbing, stinging, or other irritation occurs during the 15 minutes, swallow the food.
12	Wait 8 hours. If any ill effects occur during this period, induce vomiting and drink a lot of water.
13	If no ill effects occur, eat 0.25 cup of the same plant part prepared the same way. Wait another 8 hours. If no ill effects occur, the plant part as prepared is safe for eating.

CAUTION

Test all parts of the plant for edibility, as some plants have both edible and inedible parts. Do not assume that a part that proved edible when cooked is also edible when raw. Test the part raw to ensure edibility before eating raw. The same part or plant may produce varying reactions in different individuals.

8

FREEDOM FLOTILLA

Early the next morning found all hands on deck down at the old ferry landing bustling about and making ready to perform a rescue. Loomis and Clem got the turnbuckles off the steel cable holding the pontoon platform anchored close to shore and eventually with a lot of experimentation and work Crick and crew managed to secure the barge to the tractor and bolted the cables together. After a few tentative maneuvers to get the feel for his unwieldy craft Crick signaled that he was ready to push it up river and would meet them at the plantations landing before setting off for the rescue mission.

Preparations for today were minimalist at best, Getting ready to receive 50 or so starving people when there is so little extra food around was problematic. A big hog scalding cauldron was scrubbed out as best they could and Bertha and Rossy Ross were making a thin watery but wholesome stew out of some vegetables, two chickens and a piglet that Clem had donated to the cause. Bertha would thicken it up later with some flour dumplings and a basketful of Egyptian walking onions that Rossy had gathered from the gardens.

Walking onions are a very unusual heirloom onion. They are top-setters, which mean they produce onion seeds from the flowering green tops of the onion. The reason they are called walking onions because the top setters will fall over and re-root themselves literally walking. You can plant a patch once and have a wonderful perennial harvest for years.

Crick had brought 50 lbs. each of beans and rice and 50lbs of wheat from his stores. The preppers' survival was soon to be now measured in ounces and days at a time unless other resources were found.

Finding living quarters for all those folks was going to be problematic. There were a bunch of tents but many people had shown up with trailers and RVs and they soon would be forced to make arrangements.

One of the old shotgun style houses up by the ruins of the old plantation could be made to serve for some people without much more than a good sweeping out and the addition of a few boards after you chased the snakes and spiders out. The term "shotgun" is a reference to the idea that if you open all the doors to the house, the pellets fired from a shotgun would fly cleanly from one end to the other. Other vacant houses faired much worse and they would take considerable work to make them habitable again. There was lots of still good timber and boards around here though. The salvage of the wood and the chore of getting a dry solid roof over everyone's heads shouldn't take all that long if people treated the work like a habitat for humanity affair or just a plain good old fashioned cabin raising.

This plantation had been around a long time and had several old log cabins scattered around decaying away here and there around the massive property but the bones of a lot of them were still good and strong. The old homestead places reminded Crick of the blues singer Muddy Waters house he had once seen in Mississippi. Dovetailed oak timbers blued with age still standing strong after a hundred years or more of being exposed to the elements.

The remains of the cabin from Stovall Farms where Muddy Waters lived during his days as a sharecropper and tractor driver are displayed in the gallery. Musicologist Alan Lomax recorded Muddy on the front porch of this shack for the Library of Congress in 1941. Best known for electrifying the blues in Chicago, Muddy is represented by posters, photographs, and a life-size wax statue, displayed along with one of his electric guitars and ZZ Top's "Muddywood" guitar, crafted from one of the cabin's timbers. Now how cool is that?

Even the worst of the cabins could be made to serve some kind of function eventually. If nothing else you could just throw a tarp over where the roof used to be on the more Skeletonized ones and be well on your way to making yourself a substantial little house. Hey! How many damn preppers could even hope to flesh something out like this with nothing more than a camp axe making a family home that would serve for many generations? I know one thing, no one is going to take any time to square timbers or find the heart of an oak to make them out of while just needing shelter but the pioneers of old had the skills, the wisdom, the wherewithal and the gumption to build something once and build it right. That's the problem with society today, instant satisfaction; gratification where I need it now overwhelms what our forefathers knew that they did not want to undertake such a momentous task more than once if they could help it.

An old saying is "A man or a woman is a measure of their work." The reason that some old cabins stand the test of time and serve many generations from the days of pioneering to modern society is somebody somewhere decided that they would build something that would last for another generation in order that they would not have to spend that time on hard labor and instead have an advantage to build something further.

Some of these cabins that still exist on this plantation have oftentimes had five generations to reside in one from the first man that lived in it. He wasn't ashamed of his efforts of construction, no he was proud he had talents and was commended on his ability to make the place for himself. The generations that came after this gentleman whine and complain that they have no other finer house to live in and yet give thanks to the man who first constructed it. Hell, they don't even have a clue how to fix it as age and time makes their poor abode unlivable and yet none of the neighbors, none of the babies introduced in this next world by this one solitary man's craftsmanship is appreciated or can be reproduced by anyone of his namesakes.

Crick had shown David around the plantation a little bit and David was as excited as he was about the potentials of this place if enough people wanted to stay and work it. It was going to be hot, brutal hard scrabble community living for a while but for those willing to invest their time and effort into it was an ideal bug out location and way of life to get a new start in this dreadful apocalyptic world we were facing.

David said he could see it as a decent lifestyle possibly that was going to be slowly developing on this place that might even suit him. That is, if he just looked at sharecropping like an old hippy commune or a self sufficiency based reality survival show instead. He knew better though in many ways, back to the land living was just plain miserable for any length of time and particularly more so if all you had was a glimmer of what the old pioneers knew or had access to. Utopia it certainly was not. However, the key to survival is community and he was going to study this place more in depth, no telling what the future held for him and Julie. Having other like minded individuals and a larger talent pool to draw from had its advantages. Many hands make light the work as the saying goes.

David wondered how many folks would choose to stay and how many others would decide to take their chances elsewhere because they were better setup if they bugged back home.

David and Julie had pitched a 4 man tent out in front of Clem's house, he had an extra three man tent he told Will he could borrow to pitch at what was to be the main campground for the preppers using tents. Dang, a apocalyptic tent city, did that beat a homeless tent city? That is a hard question to wrap his head around David decided. On the one hand, opportunity and access to goods if you could afford them are readily available so David guessed homeless tent city, but the emotional and mental drains would be different. There was a lesson in pondering such a question but for now his thoughts moved on to other things.

David decided so far Will wasn't such a bad character, he was just shell-shocked and a bit strange from his experience of surviving on his own and avoiding others. Clem said he would keep an eye on him but he, like David thought that once he started having regular interaction with people he would snap back.

Loomis told Will that it would be best if he didn't mention to the other survivors anything about getting caught stealing and everyone on the plantation agreed that this secret would be safe with them. No sense having Will starting out on the wrong foot with anyone and petty jealousies and suspicions were already an endemic fact with the community that would hopefully be resolved now that everyone's futures looked a bit brighter.

David eyed the plantations landing and rickety dock and discussed with Loomis and Clem a project idea that the new sharecroppers might get around to building someday. Its construction was simple enough and Bertha and Clem could make the fish baskets easy enough using wild muscadine grape vines which seemed to grow freely around the area.

"Here comes Crick!" Beauregard called as the sound of the tractors motor was heard chugging around the bend.

Crick laid on the horn and swung the unwieldy barge around to push it towards the bank.

9

Sail On Silver Pontoon

'What in the hell do you reckon that crazy looking thing is Lowbuck?' Rod said pointing at an old barge that appeared to be being pushed along or propelled by a tractor with paddle wheels.

"I dunno but I would say its rescue arriving. That has got to be Loomis riding on that thing, check out the hat and if that is Loomis then that has got to be Crick driving that cattle boat looking thing." Lowbuck said watching the odd craft making its way towards where the fishing pier used to stand.

An excited murmur arose as the various camps started making their way towards LowBuck and Ramro's camp to welcome the craft and find out what was going on. When the pontoon barge was about mid channel Crick started laying on the horn and it looked like Loomis was doing a little jig blasting a boat air horn and waving his other hand.

"That's them!" Rod said starting to holler and wave at the rescuers and shortly thereafter a crowd formed all doing the same with various exclamations of "we are saved" and giving thanks.

Loomis made a cutting motion with his hand across his throat indicating that Crick should cut the motor off or idle it down so that he could hear Lowbuck shouting from shore and survey their proposed landing site.

Sail On Silver Pontoon

"I am not sure if you want to push that thing in over here, you might need to find a different spot. I don't know how deep or how many of those dock pilings still exist under the water over here. They might puncture your hull or something." Lowbuck called out.

"Where else do you suggest?" Loomis called out as he pondered what to do next and Crick told him he would have to start the engine back up soon or they would get caught drifting in the current.

"Throw your anchor out!" Lowbuck called watching the craft being carried sideways in the current.

The barge had two makeshift anchors Clem had made by welding angle iron to two old car tire rims and Loomis threw the bow and aft anchors out to stabilize the barge about 50 ft from shore.

Crick climbed out of the tractors cab and up on its hood surveying the shoreline that was pretty much unrecognizable from its former self after being swept clean by the flood and then further set back by the rising water.

"I can't make out how deep it is from here." Loomis called over to LowBuck

"It's hard for me to say also, the waters muddier than hell. I could wade or swim out to see about them pilings but on the far side of this butte is a sort of a sand mud bar affair that you can see the depth on. If that thing has enough horsepower you could run those pontoons aground and we can all wade to it and climb on." Lowbuck called back.

"Sounds ok as long as you all don't sink too deep when

Sail On Silver Pontoon

wading out. Meet us down there and we will check it out. We got plenty of power to get off of a sand bar as long as we don't sink the pontoons too deep. Tell folks we will come ashore and make announcement as soon as we can about what we are doing when we get to the other side but start packing up after the meeting. I figure it will take us 3 trips to get everyone off of here." Loomis called back.

"Sounds good, we are headed that way. See you soon!" Low buck called back and the herd of people on his side started making a beeline hike towards the sand bar about a quarter mile away.

Crick and Loomis after a bit of a struggle hauling up one of their anchors began following the shoreline towards their next proposed loading point. Loomis stayed up at the front of the barge looking for snags and rocks as Crick maneuvered the craft down river.

Loomis could see everyone walking down the road above the campsites heading to the sandbar and was taken aback at the sight. Shambling trudging shapes that couldn't keep up with the main body of the crowd somehow found the strength to keep a slow progress towards the rally point with a few of the healthier souls falling back to encourage or assist them, the younger healthier people out in front of the herd soon distant themselves from the rest as they quickly made their excited way to the sandbar which soon came into sight from Cricks perch inside of the tractors cab.

Crick made a wide circle in the river and slowed so that he could come on to the sandbar with Loomis's direction who soon warned for him to direct the barge hard left to avoid some obstruction. After a few moments they were aground upon a sandy bar of earth with a gravely mud mixture underneath and Loomis and Crick threw out the anchors for safety sake and

Sail On Silver Pontoon

surveyed the gap between them and shore.

The gap was not more than 25 feet or so but the slippery mud and the branches on the bottom made fording it precarious.

Lowbuck waded his way out to the barge gingerly walking on the rivers bottom and almost loosing his footing once or twice. Once he got out to the sand bar he walked over to the barge and looked up at Loomis and Crick.

"Ah hell, I was scared of this Bubba, we to far out of the water for anyone to climb on easily." Crick said looking down at Lowbuck.

"I can get up there but I just soon you all come down. Let's not worry about folks getting on that thing just yet, we can always build us a ladder or something and run some ropes across the gap for them to hold on to while wading it. I saw this is about the best we can do for now, come on down and lets chat a bit first. I am dieing for some news, what's happening on the other side? I take it you couldn't find any official help?" Lowbuck said as Loomis and Crick started to use the anchor rope to help them climb down from the barge.

"Hang on guys got a treat for you all." Lowbuck said to Loomis as his boots touched the ground after disembarking the barge, before he hollered up to the still assembling group.

"Ready preppers?" LowBuck bellowed up to the audience on the shore.

"READY!" The dull roar of the Crowd answered him back.

"THEN RESCUE!" Lowbuck yelled out in a thunderous voice and put a little zing in it by canting back his head like a wolf howling and drawing out the word rescue in a long

Sail On Silver Pontoon

warbling note.

A very loud chorus of shrill survival whistle blasts answered him that could have been heard for miles.

How's that for a celebration? Anyone who saw a boat or a group of them coming to rescue us was supposed to blow their whistle if they had one or beat on something and the rest of the group was supposed to take up the noise making and this would notify others that might be out hunting or something and attract any would be rescuers attention." A grinning Lowbuck declared.

"Sounded about as loud as a tornado siren." Crick complimented him, his own ears still ringing from the din the grinning preppers had created.

"Nobody could have missed that racket that's for sure! " Loomis declared poking and wiggling a finger in his ear to help regain his hearing.

"On a serious note guys we got lots of people to weak to come down here on their own. Funny thing about starvation, folks don't just eat anything if their starving. We got people who refuse bugs etc, you get to where eventually you just don't care and would rather not eat, and you get to feeling like you don't want to eat anything even though you know your starving. Then there is the vision thing, you know your starving when you start having problems with your eyes. Moving those folks won't be a problem but nursing them back to health in our weakened states is a huge problem. Did you find any food over there?" Lowbuck asked hopefully.

"Not much but we got a plan for food procurement. David brought some fish traps and a bunch of animal snares as well as skills to help us out some. We are setup to receive you all on an old sharecropper plantation. I haven't been to town looking for

Sail On Silver Pontoon

help yet, kind of scared to go to be honest from what little bit I have heard about cities and towns these days but we will organize something to see if there is any relief supplies to be had. Meantime everyone will be on the mainland and stay or go as they like." Crick advised Lowbuck who took a moment to take it all in about this rescue not being all it was supposed to be but in some ways better than expected.

"Crick has this idea about everyone homesteading that place for awhile however the lands overseers want to call what we will be doing as sharecropping. Don't fret none about that term, it just means they get a part in anything we brow for them helping us with seed and land and such with a bit of credit until a crop can be made. They are nice old people who have done it for generations so we are dang lucky to have their skills and the use of their land at any price, particularly now I would say." Loomis offered as an advisement.

"It ain't no utopia, nothing but a bunch of old shacks and overgrown fields but it is ideally suited for our needs at this time." Crick advised

"Sounds great, the sooner we can get some food and vitamins in folks the better. We can build us a ramp on to that boat easy enough we can even rig us a zip line to move packs and tents and such onto that barge easy enough where it sits." Lowbuck declared.

"Well that just leaves having a meeting and telling everyone about the sharecropping option and moving this pack of starving bellies over to the mainland then" Crick declared.

"I figure we can get everybody off of here in three trips, we could do it in two, but no sense overloading the barge. There is plenty of gas in these cars to siphon for the tractor if we ever need too. Hell I might want to stay over here in my trailer someday or could be we can rig that barge someway to haul the cars back and forth across the river." Loomis said speculatively eying all kinds of possibilities for upping the survivor's success given time and a bit of ingenuity.

"Now your talking, I was going to bring up ferrying back the cars some kind of way later on but it is just way too much work to consider at the moment. Crick declared.

"Don't you be thinking about putting no paddle wheels on your truck Crick." Lowbuck said only half joking.

"You never know, you just never know.. Come on guys lets get this show on the road." Crick said and waded to shore to brief the survivors about their imminent departure.

The
End!

Acknowledgements

![Ron and LowBuck Prepper photo]

Ron and LowBuck Prepper

HENRY REPEATING

My Readers Might Also Enjoy:

**THE RURAL RANGER A SUBURBAN AND
URBAN SURVIVAL MANUAL & FIELD GUIDE
OF TRAPS AND SNARES FOR FOOD AND
SURVIVAL**

By Ron Foster

The Modern Day Survival Primer for Solving Modern Day
Survival Problems! This book will teach you the techniques to
not just survive, but to use ingenuity and household items to
solve your problems scientifically with a bit of primitive know
how thrown in. A complete and detailed section utilizing explicit
drawings and easy to understand photographs covers thoroughly
the topic of survival trapping using Modern Snares, Deadfalls,
Conibear Traps, and Primitive Snares. This book is dedicated for
long term survival in the country or the suburbs to insure you
survive and thrive! Build a solar oven
or pasteurize water its all in here! Catch your dinner, then cook it
or preserve it, too! Food procurement is the name of the game
along with purified water in a survival or disaster situation. Are
you ready?

Check Out The Original Prepper Trilogy

Preppers Road March

A solar storm has just hit the world causing an EMP event.
An emergency manager visiting Atlanta GA must find his way
back home after this electromagnetic pulse has stranded him
away from his vehicle and his beloved "bug out bag". With 180
miles to go to his destination, David must let his street smarts
and survival skills kick in as food and water becomes scarce and
societal breakdown proceeds at an unrelenting pace. An

interesting and often funny cast of characters from the Deep South helps the displaced Prepper on his way, as he shares his knowledge of how to make do with common items in order to live another day. Ultimately, he acquires an old tractor and heads for home on a car-littered interstate. This is book one of the Prepper Trilogy.

BUG OUT! Preppers on the move!

Book two of the Prepper trilogy finds the disaster planner and emergency manager Dave faced with the choice of bugging out with his cohort of friends and family as he watches the societal collapse and demise of civilization around him after an electromagnetic pulse (EMP) solar storm has taken out the grid. A post apocalyptic fiction series that takes you through the trials and tribulations of survival after the predicted NASA 2012 solar super storm unravels the lives and lifestyles of a group of modern day survivalists. The preppers decide on a lake front bug out with bags in hand as well as a unique group of operating vehicles from a bobcat loader to a lawn tractor. Will they survive? Could you? Let us find out, and join the party down the desolate dystopian landscape of a new beginning in a world without lights or technology.

The Light in The Lake

Book three of the Prepper Trilogy finds our band of refugees from a solar storm safely moved into a several lake cabins and trying to work on their short term and long term survival. The lake is a beautiful place for a survival retreat, but is it safe with roving groups of lake residents all looking for what meager food resources remain after a EMP event has shut down society as we know it. Can society be recreated and restarted here, or will starvation and anarchy take over? Can a simple light in the lake be the solution to survival and the reconstruction of society, or is it merely a symbol of what has been and might be yet again?

Made in the USA
Monee, IL
13 August 2022

11033353R00292